INCURSION

ALSO BY MITCHELL HOGAN

INCURSION

THE NECROMANCER'S KEY: BOOK ONE

MITCHELL
HOGAN

ſNᄃURSION

Published by Mitchell Hogan

Copyright © 2020 by Mitchell Hogan

First Printing, 2020

PROLOGUE

THE DEAD WILL LIVE FOREVER.

That's what the necromancers taught. What Niyandrians were supposed to believe.

But the carrion birds circling overhead, the red-skinned corpses on the ground, told a different story.

Naphor, the ancient capital of Niyas, was about to fall.

Around Captain Carred Selenas, in the Avenue of Bone that led from the palace to the city's east gate, the surviving warriors of the Last Cohort were mounted, awaiting her order to flee.

Together, they watched as Queen Talia rose on a dark crest of sorcery above the invaders from the mainland pouring through the breach in the curtain walls. The Niyandrian Queen's crimson skin glowed like lava from the forces coursing through her. She looked so gaunt. Her stick limbs and frail body were swamped by the black robe that whipped and snapped around her. She resembled the *thing* the mainlanders called her: a demon. The

Necromancer Queen.

Ice formed in Carred's guts. They were not wrong in their assessment.

She had seen.

Oh, Talia.

Carred stifled her tears. Bit back revulsion.

She understood now just what it was she'd seen during the night, when she'd woken in Talia's bed. And she'd smelled the odor of decay, heard the whispering of distant voices. The image of the Queen, naked flesh rippling with unearthly light, the misty forms of women and men drifting around her, had burned itself in Carred's mind.

Talia had sacrificed too much for the power to protect her people, and still it hadn't been enough.

Carred had cried out, revealing she was awake. She'd seen the flash of anger in Talia's eyes as the Queen turned to face her and the spirits faded away. The rage had only been fleeting, replaced with tears and professions of love. And Carred had melted, believed what she wanted to believe. Talia was her queen, her life, her love.

And so, she'd welcomed the Queen back to bed and held her close, willing the warmth back into Talia's body, which had begun the slow drift into the realm of the dead.

A roar of triumph went up from the enemy charging across the plaza in front of the palace, their battle formations giving way to the chaos of a mob. It was a massacre in the name of their five-faced god.

The rose-and-star standard of the City States bobbed among them, along with the scythe-and-ox of the Pristart Combine and the golden hawk of Kaile. The yellows, greens and blues of their surcoats blurred together in one seething mass. The only semblance of discipline left in the enemy lines was among the hundreds of white-cloaked Knights of the Order of Eternal Vigilance, each surrounded by a sphere of light that could turn a blade or repel all but the most potent sorcery.

Red-skinned Niyandrians ran from their homes, some of them carrying children. Carred almost disobeyed her queen then, almost ordered the Last Cohort to charge to their aid. It would have been suicide, the outcome still the same. And she'd made Talia a promise.

The panicked Niyandrians swarmed toward the knights, howling, screaming, flinging the destructive enchantments that came so easily to their race. Silver motes sparked from the spheres around the knights. Ensorcelled blades came down. Blood sprayed.

Carred looked away, her eyes drawn to where Talia hovered above the slaughter. The air about the Queen quivered under the strain of unseen forces. It seemed that Talia grew denser somehow. Her skin danced with flames.

Carred shielded her eyes as lightning flashed.

Sparks erupted from Queen Talia's protective wards. Her eyes blazed golden as she sought out the enemy sorcerer who had blasted her. She slung out a hand, and purplish vapor whiplashed toward a red-robed man. As it struck, he putrefied in an instant, his remains splashing to the ground, bubbling and steaming.

"Yes!" Carred muttered through gritted teeth. "Yes!"

Around her, horses nickered as their riders watched the fighting with anxious eyes and slumped shoulders. They had been chosen to survive, yet every one of them would have preferred to stay and die.

A cry sounded from the end of the Avenue of Bone. The Last Cohort had been spotted. Enemy footmen poured between the shops and houses, streaming toward them.

Carred flinched as the Queen glared down at her. Though she was a hundred yards below, she heard Talia's words as if they were whispered in her ear. "Aren't you leaving it a bit late, Captain? It's time for you to go."

Tears streamed down Carred's cheeks. She'd served Talia since she was old enough to hold a sword. At sixteen, she'd been the youngest Niyandrian to join the Last Cohort. Three years later, she'd been raised to captain, always close to the Queen, ever her intimate.

Talia glanced toward the eastern gate. She'd ordered it open the moment a trebuchet's missile collapsed a section of the southern wall. Enemy soldiers surged toward the gate, ensuring no one escaped the slaughter. The Queen soared higher into the sky, spinning as she went, tendrils of dark sorcery radiating out from her, lashing, cutting, burning. Mainlanders fell screaming, yet still more came.

"Flee!" Talia commanded the Last Cohort. "Now!" Just for Carred, she added, "Hallow Hill. Don't forget." For a moment the Queen's face twisted, as if she was worried she'd made the wrong decision. "Please, Carred…don't leave me in the realm of the dead."

Concussive blasts hammered the Queen's wards, spinning her to the ground.

Carred started to dismount, but Talia rolled to her knees and stood, wreathed in emerald light.

"No," Carred mouthed.

She sat back in her saddle, kicked her heels into her horse's flanks and yelled for the rest of the Last Cohort to follow. At a gallop, she tore through the channel Talia had opened in the enemy ranks, close to thirty riders in her wake. Pressure built in her head. Sulfur and earth and coppery blood filled her nostrils—the stench of Talia's sorcery.

Enemy sorcerers fled toward the breach in the southern wall, shouting warnings. They knew what was coming. Mainland soldiers started to scatter, but it was too late—for them as well as for Naphor.

As Carred shot through the eastern gate, she glanced back over her shoulder. The Queen's emerald blaze filled the sky above the city, pulsing, throbbing, a thunderhead ready to burst. Blood oozed from Carred's nostrils. The hairs on her arms stood on end.

Riders of the Last Cohort caught up to Carred and swept to either side, shouted on by Derin Lan, one of her lieutenants.

And then the Queen's pent-up energies exploded.

The shock wave buckled the knees of Carred's horse. She flew over its head and slammed into the ground. Dazed and seeing double, she wriggled her fingers, her toes; tried to flex her arms. The chink of spurs, the clump of boots, and Derin Lan was there, helping her up.

"You all right?" he asked in a shaky voice.

Carred swallowed as she nodded, suddenly all too aware of the weight of her mail.

She looked back at the devastation. The massed ranks of the allied armies that had remained outside the walls with their trebuchets and ballistae were a frozen vignette, hands covering ears. One of their siege towers teetered precariously. Black smoke billowed above the shattered city. Scarcely a stone stood atop another.

Naphor was gone.

And so was the Queen.

The sky was leaden and there was a constant drizzle as Carred and the Last Cohort rode deep into Rynmuntithe, the great forest at the heart of Niyas. It was dusk when they came into sight of Hallow Hill.

The thirty surviving men and women drew up their horses at the foot of the ancient earthwork that covered the tombs of their ancestors. Thumbs were pressed to middle fingers—a mark of respect to Theltek of the Hundred Eyes, the god who watched over the dead until the day they would rise.

Carred dismounted and passed her reins to Derin, then took her spyglass from her saddlebag.

"You're in charge till I return," she told him.

Derin narrowed his eyes in question, but knew better than to ask. If the plans Queen Talia had hatched with Carred were to be shared with the troops, Derin would have known of them by now.

Carred couldn't have explained the Queen's designs to him anyway, as she didn't fully understand them herself. All she knew was that they began here, in some obscure way, on Hallow Hill.

The bank she trudged up was slick from the persistent rain. She slipped and muddied her hands breaking her fall. After that, she kept to the worn patches in the grass, avoiding the fragments of bone that protruded from the ground.

The ruined building at the top looked as though it had once been the base of something much larger—a tower, probably, that had long since toppled. It was constructed from the blue-gray stone that had been shipped from the Plains of Khisig-Ugtall at some distant time, when the savages that lived there had traded with Niyas. The centuries and the weather had darkened the stone and left it scabbed with yellowish lichen.

There was no entrance, nor did Carred expect one. No one

in living memory had entered the structure, nor the burial chambers said to lie within.

She moved to the brink of the hill and gazed west over the forest, where the still-smoldering ruins of Naphor were visible in the distance. Specks of light snaked across the settlements outside the city walls. She blinked, trying to focus her eyes in the twilight. The snaking lights were moving.

Extending her spyglass's brass tube, she raised the device to her eye. The lights were torches held by mounted knights—the Order of Eternal Vigilance. White-robed priests trailed them, some cradling red-skinned infants in their arms. It made no sense. Why not leave the Niyandrian babes with their families? They posed no threat now the Queen's army had been destroyed.

Carred panned the spyglass across the closest of the settlements and understood. There were bodies everywhere—in the mud-packed streets, lying in doorways, atop the roofs. And blood. So much blood, as if it had rained from the skies. Cold fury gripped her. Her hands shook, making it hard to focus as she turned the spyglass to one farmstead after another.

Dead.

All dead.

And they call us demons!

But why? Why kill civilians? Why take their children?

The whisper of the wind answered her. "They seek Queen Talia's infant daughter."

Carred stiffened. She'd heard no one approach. She had to force herself to turn. Like all Niyandrians, she'd heard the stories about the spirits that lingered at sites such as this: those who harbored grudges against the living, and whom it was prudent to appease.

A shadow detached itself from the sepulcher.

Despising the quaver in her voice, Carred said, "The Queen doesn't have a daughter."

"You are so sure?"

"I shared her bed long enough. So, yes, I'm sure." There had been no sign of pregnancy, and Talia loathed men. Hated them.

"Powerful sorcery determines what is seen and unseen," the shadow said. "What better way to conceal a child than for no one to know it ever existed?"

The figure took a step toward her, its heavy boots making no sound. There was something not quite solid about it. The breeze blowing across the hilltop didn't cause its cloak to flap, and there was nothing but blackness beneath its cowl. At its hip hung a sword that Carred would have needed two hands to swing. The hilt was wound with silver wire, the cross-guard studded with dark jewels. She almost recoiled from the musty stench coming off the figure.

Carred tried to mask her fear with anger. "You lie, wraithe."

For what else could it be but one of the ancient beings that haunted the ruins the length and breadth of Wiraya? The only evidence of their once-mighty civilization now lay buried beneath the remnants of all cultures that had succeeded them.

The wraithe glided closer, and Carred looked to one side, unable to endure the empty gaze from beneath its cowl. Only a rare few had survived encounters with wraithes. The rest met a gruesome death or simply disappeared.

"What is it you most desire, Carred Selenas?"

"Did Queen Talia give you my name?"

The Queen had hinted at her hope of an alliance with such creatures, but if Talia had been successful, that alliance had come too late. Or the wraithes had betrayed her.

The wraithe said nothing, merely watched her and waited.

What did she desire? Nothing. Not now that Talia was gone, the hope of a new Niyandrian empire shattered.

But Carred did want something, she realized, though it was as impossible as the dreams of the corpses buried all over Niyas, waiting patiently for the day of their rising.

Don't leave me in the realm of the dead...

"I want my queen back," she said. Part of her didn't. Part of her still trembled at what she'd seen last night. But she was a loyal daughter of Niyas. And she was in love, she told herself. Despite her fear of what Talia had gotten into, what the Queen had become—perhaps what she'd always been—Carred loved her like no one else. Desired her. Would have walked through fire to please her.

Still the wraithe didn't respond. She could feel it watching her, though she dared not look. Worried she'd answered incorrectly, she tried again.

"I want Niyas for Niyandrians."

"Resistance." The wraithe extended a hand. On its palm sat an engraved ring of dark metal. "Your queen wished the same thing."

"Where did you get that?" Carred demanded.

Had the ring been on Talia's finger when she battled the mainlanders? She couldn't recall. But it was the Queen's ring, of that she was certain. An heirloom passed down from Talia's father—a foreigner, it was rumored. A man Talia refused to talk about.

"Your queen gave it to me to show you. She said you would not trust easily."

"Give it to me," Carred said.

The wraithe closed its fist around the ring, seemed to consider for a moment, then surrendered it to her.

There was no weight to the ring. Carred ran her fingers over the dark metal band to convince herself it was real.

"Other payments have been made," the wraithe said. "They are sufficient for me to do as your queen and I negotiated."

"And that is?"

Its voice took on an amused tone. "What do you make of your new rulers?"

"You tell me." Carred gestured to the west and the destroyed capital. "Followers of a false god. Murderers."

"They would not agree with you."

"I've no problem disagreeing with evil."

A shiver passed beneath the wraithe's cowl. Perhaps it was chuckling. "Is it evil when cattle are slaughtered and salted for the winter?"

"We're not cattle."

The wraithe didn't respond, just watched and waited for her to say more.

"If the invaders find Talia's so-called daughter," Carred said, "what will they do? Kill the child?"

"Of course."

"And the others? The children they took? All girls, I assume?"

The wraithe was silent.

"Do you know where the child is?" Carred asked.

"Safe."

"I didn't ask—"

"Queen Talia came to an arrangement with those of my kind still abroad in the world. We will honor our side of the pact."

Carred rolled Talia's ring between her thumb and forefinger. "What exactly did she give you in return? Other payments, you said."

The wraithe ignored her question. "Trust me when I say that you and your surviving warriors must become like the mist. You know this isle better than the enemy. Foment rebellion. Strike and run. Hide so you may strike again."

"For how long?" Carred asked.

"Until the Queen returns."

Don't leave me...

So, it was possible, then. Despite their closeness, Carred knew so little of Talia's powers. But she spoke with spirits, Carred had witnessed that in the night. Just how far had Talia dipped her toe into the darkness?

Suppressing a shudder, she asked, "When? When will the Queen return?"

"You will know when the time is right."

"And her daughter?"

"The less anyone knows—"

"She should have a guardian," Carred said. "All Niyandrian heirs are warded by a guardian until they take the throne."

"You need not concern yourself. The child is safe for now. The guardian will be revealed when the moment is right, and at the same time the heir will be known."

The wraithe didn't trust her. Or was it that Talia hadn't trusted her? Unless the wraithe was lying, the Queen had kept her daughter secret from Carred all this time. It felt like a betrayal.

Bitterness threatened to swamp her and she turned her back on the wraithe.

But Talia must have had her reasons, and Carred had given her word. This was about duty now, and duty didn't care about feelings. When she'd been rising through the ranks, it had been drummed into her that duty trumped everything, even love. She thrust Talia's ring into her pocket.

"So, my orders are to fight back against the mainlanders. That's all my Queen wants from me?"

"Not all."

"What else?" Carred asked.

No reply.

"What else?" she said again.

She turned to face the wraithe, but it was no longer there.

ONE

ANSKAR DEVANTTE FELT A FIERCE itch beneath his scalp as he made his way to the stable yard for his early morning chores. Wind blasted him from the east, skirled around him, whipping up his cloak and hair, then passed him by. The odd thing was, there hadn't even been a breeze before. And there was no wind now. It was calm again.

A lantern hung outside the main stable block where the knights' destriers were stabled. Within, a dog yapped and a man let out a good-natured laugh. Anskar smiled. Larson the stablemaster liked to start his rounds early. Pages would soon arrive to tend their knights' horses, but Larson was always there first, checking their work, making sure none of the animals were neglected.

Anskar made his way to the two-stall barn he'd been given charge over. Hazel was waiting for him, her big brown head sticking over the top of the stall, ears twitching. He greeted the mare with a stroke along the white stripe that ran down her face. She was getting old—too old to be useful, so the knights said—but Larson refused to put her down. "She's family," the stablemaster liked to say, and would glare a threat at anyone who said otherwise.

Anskar bridled Hazel, opened the gate, and her to the paddock. She resisted, as she always did, and let out a loud whinny.

"Silly girl," he said, patting her flanks to reassure her. "Monty's coming. When have I ever kept you two apart?"

He shut her in the paddock, then returned to the barn's far side stall where the dappled gray and white donkey waited. Monty wasn't good around people: he'd been beaten by a previous owner and flinched at the slightest movement. But he knew Anskar well enough and dipped his head for a stroke, then rubbed up against him.

Leaving the horse and donkey to exercise and graze, Anskar grabbed a rake and went to muck out their stalls. Years of helping in the stables had built his strength, along with his regular training and exercises. And whereas many of the novice knights in his year group were still developing, Anskar was broad of shoulder, lean and muscled. Larson said the girl trainees liked to look at him, but Anskar had seen no evidence of that. Most of them were from the mainland and thought they were better than him. They mocked him to his face on account of his sun-blushed skin and long, black hair.

When he'd taken the muck by wheelbarrow to the dung pile, he filled the feed buckets with grain and led the animals back for their breakfast. Which was when he noticed Hazel was limping. Angry red bites covered her left foreleg, and Anskar cursed. Fire-ant bites. The bane of Niyas.

"I got some salve for that," Larson said, startling him. He hadn't seen the stablemaster approach. "Go see if you can find the mound and treat it," the older man added.

"Yes, sir," Anskar said, and returned to the shed. He took down a linen bag of the herb and crushed crystal ant treatment the priests of the Elder prepared, and went to search for the mound in the paddock.

Rosie, Larson's Niyandrian ridgeback hound, ambled over to join him, her nose pressed to the ground. Ridgebacks were big dogs, crossbred for their speed, size, and the volume of their bark. Niyandrian farmers reputedly used them to ward off mountain lions, and Anskar was inclined to believe it. Well, maybe not Rosie: she was too foolish for that. Too soft. As if to prove him right, she rolled over for a belly rub.

Anskar gave her a hunk of bread he'd saved in his pocket for her during supper. She wolfed it down, then followed at his side as he roamed the paddock. At first glance, Anskar couldn't see any telltale mounds of earth, but Rosie barked to let him know she'd found what he was looking for.

"Good girl," he said, kneeling beside her and stroking along the tuft of golden hair that ran in a ridge along her spine.

No wonder he hadn't seen it: the mound had been flattened by Hazel's hoof, and now hundreds of red ants swarmed all over it looking for something else to sting. He opened the linen bag, poured a measure of the glittering, pungent-smelling treatment over the mound, then re-tied the ends of the bag and returned it to the shed.

Back at the barn, Hazel had her head in the feed bucket while Larson painstakingly applied a thick salve to her bites. Rosie lay down outside the stall, tongue lolling as she panted.

"I wasn't expecting you today," Larson said as he pushed himself to his feet and shuffled to find his balance. His left leg had been mangled during a skirmish with Niyandrian rebels years ago; he was lucky not to have lost it. "Thought you'd be readying yourself for the trials."

"It's only the banquet tonight," Anskar said. "The trials don't start till the morning."

"What is it I've been telling you?" the stablemaster said. "The trials start with the banquet. You've got to be prepared. For anything. *After* the trials is when you get to unwind and have fun, not before."

"If I'm successful," Anskar pointed out, and all his old doubts returned. It wasn't just anxiety about the possibility of failing; he was just as concerned about what success would mean for him. When he ceased to be a novice, he'd be expected to go outside the citadel. In all his seventeen years of life, he'd never left the Burg, nor did he have any desire to. There were perils that lay outside, and he uttered a swift prayer of thanks to Menselas, the god of five aspects, that he was safe within. Sometimes he'd asked visiting knights from the Order's other strongholds throughout Niyas what it was like beyond Branil's Burg; whether they'd seen the sea and the mountains; whether they'd ever been to the mainland; whether there really were dead-eyes out there that feasted on corpses—after they'd defiled them.

Larson sensed the change in Anskar. He clapped him on the shoulder and led the way outside the barn. "You'll succeed," he said. "Or you won't."

Anskar glanced at him sharply.

"And if you do," Larson continued, "it's only half the battle won."

"I'll be a knight-inferior," Anskar said, and for a moment his anxiety was overwhelmed by a surge of pride.

"Which is still a step away from a consecrated knight," Larson reminded him. "Just make sure you win each bout during the first trial, and win it decisively. Don't leave it to the adjudicators to determine a winner."

"I know," Anskar said.

"To be the best, you have to beat the best," Larson continued. "The Order doesn't want mediocrity. It wants knights who'll be superior to any enemy they face. Don't be one of those spineless cretins who complains about getting the hard fights early on. In battle, you don't get to pick and choose. And don't do anything flashy, either. It doesn't matter how impressive you look if you don't win."

"I know," Anskar said again.

Larson stopped in the courtyard garden in the shadow of the citadel's keep and stooped to rub his bad leg. "Did I tell you I failed the trials the first time?" he said. "Not the fighting. I've still to meet the person who could beat me in a fair fight. Not the forging, either. Like you, I was always good at smithing. It was the sorcery that tripped me up. A simple thing like that: the casting of a ward sphere. Guess it was my nerves. Course, they also screwed up implanting my catalyst."

Larson opened his collar to show Anskar the ridged scar on his chest. "I reckon they used a flawed crystal. But you'll not have that problem, not now the Order has a new supplier."

"But you passed the second time?" Anskar said.

"Actually, it was the third, and then only by the skin of my teeth. Probably, they should have failed me then. My ward sphere flickered so much I thought the adjudicator was going to have a seizure. No, they should have thrown me out—then maybe I'd not have gotten this." He slapped his bad leg.

"You never did tell me exactly what happened…to your leg," Anskar said tentatively.

"Carred Selenas is what happened. Not her personally: the

bloody rebels she leads. I was out with my squad, culling dead-eyes, when they ambushed us. Dazzled us with sorcery, they did, and then smashed into our flanks. Big ol' Niyandrian came at me with a club. No way that should have penetrated a ward sphere, only mine failed, didn't it? Like I said, they should never have let me pass the trials. Course, I was getting old by then. My ward sphere saw me through the war, so I should be thankful for that, I suppose."

"I hate the Niyandrians for what they did to you," Anskar said.

"Don't you go hating no one on my account," Larson said. "You think the Niyandrians should lie down like sheep and let us lord it over them?"

Anskar took a step back, not quite believing what he was hearing. "No, but—"

"I might not like what Carred Selenas's rebels did in the early days of her rebellion—to my comrades or to my leg—but you have to admire a woman like that, Anskar. She's persistent, if nothing else; though these past few years the Order's turned the tide on her. She loses more than she wins nowadays, and that can't go on forever. But let's not forget, it was their land before we took it from them."

"We liberated them," Anskar said. Every tutor he'd had since childhood had convinced him of that. "Queen Talia was evil. Under her rule, Niyas was a land of horror, its people demons."

"Believe that if you like, but just make sure you don't judge them like some of us do: by the color of their skin." Larson looked pointedly at Anskar, who dipped his head in shame.

Anskar's skin had always had a reddish tint, but it was nothing like the deep crimson of the Niyandrians. Brother Tion had said it was likely a trace of Traguh-raj blood, although Anskar preferred to believe it was on account of him working so long outdoors. He ignored the fact that Larson's skin was browned by the sun, not reddened. Anskar aspired to be the perfect knight one day, the epitome of all the Order stood for—even if the hue of his skin didn't fit the image he had of what that perfect knight should look like. The Seneschal, Vihtor Ulnar, was his model: a man with the swarthy looks of a mainland noble.

"Not all Niyandrians are bad," Larson finished.

"I know that. When I worked in the kitchens—"

The stablemaster cut him off again. "You don't need to convince me, Anskar. Now, go get ready for tonight, and don't think about anything else but the trials. I'll have one of the new recruits look after Hazel and Monty the next few days. But I want to hear a full report of how you get on."

Anskar took a deep breath and nodded, but his stomach twisted as Larson turned to leave.

"You'll do fine," Larson shot over his shoulder. "And if you don't, there's always next year."

"And if I fail then?" Anskar asked.

Larson shrugged. "You're good with animals. And on the mainland, there's plenty of demand for blacksmiths. If Sned Jethryn's to be believed, you have the skills. You'll be fine. Know what I was going to do if I failed that last time?"

"Look after horses?" Anskar said.

Larson chuckled. "Sing." His eyes gleamed with remembered fondness. "I was brought up in the highlands of Valborg where everyone sings. Our bards travel the length and breadth of the mainland keeping the old songs alive. No, if the Order didn't want me, I'd already planned to buy one of them fancy Kailean guitars and take it traveling."

"I had no idea you could sing," Anskar said, but he was talking to himself. Larson had passed inside the keep.

With a sigh, Anskar turned and headed for the novices' entrance. He needed to clean up too, then grab himself something to eat. But as he crossed the garden, he couldn't stop thinking about the possibility of failure. It was all very well relying on a second attempt at the trials the following year. But what if he failed then, and the time after that? Three attempts and you were out. And what would he do then? The thought flooded him with dread. Even if he survived outside the citadel's walls, where would he go? How would he earn enough coin to eat and to put a roof over his head? All he knew was the life of the Order of Eternal Vigilance. Without it, he was nothing. No one. He didn't even have a family to turn to. Anskar had no idea who his parents had been; only that they were dead and the Order had taken him in as a baby. Brother Tion often speculated that Anskar's parents had fought in the mainland army, but if they had Larson hadn't known them.

"Morning, half-blood," a woman called. "I thought you'd be practicing for tomorrow's trial."

Anskar had been too preoccupied to notice the three novices sitting on a bench nearby: Sareya, a red-skinned Niyandrian who'd been brought to the Burg as a child; and Clenna and her twin brother Rhett, from Nagorn City on the east coast of the mainland—Nagorn City, where it was said they had yet to invent sewers. The twins were both hard as nails, Clenna more so than Rhett. Always looking for a fight. Always trouble. That either of them had come so far in their training was a wonder. Sometimes Anskar thought the Order placed more emphasis on fighting ability than on the good conduct expected of a knight.

What the twins were doing with Sareya was anyone's guess. He'd never had the impression they were friends. The fact that they all had their eyes on him only served to increase the awkwardness he always felt around Sareya. She seemed to see it as her life's work to torment him.

"You've been mucking out the stables," she said now, fanning her hand beneath her nose. "I do hope you'll wash and change before tonight's banquet, in case I'm forced to sit near you."

She crossed her legs and smoothed down the front of her shirt. The white fabric set off her berry-red skin, and her black hair—she wore it loose, tumbling about her shoulders—glistened in the early morning sunlight. For the briefest moment their eyes met. Hers were green-flecked brown with hardly any white, the pupils slanted and vertical, like a cat's. Anskar dropped his gaze to his boots. Niyandrian eyes were unnatural, he told himself. The eyes of a demon.

"Don't be shy," Sareya said. "I don't mind you looking."

Rhett seemed to stiffen, which made Anskar wonder exactly what was going on.

"You're wasting your time," Clenna told Sareya. "Anskar's incorruptible. And besides, he's one of us. Why would he be attracted to a Niyandrian?"

"Your brother is," Sareya said.

Suddenly Anskar understood. Despite the Order's rules against intimacy, everyone said Sareya was sleeping around. All the Niyandrians were, so people said. Filthy savages. Whoever had decided to allow Niyandrians into the Order had made a terrible mistake. They'd brought with them their immorality, and it was only likely to spread. And spread it apparently had: to Rhett.

"You red-skinned bitch!" Clenna spat as she stood. "You'd better not have!"

"I don't know what you're talking about," Sareya said sweetly.

"Rhett?" Clenna demanded.

Her brother's face had gone as red as Sareya's.

Clenna raised her fist, but Anskar was quicker and grabbed her by the wrist.

"No fighting, remember? Else you'll be ejected."

"No whoring, either," Clenna snarled. "Or don't you object to that, half-blood?"

Anskar let go of Clenna's wrist. His hands were shaking as he said, "I am not a half-blood."

"No," Clenna said, "you're a fucking halfwit. Everyone says so, or haven't you heard?"

Anskar found himself looking at Sareya. "They do?"

She smiled. "Oh, Anskar, you're such a child. A man in appearance, yes"—she looked him up and down—"but emotionally, a child." She stood and faced Clenna. "And no, I didn't sleep with your brother."

Rhett was still seated, his head down as if trying to hide his shame.

"Once we were done, I told him to leave," Sareya added. "I prefer to sleep alone."

Clenna's jaw dropped. Before she could recover, Sareya was entering the keep.

"You should go to the healers," Anskar told Rhett. "Make your confession before—"

"Get lost, idiot," Clenna said.

"I was only trying to—"

"Don't make me tell you twice. And Anskar: you ever grab my wrist again and you'll be spitting out teeth, got it?"

Anskar's hands clenched into fists at his sides. Heat prickled beneath his skin and he narrowed his eyes. Not trusting himself to say anything without exploding, he stormed away from Clenna and her brother.

Not to his room. Not to rest and prepare. He was too angry for that. Too close to doing something that might get him expelled from the Order.

Instead, he headed for the smithing hall, where he could take out his anger by beating red-hot metal with a heavy hammer.

TWO

ANSKAR WAITED OUTSIDE THE DOUBLE doors of the knights' refectory with the other novices. It was evening, and after spending hours expressing his fury with hammer on steel in the smithing hall, he'd returned to his room to wash and change. The violence had left him, but one wrong word from anyone could still set him off. He knew it was a failure for him to feel that way. The Five was a god of balance: Menselas despised excess in anything—in feelings above all else.

The double doors opened, and the smell of spiced meat made Anskar's stomach growl. The novices jostled each other to be first inside, but despite his hunger, Anskar was determined to be last. It showed self-control.

"Hurry up, boy," called the knight who had opened the doors.

Boy! The knight was barely out of boyhood himself, and Anskar was taller and heavier. As he passed through the doors, he saw that the knight's symbol of Menselas—a five-pointed star within a circle of Skanuric runes—was newly embroidered on his robe. Probably his mother had done it.

The novices were finding their seats at the long tables that skirted the dining hall. Some of them pointed toward the tall windows through which the manicured lawns and colorful blooms of Branil's Burg's gardens were still visible in the fading light. Others craned their necks to stare at the gilded ceiling high above, hazed by the smoke pluming from the five braziers set in a star formation at the hall's center. The resin incense sprinkled over the coals gave off an odor at once sweet and pungent.

At the table opposite the double doors were seated twelve knights in simple white robes with a crimson symbol of Menselas embroidered on the breast. They were already digging into a selection of meats and roasted vegetables, drinking wine and talking boisterously.

Vihtor Ulnar was among them. The Seneschal. Vihtor was a big man, well into middle age, dusky-skinned with fair hair and blue eyes—he may have had Inkan-Andil heritage.

Platters of roast duck were placed before the knights at the Seneschal's table. Anskar could smell sage and rosemary, garlic and onions; the yeast of freshly baked bread.

"Where's *our* food?" grumbled Orix, seated across from Anskar. Orix was Traguh-raj, from the Plains of Khisig-Ugtall, and always hungry. It showed in his girth.

"Wouldn't surprise me if we don't get none," the lad sitting next to Orix said. Naul was as skinny as Orix was sturdy, and half a head taller than any of the other novices. He was also wily for his age, as cunning as any goat-riding Soreshi sorcerer. If Naul thought they might not get fed, it was a genuine concern.

Anskar placed his hands on the table, then noticed the dirt under his nails and dropped them to his lap. But not before they were seen.

"You just come from the smithing hall?" Naul asked.

Anskar shrugged.

"Ain't you got nothing better to do?"

"Anskar's practicing his metalwork skills," Orix said, "so that when he fails the trials he'll be able to find work in a Niyandrian forge."

"I won't fail," Anskar said. "And even if I did, I wouldn't work for a Niyandrian. They don't know the first thing about metal crafting. I'd sooner work for the nomads of the Jargalan Desert." He'd been studying their techniques in his spare time. The Jargalans knew how to forge.

"They'd make a slave of you," Naul said. "And I ain't talking about hard labor neither."

"What's that supposed to—?"

The chair on Anskar's right scraped. He looked to see who it was—and groaned.

"Oh, Anskar. Are you really so naïve?" Sareya said. "Slaves that don't work?" She mimicked Anskar's tone, and the others chuckled. "Whatever could that mean?"

Anskar met her gaze before looking away. She'd dyed red streaks in her hair, which highlighted her cat's eyes.

Sareya lowered herself into her chair and gazed around the hall as if looking for someone more interesting to talk to. She was dressed like the rest of the novices, except the ties of her loose-fitting white shirt weren't laced up all the way. Anskar was drawn briefly to the swell of her breasts, then quickly dipped his head and looked away. He made a mental image of a sword, the symbol of the Warrior aspect of the Five, which was said to cut passion dead. It didn't work, and he felt heat rise to his cheeks.

Sareya pressed in close and whispered, "Am I making you

nervous, half-blood?" Her breath smelled of fresh mint from the leaves she was always chewing.

Anskar's fists clenched. "For the last time, I am *not* a half-blood."

"Of course you'd deny it," Sareya said. "I would too, if it meant accepting my Niyandrian mother was raped by a knight of the Order of Eternal Violence."

"Vigilance!" Anskar said. "And she wasn't raped."

"And you know that how?"

Anskar had no answer for that. He just knew.

"But she was still Niyandrian," Sareya said. "Or your father was. Don't be angry about it. It's what makes us close."

"We are not close."

As if to prove him wrong, Sareya leaned toward him and ran a hand through her silky black hair. Anskar caught a whiff of something at once floral and musky.

"Is that perfume?" he said, waving his hand in front of his nose and faking a cough. If it was, she was going to be in trouble. According to the statutes of the Order, the wearing of scent was lascivious.

"Brother Tion made it for me. He's not such a stick in the mud as some of the other healers. Tell me you like it."

Anskar felt the heat return to his cheeks and looked away. He closed his eyes the better to picture the Warrior's sword. Still it didn't work.

"Are you thinking of me?" Sareya asked.

"I'm praying."

Naul snorted.

"For success in the trials?" Sareya asked.

Anskar grunted in affirmation. It somehow lessened the lie if he didn't verbalize it. He *should* be petitioning for the god's aid in the trials, rather than trying to avoid thinking about what lay beneath Sareya's shirt. No one succeeded in anything unless the Five willed it.

"Say one for me," Sareya said.

"Say it yourself."

She chuckled, then slipped her hand under the table and touched between his legs.

Anskar slapped her wrist away so hard she shrieked.

Silence descended upon the hall, and Sareya lowered her eyes to the table, embarrassed. More than embarrassed, Anskar saw from the curl of her lips. She was smarting. He shouldn't have struck her, but she'd gone too far this time.

He swallowed and looked at the Seneschal to see how he would react. Vihtor met his gaze for an instant, then looked down into his half-empty wine glass.

"You all right?" Orix asked Sareya.

"No," she said, fixing her unnerving eyes on Anskar. "I am not all right. I was just teasing, and this idiot struck me." She made a show of rubbing her wrist. "Is that how it started between your father and mother, half-blood?"

Anskar didn't rise to the bait. He was all too aware of the disapproving eyes around the dining hall watching him. The flush on his cheeks was no longer the bloom of arousal, but embarrassment for disturbing the Seneschal and his knights at their meal; shame for lashing out at a peer. For whatever else she was, Sareya was a fellow novice of the Order of Eternal Vigilance, a sister in arms.

Naul mouthed, "You shouldn't have done that." It sounded like a threat.

Anskar acknowledged Naul's comment with a nod, then rose to his feet. Bowing stiffly from the waist, he said, "I'm sorry,

Sareya. I shouldn't have lost control like that." He offered his hand for her acceptance.

With a haughty tilt of her chin, Sareya sat up straight in her chair and looked down the length of the table, ignoring him.

Cutlery once more began to clink and clatter on plates and bowls, and little by little the hubbub in the hall resumed. Anskar took his seat again. His palms were damp, and he wiped them on his pants.

At Anskar's left, Blosius—the son of a noble family from Sansor in Kaile—whispered, "She'll get over it."

It was typical of Blosius, who never took anything seriously. Anskar supposed it came from being the heir to vast wealth.

"Besides," Blosius added, looking toward the door into the kitchens, "there are more important things to consider. Food's coming!"

"Thank the Five," Anskar muttered under his breath.

Sareya seemed to have forgotten their spat. She was laughing and joking with the girl to her right—Niv Allund, another Niyandrian who had been brought to the Burg at around the same time as Sareya.

Anskar's mouth watered as the servants brought out trolleys stacked with covered dishes and set them in front of the novices. Despite their hunger, no one dared to remove the pewter lids covering the plates.

The Seneschal rapped his fork against his wine glass, and the room stilled once more as Brother Tion, tonsured and robed in the Healer's white, and four priests of the other aspects processed solemnly into the hall.

Each stood beside one of the five braziers at the center, and each took turns to bestow their blessings and offer prayers for the novices' success at tomorrow's trials: Tion first; then Sister

Haldyca, who stood for the Mother; then a decrepit old man whom Anskar hadn't seen before—presumably the Elder's representative.

The old man's eyes were milky with cataracts, and the staff in his hand seemed there to keep him upright rather than for ceremony. Over threadbare pants and a woolen jerkin, he wore a moth-eaten coat with only one of its brass buttons remaining. It was difficult to hear his blessing as his voice was so rasping and thin. He rambled on until Vihtor Ulnar cleared his throat. Brother Tion ushered the old priest to one side and fetched him a chair.

All the while, the food was getting cold. Anskar glanced at the covered plate in front of him, and Orix grimaced as if he were in pain.

Beof Harril was next, the priest of the Warrior, a bearded ogre of a man who held a monstrous bejeweled mace in his shovel-like hand. Beof was the only one of the Five priests to wear armor—a breastplate of mirror-bright steel upon which was embossed a sword. Like all Beof's speeches, his prayer was brief and brutal, full of intimations of blood.

The fifth aspect was the Hooded One—previously known as Death—represented by a spindly woman in a tattered black habit with a billowing cowl that obscured her features. Slender, long-nailed fingers clutched a twisted staff of yew tipped with the skull of some kind of rodent. The woman made Anskar's skin crawl, but he couldn't stop looking at her. What had driven her to such a morbid devotion?

When the priestess of the Hooded One shuffled forward to give her blessing, she spoke in a grating whisper that reached into every corner of the hall and drew all eyes to her through some invisible compulsion. Her voice evoked images of ancient tombs and rot.

"Sweet Death, Hooded One of Menselas, Crypt Stalker, Drinker of Life, Inexorable Hand of Putrefaction, though I am but dust and ashes, hear my petition and grant unto these novices the acceptance of your uncompromising truths."

She paused, her hood panning from left to right, taking in everyone present with her concealed eyes.

"Whether on the morrow they succeed or fail makes not the slightest difference. Their only certainty is the grave, where the earth will liquefy their innards and reduce their bones to dust.

"Grant these, your victims, the clear sight to see that they consume only to be consumed; that even if they flee from you to the ends of Wiraya, you will pursue them relentlessly, until, weary of the chase, they bow their heads and receive your implacable touch."

She rapped her yew staff on the flagstones, and the hollow thud resonated around the hall.

"Well, that was uplifting," Anskar whispered.

Blosius didn't answer. His face was pale with shock, like the rest of the novices—save the Niyandrians. They were probably used to such talk. Their entire culture revolved around an obsession with death and the endless quest of necromancers to resurrect corpses.

Brother Tion coughed and clapped his hands together. "Yes, well, thank you, Sister Hathenor, for such a profound blessing. May the Five aspects of Menselas be praised and glorified. And so, without further ado, and with the fullness of the god's blessing upon you…"

Eat! Anskar willed him to say.

"Allow me to introduce the Seneschal of Branil's Burg and Governor of the Isle of Niyas, Vihtor Ulnar."

The novices stood and thumped their fists against their chests.

Rather than subject them to any further delays, the Seneschal raised his wine glass and declaimed, "Enjoy!"

A cheer went up from the novices, followed by the clatter and scrape of chairs as they re-seated themselves.

Anskar's backside had barely touched his chair before he was lifting the cover from his dinner plate to reveal…

Bread and cheese.

Stale bread, and hard cheese with a scaly white crust and the first tufts of blue mold at the edges.

He glanced around the hall to see nearly a hundred novices frozen in place, looks of surprise and resentment on their faces.

"Tomorrow, you will feast like kings," Vihtor told them. "Or starve like paupers, depending on how you fare in the opening trial. But tonight is about sacrifice and self-restraint, that you might ponder the blessings of the Five you have just received. Remember, whatever the outcome when you fight in the morning, it is the manifestation of Menselas's will, not anything you possess or lack."

Spoken like Brother Tion, Anskar thought. But if everything that happened in life was due to Menselas's will, then what was the point of study and practice? Or had he gotten it wrong? Had he missed the true meaning of Tion's words, and now Vihtor's?

The other novices were picking at their bread and chewing morosely, whereas the knights at their long table resumed boisterous talking and laughing as they drank and ate.

Anskar picked up the crust on his plate and snapped it like a twig. Some kind of beetle plopped out onto the table, and suddenly he was no longer hungry.

The banquet—if such it could be called—wasn't all bad. After abandoning his bread and moldy cheese, Anskar forsook the other novices and found Brother Tion standing by a wall and they spent the evening in conversation. Tion frequently mentioned the Widow Glaena, who he was helping get over the death of her husband in the war with Queen Talia and the Niyandrians.

When Anskar brought up the blessing given by the priestess of the Hooded One, Tion insisted on introducing them.

Sister Hathenor extended a long-fingered hand. Her nails were painted a purple so dark they were almost black. Anskar winced as she nearly broke his fingers with her icy grip. Cold seeped into his bones, and it was an effort to stop his teeth from chattering.

"The god's mark is strong with you," she said, releasing his hand.

"Thank you, ma'am," Anskar replied, for want of something better to say. It was unnerving that he couldn't see her face beneath the cowl.

"Your politeness will not save you," she said. "Death always wins."

Tion swiftly interjected: "Sister Hathenor is off to the mainland tomorrow, so she won't be here for the trials."

"Sacrilege must be answered for," the priestess said. "There will be a reckoning." And she glided away toward the door.

As she left the dining hall, Tion breathed a sigh of relief. "Never mind her, Anskar. The devotees of the Hooded One typically lack balance. Virtually all the priests of the other four aspects agree on that."

"What did she mean by sacrilege?"

Tion grimaced. "Her chapel here at the Burg has been commandeered by order of Grand Master Hyle Pausus. The Seneschal has commissioned Niyandrian stonemasons to turn it into a vault."

"Why?"

"Worship of the Hooded One is in decline," Tion said. "It's too pessimistic and macabre. Changing the name from Death was an attempt by the Church to attract more worshipers, but it's been a dismal failure. People don't like mystery. The Hooded One! Makes you wonder what's hidden beneath. A toothless crone, no doubt! With a face so covered in warts she wouldn't dare show it in public." Tion covered his mouth. "Don't tell anyone I said that. I'll confess it later."

"Maybe she's a Niyandrian," Anskar said, "given the Hooded One's dominion over death."

Tion laughed. "A good one, but not likely. I don't see the Patriarch standing for red-skins in holy orders." He shook his head ruefully. "No, devotion to the Hooded One is on its last legs. Doesn't bring in enough tithes, for one thing, and you know how the Patriarch likes his tithes. How else could he have paid for the new basilica in Sansor?"

"But why turn the Hooded One's chapel into a vault?" Anskar asked. "Is the Order moving into banking?"

"Of a sort. Hyle Pausus is very much a man of the times, and he believes the Order needs to keep up. I'm told we now have similar vaults all over the mainland. Soon the Order of Eternal Vigilance will rival the Ethereal Sorceress for the safe storage of wealth and valuable artifacts."

"And the reckoning Sister Hathenor mentioned?" Anskar asked.

"Archbishop Denalon, who oversees the priests of the Hooded One, is demanding a convocation in Sansor to accuse Hyle Pausus of desecrating the Burg's chapel. He won't be satisfied with anything less than the Grand Master's removal from office."

"Is that possible?" Anskar had been led to believe the head

of the Order of Eternal Vigilance was as untouchable as he was infallible.

Tion shrugged. "Probably not. Hyle Pausus is from one of the richest families in Sansor, and that makes him popular with the Patriarch. And it's not as though there's a lot of support for the Hooded One. Some things are just a little too grim for a cultured society like ours, and better left to the distant past that spawned them."

After Vihtor dismissed the novices, Anskar hung back to help the kitchen hands he'd worked with as a child. Jonita, once his closest friend, wouldn't meet his eyes.

"You look well," he told her—though in truth she was rake-thin and her crimson skin had lost its luster. She tried to hide it, but her jaw was swollen, and there were bruises around her wrist. "What happened? Who hurt you?"

"It's nothing. Sorry, Anskar"—she might just as well have called him *sir*— "I have to work."

"Yes," Anskar said. "I understand. Let me help."

Together, they carried piles of dirty plates and utensils back to the kitchen, where Hubin, one of the cooks, handed Anskar a piece of freshly baked bread with some not-moldy cheese on top. Anskar smiled and thanked her. Hubin ruffed up his hair like she always used to, but there was a wariness about her that hadn't been there before. In her eyes he was virtually a knight now.

Anskar finished eating in silence, then slipped away without saying goodbye. As he passed along darkened corridors on the way to his room, he played out scenes from his childhood in his mind. It had been so easy then. No one had called him half-blood, and he'd seen no difference between the Niyandrian servants and the people of the mainland. He'd been happy in a way—as happy as a child could be, not knowing their parents. Tion had been a sort of father to him; Larson even more so.

That had all changed, yet tonight was the first time he'd realized it. Was it because of his worry about the looming trials, or something else? Perhaps he was just growing up, he told himself, though he couldn't stop thinking that meant he was one more step along the road to decay. Sister Hathenor's pessimism had infected him. He was glad she was going.

A shadow stepped in front of him and Anskar yelped in surprise.

The shadow giggled. He caught a whiff of perfume.

"Sareya?"

Something struck him in the back of the head, and he staggered. He glimpsed a blur of movement—a punch. Anskar rolled his shoulder and the fist glanced off. Orix's fist!

He backed up a step, circled to his right, but then Naul barreled into him out of the dark, slamming him against the wall. Anskar grunted as air burst from his lungs. On instinct, he slung out an elbow and caught Naul coming in. Blood sprayed from Naul's shattered nose, and he turned away, clutching his face.

Orix charged, but Anskar dipped beneath his punch and stepped off to one side. As Orix turned to follow him, Anskar smashed a fist into his chin. Orix stumbled back, and Anskar kicked him in the liver. The Traguh-raj boy stood for a moment, grimacing with pain, then pitched to the floor and curled up like a baby.

A weight hit Anskar from behind. Legs clamped around his waist, an arm beneath his chin. He'd forgotten Sareya.

Anskar gripped her forearm with both hands to relieve the pressure on his throat. Sareya's other hand pressed into the back of his head as she tightened the choke. He gasped. His head swam as she constricted the blood-flow to his brain.

With a desperate heave, Anskar pulled her arm down; made a sliver of space. He found her elbow with his palm, shoved up until his head popped free, then he drove her back against the wall with such force she went limp and her legs released him. Turning, he caught her by the throat. His fist shook as he raised it.

"What do you think you're doing?" he yelled. "Fighting is forbidden!"

Sareya's cat's eyes glittered, and her lips curled into a sneer. Even now she was mocking him. "You started it, half-blood," she rasped.

Anskar squeezed tighter, and she raked at the back of his hand with her nails. He wanted so much to hit her, but his fist refused to move; just wavered in front of her face.

"Scared to hit me?" Sareya said, her voice a tortured wheeze. "Your father would have done it."

"Damn you!" He crashed his fist into the wall beside her head. "Do you hate me so much? Why can't you just leave me alone?"

He punched the wall again, and this time his knuckles split. He winced at the pain, then struck again. Sareya let out a rattling breath, and her eyes grew dull and unfocused.

"Anskar, stop!" Orix said as he climbed to his feet, bent double and clutching his side. "Let her go. She's choking!"

"You fucking lunatic!" Naul said, voice muffled where he cupped his broken nose. "By the Five, let her go!"

"Stand down!" a man bellowed from the end of the corridor.

Booted feet pounded toward them, and the white tunics of knights appeared like ghosts from the gloom—the Seneschal with them.

Anskar released his throttle-hold on Sareya and backed away.

She stumbled, gasping and rubbing her throat.

"He tried to touch me!" she wailed. "He's always lusted after me!"

"Is this true?" the Seneschal demanded.

"Sir, it's true, sir," Naul said, blood from his nose dripping through his fingers.

"Liar!" Anskar said. "Sir, they're lying!"

"No," Orix said, and Anskar flashed him a glare. "No, sir, it isn't true. Anskar was defending himself. We started it."

"Why?" Vihtor asked.

Orix glanced at Sareya. "Because she—"

"Anskar struck me at dinner, Seneschal," Sareya cut in.

Vihtor silenced her with a raised hand and looked at Orix to continue.

"She promised me…" Orix hesitated, glancing at Naul for support, but Naul merely glowered at him.

"She promised you what?" Vihtor said.

"Seneschal," Orix said, "you have to understand—"

"*She* promised you what?"

Orix dipped his eyes and said nothing.

"We didn't like what happened in the dining hall, Seneschal," Naul said. "Anskar shouldn't have hit her."

"And it took three of you to right that wrong?" Vihtor said.

"Anskar hates me," Sareya said through her sniffling. "He calls me a red-skin, a corpse-coupler. He says I'm fit for just one thing."

"I do not!" Anskar said. "I've never said any of that!"

"Don't try that act on me, girl," Vihtor snapped at Sareya. "Anskar grew up helping in the kitchens. He did so again tonight. The servants all speak well of him."

The Seneschal knew he'd returned to the kitchens after the

banquet? And he'd taken notice of what Anskar had done as a child? It had been Brother Tion who'd sent Anskar to work in the kitchens initially. But Vihtor had known?

"I'm not blind," Vihtor told Sareya. "I saw what happened at the banquet, before you were rightfully slapped. Don't think I don't know what you are. Save your passions for when you're consecrated, and then indulge them *outside* the Order, like the rest of us."

"Seneschal, please," Sareya said, and now she was really sobbing. "I was teasing. I've made mistakes, I know that now, but I've changed. You have to believe me."

"Dry your tears and wipe your nose," Vihtor said. "Maybe you don't set much stock by the Order's code, but, by Menselas, I do. Touch a comrade like that one more time, and you're out. Is that understood?"

Sareya sniffed as she nodded.

"Get out of my sight," Vihtor said, and she turned and fled.

To Naul, Vihtor said, "Idiot." Then to Orix: "I respect your honesty. You're from the Plains of Khisig-Ugtall, aren't you?"

"City of Ivrian, Seneschal," Orix said.

"You do your people credit. But in future, make sure you fight for the right reasons."

Vihtor turned to regard Anskar.

With a lump in his throat, Anskar said, "I'm sorry, sir. I shouldn't have lost control the way I did."

Vihtor stared at him for a long moment, then said, "No, you shouldn't. As a knight, you'll be expected to show restraint and understanding. Sareya was taken from her family as a child and brought here to the Burg. Though necessary, such things scar a person deeply. You'd do well to remember that."

Moonlight spilled through the narrow window above Anskar's bedhead, splashing the sheets and his naked torso with crimson. Jagonath, the red moon, was in the ascendancy tonight: the bloodshot eye of Menselas, the priests of the Elder called it. The avenger moon. The destroyer of dreams. Anskar lay on his bed, unable to sleep, worries about the pending trials wrapped up with anger about Sareya and her lies, and the feeling he had disappointed the Seneschal.

He tried praying to the Elder aspect of Menselas—the font of wisdom and control—but it did no good. He couldn't focus. He felt lost, a failure, as if he'd been on the brink of greatness and let it slip away from him. Nonsense, he knew, but the realization didn't help.

He gave up on the Elder and switched instead to the Litany of the Healer, which Brother Tion had made him learn as a child. Anskar struggled with the ancient Skanuric words, and still barely understood them, but the familiar rhythms of the prayer always seemed to soothe him.

Menselas would forgive his loss of control—Menselas always did—and come morning, maybe things would look different. If morning ever came.

The flutter of wings outside his window startled him, and he pushed himself up on one elbow, craning his neck to see. There was nothing, just the dark background of night saturated by the moon's ruddy glow. Probably an owl, he told himself. Or a bat.

He held his breath, listening for any sound, but none came. He slumped back down on the bed, and straight away all he could think of was Sareya. By the Five he hated her. When he closed his eyes, he could see her smirking face reveling that she'd brought him down to her level.

But it wasn't just anger he felt. He saw Sareya's image in his mind again, her unlaced shirt, the lingering scent of her perfume…

Anskar rolled over onto his side and buried his face in the pillow, ashamed by the pressure growing in his groin. It wasn't his fault, he told himself. She was the one making him feel this way. That's what Niyandrians did. They were sorcerers through and through. She'd beguiled him.

He formed the sword of the Warrior in his mind's eye, and this time it blazed golden, so clearly it was almost solid. He imagined himself grasping the hilt; pictured Sareya as a red-skinned and bat-winged demon; saw himself drive the blade between her breasts so that blood bubbled from her mouth and she wailed and twitched till she stilled.

With a mumbled prayer of thanks to the Warrior, he rolled onto his side and let his head sink into the pillow.

THREE

THE NOVICES WERE SPLIT INTO twelve groups of eight and told to sit quietly in the antechamber outside the Dodecagon, the great hall in which they were to face the first of the trials. Anskar sat at the end of the stone bench allotted to his group, nursing sweaty palms and repeatedly wiping them on his pants. Brother Tion would no doubt say there was virtue in patience, but why couldn't they just get on with it and let the trial begin?

He was tired from lack of sleep, and had only managed to eat a few spoonfuls of porridge at breakfast. He wouldn't have been able to keep down any more than that. But now all he could think about was how sluggish he felt—and the ramifications of failure. It didn't help to remind himself that this was the first of three attempts at the trials. Failure—any failure—was absolute to his way of thinking. You didn't get three chances in battle. One mistake, and you were dead.

Of course, Larson had admitted to failing the trials at his first two attempts, and the stablemaster had slipped up in battle and lived to tell the tale, albeit with a mangled leg. So, maybe the Order was right to be lenient; but Anskar wasn't interested in just getting by. He bet Vihtor Ulnar never failed the trials, nor the Grand Master, not anyone else high up in the Order. That was the difference between Anskar and the other novices: they wanted to be knights. He wanted to be the best.

He licked dry lips and tried to swallow but couldn't make enough spit. Today's trial should be easy, he told himself. A simple test of sword play. None of the others practiced as much as he did, nor had they grown up with the knights. None of them had his natural gifts.

Unable to bear the waiting any longer, he stood and shook out his arms, then went through a sequence of footwork drills. As he limbered up with slips and pivots and stance switches, he cast surreptitious glances over his group. Blosius, the rich boy from Kaile, looked as though he were going to be sick. He watched Anskar's exercises as if he knew he should be doing them himself but didn't think there would be much point.

The twins, Clenna and Rhett, whispered to each other and sneered whenever they met Anskar's gaze. They were both skilled with the blade and showed quick footwork, but Clenna was stronger mentally. She had the flat eyes of a killer.

Anskar didn't know the other four in his group but had seen them around. They were all older than him, having failed the trials before. It could be that this was their last chance. By the defeated looks on their faces, a couple of them could already hear the dead-eyes outside the Burg sharpening their talons.

The sound of hammering and occasional crashes and shouts from beneath the marble floor drew worried looks from the novices, but Anskar knew it must be the Niyandrian masons converting the Hooded One's chapel into a banker's vault.

He caught Sareya and Niv watching him and immediately looked away, pretending to take an interest in an oil painting above the blackwood double doors to the Dodecagon. The painting combined the emblems of the City States, the Pristart Combine, and Kaile—star, ox and scythe, and hawk—and above them, the silver gauntlet of the Knights of Eternal Vigilance, fingers and thumb splayed to denote the five aspects of Menselas. Of course, in recent years, the Order had adopted a five-pointed star in place of the hand: it was less intimidating to the vanquished locals, they claimed, who were learning to live under mainland rule. The priests of the Healer had taken the theory a step further and preferred the symbol of a five-petaled rose.

The painting was a reminder of when the rival mainland nations had come together to save Wiraya from the Necromancer Queen. The allies had gained their first foothold in Niyas here at Dorinah, besieging the city for weeks until it capitulated. Branil's Burg—Anskar had no idea what it had been called before—had been swiftly garrisoned, and formed the bridgehead for the final push toward the capital, Naphor.

Anskar sat back on the end of his bench, only to find Naul glaring at him from the bench opposite. The dried cast of one of Tion's poultices covered the skinny lad's broken nose.

Orix was in another group, shoulders bunched up about his ears. He seemed lost in contemplation, which was absurd, given that contemplation required a brain. Still, built like he was, Orix wouldn't need much of a brain to pass the first trial. But come the second trial, he was finished.

The second trial was to take place in the smithing hall, where the novices would be asked to forge a sword using the techniques that made the Order's weapons the most desired—and the most expensive—throughout Wiraya. Like most Traguh-raj, Orix didn't know an anvil from a slack-tub, despite years of lessons.

Metal-crafting had always been Anskar's first love—even more than fighting. Most candidates didn't commence the disciplines of the Order until the mark of the god had manifested in them—usually around ten or eleven for the girls, and a little later for the boys. But Anskar's mark had been there since birth, so Tion said. It was likely the reason he'd been brought to the Burg as an infant after his parents had perished in the war.

Someone tugged at Anskar's sleeve—Blosius. Anskar could feel his hand shaking.

"I was just thinking," Blosius said, "what are the chances we'll end up fighting? Wouldn't that be something?" He let out a nervous laugh.

"Well, seeing as we're in the same group of eight, I'd say it's pretty likely."

Blosius let out another laugh, following it up with a couple of feigned punches. "I've had my eye on you for some time, Anskar. Like to keep myself apprised of the competition. You're a good swordsman. More than good. I had thought of asking you to give me private lessons—you know, work on my parry, and on speed and extension with my thrust. I would have paid you handsomely, of course."

"I can't take your coin," Anskar said. "It's not allowed." Novices had been thrown out for less. "And besides, there's not much I could teach you."

Blosius was good. The problem was, he didn't know it. But he wasn't a fighter, not in the head, where it mattered most.

Anskar gave him a reassuring pat on the shoulder. "You're better than you think, Blosius. Pray to the Warrior. Ask him for the grace to excel in your bouts this morning."

"Good idea. Thank you. I'll give it a try." Blosius interlaced his fingers and bowed his head.

Oddly, encouraging Blosius helped to quell some of Anskar's own anxiety. Taking his own advice, he closed his eyes and made a mental image of a silver sword etched with Skanuric runes, its cross-guard embellished with gold filigree, its hilt wound with a continuous strip of sea-ray skin. It was an image from an illuminated manuscript Brother Tion had made him study in an attempt to teach him Skanuric. A year on, and Anskar could still only recognize a smattering of words—and the grammar made no sense to him at all. But the vividly inked illustrations had burned themselves into his memory and often formed the focal point for his prayers.

He began to recite the litany of petitions to the Warrior that he'd learned by heart—in common Nan-Rhouric, not the original Skanuric:

"God of Battle, temper me. God of War, sharpen me. God of Slaughter…"

He trailed off as he heard the clunk and thud of bolts being drawn back, and looked up to see the blackwood doors open inward. A ripple of nervous breaths came from the waiting novices.

Gripping the hilt of the wooden practice sword sheathed at his hip, Anskar mouthed a quick final petition for the Warrior's favor, then joined the line of novices filing inside behind their trainers.

As Anskar crossed the threshold behind Blosius, he was overwhelmed by the clouds of sweet-smelling incense and the chanting of dozens of robed and cowled priests.

The light inside the Dodecagon had a peculiar rosy tint, caused by the high stained-glass ceiling—twelve lead-framed panels that converged in a point at the apex. To Anskar's shock, each panel depicted red-skinned Niyandrians with nothing on save for skull masks.

He wasn't the only one to notice. The orderly procession into the Dodecagon halted as the trainees gawped at the ceiling, some passing their forearms in front of their faces—the Mother's ward against immorality. The Niyandrians, though, just seemed curious.

Vihtor Ulnar's voice rang out, calling the novices' attention back to the moment. "Ignore the Niyandrian decor. Recall why you're here."

The Seneschal was seated upon a carved blackwood throne atop a half-dais in front of one of the chamber's twelve walls. Each of the other walls had its own dais and throne, upon which was seated a senior knight in the silver mail and white surcoat of the Order. These twelve were to judge the groups of combatants.

Beneath each throne was a long bench, where the groups of novices were directed to sit. Anskar's chest grew tight with excitement as his group took its place at the foot of Vihtor's throne.

The blue-and-white tiled floor formed a mosaic of a grinning death's-head, another testimony to the Niyandrian culture that had built Branil's Burg. The floor space had been divided by ropes into four fighting squares, which gave enough room for movement, but not so much that you could avoid your opponent for the entire five-minute bout.

Beside Anskar, Blosius continued to mutter prayers, but stopped abruptly when Beof Harril, the senior representative of the Warrior on Niyas, separated out from the chanting priests and raised his mace. The Dodecagon pitched into silence.

Beof called the names of pairs of combatants from four of

the groups. Among them were Naul and Orix. Anskar's hands clenched into fists as he suppressed disappointment. He'd wanted to be among the first to fight.

Blosius sucked in a deep breath, then let it out with a rush. "Shame. I thought we were on. Still, can't hurt to watch, pick up a few pointers, eh?"

There were obvious nerves on display among the first eight combatants as they stepped into their squares, while four knights came down from their thrones to act as adjudicators.

Orix faced off against an older lad who had a reach and height advantage. At first Orix could find no way through his opponent's defensive thrusts, and finally decided to take a blow from the other's practice sword in order to deliver one of his own. Wincing at a jab to his ribs, Orix smashed his blade into his opponent's face then barreled him to the floor, pounding the hilt of his wooden sword into the bigger lad's face until the knight-adjudicator pulled him off.

Anything it took to win, Anskar knew. In sparring, they had never been permitted to go all-out, but he'd often imagined real bouts like this, and his scuffle with Sareya, Orix, and Naul last night had convinced him he was ready.

Anskar had been so caught up in Orix's brutal victory that he'd not been following the action in the other three squares. Now he saw that Naul and his opponent were evenly matched. The young woman wasn't as tall as Naul, but she was broader and possessed of a ferocity that initially threatened to overwhelm him. But Naul was as crafty as they came.

She lunged and thrust—easily turned aside by Naul, who retreated a step. Her next attack came swift and hard after a feint. Naul parried and dropped into a crouch. Her sword slashed at his legs, forcing him back, then Naul launched a flurry of blistering blows. His opponent deftly dodged and parried them all, but staggered and almost tripped.

Having seen enough to know how she'd react, Naul stepped in suddenly, feinted a thrust and punched her full in the face with his free hand. As she staggered back, he tripped her, then rammed his sword into her chest where she lay. With a steel blade, she'd be dead. Even with a blunt wooden sword, she cried out in pain and curled into a ball. When Naul proceeded to beat her with the flat of his blade, the knight-adjudicator stepped in to end the bout.

I'll not lose like that, Anskar told himself, but his mouth was dry again, and his stomach felt queasy. He had a vision of hammering out horseshoes and repairing plows for the rest of his life.

The four losers were escorted from the Dodecagon, and the winners returned to their benches. Beof announced the second set of bouts. This time, two were called from Anskar's bench: Rhett and his sister Clenna.

Always full of insolence, Clenna immediately protested to Vihtor Ulnar. "It's not fair to pit me against my own brother in the first round. I won't do it!"

"The lots were chosen at random," Vihtor said. "Fight or fail. Your choice."

"My family in Nagorn City will hear about this," Clenna said.

Anskar expected a mocking retort from the Seneschal. Everyone knew Nagorn City was a stinking mound of dung whose wealthiest families were poorer than the servants in Kaile, where Vihtor hailed from. But to his surprise, the Seneschal didn't even roll his eyes.

"Very well, sit this round out," Vihtor said. "It's not like you two haven't fought each other before."

He wasn't wrong there. Clenna and Rhett were always at each other's throats, though you'd have thought Rhett would have learned his lesson by now.

In Clenna's place, Vihtor selected an older lad called Shenk, who looked as though he might have a trace of San-Kharr blood, judging by the grayness of his skin.

The other three fights were well underway by the time Rhett and Shenk faced off in the square closest to Anskar, with Vihtor adjudicating.

It was immediately clear that Shenk wasn't a good swordsman: he tried to muscle his strokes, using wide, sweeping arcs that left him open to counters down the middle. Rhett took full advantage, jabbing Shenk in the midriff with well-timed thrusts. Each strike knocked the air out of Shenk's lungs, and soon he was backing up, gasping for breath.

Shenk rallied for one final assault, all rage and no finesse. Rhett sidestepped and struck him on the side of the head with the hilt. Shenk's knees buckled and he went down. He didn't even bother trying to get up. He knew he was outmatched and, judging by his shameful lack of heart, looked already resolved to pursue an alternative career.

"That's him gone," said an older novice, confirming what Anskar had deduced: fail at the first trial in any given year, and you didn't advance to the second trial. Fail three years, and you were out. Permanently.

The other three bouts went to decisions. Points were allotted solely for swordsmanship, so it was a good idea to score hits with the practice sword rather than with punches, kicks, and elbows.

Anskar was itching to get up from the bench by the time his name was called. He strode toward the fight square, drawing his wooden sword and going through his forms, only looking up as his opponent stepped into the square. It shouldn't have come as a surprise, but it did, and for an instant it deflated him. He'd come to like Blosius.

It was a fleeting regret. The instant Vihtor stepped into the square between them and signaled for the bout to begin, Anskar saw Blosius only as an obstacle in his way.

They circled each other, swords ready, eyes locked. Blosius said something—a curse or a challenge, Anskar couldn't tell. Maybe he was asking Anskar to go easy on him.

Blosius's first lunge came hard and fast, and wood clacked against wood as Anskar parried and stepped aside. Blosius gave an apologetic smile, but Anskar gave him nothing in return. He needed to be careful: he'd started to underestimate his opponent.

Anskar thrust once, twice—feints to see how Blosius would react. The rich boy didn't bite, just kept his eyes on Anskar's and circled away to his right.

Anskar let his blade drop and Blosius swung for his head, but he was at the extent of his range and Anskar swayed back out of the way then sprang forward with a counter. Blosius blocked, and Anskar angled away to the side.

There followed a sequence of thrusts and parries, neither willing to overcommit, but then Blosius pressed forward, aiming low, then going high, forcing Anskar back. The rich boy was breathing hard now, putting everything into his offensive, but Anskar just parried as he circled away, conserving his strength, waiting for Blosius to tire himself out before he countered.

As Anskar stepped to his right, Blosius moved with him. Back the other way, and Blosius was there again, more measured now with his strikes: thrusts down the center; hacks either side to prevent Anskar from circling out of danger.

When Anskar's back touched the rope that defined the fight

square, Blosius unleashed a ferocious combination. Anskar blocked desperately, then stepped beneath a swing and pivoted off to one side. Blosius turned and only just ducked beneath a vicious swing from Anskar.

Blosius retreated a step, keeping his blade in the high guard position.

Now it was Anskar's turn to stalk him, and Blosius backed up in a straight line. Each time he tried to angle off to the side, Anskar was one step ahead of him. Blosius's breaths came out ragged now, and he wiped sweat from his eyes.

Anskar's heart thumped wildly in his chest, goading him to launch an all-out attack and finish this. And he almost did. Almost fell for it.

Blosius stumbled as he retreated, and Anskar darted forward; but it was a ruse. Blosius dipped his knees and thrust for Anskar's chest. With speed his only defense, Anskar smacked the stroke away and sent a riposte at Blosius's face. Blosius dipped and pivoted, but before he could take advantage of the angle, Anskar stepped back out of range.

They circled each other more warily now, and then Anskar broke the rhythm of their steps with a swift thrust at Blosius's throat, at the last instant bending his knees and going low. Blosius parried and countered with a slash that left him wide open. Anskar thrust for Blosius' exposed chest—just as he was supposed to. Blosius swayed back so the tip of Anskar's sword barely missed then returned a thrust of his own. Anskar blocked, and Blosius separated, chest heaving.

Not giving his opponent time to recover his breath, Anskar closed the distance with three deft thrusts to stomach, chest and throat, then slashed at Blosius's legs. Again, Blosius parried, but Anskar went high, his wooden blade grazing Blosius's cheek.

This time, Blosius didn't break off, but instead slammed blow after blow into Anskar's sword, trying to knock it from his grasp.

Anskar fell back under the assault, knowing all he needed to do was weather the storm. Blosius's strikes grew weaker and weaker, but then he tried a sudden jab at Anskar's body. Anskar swayed aside and Blosius stumbled past him, pitching to one knee.

Anskar could have ended it there: could have hit the rich boy in the face as he tried to turn and stand, but instead he backed up and gave Blosius a second to recover.

Jeers sounded from the benches, but when Anskar glanced round, his eyes met Vihtor's. He'd all but forgotten the Seneschal was adjudicating the bout. Vihtor gave a barely perceptible nod of approval, but then his eyes widened and Anskar turned just in time to block Blosius's attack, which was designed to split his skull down the middle.

Anskar responded with deft stabs that drove Blosius back against the rope, then he abandoned finesse for power, hacking apart Blosius's defense as if possessed by a demon.

Blosius pivoted out of danger, but his mouth hung open and he gasped for every breath. But when Blosius let his sword hang limp as if he were too exhausted to lift it, Anskar didn't fall for the trick. Instead, he forced Blosius back across the square with relentless pressure.

As his back hit the rope on the other side of the square, Blosius tried to regain the initiative with three quick thrusts, but there was no sting in his attacks.

Anskar's confidence soared, and he felt as fresh as he'd been at the start of the bout. He kept just out of range, then lunged in and stabbed Blosius in the sternum. Blosius grunted and pitched backward into the rope as his sword clattered to the floor.

Anskar stepped back. "Pick it up," he said.

Blosius shook his head, then bent over, exhausted, hands on thighs. "I'm done," he said. "Really, I'm done."

A look of disgust on his face, Vihtor announced Anskar the winner and shook his head at Blosius before leaving the square to call for the next fight.

Blosius straightened up and offered his hand to Anskar. "The best man won."

"You fought well, Blosius."

"Not really. I hung on in there as long as I could, but that's all I was doing: barely surviving."

"Not true," Anskar said. "You had me in trouble. With more stamina, more belief in your abilities… Learn from this, Blosius. Don't give up."

"I won't," Blosius said, but there was no conviction in his voice.

Clenna stepped into the square, ready to fight, glaring at them for lingering too long.

"Perhaps I'll take up running," Blosius said unconvincingly. "Who knows, with another year to train…"

"You'd still lose," Clenna said. "Rich bastards like you can't fight. You've never had to."

Blosius looked relieved as he headed out through the blackwood doors, and Anskar wondered if he had it in him to enter the trial a second time.

As Anskar turned back to the bench, he almost bumped into Vihtor, who was waiting to adjudicate Clenna's bout. The Seneschal nodded, his mouth curling into a half smile, and Anskar beamed with pride.

Clenna was up against a frightened-looking youth who was clearly older than her, and possibly on his last attempt. The lad had no meat on his bones and was right to look scared. Clenna smirked at him, virtually licking her lips at the prospect of beating him senseless.

It didn't take her long to destroy the skinny youth, and she continued to spit and curse at his unconscious form even as the Seneschal dragged her from the fight square.

"Enough, girl!" Vihtor shouted. "By Menselas, you demean yourself. Start acting like a knight, if that's what you want to be. Another show of behavior like that, and it'll be the lash for you."

Clenna's eyes narrowed and her hands clenched into fists, but she gave Vihtor a curt nod before moving back to her seat. She sat sullenly, breathing heavily, and stared at the ground. They'd all felt the sting of the lash for infractions, even Anskar.

A short recess followed so the combatants could visit the latrines and drink from the jugs of water Niyandrian servants brought around.

Head bowed, hair obscuring her face, Jonita poured Anskar a drink. He knew it was her from the welts on her wrists. He longed to say something to his old friend but had no idea what and started to move away.

"You fought well, Anskar," Jonita murmured.

"You saw?"

She lifted her head, and through her unruly hair, Anskar could see that she had a black eye to go with her swollen jaw. "I always knew you'd amount to something."

"Who did this to you?" Anskar asked.

"It's nothing."

"Tell me who it was and I'll—"

"You were always kind to me," Jonita said, meeting his gaze. She looked older than she was, wise beyond her years. "But that was another world, a world you've left behind."

"Jonita…"

"Don't lose your focus," she said. "You still have two bouts remaining. Pass the trials. The other kitchen hands and I, we're all cheering for you."

You are? Anskar wanted to say. He swallowed a lump in his throat. "I..." But once more he was speechless.

Jonita smiled and touched his cheek. "Go on. If not for yourself, do it for us."

"I will," he said. "Thank you, I will."

As he turned away, an older novice caught his eye—a lad by the name of Unther he'd sparred with once or twice.

"By the Five, did you see Clenna fight?" Unther said as he handed a water jug back to a Niyandrian servant. "That is one wild bitch! Thank Menselas she's not in my group."

"No," Anskar said, "she's in mine."

"Yes, well, good luck there," Unther said. He nudged Anskar with his elbow. "Say, do you think she's as ferocious in other activities?"

"What do you mean?"

"You know!"

"Sorcery?"

Unther rolled his eyes and looked about to give up, and then Anskar understood what he was getting at.

"You know the rules, Unther."

"I do, but does she? That's what you have to ask yourself. Imagine, though!" He gulped down his water. "Actually, don't. There's a sin in there somewhere, though you'd know better than me."

"I doubt that," Anskar said with a shake of his head. "But you're right about Clenna's wildness. There's something... broken about her."

"And you're the one to fix it, eh? Do you think she needs taming?"

"No, that's not what I mean," Anskar said. "But all that rage...
on a battlefield... Either she'll learn to temper it, or she'll die
long before her time."

Unther grunted his agreement. "We'll probably all die before
our time. It's not like we're training to work in the kitchens."

"Don't knock what you've not tried," Anskar said. "The
kitchens aren't so bad."

When the time came for his second bout, it was Rhett waiting
across the square from him. As Anskar took his place, he heard
Clenna mutter, "Hope you die, half-blood."

She was goading him, Anskar knew, in the hope that he would
make a mistake that her twin could capitalize on.

Anskar immediately took control of the center of the square,
willing himself to relax and allow his movements to flow.

Rhett tried the same tactic he'd used on Shenk in the first
round: he feinted a thrust, trying to lure Anskar into an attack
so he could counter. Anskar circled to the right, always an inch
or two out of range. Whenever Rhett edged forward, Anskar
retreated the same distance, then pivoted and worked his way
back to the center. It was a game of patience, both wanting the
other to strike first.

But when Clenna called out from the bench, "Get on with
it!" it was her brother who attacked. Rhett feinted low, then
launched a cut at Anskar's head.

Anskar ducked beneath the wooden blade and slammed into
Rhett, tripping him and sending him crashing to the floor. Rhett's
sword jarred from his grip and skittered away across the tiles.

Anskar abandoned his own blade and dropped his weight on
Rhett, pinning him from the side. Rhett tried to twist into him,
but Anskar rammed a shoulder into his face and forced him to
look away, then put a knee on his stomach and transferred all his

weight there. Rhett winced and gasped for air.

Anskar slid his knee across so he was fully mounted, clamped a hand over Rhett's nose and mouth to hinder his breathing, then started to pound away at his ribs.

When Rhett brought his hands down to defend, Anskar elbowed him in the face. An angry cut opened up on Rhett's forehead, gushing blood. Anskar hit him again and again, each time smacking Rhett's head against the floor until Vihtor pulled him off.

Rhett was no longer moving.

Anskar glared at Vihtor as he resumed the bench. The Seneschal should have stopped the fight sooner.

Clenna looked as though she was barely restraining herself from leaping at Anskar. He could see her hands clenching and unclenching as she leaned toward him.

"I'm going to gouge your eyes out, half-blood. I'll do it quick, before they can stop me."

"Try it and you'll get the same as your brother," he replied with more bravado than he felt.

Clenna sneered and turned away.

It wasn't long before she had the chance to vent her anger in the square. Her opponent was Lalea, a girl Clenna's own age who came from a wealthy family in the City States and tended to keep herself aloof from the other novices. By the end of Clenna's furious onslaught, Lalea's nose was shattered, her front teeth broken, and her once unblemished face was a mess of crimson. The healers had to carry her out of the Dodecagon.

Clenna stalked toward the bench, crimson speckling her face. "Just you and me now, half-blood," she told Anskar.

For the first time since the trials had begun, Anskar felt a stab of doubt. More than doubt. Fear. Clenna had a quality that couldn't be taught: a predator's instinct for pinpointing a weakness and knowing when to pounce. And she had the kind of rage that could overwhelm a more skilled opponent.

Orix and Naul both won their next fights and emerged triumphant in their groups. As did Sareya, which was a surprise to Anskar. The Niyandrian had always looked average during sparring, but the contest had brought the fight out of her.

Perhaps an even bigger shock was that Myra DeYenté came out on top of her group. Myra was infamous for never eating—at least in public—and had a lean frame to show for it; but she'd shown great composure in each of her bouts, and a sharp, strategic mind.

Anskar's fight with Clenna to decide the winner of their group was the last bout of the day. His muscles ached from his previous two fights, and he'd grown stiff and weary from sitting around watching the others. Clenna, though, was itching to fight, and she prowled the square, glaring hatred at Anskar as he took his place.

At the commencement of the bout, Vihtor, who was again the adjudicator, gave Anskar an almost imperceptible nod.

Anskar came out fast, trying to command the center as he'd done against Rhett, but Clenna would give no quarter. She blocked his thrusts with efficiency and ease, always moving laterally to take herself off the center line. Anskar had the sense she was feeling him out, gauging his timing and his reactions to her feints.

Clenna launched into a series of thrusts and slashes, which Anskar blocked as he backed away, but she managed to rush in close and caught him on the jaw with a left hook he'd not seen coming. She followed up with a low kick to his thigh that almost buckled his knee.

He was learning the hard way that Clenna had a lot more to

her than blind rage.

She went to kick again, and Anskar raised his shin to block, but it had been another feint. The tip of Clenna's sword slipped past his guard and punched into his sternum so hard he couldn't breathe. Staggering back, he flailed around with his blade, trying to create space, but Clenna walked through his blows, punched him in the mouth, then swung her wooden blade at his neck.

Anskar ducked…straight into a well-timed knee that jolted his head back and rattled his teeth. She grabbed a fistful of his hair and held him in place for another knee, and another. Anskar's vision blurred, and with each concussive impact, the will to fight sluiced out of him.

He was about to concede, but then he heard Jonita's voice in his head: *Do it for us.* He pictured her black eye, the welts on her wrist. Her swollen jaw. Anger sparked inside him; ignited in his veins.

As Clenna threw another knee, Anskar swept her back leg out from under her. She flipped as she fell, landing in a crouch, still facing him. He kicked her in the chest to drive her back, and she shrieked with fury as she launched herself at him, swinging her sword at his head.

Anskar parried then sent a riposte into her temple. She staggered, momentarily stunned, and he pressed the advantage, movements flowing swifter than he could think. A kick to her knee, a hack to her forearm that sent her practice sword clattering to the floor. Then he cracked an elbow into her face. Blood sprayed and Clenna stumbled back—but only a step.

Her face was a bloody mess as she started to stalk him again, eyes reading his every move, hunting for openings. Even without a sword, she still thought she could win.

Clenna lunged forward, dipping under his thrust, and swung a wild hook that Anskar blocked with his forearm. But the punch was a feint for a spinning kick that just skimmed the top of his head as he ducked.

Anskar switched stance and countered with a roundhouse kick to her ribs, which crumpled Clenna to her knees. He smashed his blade into her head, pitching her to the floor, where she sprawled on her back.

Anskar stood over her, the tip of his wooden sword pressed against her throat.

Clenna cursed and spat, but that only made Anskar press harder. Her face grew purple with the effort to breathe, but still she struggled.

Anskar narrowed his eyes. It might only be a wooden blade, but with enough force behind it, it would crush her windpipe.

"It's only a trial," he said through clenched teeth. "You have two more attempts."

Clenna hissed and thrashed and swore.

"Your choice," Anskar said, steeling himself for the final thrust.

But a strong hand on his shoulder pulled him back, and Vihtor raised Anskar's arm in victory.

The applause from the watching knights and novices was muted. They were shocked at what they'd witnessed.

Anskar braced himself as Clenna climbed to her feet, gingerly feeling her throat. The blood flowed down her face in rivulets that stained her white shirt crimson.

Vihtor stood between them, holding up a hand for Clenna to desist. But instead of a renewed attack, she dipped her head to Anskar.

"Good fight," she said.

Anskar let out a sigh of relief.

FOUR

ANSKAR SCREAMED HIMSELF AWAKE. STABBING pain radiated from his chest to his back and both arms. In his dream, a spear had ripped through his defenses and pierced his heart. His attacker was a woman—a Niyandrian. A jagged scar ran from beneath one eye to her chin. She spat hatred at him and yelled betrayal before she thrust.

Brother Tion hurried to his bedside, and Anskar realized he was in the infirmary, where they had brought him last night to tend his injuries from the trial.

"Here," Tion said, holding a moistened rag to Anskar's lips. "It's soaked in herbs that will ease the pain."

Anskar bit down on the rag, gagging at the bitter taste. Warm fluid filled his mouth, and he swallowed. Within moments the crushing pain in his chest had reduced to a dull ache.

"Your sternum is badly bruised," Tion said. "But it will heal."

Anskar spat out the rag and wiped its taste from his lips. "I dreamed I'd been stabbed through the heart…by a woman—a Niyandrian."

Tion chuckled. "Dreams play odd tricks on us, though the Five only knows why. Clenna's certainly no Niyandrian." He leaned in so he could whisper. "And I'm not even sure she's a woman; the way she fights, she might be part demon."

Anskar realized he couldn't feel his face. He probed with his fingers and felt a cold, sticky layer covering his cheeks and forehead.

"One of my poultices," Tion said. "For the bruising. There's one on your chest too, though it's yet to make a difference."

With a grunt, Anskar forced himself to sit up. He pulled the sheets down to reveal a purplish bloom covering his entire chest as far as his navel. Clenna had caught him good.

He saw her in the bed opposite, propped up against her pillows, the trace of a smirk on her face. She must have taken some satisfaction from hearing him scream.

"A fraction more force and you might have fractured or broken ribs," Tion said. "Just thank Menselas it was only a practice sword. Lie back now and rest. You need to be at least partially recovered for the start of the second trial tomorrow."

Once the healer had shuffled off, Clenna said, "I should have beaten you."

"You almost did," Anskar conceded.

He heard Clenna sigh and the creak of her bed as she rolled over. Then she muttered, "Almost isn't good enough."

Anskar closed his eyes and let his head sink into the pillow. He had no doubt Clenna would have emerged victorious in any of the other groups. It seemed unfair that she—arguably one of the best two or three fighters among the novices—would have to wait until next year to try again.

He tried to sleep but wasn't able to find a comfortable position. He watched what was going on in the infirmary instead. Half the beds were occupied by injured novices from the first trial, and priests of the Healer flitted about, pushing wooden trolleys that held jugs of water, towels—both bloodstained and fresh—sharp knives, jars of honey, and pouches of herbs.

Some time later, Tion returned with a bowl of steaming broth—chicken giblets and a blend of pungent herbs he claimed as his closely guarded secret. Whatever it was, it worked. Anskar spooned it down greedily, and within the hour was in one of the private rooms in the bath house, soaking in a tub the healers had filled with salted water for him, letting the aches ebb from his body.

After he'd dried off and dressed in a fresh shirt and pants, he took a gentle walk around the bailey with Tion. Glistening dew still covered the grass, though it was close to midmorning. A cold wind blowing in from the Simorga Sea filled the air with the tang of brine.

"Clenna was certain she had you beaten," the priest said.

"So was I."

Tion stopped him with a hand on the shoulder. "What happened?"

"I'm not sure. I remember thinking about the kitchen servants; not wanting to let them down."

"And that's all?"

"Maybe the Warrior blessed me?"

Tion sniffed, unconvinced. "I've no doubt he blessed all of you—at least those who bothered to pray beforehand. But I've never heard of anyone getting a second wind like you did against Clenna. Surely, you don't really believe it was divine intervention?"

"I don't know. Why would the Five aid me and not Clenna?"

"That, my dear Anskar, I would have thought obvious. But seriously now, describe it to me: everything you felt."

Anskar pinched the bridge of his nose. It was all still a blur of sensations muddled by pain. "Something like a cold flame erupted inside me. After that, I couldn't put a foot wrong. My movements just flowed, and Clenna's seemed so slow."

A shadow of concern passed behind Tion's eyes. "Perhaps you should speak with Beof about this. I know little of the Warrior's gifts, but I suppose it's possible you could have felt his touch."

There was more the priest wasn't saying—something else he'd considered and rejected, or some specter he'd not wanted to raise.

"What is it?" Anskar asked.

"Nothing to worry about. Just be thankful that whatever happened, happened. Either the Warrior touched you or he didn't. The important thing is that you passed the first trial. And if it wasn't one of the aspects of Menselas, then whatever was unleashed within you is either perfectly natural or best left well alone. It's a pity Sister Hathenor's returned to the mainland; I'm sure she would have had something profound and uplifting to say on the matter."

On Tion's instructions, Anskar removed the poultice the following morning. His face was a mass of yellow bruising, and still swollen around his cheek and jaw; and there was a knot at his temple—but nothing that would prevent him from continuing with the trials.

A shard of gray light came through the narrow window above his bed, illuminating the books stacked on his writing desk. He'd borrowed them from the Burg's library: tomes on the techniques of metallurgy, blacksmithing, arms and armor, military tactics; and Duin's *Cants and Calculations*, which was required reading for novices commencing the study of the limited sorcery the Order condoned for defense.

The shirt and pants he'd worn for the combat trial had been washed and left folded atop his bed by one of the Niyandrian servants who oversaw the novices' rooms. He changed into them, then sat at his desk and leafed through *Secrets of Jargalan Crafting*. The Order had been trying to emulate the Jargalan swordsmiths for decades, and while they'd made great progress, there was still a way to go before they would be able to produce blades that could never be broken, and were as flexible as they were strong, with a cutting edge as hard as diamond.

Removing the sketches and notes he'd made for the second trial, he glanced over them one last time then folded the piece of parchment and put it in his pocket.

After a breakfast of baked oats mixed with dried fruit and honey, Anskar hurried to the vast smithing hall that was the heart and soul of Branil's Burg, where he joined the other eleven novices who'd passed the first trial.

Several forges were already in use when they arrived. Anskar covered his ears against the clangor of hammers on anvils—too loud for so early in the day. He wiped sweat from his eyes. Outside, there was a cool breeze blowing, but the smithing hall was stifling, hotter than the abyssal realms.

"Nervous?" Sareya asked him. Her white shirt was damp in patches that clung to her curves.

"No," Anskar said, averting his gaze. If anything, he was concerned that he was too relaxed. The forges felt like home, and he'd prepared for this trial above and beyond what was expected.

"You noticed?" Sareya asked.

He shook his head, thinking she meant her damp shirt.

"Not that, silly. I didn't call you half-blood."

"Why's that, then?" *What is it you want?*

She shrugged. "I prayed about it."

A likely story. "And Menselas answered, did he?"

"Maybe."

Anskar pretended to take an interest in the familiar surroundings of the smithing hall. Whatever had been in the hall in the Niyandrians' time had been stripped out long ago and replaced with slatted vents built into the walls, and flues that exited the ceiling above each of the twelve forges dotted about the space. There were slack-tubs for the cooling of hot metal, grindstones, and an iron quench press for holding large pieces of metalwork that needed to be plunged into water in a sunken trough big enough to swim in. Tools hung from every wall—hammers, mallets, pincers, tongs, chisels, fine-toothed metal saws. Cupboards were filled with thick leather gloves, aprons, and the wax balls the smiths used as earplugs.

The other novices stood in a group, feet shuffling, casting nervous glances at each other. Sareya had her back to Anskar now and was in whispered conversation with Naul.

Smoke hung thick in the air; with so many forges in use at one time, the vents couldn't clear it fast enough. Six forges had been allocated to the novices, each banked with charcoal in various stages of heat from red to white. At the other forges, knight-smiths were hard at work on orders from the mainland; the smithing of tools and weapons was a mainstay of the Burg's income.

The tang of hot metal bit into Anskar's nostrils above the stench of coal smoke and sweat. Water within a slack-tub sizzled and steamed as the glowing iron of an axe head was plunged into it. Sparks flew from an anvil where a knight-smith was drawing out the spine of a short sword, making it thinner and longer, but delivering his hammer strikes with great precision to keep the width even.

Despite the heat and the noise, this was an atmosphere Anskar had come to love. For several years, all the novices had received daily instruction and practice in the craft of smithing, but none had put in long hours after the evening meal like he had. Sometimes the only reason he left the smithing hall for his bed was because the Forge Master, Sned Jethryn, dragged him out by his ear.

The novices hadn't only been taught basic techniques, hammering out weapons of bronze, then iron, then steel; they had also learned the Order's secrets for bonding hard and soft metals together by heating and quenching them at just the right temperature and for the right amount of time. Then they had moved on to more complex techniques, such as folding one metal into another, and heat welding—but many had not fully mastered these. Even Anskar, who obsessively practiced his designs and the exacting methods he'd been taught, had only achieved limited success.

To pass the trial, the trainees must craft a functional sword, though the appearance of the weapon and the care that had gone into its design would also be factors. For many trainees, the safe option was to make a serviceable blade from iron, which was softer and easier to work with. Better a simple weapon well made, they reasoned, than a complex one made poorly. Anskar had wrestled with which approach to take for weeks but had known all along he had no real choice. He wasn't given to half measures.

"Right, then," Sned yelled above the din. "Let's get you started."

The Forge Master gave the impression of being broader than he was tall. His shoulders were so huge he seemed to have no neck, and his forearms—scarred white from metal burns—were as thick as thighs. Sweat glistened from his bald head, and his mustache was slick with it. His left eye permanently squinted— he'd caught a red-hot splinter in it years ago.

Sned assigned each of the trainees to a forge—two to each— then told them to face him at the center of the hall so he could go over the rules.

"Now, you should already know them," the Forge Master said, "but like as not, half of you probably weren't listening. Am I right?" He raised a wooden mallet he kept on him to ensure people paid attention. One or two novices flinched.

"Five days you've got to finish the trial," Sned said. "But if you want to finish early, be my guest. Just don't blame me when you fail."

Orix raised his hand.

"Yes?" Sned said.

"Sir, is it only steel we can use?"

Sned raised his mallet and Orix ducked behind his raised arms.

"Use what you like. Use wood, if you don't care about passing. Use horse shit. So long as you make a sword out of it, I don't care.

"But just to clarify for the rest of you cloth-eared wasters: there's no restriction on the number and types of metal you can use. There's a variety of woods and leathers for hilts, along with sea-ray skin, which is a bastard to work with but gives the best grip. Wax earplugs are in the cupboard for those who want them—and only a fool wouldn't. There's more than enough charcoal. My folks"—by which he meant the old men and women among the knights who helped out with Branil's Burg's principal industry—"have been slow-burning wood in piles for weeks, just for you. There's plenty of ingots too. Just don't waste any, because if you do," he said, hefting his mallet, "I can hit you in the back of the head at twenty paces.

"Any questions? Good. Because if you don't know the answers by now, you never will."

When Anskar took out the folded piece of parchment upon which he'd sketched his design, he caught Orix watching him from the adjacent forge.

"What's that?" the Orix asked, as the knight-smiths pulled hot steel from their forges and renewed hammering.

Anskar held up the parchment to show him. He'd drawn a long, slightly curved blade with a grip that could be held with one or both hands. The bow in the steel was a risk he'd decided to take; up to one third of swords made this way were ruined during the quenching and tempering process. There was a single, narrow fuller running along the center of the blade, and around the picture he'd written out the dimensions and listed the materials he planned to use: iron; steel; ash for the handle; sea-ray skin for the grip. Anskar had painstakingly copied out the instructions on what was known of Jargalan smithing and committed them to memory. He'd practiced the techniques time and again during his night sessions at the smithing hall.

"I didn't know we were meant to make a design," Orix said.

Even for a Traguh-raj savage, Orix was slow. Their smithing tutor, Adsila, had urged them for weeks on end to come prepared. She'd even gone so far as to show them the designs she'd made for her own trial more than a decade ago—and the finished weapon.

"You'll just have to do your best," Anskar said, heading for one of the cupboards to get himself some earplugs.

When he returned, Sned was with Orix, asking him what

materials he planned to use. When Orix shrugged, Sned asked to see his design. Orix swallowed thickly and looked miserable.

Shaking his head, Sned turned his back on him and caught Anskar's eye. "What about you, Assling? Surely if anyone has a clue what they're doing, it's you."

If anyone else had called him Assling, Anskar would have broken their nose, but with Sned the nickname was a term of affection.

The Forge Master took the parchment from Anskar and held it above the glow of the forge to examine it. He handed it back with a sniff.

"Too complicated. You'd be better off with something simpler. Pass the trial first. Experiment later. But don't listen to a word I say," he threw over his shoulder as he ambled away to the next forge. "No one ever does."

Anskar took his time selecting the steel for the spine of his sword, eventually settling on the hardest the Order had to offer. He caught some of the novices shaking their heads at him, knowing how hard it was to work such steel, but Anskar was no stranger to difficult forge work and the accompanying ache in his muscles.

He began by laying the steel bar in the coals to heat, adding air from a bellows and waiting till it was white-hot. Sweat dripped from his brow into his eyes. He'd barely even started and he was dying for a drink. Later, he told himself. Five days might have sounded a lot, but with a sword as complex as the one he had in mind, he could have used an entire week.

When the steel was ready, he put in his earplugs and began to hammer out the bar on an anvil. Sparks flew, and the steel rippled white and red as he drew it out with rhythmic blows. The ring of steel on steel could be heard even through his earplugs, and with each strike vibrations traveled up his arm.

Anskar returned the bar to the heat while he found a heavy chisel, then brought the tool back to the anvil, where he scored a groove across the bar's center so he could force the metal to bend with powerful strikes of the hammer.

After more heating and hammering, he got the bar to fold fully back on itself. Then he heated the steel to white again and forge-welded the pieces together before starting to draw out the steel once more.

He'd folded the metal only twice before he needed a break. The skin of his palms ached from gripping the hammer, and sweat was pouring off him and pooling on the floor. He rubbed his sore forearms, then grabbed himself a cup of water from the jug by the entrance.

As he drank deeply, Anskar tried to get a good look at what his peers were working on.

Orix was scratching his head and staring balefully at the misshapen iron bar he'd somehow managed to fuse to the tongs he'd used to hold it in the coals.

Naul had already forge-hardened a bar of iron and shaped a broad, tapering blade complete with a tang. Naul knew what he was doing. Nothing fancy: just enough to pass the trial.

Sareya had also taken the easy option of working with iron, and her sword had a decent shape. At the rate she was going, she'd be finished by tomorrow. He wondered if she'd forge-hardened the metal enough so it wouldn't bend or shatter under stress.

She wiped her brow with her forearm and saw Anskar watching her.

Her eyes flashed with what he took to be annoyance, but then her lips parted in a smile that was, if anything, the opposite.

He looked away and ignored her.

The novice at the forge next to Sareya was clearly copying her design, though he was still drawing out the iron to the required length.

Sned saw Anskar looking and lumbered over to him. "What a goat turd. If he thinks just hammering out an iron bar is going to stand up to my tests…"

Iron or not, at least the novice had something that vaguely resembled a sword, whereas Anskar had slaved away all morning and only had an unformed block of steel to show for his efforts.

A couple of novices took off their leather aprons and gloves and stowed away their work. Judging by the sun's position through the windows, it was past midday.

"You breaking for lunch, Assling?" Sned asked.

"I'd sooner keep working."

"Thought as much." Sned took a pewter flask from his pocket and swigged the contents, then wagged a finger at the block of folded steel on Anskar's anvil. "Too complicated. You know how long it takes the Jargalan nomads to make their curved blades?"

"Just over a week," Anskar said. All the books agreed on that.

Sned raised an eyebrow, then took another swig. "That's with three smiths working on it. You've got five days."

"I'll be fine," Anskar said, though he was far from certain. "I was planning on working through the night."

"Not tonight you can't. The external adjudicator of sorcery is arriving, and the Seneschal wants you novices in the bailey to greet him."

"External adjudicator?"

"Frae Ganwen's job is to teach, but she can't very well assess you as well, can she? That needs someone independent. Same as I won't be the one to test your swords."

Sned screwed the top back on his flask and stowed it in his

pocket.

"And this adjudicator is a sorcerer?" Anskar asked.

The Forge Master touched four fingers and a thumb to his forehead. "One of the few real sorcerers the Church permits us. The Order has a contract with him. Bringing astrumium with him, he is, among other things. These fools won't be happy when they have to hammer their work out tomorrow so they can meld astrumium shards to the iron and steel."

"Astrumium?" Anskar said. "That's an alloy of orichalcum and star-metal, isn't it?"

"Good boy, Assling. I see all that reading's been paying off. Without astrumium, the swords won't hold the sorcery that stops the edge from blunting—which is the whole point of the second trial."

"How come you let everyone shape blades, knowing they'd have to start again in the morning?"

"They should have watched what you were doing. They've all been told repeatedly about the importance of bonding metal to make it hard without being brittle, so there's no excuse. What were they thinking—that I'd pass them just for turning up, or because their sword has a pretty shape? No place for slackers in my smithy, Assling."

Sned ambled to the center of the smithing hall and addressed the group of novices. "Besides Assling here, who's been diligently preparing his metal rather than rushing to shape it, you'll all be starting over in the morning."

Orix palmed his face. Naul narrowed his eyes at Anskar and shook his head. Sareya looked as though she were going to cry. The two novices who'd already packed up for lunch started to grumble, but stopped when Sned picked up his mallet and flipped it from hand to hand.

"There's a mainland sorcerer arriving by ship tonight," Sned said. "Besides the astrumium he's bringing for your swords, you'll be pleased to hear he has a gift for each of you."

Glances passed between the novices, and a few covered their eyes with their forearms. They all knew that Menselas despised sorcerers. But the Order's relationship with them, so it seemed to Anskar, was more complicated than that.

FIVE

IT HAD BEEN SIXTEEN YEARS since Carred Selenas had been to Hallow Hill. The day Naphor had fallen. The day she'd learned her lover, Talia, had a daughter. The day the Queen had died. It had also been the start of Carred's long wait for the daughter—and her guardian—to be revealed.

And still she was waiting.

Her ragtag force of fifty were among the trees skirting the base of Hallow Hill. They remained mounted while their horses cropped the grass. None of them had offered to accompany her to the top. She knew they muttered behind her back. Knew they no longer believed in her promises. She didn't blame them. Her promises sounded hollow even to herself.

There seemed no goal to anything she and her rebels had done all this time—just hit the enemy then flee and hide, only to do the same again and again the length and breadth of Niyas. There was no rhyme or reason to their attacks. All they were was a long, drawn-out act of defiance, a reminder that not all Niyandrians had rolled over and accepted mainland rule. Sometimes it felt as if she were just passing the time till Queen Talia's heir revealed herself.

But what if there was no heir? She only had the word of a wraithe to go on. At least if she'd been told who the heir was, her hope would have been more tangible. More so, if Carred had been named the guardian. She'd give her life to protect Talia's child—the future of Niyas. But, apparently, giving her life wasn't good enough.

The ox-drawn cart they'd brought with them groaned and clattered to a halt on the mud-churned road that led to the hill. The two Last Cohort veterans responsible for keeping the cargo stable climbed out the back and signaled to her that everything was all right. The cart was stacked with kegs of black powder and volatile alchemicals. Carred had paid good coin for the explosives, which her agents had procured from the caliphate of Sohrah in the Jargalan Desert. She'd paid more to smuggle the dangerous goods through the Order's naval blockades.

Coins well spent, she had to hope. Niyandrians needed a victory more meaningful than the burning of mainlander settlements. *She* needed one. More than that, her people needed a cause to rally behind.

And the Order of Eternal Vigilance had given them that cause when they began construction of a new stronghold on the site of the old capital of Niyas.

Strike and run, the wraithe had told her all those years ago. *Hide so you may strike again.* Well, she'd been doing just that, but not any longer. Not today. Maybe she was breaking Queen Talia's orders, but how could she know? She'd been kept in the dark about virtually everything. She'd been given the thinnest of hopes and then told to be patient. But she'd be damned if she was going to allow mainlanders to claim the ruins of Naphor as their own. She'd not stand idly by while her enemy built a city at the very heart of Niyas. It was an affront to everything Niyandrian. A desecration.

She pulled out the dark metal ring she wore on a chain around her neck—Talia's ring—and made a fist around it. She'd sworn to herself never to put it on, but nor would she be without it until her Queen returned to claim it. "Talia, if you can hear me, give me strength," Carred muttered as she set foot on the weathered track that led to the summit. "Because I'm getting too old for this."

She allowed herself a rueful smile as she tucked the ring back beneath her shirt. She was nowhere close to being considered old for a Niyandrian, but as she made the ascent, the area around her right hip stiffened, forcing her to limp slightly. Her body was riddled with aches and pains and unsightly battle scars. No one could fight forever, and she'd been a fighter for more than half her life. She'd taken an arrow in her hip several years back— it had hit her in the front, the head exiting behind. Eadgith, the cohort's necromancer, had removed the shaft and banished the rot with an influx of the earth-tide that powered her sorcery. The wound had healed into a puckered scar front and back. The whole area was numb, but arduous walking, or too long in the saddle, caused the joint to stiffen.

When Carred reached the top of the hill, the mist was so thick she could barely see her hand in front of her face. She moved with caution through the gloom, expecting at any moment a shadow to emerge. If it did, would the wraithe strike her down for her disobedience? Or was she supposed to be here? The mist seemed to amplify her heartbeat till it pounded in her ears. It brought back memories of the siege of Naphor and the panic instilled by mainland war drums.

Gradually, the outline of the squat building atop the summit began to take shape within the mist. Carred gave it a wide berth and made for the far side of the hill. There, she knelt on the damp grass to wait for the mist to lift.

While she waited, she closed her eyes and spoke to Talia. It was a ritual that had started as an outpouring of grief, but with the passage of time, the words of loss and longing had taken on the nature of prayer. As her lips moved in a silent litany, she felt once more the coldness of Talia's skin against hers, the kiss of her bloodless lips.

Carred sniffed back tears, not understanding why, after all this time, she still wept. It felt like someone else's grief, or a grief too great to call her own. It was Niyas she wept for, she told herself. But she couldn't shake off the feeling that she wept for herself, for half a life passed in service to nothing more than a fading dream.

Talia's final words rang in her head again: *Don't leave me in the realm of the dead…*

The necromancers of old spoke of a time when death would be conquered once and for all, but most these days used the earth-tide to stave off infection or add a few more years to their lives. Talia, though, had still believed. There had been a contagious certainty in her pursuit of immortality. Since Naphor, Carred had wanted to believe the Queen had been successful, that it was only a matter of time before she came back. But hope was a fragile thing, and the years of waiting had worn away the edges of her certainty.

She knew that the Knights of Eternal Vigilance who now had the run of Niyas called her the priestess of a cult of fanatics, but what else did she have? And now the mainland overlords wanted to obliterate the last vestiges of Niyandrian culture by appropriating the former capital. Carred and her people were doomed to a life of oppression, if they were left any life at all. They lacked the might to repel the mainlanders, even if they mustered the will. All they had left were myths and promises.

Carred took in a long breath and opened her eyes. The mist was thinning, and in the distance she could see the scorched earth of Naphor. At the center of the devastated city, where Queen Talia's palace had once stood, a huge citadel was under construction. Carred took out her spyglass, extended the tube, and surveyed the scene.

Even at this early hour, workers made their way through the remnants of streets toward the construction site, overseen by a scatter of knights in armor that glinted in the rising sun's pinkish rays. The workers were Niyandrians—either slaves or traitors. Either way, their unparalleled skills in masonry would benefit the Order and make their citadel stronger than any on the mainland. Only Crac Tholanoth at Dorinah, which the knights had renamed Branil's Burg, could rival it.

Carred made out wagons within an enclosure, stables and a corral in the near distance. And all about, mountainous piles of stone taken from the ruins of the old city. There were small buildings under construction around the citadel too. The knights were rebuilding the city. It was another violation she could not permit.

She took note each time she saw a knight, and looked in vain for any sign of a garrison significant enough to oppose her force of fifty. She estimated a few hundred workers, but fewer than twenty knights.

She'd seen enough. Closing the spyglass, she returned it to its sheath at her belt, then made her way back down the hill to where her soldiers waited.

"Get some rest," she told them. "We attack at dusk."

Just before the sun set over Naphor, wagons filled with Niyandrian laborers departed the construction site. From the edge of the forest, Carred watched them through her spyglass. Within the charred ruins of the old city there was little movement, just a handful of guards posted beneath the scaffolding that surrounded the citadel. She counted four, armored head to toe and carrying shields and swords. There would be more in the makeshift barracks behind the stables.

She returned to her men and women and nodded that it was time.

As Carred untethered her horse and mounted, it snorted and shook its mane. The beast was nervous. It knew what was coming.

With a raised hand, she motioned her small force forward.

Griga the sorceress went first, uttering a cant that created an obscuring bank of fog before her, which expanded to cover all the riders. If Griga could be relied on, the fog would also muffle the sound of their horses' hooves.

Griga was one of the moontouched: those Niyandrians born with an exceptional capacity for sorcery who were selected for a life dedicated to the arcane arts. She was a lean, hawkish woman of maybe twenty years, her scrawny body clad in a gossamer dress that seemed woven from spider's silk. Her hair was braided into thick ropey locks bound with silver, copper, and gold thread, and her arms were sleeved with snaking tattoos and swirling script.

Behind the shifting wall of fog, the fifty rebels left the cover of the woods. At their rear came the horse-drawn cart laden with the black powder and alchemicals. The intention was to get as near to the citadel as they could without being seen, overrun the guards, and create sufficient chaos to give the team with the powder opportunity to work their destruction. In the meantime, Carred and the others would deal with the knights coming from the barracks. A simple and direct plan, with everyone knowing their role.

Griga paused in her incantation, flicked a glance at Carred and pointed to the east. A light could be seen through the fog—a silvery sphere that bobbed as it grew steadily larger. Carred stared at it as she rode, and Griga resumed her chanting.

The pace of the horses increased, matching the fog that went before them.

Ahead, a cry went up, and was echoed by another. Griga's sorcery had bought them time, but the knights had seen the sorcerous fog bank for what it was and sounded the alarm. A horn brayed, and Carred yelled the order to charge.

Hooves pounded in her ears as she leaned low over the saddle and drew her sword. Griga screeched a command and the fog instantly vanished. A flash drew Carred's eye. Behind her, a sphere of coruscating silver smashed into the flanks of her charging rebels.

In front, protective wards flared around the four knights converging on her.

As planned, Griga spoke a cant, and a fist of fire hammered into one of the knights, punching through his ward sphere and knocking him from his feet. The remaining three grouped together, their wards interlocking to become a single lucent dome that repulsed Griga's flaming fist.

Realizing the danger, Carred veered to the left, taking her

horse in a wide loop around the three protected knights. As she wheeled, she glimpsed more of the enemy—men and women, some armored, some not—streaming from behind the stables, swords in hand. Wards sprang up around them, silver suns that punctuated the gloom.

Carred came around behind the three knights beneath their luminous dome and saw the chaos amid her riders. The silver sphere she'd first glimpsed during the charge was now clearly visible as a warded knight mounted on a white destrier. The horse reared, kicking out with its hooves as the rider slashed his sword into the face of one of her cohorts. The brilliance of the ward surrounding him caused the knight to flicker as he moved, giving the impression his sword was slow and stuttering, yet the devastation it wrought gave lie to the illusion. He was a big man, armored in shimmering plate, a great helm covering his head with only a narrow slit for the eyes. She'd seen him before: Eldrid DeVantte, the bane of her rebellion. She'd lost count of how many of her attacks DeVantte had scuppered, and now she feared he would thwart her again.

Eldrid hacked left and right at the Niyandrians surrounding him. Already half a dozen were down. Four riderless horses galloped for the woods. One writhed and screamed on the ground atop its rider. The lone knight had broken the momentum of the charge.

A glance over her shoulder showed Carred the number of defenders was continuing to swell. She estimated upward of thirty knights now, all of them warded, and still more were coming. She'd been mistaken in her initial assessment.

No, she'd been tricked.

Griga spurred her mount to the east, then looped back toward the trees. Carred opened her mouth to yell "Coward!" then realized Griga was right. The moontouched woman had seen into the future with no need for sorcery. The day was lost.

"Withdraw!" Carred shouted over the clangor of steel on steel.

Behind her, the gathering knights sprinted toward the fray. In front, Eldrid DeVantte continued his slaughter as Carred's riders tried to break off. Niyandrian swords scraped uselessly off the knight's ward sphere amid showers of sparks.

"Flee!" Carred screamed, kicking her horse into a gallop toward the woods, past the abandoned wagon with its cargo of black powder and alchemicals. It had taken months to arrange for delivery of the deadly cargo, and more gold than she could afford. All wasted. All for nothing.

She reached the tree line behind Griga and a clutch of riders, and turned to see another twenty or so of her force galloping her way. Eldrid DeVantte sat tall upon his steed amid a carpet of dead horses and riders. He looked straight at Carred and his ward sphere dissolved, as if he feared nothing she or her Niyandrians could do.

Griga raised a clawed hand and started a cant, but Carred grabbed her wrist.

"Don't," she said. "It's too late."

Even as she spoke, mounted knights poured out of the stables—dozens of them, an entire garrison that had somehow remained hidden from her. A score of wards flared silver in unison, a great shimmering wall of light.

Carred had seen enough. Beaten, close to despair, she ordered the remnants of her force to split up.

Alone, she galloped recklessly through the trees, ruing the day she'd been tasked with leading the resistance, cursing the wraithe for filling her head with lies, hating Queen Talia for her impotent scheming.

If it was possible to return from the dead, Talia would have done it by now.

And still there was no guardian.

Still there was no heir.

SIX

ANSKAR SAT ON A STONE bench in the bailey, mesmerized by the pinpricks of starlight speckling the darkening sky. The priests of the Elder taught that stars were the suns of other worlds, but tonight they seemed to Anskar like puncture marks in the dark through which seeped strange and occult energies. The Elder's priests would probably call such an idea heresy.

The inner doors of the barbican stood open, a fully armored knight on either side. The portcullis was raised and the massive blackwood doors beyond were open to the world outside. Through them, Anskar could see knights standing in columns on the narrow road that led to and from Branil's Burg, each holding a flaming torch to provide a beacon of welcome for the guest who was still to arrive.

A bat flittered overhead, and in the distance something moaned. Anskar shuddered as the sound distorted in his mind from the hoot of an owl into the cry of a ghoul, or perhaps a dead-eye. A whole day of smithing had pushed him to his limits, and maybe a little beyond.

Orix slumped down beside him on the bench, and Anskar braced himself for trouble. He glanced around, expecting Naul and Sareya to be lurking nearby. To his surprise, Sareya was standing some distance away, apart from the rest of the novices and apparently lost in thought. Naul was with two other lads, looking thoroughly bored by their banter.

"Don't worry," Orix said. "They ain't friends with me anymore. They said I was a snitch for telling Vihtor the truth."

"Better that than an idiot for letting them talk you into attacking me," Anskar said.

"They didn't. I mean, it was my idea."

"Why?"

Orix shrugged. "Because I don't fit in here. Traguh-raj are savage scum. Just you ask any mainland knight."

"Better that than a Niyandrian," Anskar said.

Orix chuckled, but there was no humor in it. "Must be tough to be a Niyandrian. Don't know how they put up with it."

Anskar turned a searching look on him. "Are you saying you acted out of pity for Sareya?"

The flush of Orix's cheeks told a different story.

"Don't tell me, you were trying to impress her? Whatever she's offering, Orix, it's against the rules of the Order."

"I know." Orix sighed. "And I know I'm a fool."

Anskar studied him for a moment longer, then said, "Thank you for telling Vihtor the truth."

"Couldn't help myself. If my mom heard I'd been telling lies, she'd clip me round the ear. We Traguh-raj might be savage scum, but we hate lying. That's why we lost so many wars in the past. Honesty puts us at a disadvantage." He looked Anskar in the eye. "So, am I forgiven?"

Anskar offered his hand and Orix shook it. "Yes, you're forgiven."

"Then, we can be friends?"

"Are you really that unpopular?"

"No!" Orix said, then added miserably, "Yes. But I thought—"

"I'm joking. Of course we can be friends."

"Good, because I wanted to ask you…" Orix looked suddenly pensive. "I ain't got a clue what to do in the smithing hall."

"Were you asleep during the lessons? You were in the same classes as me, and you saw the same practical demonstrations."

"And I did all right with them. But that was basic stuff, not enough to forge a half-decent sword. I need more time to learn. I weren't raised here with the knights like you was."

"But the readings Adsila gave us…"

"Not everyone comes from a rich family that can afford tutors, and you had Brother Tion learning you letters when you was young."

"You can't read?" Anskar said.

"No call for it in the Plains, and when I came here I was already thirteen."

"So, all this time you've gotten by and no one suspected?"

"They just thought I was being lazy, or difficult," Orix said. "So, I just went along with it. It weren't hard to pull the wool over the teachers' eyes, but now…"

"Well, you know how to forge weld, don't you?" Anskar said.

Orix nodded.

"All right, then here's what you need to do. The iron you're working with is too soft. At the end of the trial, our swords will be put through some kind of durability test, and yours will bend out of shape. It's more difficult, but you should select harder bars of iron and forge weld them till they're soft, then beat them into a blended whole. The hammering will also work-harden the metal. The tempering is hard to explain, though."

"Hold your horses!" Orix said. "You're going too fast. Can't you just show me?"

Anskar felt a pang of guilt as he wondered if the Five would punish him for breaking the rules of the trial. But Orix had done the right thing, telling the truth to Vihtor. And he'd made Anskar an offer of friendship. Most of the novices shunned Anskar, when they weren't mocking him. They thought he was too much a stickler for the rules.

"Make sure you take water breaks whenever I do," Anskar said. "So long as Sned's not around, we'll be able to talk. I can check your progress and give you tips."

The clatter of cartwheels and the clop of hooves caused them to look round. A single horse pulling a covered wagon entered the barbican. A dwarfish woman in a motley jacket and pants and a tricorn hat was at the reins. Beside her on the driver's bench sat a tall, spindly man wearing a black coat with silver buttons and a hat like a crooked chimney. He had a long, pale face with dark cavities where his eyes should have been.

As the wagon emerged into the bailey, catching the light of the ensconced torches around the walls, Anskar saw that he'd been mistaken. Not cavities: the man wore round lenses of black glass over his eyes. It was a wonder he could see through them. If it was a toss-up between the dwarf and the man in the black coat, Anskar assumed the latter was the sorcerer Sned had spoken about.

The knights who'd waited outside with the torches processed through the barbican behind the wagon. Slowly, the blackwood outer doors were closed and the portcullis began to descend. Only when it clanged back into place did Anskar fully relax, although he knew he was going to have to face his fear of the unknown sooner or later. If he passed the trials and became a knight-inferior, he'd be expected to visit other strongholds throughout Niyas, and might even be sent all the way to the mainland.

The wagon came to a stop on the grass, where the Seneschal and three senior knights waited. The sorcerer climbed down, grunting as he stretched his back. He was older than Anskar had first thought, his face riddled with wrinkles. When he removed his hat to offer Vihtor a shallow bow, his bald head resembled a skull, the skin was so taut and so thin.

Pitching his voice so that all could hear, Vihtor said, "It is my honor and privilege to welcome to Branil's Burg the external adjudicator of sorcery, Master Luzius Landav from the Ymaltian Mountains."

So, the adjudicator was Soreshi—a race of natural-born sorcerers from the far north of the mainland.

"Never listen to rumors, Seneschal," Landav said with a pronounced lisp. "While it is true that I spent many years among the Soreshi to learn what they would reveal of their lore, I am, alas, a citizen of the City States."

"I see," Vihtor said skeptically. "Well, the City States are fortunate to have you, as we are fortunate that such an esteemed sorcerer has come to assess our novices and bring the materials necessary for the successful completion of their trials."

"Indeed you are, Seneschal," Landav said. "Fortunate, I mean. I usually leave these things to my underlings, but as I already had business in Niyas, I thought I'd kill two birds with one stone."

"What business?" Vihtor asked. As Governor, as well as Seneschal, the affairs of the island were his concern.

"Carred Selenas. The Order's mainland donors are keen expand their interests in Niyas, but this niggling rebellion is the enemy of commerce. Which is why the Grand Master has asked me to bring it to an abrupt end."

"You seek to do what we could not?" Vihtor said.

"It has been how many years, Seneschal? Hyle Pausus has been patient, and as you know, he is not a patient man."

"We will speak of this later," Vihtor said, his face hard.

"Of course. I shall look forward to it."

To the novices Vihtor said, "You may use the next few hours as you see fit, but don't stray far. Once he has settled in, Master Landav will need to meet with each of you individually."

Anskar wondered why. Surely the sorcerer didn't need to hand over the astrumium to the novices one by one?

He looked around at his peers to gauge their reactions, and found himself face to face with the dwarf, who was still perched on the wagon's driving seat. She, too, was much older than she'd appeared from a distance. Her eyes sparkled with mischief, and she was grinning at him, the brownish stubs of her teeth exposed.

Anskar swallowed and looked away, but just before he did, she stuck her tongue out at him.

"Come!" Luzius Landav called when Anskar knocked at the door.

The room was dark, save for the light of a single candle on a long table. The sorcerer was little more than a dense shadow seated in an armchair. There was a heaviness to the air that couldn't possibly be attributed to candle smoke. It had a tang to it: astringent, and cut with lime or lemon.

Landav leaned forward to get a better look at Anskar. He still wore the dark lenses—spectacles Anskar had heard them called. "Quite a mark you have. Deep and gaping. A little rough around the edges, but that's to be expected. A small matter of refinement."

"The god's mark?" Anskar asked, still standing by the door. Brother Tion never tired of telling him he should have been a priest, not a knight; that the mark of Menselas was inscribed indelibly upon his soul.

"Your sorcerer's mark. It's why they brought you into the Order."

"You can see it?"

Landav chuckled and adjusted the lenses on the bridge of his nose. "Clearer than I can see anything else. Did you ask the priests the same thing about your god's mark? Did they explain why they can see it when others cannot?"

Anskar hesitated, not sure how to answer.

"I can see I have unsettled you," the sorcerer said. "I will tell you what I believe. The mark of the god and the sorcerous mark are the same thing, only viewed from a different perspective."

"That can't be," Anskar said. "Menselas forbids sorcery."

"Save when it comes to his knights using it for warding, or to keep their renowned blades from blunting."

Silence settled between them, thick and clotting. When Landav showed no sign of breaking it, Anskar took the initiative.

"Why do you wear those lenses?"

Landav moved to perch on the edge of his chair, his bald head reflecting the candlelight, face wreathed in long shadows. "You would like me to remove them?"

Something crawled up Anskar's spine, and his mouth was suddenly too dry to speak. He shook his head.

"There's really nothing to see," Landav said. "Just cavities where once were eyes."

"What happened?"

"I no longer needed them."

Landav settled back in the armchair again, hands folded in his lap. He wore an ankle-length black robe, cinched at the waist by a braided cord of silver. Each of his long fingers was adorned with a heavy ring set with gemstones that glittered in the scant light.

"The loss of my eyes was painful, but a necessary sacrifice. I see what I need without them. And there's nothing wrong with my nose…or my ears. Your accent, for example, is a mix of Kaile and the City States. That is nothing unusual. But you weren't born there, were you? Where are you from originally?"

"Niyas," Anskar said.

"So, you are Niyandrian?"

"No! My parents fought in the war against the Necromancer Queen."

"Describe yourself."

"Describe?"

"It's a simple enough instruction."

Anskar licked dry lips and swallowed. "My hair is black—"

"Which is by no means unusual for a Niyandrian," the sorcerer said.

Anskar clenched his fists at his sides. "But my eyes are gray, and they are not slanted. My pupils—" He was about to say they were the same as Landav's but caught himself.

The sorcerer smiled. "Your pupils are round, not at all like a cat's?"

"That's right. And I have dark skin." He didn't want to tell Landav about its reddish cast, as that would prompt more questions he didn't know the answers to. "So, I'm not a Niyandrian."

"You make an excellent case. Forgive my line of questioning, Five, but it is rare to perceive such a potent mark of sorcery in someone of mainland descent. Could there possibly be a trace of Soreshi in your ancestry?"

"How should I know? But why did you call me Five?" It sounded like blasphemy. Only Menselas was worthy of that title.

Landav waved away the question. "It is merely your number in the line. I've seen four of your peers before you, and still have seven to go."

"Oh," Anskar said, feeling foolish. "Forgive my surliness, sir. I don't know my ancestry, and I never knew my parents. They died during the war."

"And no one has told you who they were. Why?"

"I don't know."

"Perhaps they fell into disgrace? Maybe they were traitors? Or maybe they weren't knights at all?"

Anskar's anger flared and he took a step toward the sorcerer, but when Landav whipped off his lenses, he froze on the spot. Twin pits of emptiness stared right at him. Try as he might, he couldn't look away from those dark cavities. They scoured his depths, probed him inside and out. Anskar felt diminished, as though he were being liquefied and slurped through a reed straw. Something within seemed to unbind itself from his very marrow and stream toward the voids where Landav's eyes had once been. Anskar was nothing, a thing of meat and bone that had deluded itself into believing it was a person. A desiccated husk, drained of blood, of essence. Empty. Pointless. Worthless.

"Such a demonic temper for a young man," Landav said. "How ever do you get through each day without a fight? Perhaps you don't, and maybe that's a good thing. This is, after all, a military Order."

Landav replaced his lenses, and Anskar gasped as all that he had lost came flooding back.

"I will not be threatened," the sorcerer said amicably. "I'm glad we see eye to eye on that."

He chuckled at his joke, stood and crossed to where his coat hung on the stand. He took a slender vial from one of its pockets, unstoppered it and drank the contents, before returning it to the pocket. He coughed, thumped his chest, then turned to the table, running a finger along its length.

Now, Anskar made out a collection of small square wooden boxes and drawstring pouches lined up atop the table—eight of each.

"Has anyone explained to you how to make metal absorb and hold a sorcerous charge?" Landav said.

"Yes," Anskar answered. "Sned the Forge Master. And I've read about it."

"Oh." Landav seemed put out. He probably enjoyed lecturing novices on the subject. "Then I shan't bore you any further."

He picked up one of the drawstring bags and slung it across the table toward Anskar.

"Astrumium shavings, comprised of orichalcum and star-metal mixed in the correct ratio. The addition of the alloy will only keep a sharp edge from blunting if the sword is well crafted, mind. It will do nothing for copper and very little for bronze—or am I telling you things you already know?"

Anskar shook his head. "Thank you. I'm grateful for your advice, sir." He slipped the pouch into his trouser pocket.

"I'm sure you are."

Landav lifted one of the wooden boxes, and Anskar saw it was made from blackwood, which was said to repel sorcery. The lid and four sides were carved with Skanuric writing.

"You understand what this is?" Landav said, opening the hinged lid and tilting the box toward Anskar.

The inside was lined with an orange metal—which had to be orichalcum. Upon a cushion of black velvet sat a multi-faceted crystal the size of a thumbnail, illuminated from within by a silvery glow.

"A catalyst?"

"*Your* catalyst. To be embedded beneath the skin." Landav tapped his own chest. "Not now, though. First you must learn to use it externally. When you have finished forging your blade, you will set the crystal in its box beside it. You have learned the cant for retaining a sword's sharpness?"

Anskar nodded. Besides the calculations required for casting a sorcerous ward, the cant was all the Order's knight-sorcery tutor, the elderly Frae Ganwen, had taught the novices.

"A cant without a catalyst is like eating too many eggs." When Anskar frowned, Landav added, "You have never been constipated? It's all right, Five, don't answer. A catalyst is a sorcerer's purgative, unbinding the dawn-tide, the dusk-tide, and…" He gave a double cough. "It unbinds the dawn- and dusk-tide forces we store within our mental repositories. You are aware of your repositories, I assume?"

Instinctively, Anskar touched his temples. "Yes."

Landav's dark lenses fixed on him for a long while. "Yours are ripe. Full and virginal. And now you must learn to access them. To do that, you will have to fathom how to connect your repositories to your catalyst—well, one of them: the dawn-tide repository. It's really quite simple, but you will have to work it out for yourself. A clue: emotion is key. Furthermore, you must wait to access your repository until the moment you are ready to ensorcel the sword. Otherwise you may empty it of stored dawn-tide essence, and I daresay your tutors have not yet broached the matter of how to replenish it."

Anskar shrugged. He had no idea what the sorcerer was talking about.

Landav handed him the open box.

Anskar immediately sensed a palpable vibration coming through the blackwood, which was matched by the subtle pulsing of the crystal. He saw that the silver glow was in fact thousands of glittering motes coursing through each of the crystal's facets, like blood leaving and entering a heart.

"Such pure sorcery," Landav said, then laughed gleefully. "Be careful not to taint it, Five."

He dismissed Anskar with a wave.

Unable to take his eyes from the crystal, Anskar turned and headed for the door. He was suddenly overcome with an irresistible need to hold the crystal close to his skin, and a contrasting desire to shatter it underfoot. Quickly, he closed the lid of the box, and relief washed over him as the odd compulsions ebbed away.

"Look where you're going!" a voice said in a grating rasp.

Anskar had almost walked into the dwarfish woman. He hadn't seen her when he came in, nor had he heard her enter after him. She had a fierce scowl on her wizened face, but her eyes still glittered at some private joke. As she stood aside and opened the door for him, she raised an eyebrow and smiled—as if she knew him somehow.

Or knew something about him.

Back in his room, Anskar shut and locked the door. He lit the oil lamp on the nightstand, waited a few moments for the sooty smoke to disperse, then turned up the flame as bright as it would go.

He sat on the edge of the bed, the drawstring bag filled with orange-tinged astrumium shavings beside him. The blackwood box containing the catalyst he held in his lap.

He could feel the rapid patter of his heartbeat against his chest. It seemed impossibly hot for this time of the evening, oppressive and sweltering. With the back of his hand he wiped sweat from his brow, all the while not taking his eyes from the box.

Should he open it now, try to make the connection between the catalyst and his repositories? Luzius Landav had warned him not to, in case he used up the dawn-tide energy in his repository and was unable to continue with the trials.

He decided not to risk it and shoved the blackwood box beneath his pillow in the hope that would dampen the crystal's call. Because that's what it felt like: an invitation to take the catalyst within his body, so it and he could be one.

It made him wonder why Menselas hadn't made his believers capable of sorcery without the need for a crystal embedded beneath the skin. Surely it was more evidence that the Five had never intended for people to use such powers? Yet even the priests justified the use of the dawn-tide and condoned the casting of sorcerous wards by the knights.

Anskar thought he would never understand religion. Either there was a right way to do something or there wasn't: a simple case of black and white. All these shades of gray in between reeked of half-truths and compromise. He had no use for either.

Tugging his boots off, he lay back on the bed and turned down the oil lamp to a faint glow. Shutting his eyes, he tried to sleep, but he kept picturing the mocking face of the dwarf woman, and Landav's empty eye sockets boring into him. He tossed and turned, then gave sleep up as futile.

Grabbing the bag of astrumium shavings, he pulled his boots back on and left his room.

There were better things he could be doing.

SEVEN

AN ORANGE GLOW STILL CAME from the forges. Anskar used it to find his way across the darkened smithing hall to light an oil lamp. Taking the lamp with him to his work space, he fired his forge, added some charcoal from the scuttle beside it, then retrieved from a workbench the steel bar that was destined to become his sword.

It would be a while before the coals were hot enough, so he used the time to study the contents of the drawstring pouch Luzius Landav had given him.

The astrumium shavings were a reddish silver, and many times more valuable than gold. Orichalcum was mined in the depths of the Jargalan Mountains, according to the appendix in Duin's *Cants and Calculations*, and the star-metal came from rocks that had fallen from the sky. Both were difficult to procure—the desert nomads protected their lore fiercely. It was only when the Order first made inroads into the nomads' sacred lands that the chieftains had agreed to relinquish some of the precious metals in return for a treaty guaranteeing the knights would leave and not return. That had been close to fifty years ago, during which time the Order of Eternal Vigilance's reputation for crafting superior weapons had been enhanced tenfold due to the astrumium's ability to hold a sorcerous charge that maintained a blade's sharpness.

Anskar decided the best method for adding the astrumium to his sword would be to sprinkle shavings atop the steel bar, melt them in the coals, then refold the metal, hammer the bar out again, and repeat the process until all the shavings were used up. That way the astrumium would be perfectly blended with the steel, and any sorcery it was imbued with would permeate the entire blade. In theory, the astrumium would be buffered by the surrounding steel, which would slow the inevitable bleed of the sorcery it held. If Anskar was right, the cant to render the edge of the blade impervious to nicks and blunting would probably last a lifetime.

Once the forge was hot enough, he worked obsessively, adding astrumium, heating and hammering, folding the steel, and repeating. It was hot, sweaty, agonizing work. The skin on his palms and fingers burned, and patches became shredded and raw, so much so that he had to stop to apply the salve and bandages the healers had given him. Blood quickly stained the bindings. Sweat slicked his arms and dripped from his forehead to sting his eyes. Each time he lay the steel back on the coals to reheat, he drank water to replenish what he'd lost.

Finally, when he'd added all the astrumium and was satisfied he'd folded and hammered the steel to perfection, he began the arduous process of drawing out the blade. Again, he struck it upon an anvil, but was careful to keep the width even—save for the tang that would form the spine of the handle, and the taper toward the tip.

He wanted so much to rush ahead, to get to the fullering of the groove along the blade's center, the tempering of the steel, and the steps that came after to finish the sword; but the desire only made him proceed with more care and caution. He didn't intend to make a sword just good enough to pass the trials. He wanted a blade for life; a sword fit for heroes and kings.

He'd drawn the blade out to about the length of his arm, with a solid tang and a graceful taper, and had just set it back in the coals to regain its white heat, when he heard the scuff of boots at the entrance. He glanced round, expecting to see Sned come to reprimand him for working so late. But it wasn't the Forge Master.

"Sareya! What are you doing here?"

She emerged fully into the orange glow of forge. "Did I scare you?"

"Of course not." Anskar set the hammer down on the anvil with a clang. "I thought you were Sned."

"Do I look like Sned?"

"Save for the mustache."

He expected her to at least roll her eyes, but Sareya continued to stare at him, a faintly quizzical look on her face. In the light of the coals, her skin glowed crimson. With the slitted pupils of her eyes, it should have made her appear demonic, but instead Anskar was struck by her beauty.

He looked away, pretending to monitor the heating of the sword he'd left in the coals, but in his mind's eye he could still see her smooth, unblemished skin shining in the forge's light.

He felt rather than heard her approach from behind. Above the smell of hot metal, he breathed in her musky scent.

Voice tight, he said, "I'm busy right now."

"I can see."

He could feel the weight of her presence behind him.

Anskar waited till his sword was white-hot, then gripped it with the tongs. "Mind out," he said, turning to take the glowing metal to the anvil.

Sareya stepped back, then watched as he picked up the hammer and resumed drawing out the blade. His blows were harder than before, more urgent. He hoped the din would drive her away.

When he paused for a moment to wipe sweat from his eyes, Sareya asked, "Would you like me to fetch you some water?"

All he could manage in reply was a nod and a grunt.

She returned with a mug for each of them, and sipped at her own before asking, "Have you added the astrumium alloy?"

Another grunt.

This time she smiled.

"I wish they'd told us about this in the lessons," she said, untying her pouch of shavings from her belt. "Do you think Sned will show us what to do with it in the morning?"

"I doubt it," Anskar said, setting his glass down on the edge of the slack-tub.

"Oh. But he showed you, didn't he?"

Anskar took up the hammer again. "No. I read about it in a book. I just figured it must be the same as bonding any two metals."

"Yes?" There was an eagerness in Sareya's tone. She'd not stayed to taunt him, he realized; she'd stayed to learn from him. She was frightened she might not pass the trial.

"You know how to forge weld," he said simply. They all did— or they should do.

"Kind of," she said. "But I thought I wouldn't need to if I just made an iron blade."

"You've hammered your iron enough to work-harden it, right?"

Her blank look told him she hadn't.

"Without enough hammering, your sword will be too soft. It will bend under stress."

"Perin just shaped his blade," she said. "The lad at the forge next to mine. He said that once we imbued the blades with sorcery, it wouldn't matter."

"Well, you know what Tion always says about the pupil of a fool."

"You think Perin's a fool?"

"I don't know him well enough," Anskar said. "But if he's hoping to pass the trial with a sword of iron that hasn't been hardened properly, he's certainly going to look like one."

Sareya stepped closer to him, so they were almost touching. "But you're no fool, Anskar. You could teach me what to do."

"Didn't you forget something?" he asked.

Sareya set her glass next to Anskar's on the slack-tub. "Forget what?"

"To call me half-blood."

"Fine," she said, turning away. "I'm not going to beg."

Anskar heard her sniff back tears

"Wait," he said. "I'm sorry."

She turned to face him. "You were quick enough to forgive Orix."

"I said I'm sorry."

"Then you'll help me?"

They shared the forge Anskar had running, and he helped Sareya hammer out the iron, and even folded and forge-welded it once for her. Once was fine, he told himself. To do more would take too long, and he wasn't going to do the work for her. He left her hammering her iron while he returned to lengthening his own sword. She stopped every minute or two to wipe her forehead and rub her aching forearms, but she persisted despite her discomfort.

His eyes wandered to the sweat-stained back of her shirt, then the tightness of her pants around her buttocks. Swallowing, he returned to his own work and tried not to think about it.

When Sareya had finished, she came to stand behind him as he worked on the tip of his blade. The length now was about right—a good foot longer than his entire arm. He'd managed to keep the sword straight, thicker on one edge to bow the steel when quenching, and it had a sturdy tang ready to be fitted with a wooden handle.

"Hammering, hammering, hammering," Sareya said. "It's exhausting. When can I stop?"

"When it's hard enough."

Sareya raised an eyebrow. "Really?"

"Don't start," Anskar said, though he was almost disappointed when she desisted.

"Could you show me what to do with the astrumium now?" she asked.

Anskar glanced up at a window. Both moons had left the night sky, and dawn would come in a few hours. "We'll have to be quick."

"I don't mind quick," she said, then held up a hand in apology.

Adding astrumium to Sareya's blade was a simple matter, and under Anskar's direction she completed the bonding in less than an hour.

"You're ready to draw the blade out again during the morning session," he told her. "Unless you want to fold it a few more times."

Sareya looked relieved. She also seemed back to her old self as she pressed up close to him and breathed, "What if I want to draw it out right now?"

When Anskar didn't flinch, she ran her hand up his thigh. He held his breath as she neared his crotch, then grimaced as she moved her hand away.

"You don't really believe all that moral stuff Tion talks about, do you?" she said. "Because he certainly doesn't."

"He's a good man," Anskar said weakly.

"I didn't say he wasn't." A hard look came over Sareya's face. "More of a man than most."

"You haven't…?"

Sareya didn't answer.

Anskar shook his head with disapproval. "That would be an insult to Menselas."

"Fuck Menselas," she said, her voice little more than a whisper. "Fuck all five of him."

Anskar backed away from her, mouth open in shock.

"I'm sorry," she said. "I shouldn't have said that."

"But you're sworn to Menselas," Anskar said. "We all are. He's the divine patron of our Order."

Sareya dipped her head so he couldn't see her eyes. "I hate the Order and everything it stands for. I don't expect you to understand."

"I don't," Anskar said. But he wasn't being strictly truthful. He'd had his doubts too, his struggles; and it was only fear of being cast out of the Order that kept him from questioning more, challenging the things that made no sense to him.

Sareya met his gaze now. "And I wasn't merely taunting you about being a half-blood, Anskar."

Immediately, he stiffened.

She stepped in close, touching his cheek with her fingertips. "I know a Niyandrian when I see one."

"No, you don't." Anskar peeled her hand from his face. Her nails were long, perfectly manicured and painted yellow, each with a swirling black symbol in the center. Despite his anger, his curiosity was piqued. "What do they mean?"

"Blackwing," she said, holding her nails up. "In the language of Niyas. In case I forget."

"Blackwing?"

She closed her eyes, the trace of a smile curling her lips. "A Niyandrian secret. The spirit name of Queen Talia."

Anskar pulled back again. "The Necromancer Queen? You support Carred Selenas and the Last Cohort?"

"No! Nothing like that. It just reminds me of who I am, where I came from. I remember my parents. I was old enough to be terrified when the knights took me from them. By the time that cow of a priestess, Haldyca, decided I wasn't Queen Talia's daughter, it was too late. I'd been too long inside Branil's Burg, exposed to the Order's way of life and their stupid lore. They said I could never leave, then told me how Menselas was merciful; that if I served the Five and trained to be a knight, I might yet be saved from the taint of my Niyandrian blood. Idiots! I had no choice, and so I went along with it. But I promised myself I would one day expose the Order for the sham it is."

"By sleeping with Tion?" Anskar still couldn't get the thought out of his head.

"He was the first."

"The other priests too? The knights?"

"Very few. Most of them believe their own lies. But the novices are still corruptible, and they are the Order's future."

"Rhett," Anskar said.

"And others."

"I should report you to the Seneschal."

She smiled. "Maybe you'd be believed. Though I doubt Tion would bear witness against himself, and neither would Niv and the rest of them."

"Niv?"

"You don't approve?"

Anskar didn't approve of anything she was telling him, but Sareya and Niv—two women together? He'd never heard of such a thing.

"You have to understand," Sareya said, "all the Niyandrian trainees were abducted as children. Those of us old enough to know our mother language were beaten for using it. Our history was obliterated, and we were told our people were savages, demons, worshipers of corpses. They even blasphemed against Queen Talia."

Anskar scoffed at that. "Blasphemy is only possible against a god."

"I know."

Anskar shook his head, trying to make sense of it all. He could understand Sareya's bitterness at being taken from her family, but at least she'd had a family. And so what if her culture had been beaten out of her? It was an act of mercy. The Order was simply doing Menselas's will.

"Why not leave?" he asked. "Why not join Carred Selenas?"

"Do you think I wouldn't if I had the chance? We're prisoners here, Anskar; you know that more than anyone. You've been here the longest. Why do you think you've never been allowed outside the citadel? You think I'm taunting you when I call you half-blood, but the red of your skin gives it away. I'd bet my life the better part of you is Niyandrian."

"You're wrong. And it's not just me who can't leave the Burg. It's everyone, all the novices. For our own safety, because of the dead-eyes and other dangers in the wilderness."

Sareya just raised her eyebrows skeptically.

"Look," Anskar said, "you came here tonight for my help, but if you're so desperate to go back to your people, why not fail the trials? Fail again next year, and the one after that, then you'll be expelled."

Tion had told Anskar that the Niyandrians who were expelled from the Order were sent back to their own people so they could carry the Order's learning with them, and little by little the depraved culture of Niyas could begin the process of civilization. "Not all wars are won on the battlefield," the healer had said.

"When did anyone expelled from the Order ever come back to tell us how things are going in the world outside?" Sareya said. "And even if I were allowed to return to my people, do you really think Niyandrians are so stupid as to allow those of us infected by the Order's teaching to live among them and risk the destruction of their culture? We would be outcasts at best."

Pressure built in Anskar's skull as he tried to grasp the implications of everything Sareya was telling him. Until now, he'd never considered himself a prisoner. He'd merely thought of the citadel as his home; a safe haven.

"If I'm part Niyandrian," he said, "why would the Order have brought me here? I'm not a girl."

Sareya shrugged. "It seems obvious one of your parents was a mainlander. I wasn't joking about rape. Knights of the Order have done far worse. And you know how guilty Menselas makes the good ones feel. Raising you was probably the Order's penance."

It was like arguing theology with Tion: she had an answer for everything.

"So," he said, "you're not Talia's daughter. That must have come as a relief."

Sareya said nothing, and Anskar wondered if he'd offended her. He *cared* that he might have. It made no sense. She'd had no qualms about mocking him. And yet he was starting to feel that, at least to some extent, she'd believed what she was saying.

"All this time," Anskar said, "and still no one has found the Necromancer Queen's daughter. How do you know she even exists?"

Sareya shrugged. "That's what Niv says. She believes the Order uses Queen Talia's daughter as a pretext for bringing Niyandrian girls here as part of a program for breeding our culture out of us."

"Do *you* believe there's an heir? And a guardian?"

"Why wouldn't I?"

Anskar narrowed his eyes. Had she been lying when she'd said she knew her parents? "But it's definitely not you?"

Sareya chuckled. "If it is, the Order and their priests are even more incompetent than I thought. If they believed I was the heir to Niyas, I'd already be dead, and my head would be paraded around the isle to take the sting out of the rebellion. And where's my guardian to protect me? I think Queen Talia was too clever for them; that she had ways of concealing her child. We Niyandrians are born to sorcery, Anskar. It's the fabric of our culture.

"Oh, you look disappointed. Would you like it if I *were* the Queen's daughter?" She twined her fingers in his hair and pressed her face close to his. "Would you serve me? Desire me? Does the idea of being with a princess excite you?"

She tilted her head and kissed his neck. When he didn't pull away, she nipped at the skin with her teeth. Anskar groaned. Pressure built in his groin.

"You like that?" Sareya said.

Without waiting for his reply, she returned her mouth to his neck, alternately sucking and biting. Her hand found its way between his legs, and this time he didn't lash out. Between her nibbles, she gave a throaty chuckle.

He didn't resist when she unlaced his pants and pulled them down around his ankles. He tried to summon feelings of guilt and shame as she kneeled before him, tried to find the will to break away, to flee from the smithing hall with his soul unblemished. But as the hot wetness of her lips engulfed him, he could only moan in pleasure.

She removed her own clothes and then stretched naked before him, letting him drink in her beauty. Anskar kneeled, his hands found her soft skin, tentatively rose to her breasts, seeking permission—which she granted with a breathy sigh and a brazen smile.

Then she grew suddenly urgent, pressing him to his back on the cold stone floor and lowering herself onto him. Sareya's movements grew faster, almost violent. She grunted and cried out as she ground herself against him.

For a blessed moment, the shackles of the Five were washed away by a torrent of force so powerful it could only have been sorcery.

Sareya rolled off him, a tight smile on her face—it looked fake to Anskar. Was she mocking him, comparing him to all her former lovers? "What's the matter?" she asked. "Feeling guilty?"

And in an instant, Anskar felt the snap of old shackles refastening. A lifetime of pious stories, of morals and prayers, could not be cast off so easily. Already the heat that had flooded his skin was ebbing away, to be replaced by an inner chill that belied the warmth coming off the forges.

Unable to look at Sareya, he stood on wobbly legs, laced up his pants, and headed for the door.

EIGHT

ANSKAR KNELT AT THE FOOT of his bed and begged the Five's forgiveness. It didn't matter that Tion didn't live up to his own preaching; the *Book of the Five Aspects* was littered with stories condemning hypocrites and lukewarm followers of Menselas. They were the ones whose negligence had paved the way for the coming of the demon lord Nysrog, who had nearly devastated the ancient world. They were the ones dragged kicking and screaming into the abyssal realms as punishment. He sobbed as he prayed; felt sullied inside and out. And yet he couldn't stop thinking about what he and Sareya had done in the heat of the forge.

After dawn, he took himself off to the communal bath house. Relieved to find it empty, he stripped off and plunged into the water. The massive tiled bath was yet another testimony to the craftsmanship of the Niyandrians who had built Branil's Burg. He held his breath, staying below the surface until his lungs burned with the need for air. When he came up, he waded to the edge of the bath and took up a brush and soap so he could scrub himself clean.

When he emerged from the water and toweled himself off, he no longer smelled of Sareya and what they had done. He threw on his clothes, not minding that they stank of the forges. That, at least, was an honest smell; one he could live with.

Bathing did nothing for the way Anskar felt inside, though. He'd betrayed Menselas, betrayed everything Tion had taught him about right and wrong. Tion would have told him confession would fix the problem, set him right with the Five once more; but the thought of telling another what he'd done filled him with shame. Instead, he did what he always did when he was troubled.

"Thought I told you not to come till after the trials," Larson said from his chair outside the dry paddock. He liked to sit there and watch the horses exercise while he smoked his pipe. His bad leg was elevated on a hay bale, and Rosie was curled up on the ground beside him.

"Did you find helpers among the new recruits?" Anskar asked.

"Not yet, but I'll manage." When the Niyandrian ridgeback lifted her head at the sound of Anskar's voice, Larson added, "We both will, won't we, girl? Don't you worry, Hazel and Monty don't miss you in the slightest."

Anskar crouched down to pet Rosie then went to lean on the wooden fence to watch the four horses being exercised in the paddock.

"Chestnut's a Kailean palfrey," Larson said around the stem of his pipe.

"From Kaile on the mainland?"

"That's why I said Kailean. Lot of wealth in Kaile, and wealth makes for the best breeding. Palfreys like this one are the most sought-after for the races in Sansor. You wouldn't believe the prices the toffs there are willing to pay just to say they own one."

"Whose is it?" Anskar asked. The palfrey was a hand and a half taller than the other three horses; she trotted ahead of them almost disdainfully, then came to a stop in front of Anskar. The great horse rested her head atop the fence and didn't flinch when Anskar reached out to stroke her.

"A rich toff, of course, or weren't you listening?"

Anskar chuckled. "Which rich toff?" The only one he knew personally was Blosius.

"Dead now. Killed by the same sort as did this." Larson tapped out his pipe on the long leather boot that covered his mangled leg.

"Niyandrian rebels?" Anskar asked.

"Few weeks back. You must've seen him: swaggering prat with a pole up his—"

"That could be anyone with mainland coin," Anskar said.

"Had a feathered plume on his helm. Blue it was, like the sky. Paid to have Fellswain here shipped from Sansor with him. Weren't here long. Reckon ol' Vihtor couldn't wait to see the back of him. Thought he'd make a name for himself in a quiet backwater like Niyas. Only, Niyas weren't as quiet as he'd heard. Got to hand it to the poor fellow: he knew how to pick a good horse. Fellswain brought his body back to the Burg. That big ol' horse was the only survivor. It's a whole different world beyond these walls, Anskar. Dead-eyes ain't the half of it."

Fellswain nudged Anskar through the fence.

"Can I feed her?" he asked.

"That why you're here? And there was me thinking you was offering to muck out the stalls."

"I am. I mean I will, if you like."

Larson chuckled. "Done it myself earlier. Hazel and Monty's too. Sure, you can feed her—just a handful of oats, mind. Don't want her growing fat in case I have to sell her to some bigwig in Sansor."

"You're going to sell her?"

"Maybe. Maybe I'll keep her for myself. Might even let you ride her, if you tell me what's up?"

"Nothing's up," Anskar said, but his cheeks burned with the shame of his denial as much as with what he'd done with Sareya.

Larson studied him for a long while but didn't push the point. "Remember that first day you came to the stables?" he said.

"I hid in a stall."

"From those bastard City States boys, I know." Larson started to refill his pipe bowl. "Tanned their behinds raw, I did. Bet they never touched you again."

"They didn't."

"But plenty more did, eh?"

"It's mostly just words."

Again, Larson gave him a long look. "What is it, the trials got you down, boy?"

"It's stressful," Anskar admitted.

"Course it is. We all hate it at the time, but after, when you become a knight…" Larson trailed off, remembering. "Well, it was good at first, till I got this." He slapped his bad leg.

"There's…" Anskar stopped.

"More? With you there always is," Larson said. "You want to tell me?"

Anskar dipped his eyes to the ground. He did want to, but where to start?

"No need," Larson said. "I know you, boy, like you were my

own son. Whatever it is, it can wait. It won't change a thing I think of you." He nodded toward the palfrey. "You can take her for a ride, if you've got time."

Anskar saw that Fellswain was watching him with her big brown eyes, as if she understood the conversation, knew what he'd done, and like Larson, didn't judge him for it.

"I can?" he said.

"Be doing me a favor; keeping her trim for the races."

While Larson headed off to prepare horses for a group of knights who were riding to one of the new strongholds under construction, Anskar led Fellswain from the paddock to her stall in the main stable block. He brushed the palfrey's flanks and fed her a handful of oats, then slung on her saddle and bridle. Fellswain was well-trained; he could tell that from how she patiently stood while he mounted her, then set off at a plod with the merest touch of his heels.

Anskar rode her the length of the sward that formed much of the bailey, passing a dozen or so grazing horses who looked up with apparent interest. He could feel the palfrey straining to be unleashed, wanting to exercise her great muscles. Riding at full tilt on a horse like Fellswain was something Anskar had often dreamed about, but there was no galloping within the Burg. Instead, he steered a course along the cobbled path that skirted the inside of the citadel's walls, then had to duck as Fellswain passed beneath the archway that led to the eastern quarter.

The early morning sunlight limned the battlements in hues of gold. The moons, white Chandra and red Jagonath, lingered in the sky, insubstantial as ghosts. Knights in white robes stood around talking in small groups, from where they daily congregated to greet the dawn then recite the litanies of the Five. Some of them whistled with appreciation as Fellswain passed, muttering among themselves; they knew what the palfrey was worth.

Anskar rode a full circuit of the bailey and began another, when he heard a commotion from beyond the walls and saw a flurry of activity atop the parapet. He reined in Fellswain the better to listen. It sounded like a crowd—or maybe a mob—in the streets of Dorinah, outside the citadel.

He shot a questioning glance at one of the knights, who replied with a shrug. "Some of the locals are unsettled. Nothing to worry about; you'll get used to it when you're consecrated. Just like you'll get used to waking before dawn every day."

That was something none of the novices looked forward to.

Then the shouting was drowned out by the clop of horses' hooves.

"That'll be our people, come to quieten things down," the knight said.

Anskar returned Fellswain to her stall, gave her fresh hay, and thanked Larson, who was busy fitting tack and saddles to six horses. Then he made his way to the refectory, where the other novices were already forming a long line for a cooked breakfast of eggs, ham, toasted bread and hot tea. Anskar seated himself at an empty table and waited for the queue to go down. He found himself nodding off, and his head almost hit the tabletop. Eventually, he gave up fighting his fatigue and pillowed his head on his arms, but jumped awake when a tray was slapped down on the table in front of him.

"Dig in," Orix said, seating himself next to Anskar and setting his own tray before him. "You look like you could do with a good feed."

Anskar smiled his thanks and raised the mug of steaming tea to his lips. By the time he'd emptied the mug, he felt alert enough to pick at his food.

"Working late?" Orix asked through a mouthful of scrambled eggs. He slurped his tea, and Anskar winced at the noise. It wasn't just Orix; every clatter, clang and raised voice in the refectory was an assault on his tired brain.

"I couldn't sleep," he said.

"Me neither. I've got a bad feeling about this trial, like I ain't gonna pass it."

Anskar caught sight of Sareya lined up for her breakfast. She glanced his way, but her expression was hard to read. Had he offended her, running off like he had? Or had she lost interest now she'd done what she'd set out to and corrupted him? His grip on his fork tightened. Well, she wasn't going to bring him down. Menselas would forgive him.

He returned to his breakfast, but an image of Sareya's naked flesh broke into his mind. He tried to banish it, but that only brought on an even lewder picture. This time he relived the sensations he'd experienced with her, and his body started to respond. Laying down his knife and fork he stood, chair scraping on the flags as he pushed it back.

Sareya looked at him as she approached with her tray. The merest frown furrowed her brow.

"What's up?" Orix asked Anskar.

"I'm not hungry."

As he headed for the door, Orix called after him, "Mind if I eat yours? I'm starving."

Anskar found a wooden bench amid the olive trees in the Burg's gardens. Already, the bees were at work, buzzing in and out of the roses opposite where he sat, and the gentle breeze carried with it the mixed scents of the healers' herb garden. He closed his eyes, enjoying the sound of insects, the smells, the cool touch of the breeze on his skin, and slowly he began to relax.

"Can I join you?" Blosius asked, sitting on the bench beside him.

Anskar opened his eyes and did his best to smile in welcome. He noted the bruising on Blosius's face from their bout. "I'm sorry," he said.

"Sorry you beat me? No, you're not."

"Sorry that I hurt you."

"That's the nature of the game."

"Game?"

"Fight, game: it's all one and the same. None of it's really serious, when you look at it." Blosius watched the bees amid the flowers.

"It's serious to me."

"Personally, I'm glad to be out of it." Blosius chuckled, but there was a sadness to his eyes.

"What will you do now?" Anskar asked.

"My father won't hear of me dropping out. Oh, the shame! No, I start my new class this morning. Two more failures left, and then Father can go hump a goat."

Anskar frowned.

"Figuratively speaking," Blosius said. "And I'd never tell him that to his face. But in two years' time, I daresay I'll be considered good for nothing save banking or trading, which is all I've ever wanted to do anyway. I'm not cut out to be a knight, Anskar. Not like you."

"You're a good swordsman."

"Ah, but is that enough? I'm no fighter. You know that. And truth be told, I'm not sure learning sorcery is for me, either, even though I have the mark."

They sat in companionable silence for a while, until Anskar's mind returned to last night. He might have scrubbed Sareya's scent from his body, but it still clung to his nostrils.

"Have you…" he began awkwardly. "Have you had much experience with girls?"

Blosius let out a loud hoot. "Oh ho! The young ladies, eh? There's some beauties here, wouldn't you say? Personally, I'm rather partial to the Niyandrians. I know they're the spawn of demons, but that red skin…" He blew air through his lips, then grew suddenly self-conscious under Anskar's gaze. "Not like yours—deeper, more vibrant. Crimson. No," he said sheepishly. "I've not had much luck in that department. You'd have thought girls would be drawn to wealth like flies to honey, but alas no. Must be the Order's rules. Can't abide it, myself, all that piety and self-regulation. No one really believes in those things back home. Not even the bishops," he added with a wink.

"Nor do the bulk of the novices," Anskar said, doing his best to sound disapproving. "And some of the priests here too."

"Really? I mean, I've heard one or two things about a certain priest, but novices? Are you sure?" Blosius sounded disappointed, or perhaps put out that everyone other than him seemed to be doing it.

"Anskar!" Brother Tion's voice came from the direction of the herb garden.

"I need to go," Anskar said to Blosius. "I don't want to be late."

Tion called after him again, but Anskar pretended not to hear as he hurried off to the smithing hall.

He was angry at the priest for not practicing what he preached. Tion was supposed to bestow the balm of Menselas's healing on the novices, not use the novices for his own needs.

But even that judgment was a smokescreen, Anskar realized. The truth was, the thought of Tion and Sareya lying together made his blood boil.

Anskar spent the morning shaping his blade by repeatedly heating it and hammering the metal as it cooled. His progress was much slower today, on account of his fatigue and the soreness in his hands. He was frequently distracted, wanting to see what the other novices were doing. Most were in the process of adding their astrumium shavings, though none of them went to the extra effort of folding the alloy into the metal the way he had. They simply applied one layer of shavings and left the rest in the drawstring bag. Maybe it would be enough to hold a sorcerous charge; maybe it wouldn't.

Several times he glanced at Sareya's back as she reheated her blade, but when she turned around to draw out the length on her anvil, Anskar looked away. He thought he felt her eyes on him now and again, but he couldn't bring himself to face her.

During the evening meal, he ate sullenly beside Orix, who again wolfed down Anskar's leftovers. Blosius waved from where he was comfortably ensconced with his new classmates, most of whom had also failed the first test. The twins Anskar had defeated in the first trial were among them. Rhett was a scowling presence who couldn't meet Anskar's gaze, but Clenna acknowledged Anskar with a nod. He saw none of the familiar scorn and rage in her eyes, merely a simmering determination. *You win or you learn*, the priests of the Warrior were given to say; and it seemed as though Clenna was taking that aphorism seriously. That was a good thing; it showed Menselas was at work in her, still guiding her along the path to consecration. She'd pass next year, of that Anskar had no doubt. And maybe failure this year would serve only to make her a better person, a more formidable knight. It came as a surprise to Anskar that he found he hoped so.

He glanced about for Sareya, but she didn't appear. He assumed she was working late in the smithing hall. The thought brought him a warm glow. Since he'd shown her what to do, she'd worked far more diligently than any of the others. It was a quality he hadn't expected to see in her, and one that he admired. And as he thought about her, he came to understand the cause of his sour mood: he felt her absence acutely. Jealously.

Sliding his plate in front of Orix, he rose from the table and strode from the refectory, intent on confronting Tion. He found the priest in the Healer's chapel, but he wasn't alone. Seated on the pew next to him was a woman who was muttering and sobbing.

Anskar assumed it was the Widow Glaena, who Tion had been helping with her burden of grief. But when the priest turned to face him, Anskar caught a glimpse of the woman's red skin, the flash of cat's eyes glistening with tears.

Sareya.

Anskar stormed out of the chapel. He heard Tion's footsteps following, and the priest called for him to wait, but Anskar didn't stop until he reached his room and slammed the door behind him.

He kicked off his boots and threw himself down on the bed, cursing as he hit his head on something hard. He slung the pillow aside to reveal the blackwood box containing the catalyst, where he'd left it the previous night. Instantly, his anger was subsumed by a different feeling: it was akin to hunger—a longing, a need.

With trembling fingers, he began to open the box, but a sharp rap on the door stopped him.

"Go away!" he yelled, knowing it had to be Tion.

"It's me," Sareya said. "Let me in. Please."

Anskar placed the catalyst's box on his nightstand and rolled from the bed, bare feet slapping against stone as he crossed to the door and opened it.

Sareya slipped through the gap, then pressed the door shut by leaning against it. Her eyes were puffy from crying.

"What?" Anskar said, and she flinched at his tone.

"Whatever you're thinking, Anskar, it's not true."

"You can read my mind, can you?"

"It's not so hard, especially when you storm off like that."

"What did you expect me to do—join in?"

She let out an exasperated sigh and playfully shoved him in the chest. "Do you think so little of me?"

"You gave yourself to him before, so why not again?"

"Tion isn't like that any more, at least not with me. He's in love with the Widow Glaena. I've never seen him so happy, and Glaena is too. Tion intends to tender his resignation to the bishop next time he visits the mainland. They're going to marry."

"So, you didn't…"

"I know what you must have thought," Sareya said. She stepped closer until he could feel the heat of her body, smell the sweet mint on her breath. "After working in the smithing hall, I couldn't face eating. There was a heaviness in my heart I've never known before, or at least not for a long time. I shouldn't have tempted you. You know I despise Menselas and all he stands for, but you don't. I wanted the Five to forgive and bless you. That's why I went to Tion."

Anskar's voice was hoarse as he asked, "Then why? Why did you do it?" He didn't have the courage to ask himself why he had so easily succumbed.

"Because I could. Because I wanted to. Because I have a need to ruin things, to sabotage. But this time—with you—it felt wrong."

Anskar frowned. "You didn't like it?"

Sareya touched his cheek. "I liked it very much, but you are— you were—so innocent, Anskar. And I went and ruined that."

Anskar ran his fingers through her hair.

Her eyes widened, and he couldn't tell if she was relieved or disappointed in him.

"I should go," she said, but made no move to disengage.

Anskar knew he ran the risk of being disciplined by the Order if they found out about him and Sareya, but he couldn't bring himself to separate from the warmth of her presence.

They simply stood there, him stroking her hair, Sareya tracing the outline of his face as if she were a blind woman trying to see.

Then she led him by the hand to his bed, and Anskar didn't resist.

Sareya left first thing in the morning, so she wouldn't be seen departing Anskar's room. He missed her at once; felt cold and empty without her. But at breakfast he barely even looked at her, as they had agreed. It wouldn't go well for either of them if suspicions were aroused.

During the meal, Beof Harril, priest of the Warrior, announced that the novices were all to assemble in the bailey. The brave knights who'd died defending the new stronghold under construction at Naphor were coming home to be put to rest.

There was a fine drizzle as the novices and upwards of two

hundred knights stood to attention to watch the solemn cavalcade pass through the barbican. The sorcerer Luzius Landav was there too, and Anskar saw him tip his tall hat as the first coffin was unloaded. His dwarfish assistant sat apart on a stone bench, flicking acorns at the sparrows pecking the soft earth for seeds and insects.

As was the custom, each coffin was draped in the flag of the Order—the five-pointed star of Menselas—and left beneath the awning erected for the purpose for the remainder of the day and night. The knights would pay their respects to the fallen during a vigil. After that, the coffins would be taken for burial in the knights' graveyard.

Riding at the head of the procession was a man armored in full plate speckled with blood. He carried a great helm under one arm, and had a dark, square-jawed face with a blade of a nose and deep-set eyes of sparkling blue. His hair was cropped short, mostly black, but showing flecks of gray. More even than Vihtor, he seemed to Anskar the epitome of knighthood.

By the time the last coffin had been unloaded and draped with the Order's flag, Anskar was soaked through and shivering.

"Freedom," Vihtor declaimed, so his voice would carry. He allowed the word to linger as he walked among the coffins, pausing to touch each lightly with his fingers.

Anskar had the sense the Seneschal was praying silently for each of the fallen, and that if he didn't, some terrible fate would await their souls. The thought struck him as irrational; Vihtor had no such sorcerous powers, and if it was necessary to invoke the Five's aid for the dead, surely a priest would have been better suited to the task. But Vihtor continued to touch the coffins as he spoke, and whatever the truth of the impression this gave, Anskar was glad that he did it.

"Balance," Vihtor said next, and the two hundred knights lined up before him touched five fingers to their breasts, the clink and grate of so much armor punctuating the Seneschal's voice.

The knight in the blood-speckled plate made the same gesture while seated upon his horse. Behind him, the remnants of the force he led were hazy and indistinct in the dismal rain: blurs that seemed more ghost-like than human. It was difficult to gauge their number in the downpour; upwards of sixty men and women, Anskar guessed.

"Service," Vihtor concluded as he touched his fingertips to the last coffin. "These sons and daughters of Menselas gave their lives in service to the Five and to the balance and law and order that is the seedbed of freedom. Freedom for their homes in Kaile, the City States, the Pristart Combine. Some few hailed from the Kingdom of Thousand Lakes. Others still were from Nagorn City.

"Menselas has no sword to strike down tyranny but ours. No fist to defend the weak and the oppressed but the very fists he gave us.

"During the persecution of Queen Talia, when she ravished her own lands and those of Niyas's neighbors—her reach always expanding, her lust for power as insatiable as her lust for depraved knowledge—the Order of Eternal Vigilance was all that stood between our mainland home and conquest. Without the steadfast service of men and women like these—like you…" he said, pausing to take in the assembled knights before him, then turning to include the survivors of the cohort behind. "…ancient evil would have risen from the very earth to consume us. The bodies of the dead would have returned to life, though with a thirst for the blood of the living: you," he said again. "Your parents, husbands, wives. *Children*. Is this what you want?"

"By the Five, no!" close to three hundred voices cried.

"This"—Vihtor swept out his arm to encompass the coffins—"is why they died. This is why, over the years, so many of our brothers and sisters have died. Queen Talia's evil did not end with the fall of Naphor." The Seneschal's face contorted into a grimace—either of pain or a memory disinterred. He looked over the assembled knights and novices; briefly met Anskar's gaze. "It endures even today. It lives on in Carred Selenas and her rebels: fanatics whose goal is the return of the Necromancer Queen. These knights, these servants of Menselas, died to prevent that from happening. All of us here"—Anskar noticed that Luzius Landav was engaged in a hushed conversation with his dwarf companion, who may even have been chuckling—"would give our lives to stop such horror from ever again threatening our world."

Once more, hands touched breasts in the sign of the Five, and when Anskar did the same, he felt a complex surge of emotion: hatred for Carred Selenas and her rebels; loathing for the Necromancer Queen; grief for the Order's fallen heroes; and pride that he was their brother in Menselas; that one day, the Five willing, he'd take his place as a consecrated knight.

Pride swiftly turned to regret, though; disappointment that he'd sullied himself and that, rather than confess to a priest, he'd repeated the sin and wasn't sure he could stop from sinning again, even if he wanted to.

The knight in the blood-spattered armor suddenly seemed the embodiment of the Five's chastisement as he dismounted and embraced Vihtor. That seemed to be the signal for the survivors and their comrades from the Burg to come forward and console one another.

A woman with a dented shield and much-patched mail approached Anskar. A bloodstained bandage was wound about her head, and her right arm was in a sling. Tears and pride glittered in her eyes as she leaned toward him, and he held her in an awkward hug, patting her back. He fumbled for the right words to say, but before he could find them, she separated and went to her next embrace.

Anskar dutifully greeted all who came to him, settling on a simple, "May the Five bless you," for his words of comfort.

When at last the consolations were over and the knights re-formed in their ranks, he glanced at Sareya. She was tight-lipped, her expression inscrutable, and he felt a flash of anger at her that he knew was unfair. She might have come to the smithing hall with the intention of seducing him, but it had been his lack of sanctity that made him succumb. And last night, in his room, he'd not wanted her to leave.

Sareya looked at him then, as if she'd read his mind, but she merely smiled and lowered her eyes.

It was midmorning by the time the novices returned to the smithing hall and resumed work on their sword-crafting. Anskar refrained from observing what his peers were up to. His hands ached, but he wanted to get ahead, to ensure he had enough time to hone his sword to perfection before he imbued it with sorcery.

First, he selected a swage block—an anvil with a raised ridge in its center over which a blade could be hammered in order to fuller a narrow groove along its length. He took the corresponding fuller, a six-inch bevel-faced tool that would enable him to groove both sides of the blade at the same time, and attached it to the swage block with a peg. He then sandwiched the reheated blade between fuller and swage block and hammered the grooves into each side, gradually pulling the sword through with tongs until the entire groove was the correct depth and shape. It was painstaking work that required frequent reheating of the steel.

The flash that formed along the edges of each groove due to metal displacement he shaped with a finer swage tool, thereby creating thicker areas in the cross-section that would strengthen the blade.

Anskar skipped lunch, working instead on hardening and tempering. He heated the entire length of his blade, careful not to overheat the tip, until it reached the desired red-orange temperature where a lodestone was no longer attracted to the metal. Then he submerged the blade in an oil-quench, resulting in a hissing rush and a fierce bubbling. Anskar drew back from the rising steam, face stinging, lungs burning.

It had been Sned who'd told him that if you cooled steel too quickly you rendered it hard and brittle, whereas slow made it softer and resilient. The trick was to maximize both the cutting edge and the spine, one hard, the other softer.

Gradually, the other novices made their way back from lunch, not a few of them murmuring together as they looked Anskar's way. He did his best to ignore them, the same as he ignored his mounting hunger. They could think what they liked, but at least he was taking the trial seriously and giving it his all.

Anskar sanded off the black scale on the metal to make it easier for the clay to stick. He painted on layers of specially formulated slurry, a thin coating on the edge, thicker along the rest of the blade. In the heat of the forge it dried quickly, allowing him to build it up swiftly. The theory was to cool different parts of the steel at dissimilar rates using clay as an insulating layer. Doing this would cause the blade to curve as it cooled, and give the steel a tempering line—if it didn't shatter.

He checked the quenching water temperature and found it warm enough, then carefully placed the entire blade in the forge to heat. Once he judged the steel ready, Anskar plunged it into the water quench. His heart skipped beats as he waited for the steel to shatter as it bowed; then he muttered a prayer of thanks to Menselas when it didn't.

Taking out the blade, he scraped then scrubbed the clay away and checked for cracks and other imperfections. There were none. And the blade now had a graceful curve. Firelight reflected in gleams of orange and gold on the metal. Thus far, it was perfect, but there was still more he needed to do.

The next step was easy. The edge was now too hard and had to be slightly softened. Anskar placed the blade in a cooler section of the coals, keeping it uncovered so he could see the color change, and frequently turning the sword. When the metal shimmered yellow, he removed it and left it to cool. Now his blade was tempered, the edge had just the right hardness, and the spine was strong yet resilient.

As the hours wore on, he carved the two halves of the handle from ash and attached them to the tang with an adhesive resin and iron rivets. He wrapped the handle with sea-ray skin, then took the sword to a grindstone operated by a foot pedal and proceeded to hone the edges of the blade, testing it with his index finger until the skin popped with the merest touch. He sucked his fingertip, tasting blood.

Sned handed Anskar an adhesive bandage, then nodded toward the sword. "May I?"

The Forge Master hefted it, testing the balance, then stuck out his bottom lip, which Anskar recognized as a mark of approval. "Might turn out all right, Assling, once you've polished the blade."

Sareya and Orix were chatting together at a work bench while they hand-polished their swords. Anskar joined them, gladdened that they seemed to be getting along again, but Orix grew suddenly awkward, as if he'd been caught betraying his new friend. He turned his back on Sareya and made a show of inspecting Anskar's sword. Sareya seemed about to say something, then remembered their agreement and focused on her polishing.

Orix's and Sareya's blades looked serviceable, Anskar thought, but lacked fullered grooves. Orix's was slightly misshapen at its tapered end, and the wooden handle was ill-fitted, causing the leather binding to stick up in places. Sareya's broad sword must have weighed a ton. Probably, she'd have to wield it two-handed, but at least it shouldn't bend, given the work-hardening she'd done.

Anskar's stomach grumbled as he returned to his task, running his blade repeatedly over the water-stone blocks of progressively finer grit set into the tabletop. For the finest weapons, the knights used up to seven grades of stone, before moving on to hand-polishing the blade section by section with slivers of water-stone. The process took many weeks, far longer than the actual crafting of the sword itself, and with tomorrow being the last day of the trial, there wasn't enough time. Even so, as the day's work drew to a close, Anskar's blade had a good shine, contrasted by the matte finish he'd retained for the fullered groove and the sharpened edges. This time he did nothing to quell the swell of pride he felt as his peers pressed around him for a closer look.

Some of them looked worried that their own swords might not pass the trial, and others were clearly envious, but Orix bobbed his head in awe, and Sareya flashed Anskar a smile so brilliant he wanted to kiss her then and there. Orix gave him a narrow-eyed look, and Anskar inwardly cursed himself. He'd been swept away by pride in his sword and had let his guard down. He needed to be more careful. He and Sareya both did.

"Good work, Assling," Sned said. "Makes me wonder what you could achieve with more time. What's she called?"

"Sir?"

"A sword should have a name, especially one as lovingly crafted as yours."

"I hadn't thought of that," Anskar said.

"See what you come up with tonight." Sned turned to the others. "Right, you goat turds, get your things packed away, eat a good dinner, then revise your sorcerous calculations. In the morning, you'll be placing a cant on the blades, and after that, Brother Beof gets to test them."

NINE

SAREYA VISITED ANSKAR'S ROOM AGAIN that night. They were taking a big risk, but he was powerless to resist her. Their lovemaking grew better each time. Under Sareya's direction he learned how to please her, and she showed her gratitude in ways he would not soon forget.

When they were finished, he lay beside her and played with her hair before speaking. "I'm worried that you might fall pregnant. It would mean expulsion for us both. But I won't abandon you, or our child."

Sareya laughed, then grew serious. "Tion provides me with an alchemical elixir steeped with herbs, so I don't think we'll have to run off in disgrace. But thank you." She kissed him and nestled her face in his chest.

"I find it odd that Tion would aid you in this."

"He's a realist, Anskar. Wasted on the Church."

"But aiding a Niyandrian...in this manner."

"Not everyone from the mainland agrees with what has been done to us Niyandrians."

"Tion sympathizes with Carred Selenas and her rebellion?"

"Rebellion? This is her country. My country." Sareya turned her back on him.

"I'm sorry," he said. "I don't know what to believe anymore."

For a moment Sareya remained perfectly still, but then she rolled over to face him. She'd been crying. Anskar wiped away her tears with his fingertips.

"Thank you," she said.

"Perhaps we should try to sleep?" Anskar suggested.

"No. Keep talking. I find it comforting."

And so they spoke—about nothing very much, just trivial things, and that seemed to please Sareya. Eventually, though, she brought up the subject of their newly forged blades.

"I've named my sword 'Lump'," she said, "on account of its elegant construction."

Anskar frowned, but then noticed the sparkle in Sareya's eyes. "You're being sarcastic."

"Clever boy."

"Sned told me I should name mine," Anskar said, "but I've no idea what."

"*Kaythe Nurglich.*" At Anskar's bewildered shrug, she added, "It's Niyandrian. In Nan-Rhouric it would be 'Corpse Maker.' It's the name of one of our Elder gods."

"Definitely not!" Anskar said, and Sareya laughed.

"Then think about what's important to you. What does the sword remind you of? What will you achieve with it in your grasp?"

He thought about the polish he'd given the blade and said, "Sunbeam?"

Sareya wrinkled her nose.

"Starlight?"

She shook her head.

"Dawnblade?"

"Getting worse. Focus on its shape. See what comes."

He tried to concentrate. "All I see is a sword," he complained. "It doesn't look like anything else."

"Are you sure?" she said, and he gave her a playful shove.

Thinking about the tapered end, he said lamely, "Leaf?"

She rolled her eyes.

"All right then, what's your spirit name? Queen Talia's was Blackwing, you said. Don't all Niyandrians have one?"

"Moontouched," she said. "The moons are sacred to my people. Someone touched by the moons is set aside by the gods to be a great sorcerer." A look of sadness came over her. "I have the mark, otherwise the knights would never have brought me here, but how much of a mark and what I can do with it…"

"Have you spoken to Luzius Landav?"

She snorted. "He said I was nothing unusual for a Niyandrian. I couldn't wait to get out of his room. That dwarf with him unsettles me."

Anskar nodded, but he was thinking about something else. "What is 'Moontouched' in Niyandrian?"

She fixed her eyes on him, daring him to mock her. "*Amalantril.*"

"Does anyone call you that?"

"No, but my family would have—if I'd stayed with them and grown into the role the gods had ordained for me."

"I thought Queen Talia was your god."

She flashed him an angry look.

"I'm being serious," he said.

"If the Queen had told me what to do with my life," Sareya said softly, "I would have done it without hesitation. Yes, she is a god to us. We have many gods, most of whom have walked the surface of Wiraya at one time or another."

"*Amalantril*," Anskar whispered. He leaned in and kissed her. "I like the sound of that."

"Then take it for your sword. It's no good to me now. Perhaps one day you'll remember me by it."

"I will. Use it for my sword, I mean. But I won't need to remember you. I'll never forget you. I don't ever want to be without you."

She touched his face then. Moisture glistened in the corners of her eyes. "My sweet, innocent Anskar. So much to learn."

He tried to lighten the mood, cupping her breast and saying, "Then teach me."

She seemed uninterested at first, but then her melancholy broke, and she pushed him down on the bed.

Her lovemaking this time was urgent, almost violent. When she shuddered and slumped forward over him, Anskar stroked her hair as she trembled.

Anskar went ahead of Sareya to the smithing hall next morning, only to find the forges cold and the windows shuttered. Four long tables had been arranged in a square at the middle of the hall, and Luzius Landav, wearing his tall, crooked hat, stood within the center of the square. A glowing amber sphere hovered above each table, connected by a glittering thread to the fingertips of the dwarf woman. She was sitting cross-legged against a wall, chin resting on her free hand, an expression of supreme boredom on her face. Her only amusement seemed to be making the spheres of light bob in the air by twitching her fingers.

Sned stood just inside the doorway, directing the novices to stand next to their swords, which had been placed at intervals on the tables. Each trainee carried their blackwood box, which Sned instructed them to set down on the tabletops without opening them.

Sareya arrived late. Anskar glanced at her as she came in, both relieved and disappointed that she was stationed at an adjacent table, between Naul and a mainland girl named Janil.

Luzius Landav reached into the pocket of his long black coat and produced a tiny metal box. He opened the lid, sprinkled brownish powder onto the back of his hand, and raised it to his nose. He inhaled the powder with a long, noisy sniff, shuddered, then snapped the lid shut and dropped the box back into his pocket.

Turning, so he could take in each of the twelve remaining novices, Landav said with his pronounced lisp, "Splendid. You are all here, and not a single one of you has forgotten to bring their catalyst. Most impressive, Master Jethryn," he said to Sned, who looked decidedly uneasy under the glare of the sorcerer's dark lenses. "You have them well trained. Now, open your boxes."

Around the tables, the silvery radiance of twelve catalysts added to the illumination of the dwarf woman's spheres. Anskar felt an immediate wrench in his guts, then a succession of pinpricks inside his skull.

Landav spun to face him. The sorcerer gave Anskar a thin-lipped smile and nodded.

"I have spoken with Frae Ganwen, your more-than-adequate sorcery tutor," Landav continued, addressing the group again, "and I am satisfied you have been taught the requisite knowledge;

but let me tell you, there is a wide gulf between theory and practice. It is the same with any discipline. Just ask the knights here. There is a world of difference between learning how to thrust with a sword and actually burying your blade to the hilt in an opponent's chest. I'm not just talking about having the nerve to do it, but the force required to penetrate the protection offered by the ribcage; the manner in which to twist the blade to cause maximal internal injury… These are things it is not possible to teach. They must be learned through trial and error; through experience.

"Sorcery is the same, only infinitely more complex and more nuanced. What is it, you must ask yourselves, that bridges the gap between mental calculations and the physical manifestation of your intent? And how does a glowing crystal in a box go from being a pretty bauble to a virulent igniter of the dawn-tide power?"

He made no mention of the dusk-tide, Anskar noted; but why would he when the knights, as devotees of Menselas, were forbidden from using it?

"Yes, you know the answers," Landav said, "but do you really *know* them? This morning we will find out. Now, any questions?"

A few hands went up.

"Well, there shouldn't be, not at this stage," the sorcerer snapped.

The hands went down again, and the novices exchanged anxious looks.

"Master Jethryn," Landav said, and Sned began a slow walk around the perimeter of the tables.

"You all know what's required," the Forge Master said. "The astrumium you've added to your swords, hopefully in sufficient quantities, will absorb the sorcery of your cants, but only if you're able to awaken the latent dawn-tide energy stored within your repositories"—Sned tapped his temple—"by effecting a connection with the catalyst crystal in the box before you. How you do that, as Master Landav has said, is a little trickier than it might sound in theory."

Anskar chewed his bottom lip. Frae Ganwen had taught them that imagination played a part, and Landav had said that emotion was the key. But which emotion, and how was it to be used?

"You have until the lunch bell rings," Landav said.

The sorcerer now stood on the outside of the square of tables, but Anskar hadn't seen him move, and there was no gap between the tables for him to have passed through. Landav caught Anskar's astonished look and raised his eyebrows in amusement.

The dwarf woman stood and released the threads trailing from her fingers. The glowing spheres drifted up to touch the high ceiling, their threads dangling like gossamer tails.

Landav and his assistant left, and Sned pulled up a chair by the entrance and settled down to monitor the novices. Almost at once, the hall was filled with the muttering of Skanuric cants.

Anskar watched as some novices took the catalyst crystals from their boxes and closed their fingers around them. Others laid their hands over the box, leaving the crystal inside. Some closed their eyes; others kept them wide open but staring at nothing.

Anskar knew the cant of durability and sharpness inside out, and although the ancient Skanuric language didn't come easily to him, he'd learned the pronunciation of the words as thoroughly as he could. But it was inspiration he needed now; intuition as to how to effect the connection with his catalyst.

He glanced at his own crystal, still in its box, and winced at the sudden pain in his head. Not so much pinpricks this time as barbs that sank deep and took hold. He knew the catalyst was calling to him; it wanted him to hold it. He glared at it and shut the box's lid. The barbs withdrew.

Sareya looked over at him. He could see the glow of her crystal bleeding between her fingers. She opened her hand so the catalyst sat on her palm and, still looking at Anskar, raised it to her lips. Her eyes widened, pupils narrowing to vertical slits, then she shut them, covered the crystal with both hands and pressed it to her heart. She swayed in place, head thrown back, lips parted, chest rising and falling rapidly, like it did when they made love. Anskar watched her spellbound, dimly aware of the arousal blossoming within him.

Suddenly, Sareya stiffened. When she opened her eyes, she looked not at him but at her sword on the table before her. Slowly, deliberately, she began to speak her cant.

That was it! Anskar realized: the insight he needed.

Opening his box, he took out the catalyst. Barbs again latched onto his mind, but this time he imagined them as Sareya's fingernails raking his back. He clutched the crystal to his breast, closing his eyes, and remembered the warmth of her touch; the hot wetness of her lips; the first time he had entered her. White heat blazed behind his eyelids. Fire coursed through his veins. The crystal clutched to his chest began to pulse like a second heart.

He sent out a questing thought, and the crystal responded with a rhythmic thrum. He sighed, and the catalyst seemed to echo him. He knew he'd done it then. He had a connection.

Flashing a grin at Sareya, who appeared to have finished and was running a finger along the keen edge of her sword, Anskar extended his hands over his own blade and began the Skanuric cant.

That evening the novices returned to the Dodecagon with their swords. Anskar left the blackwood box containing his catalyst on the nightstand beside his bed. It no longer called to him. Instead, when he was close to it, the crystal emitted a soft, contented purr. Its center, though, appeared cloudy, slightly discolored, which caused him to wonder if he had erred when establishing the connection. But his sorcery had worked: the edge of his blade was razor-sharp and hadn't blunted even when he'd taken a hammer to it.

Vihtor and the other eleven senior knights had resumed their thrones around the chamber's twelve walls. The wooden benches the novices had occupied during the combat trial had been removed, as had the cordoned-off fight squares. Sned looked uncharacteristically solemn at the center of the Dodecagon, next to Beof, the priest of the Warrior, who held his jeweled mace reverently in both hands.

The sorcerer Luzius Landav stood at the foot of Vihtor's throne. Despite being indoors, where the heat from half a dozen braziers took the chill off the air, he wore his tall hat and long black coat. His dark lenses shimmered in the flickering glow of the braziers. The dwarf stood sullenly at his side and rolled her eyes as the trainees entered.

Sareya was at the front of the group, with Naul, Orix, and Janil behind her. Anskar was the last to enter, not wanting to draw attention to his and Sareya's relationship. As far as everyone else was concerned, they still hated each other, although Orix was starting to suspect something.

Sned lined the novices up in the order in which they'd entered, then invited them one at a time to come forward with their swords.

To Anskar, Sareya looked frail and tiny when she was

directed to defend herself against the massive Beof. The sense of trepidation coming from the other novices was palpable.

Sareya rolled her shoulders and widened her stance. Her balance looked good, and she took a double-handed grip on her sword. Just in time, for Beof stepped in and delivered a murderous blow toward her head with his mace. Sareya pivoted and brought her blade up to parry.

There was a collective intake of breath, and Vihtor even leaned forward from his throne. As Beof stepped back, all eyes were on Sareya's sword.

It was still straight, not a nick in its sharpened edge.

"You now," Beof said, and Sareya hacked at his waist. The mace came down to block her. "Again!" Beof shouted.

Sareya aimed high, and there was a resounding clang as her sword was met by the iron head of the mace. Beof swung for her in a wide arc, but Sareya ducked beneath it.

Anskar winced. Beof's strike had been a ruse, and the mace was already coming back the other way. Sareya got her sword up just in time, but the force of Beof's blow spun the blade from her hands to clatter away on the floor.

When Sareya launched herself at Beof and locked her hands around his back, determined to take him to the ground, Vihtor stood, laughing, and called an end to the bout. He came down from his throne, picked up her sword and handed it back to her with a nod of respect.

Sareya, shaking from the fight, was unable to keep the joy from her face. No matter what she felt about the Order, she was clearly proud that the Seneschal was pleased with her performance. Anskar envied her at that moment, but then resolved he would do even better when his turn came.

Sned examined the edge of Sareya's blade, then nodded to

Vihtor. "Not a mark on it, and it holds its keenness."

"Congratulations," Vihtor said as he resumed his throne. "You have passed the second trial."

Next up it was Naul.

Whether Beof had something to prove after the good show Sareya had put up, or whether Naul was beset with nerves, the bout did not go well. Naul held his sword in a white-knuckled hand, and his stance was stiff and too upright. When Beof stepped in and swung, Naul wasn't ready. He tried to sway aside, but the mace smashed into his jaw and he went down hard, his sword skittering from his grip.

Sned glared at Beof then knelt beside the prone Naul. Looking up at Vihtor he said, "He's still breathing."

Vihtor shook his head and commanded the knight on his left to fetch the healers. He told the novices to wait outside.

It seemed an age before a trio of priests of the Healer came, two of them carrying a stretcher. The third was Tion, who offered Anskar a weak smile as he opened the blackwood doors and went inside.

Anskar sighed and looked the other way, straight at Sareya, who held up her sword and mouthed, "Thank you."

Naul was conscious when the healers brought him out on the stretcher, his sword cradled to his chest like the carvings of knights on the lids of the sarcophagi in the cemetery.

"I passed," Naul said in a drunk-sounding voice. "The Seneschal himself tested my sword against Beof's mace, and it held up."

"But don't forget what he told you," Tion said testily. "About protecting yourself at all times. Still, at least your jaw now matches your broken nose." The priest's eyes sparkled as he glanced at Anskar, but Anskar was in no mood for humor. His palms were slick with sweat, and he couldn't stop wondering if he'd forgotten something in the forging process; made some fatal mistake.

When the trainees filed back inside the Dodecagon, Orix was next to test his blade. After blocking Beof's initial blow, Orix countered with three powerful strikes that drove the priest of the Warrior back. Beof dug in and delivered a fierce counter that Orix caught on his blade, and the two pushed against each other, neither giving ground until Vihtor called a halt. Sned inspected the blade and declared Orix successful.

Perin, the lad who'd worked at the forge next to Sareya, stepped up to take his turn with a confident swagger. His iron sword looked magnificent, its polished blade dazzling in the glow of the braziers. His stance was wide and low, and he brought the sword to bear on Beof with an impressive flourish he must have practiced for long hours in front of a mirror.

As Beof surged forward and swung his mace overhead, Perin braced himself beneath the arc and brought his sword up with two hands. Iron met iron in a clash of sparks, and Perin's sword lost, shattering in two.

Beof bellowed a deep belly laugh, and Sned snatched the hilt of the broken sword from the stunned Perin and slung it across the hall in disgust. Without saying a word, Sned pointed to the blackwood doors. Perin couldn't exit fast enough.

Anskar risked a glance at Sareya. She kept her face impassive, but he could see she was trying hard not to laugh.

Two more trainees failed the test, one's sword bending, lucky not to break as Perin's had, and Janil's steel blade showed signs of blunting. Both left the Dodecagon in shame.

Finally, it was Anskar's turn. Sned gave him a reassuring smile, and Vihtor was on the edge of his throne, watching intently.

"Pretty, pretty," Beof said, sneering at Anskar's gracefully curved blade.

The sword was gleaming, save for the matte finish that made the keen edges stand out. The sting-ray grip felt secure in Anskar's hand, not only from the abrasive roughness, but because it absorbed sweat.

Beof shoulder charged, catching Anskar off guard, then swung before he could regain his balance. The mace came thundering toward Anskar's head. Faster than his stunned mind could register what was happening, *Amalantril* came up like a streak of lightning and sheared straight through the haft of Beof's mace. The mace head hit the floor with a terrific thud that cracked the flagstone. Beof was left staring dumbly at the cleanly severed haft in his hands. It hadn't just been wood; it was wrapped with iron.

Vihtor stood and gestured for the other eleven knights to do so too. Then the Seneschal began a slow handclap that was picked up by everyone in the Dodecagon. Everyone save Beof, whose eyes smoldered with hatred before he picked up the head of his mace and stalked from the hall.

The heat flooding Anskar's veins and flushing his face was only partly assuaged by the feeling of triumph. His pounding heart began to slow, but already he was worrying about what his success here meant. He hadn't just completed the trial, he had humiliated Beof, and priests of the Warrior weren't exactly known for their forgiveness and understanding.

When the applause died down, Vihtor congratulated the nine novices who had passed the trial, presenting each with a lacquered wooden scabbard Sned had selected as close to the specific dimensions of their swords as he could find in the Burg's armory.

As Anskar fitted his scabbard to his belt and sheathed

Amalantril, he couldn't contain his elation. He was one step closer to being a knight.

When Luzius Landav shook his hand, it was like clutching a dead fish.

"I am impressed," the sorcerer said. "And it takes a lot to impress me, doesn't it, Malady?"

The dwarf woman scowled, which Landav seemed to find amusing. It was a relief when the sorcerer and his assistant left the Dodecagon.

"I did it!" Orix said, throwing his arms around Anskar and nearly crushing him in a bear hug. "Thanks to you."

"The work was your own," Anskar said, extricating himself and gingerly feeling his ribs. "How did you effect the connection with your catalyst? Your blade weathered everything Beof threw at it."

"I don't really know," Orix said. "I was on the verge of giving up. Thought I was too stupid for this life. I started missing my home, my family, and almost cried like a baby, but then I felt a change. The crystal seemed to sing to me."

That was interesting. So, emotion was indeed the key. The question was, did it matter which emotion? Was there a qualitative difference?

Anskar wanted to ask Orix about the state of his catalyst afterwards: had the crystal clouded over or changed color? But he didn't get the chance.

"Same thing happened to me," Cail Hexal said—a City States lad who always seemed so irritatingly carefree. "Though my thoughts were of happy times."

"It was easy," Sareya said. "Nowhere near as difficult as the forging." She beamed at Anskar, and there was no artifice in the look, merely unmitigated gratitude and affection.

Before he could stop himself, Anskar was grinning back at her, but the grin swiftly fell off his face.

Vihtor had noticed, and he fixed Anskar with a stern glare.

Anskar felt sick to the stomach. He felt as though the Seneschal could see right through him; that he knew exactly what Anskar had done with Sareya.

Clenching his jaw, Anskar backed out of the group of novices. As he walked away, he heard Sareya hiss his name, but he ignored her.

This had to stop.

He needed to see Tion and confess his weakness, and hopefully Menselas would forgive him.

And not just Menselas, but the Seneschal as well.

TEN

THE WARMTH OF THE FIRE crackling and spitting in the hearth, the taste of mistberry wine on her lips, the light touch of a lover's hand on her thigh: like the temptations of the abyssal realms, they all felt good enough to keep Carred here forever, but in equal measure filled her with guilt.

She should have been among the fallen at Naphor, for it had been her plan, and she'd been rash. No, she'd been outmaneuvered once more by Eldrid DeVantte and the cursed Order of Eternal Vigilance.

The only wonder was that her resistance had lasted as long as it had. Truly there was mystery in that. Fate. The determination of gods. Or Queen Talia.

As if. More likely, it was luck, or the knights lacking the resolve or the resources for an all-out assault. Probably, Talia had nothing to do with it. Probably, Talia was gone, and gone for good. Despite the whole of Niyandrian culture being built upon the idea of resurrection—in the sorcery of the dead, which would one day be used to grant eternal life to all who paid the price—no one had ever come back from the dead.

The shades with which Carred had seen the Queen communing the night before Naphor's destruction were no more than impotent spirits consigned to the realm of the dead. Probably.

"Why so pensive, love?" Marith asked.

Carred responded with a grunt and a shake of her head.

Marith gave her a sympathetic frown and wrapped her robe more tightly around herself, as if she were cold in spite of the heated room. Like Talia, Marith was always cold. Had been ever since she lost her husband, Jared, in the war. More so since her daughter, Kyra, had died from lung rot that the best necromancers in the region had been unable to reverse.

Marith topped up Carred's wine glass. "It's curative," she said with a wink. "Drink up now."

For two days they had danced around the same conversation, in between hot embraces in Marith's four-poster bed, Carred brooding over her losses, her guilt; Marith reassuring her she had nothing to be ashamed of. It was why Carred had come to the farm after the botched attack on Naphor: because Marith loved her, and always managed to restore her to what she ought to be. A leader. A hero of the Niyandrian resistance. Only it wasn't working this time. The losses were too severe, the setbacks too many. Unless Carred won a victory soon, recruits would stop coming to her cause.

Already, old allies had shut their doors to the rebellion she'd built on the remnants of the Last Cohort. They wanted no more of it and were instead paying taxes and seeking favor with the oppressors. Another reason she couldn't abandon her hope in Talia's promises: she needed to know that justice would be done.

And these traitors would certainly get what they deserved, if and when Talia appeared as a goddess among them and rewarded them with smoke and flame.

Carred sighed and took a sip of wine. "I can't stay here forever, Marith."

"That's up to you."

Not really. If it were, she'd never leave. Not just because of Marith, whom she loved dearly, but because of the cozy cabin high on the escarpment, and the acres of pasture surrounding them, hemmed in by miles of forest. Besides the sheep and cattle, the chickens, pigs, and horses—and the hired hands in their cottages a good distance from the cabin—they were as good as alone. It was all Carred could have wanted. In some ways she wanted it even more than the return of her queen. But she'd given her word.

Carred rose, taking her wine with her, and walked to the window so she could stare through the slats of the shutters. It was late, but the spectral faces of both moons cast a silvery-red sheen across the pasture, and the stars were a scatter of light against the backdrop of night.

She heard Marith move, felt her hand on her shoulder, the warmth of her belly against the small of her back.

"You still think you were followed?"

Carred shook her head. "I never really did. It's always the feeling I get after a fight."

"I can understand that," Marith said, her breath hot on Carred's cheek.

Carred turned and kissed her lightly on the lips, and before she knew it, Marith was leading her to the bedroom.

After their lovemaking, Carred lay with her head on Marith's breast, enjoying the sensation of her hair being twirled between her lover's fingers.

"What are you thinking about?" Marith asked.

"Her."

A moment's silence, before Marith said, "Queen Talia?" And as they'd done a thousand times, they commenced another favorite game. Whimsically, Marith asked, "Was she…better than me?"

Carred rolled on top of her, bit her neck and kissed her lips. "No one is better than you."

She said the same thing to each of her lovers dotted about the island, and yet in Marith's case she was telling the truth.

But with Talia it had been different. The Queen had compelled love with the powerful allure of her personality, the sorcerous attractions she surrounded herself with. Making love with her had been blissful, but also tainted with fear and subservience. And it had been necessary, the only remedy for Talia's ever-growing physical coldness as, daily, her exertions bled more of her away into the realm of the dead. Making love with her queen had been a duty for Carred as much as her command of the Last Cohort. She and Talia were not friends; they were subject and ruler. Although, within the rules of that relationship, something akin to friendship had blossomed. Carred hadn't only revered Talia; she'd grown infatuated with her. Not for the first time, she wondered if what she'd felt was any different to the loyalty of a dog for its master. But did she still feel that way, after all these years struggling to keep the resistance alive?

Marith slipped out from underneath Carred, reversing their positions. Heat radiated from her red skin as she pressed herself tight against Carred, nipping and scratching, leaving wet trails with her tongue. Carred responded with passion.

This time when they finished, they were both tired. Marith

lazily traced the puckered ridge of the scar above Carred's hip. Instinctively, Carred winced at remembered pain from where the arrow had pierced her right through.

Marith must have thought she was self-conscious about the mark. "Your scars are beautiful," she said. "Your scars are you."

Around the edges of a yawn, Carred said, "Pervert."

"That's what you like about me."

Carred smiled and snuggled into her, pulling up the sheets for warmth. She closed her eyes, already feeling the gentle tug of sleep, when she heard a muffled thud from outside. She sat up, instantly alert.

"It's just the cat," Marith said drowsily. "Running across the porch."

Carred strained to listen, but there was nothing more. As she lay back down, her hand went to the ring she wore on a chain around her neck—a superstitious habit and a comfort combined—but it was gone. She immediately sat back up and started searching amid the sheets for it.

"What is it?" Marith asked.

"My ring—Talia's ring…"

"Under the pillow," Marith said, indicating which one with a lazy flap of her hand. "The chain must have come undone when we were—"

Carred fished out the ring and fastened the chain around her neck.

"I thought you were going to get rid of it," Marith said, propping herself up on an elbow.

"Is that why you hid it under the pillow—in the hope I might forget it?"

"Carred, it's ensorcelled void-steel. That ring of yours is worth more than the two of us together could earn in a dozen lifetimes.

Only a demon lord of immense power could create such a thing."

Had Talia found the ring, or been given it? "Talia was no demon."

"I never said she was."

"You've been listening to the slander the mainlanders put about!"

Marith spoke in a voice of mock horror: "About the Necromancer Queen. *Your* lover."

"You're just jealous."

"Of course. You'd be worried if I weren't."

Carred smiled at that, but she felt shaken, close to tears. She made a fist around the ring. Even after this time, she was surprised by its weightlessness.

"Ensorcelled void-steel nullifies sorcery, Carred."

"And you know that how?"

"I'm a born sorcerer, silly, like I keep telling you."

"A succubus, more like."

Marith settled back into her pillow. "Before I married Jared, I was marked as moontouched."

"You're joking?" Carred lay down beside her lover and snuggled against her back for warmth.

"It was either marriage or a life as a celibate witch. Hence my choice of Jared. But the gift of being moontouched isn't lost along with virginity. I still have it."

"And why am I only hearing about this now?"

Marith rolled over to face Carred and grinned. "If I'd told you before, you might have resisted my enchantments of beguilement."

"I seduced *you*," Carred said.

"Keep telling yourself that, if it makes you feel better."

Carred shook her head. She wasn't going to win this one.

With Marith, she never did.

"Is that why you wanted me to get rid of the ring?" she said instead. "Because it nullifies your powers over me."

Marith didn't roll her eyes or give a wry smile like Carred expected her to. For her, the joking was over.

"It has no effect on the dawn- or the dusk-tides," she told Carred.

"The dark-tide, then? Marith, what have you been doing?"

"I thought I mentioned I dabbled. I didn't? Oh, well. Now you know. I suspect your beloved Talia dabbled too. More than dabbled."

"She…" Carred had been about to tell her about the night she'd seen Talia surrounded by the spirits of the dead, but the mere thought of divulging her secret made her heart thud hollowly in her chest. There had been anger in Talia's eyes. Carred wasn't meant to have seen. What if she wasn't supposed to tell? Instead, she asked, "But why would Talia have a ring that repelled her own sorcery?"

"You tell me. Maybe she took it off when she called upon the dark-tide? Maybe she was afraid of demons? After all, demons are said to be imbued with the dark-tide."

A frown tugged at Carred's face. It wasn't demons Talia had feared. It was *a* demon. One that shadowed her dreams and caused her to wake screaming. Any more than that, the Queen would never say. It was too hard to speak about, she'd sob as she lay in Carred's arms. Were the dreams why Talia wore the ring? But then why had she left it for Carred? Or had she? The wraithe at Hallow Hill had been reluctant to part with it. At least, it had seemed that way.

"Shall I tell you what I'd do with it?" Marith asked.

"No, but don't let that stop you."

"Sell it to the Ethereal Sorceress. They say she has a depot in the city of Ivrian in the Plains of Khisig-Ugtall. It'd be well worth the trip."

"And then what? Buy an island in the Simorga Sea and live there with you?"

"The thought never occurred to me."

"But Niyas—"

"Is lost, my love. It has been since the fall of Naphor."

Carred clutched at the ring between her breasts. Her heart fluttered. She felt hollow inside. "I gave my word, Marith."

"To Queen Talia. I know." Marith sighed. "What will happen to me if she returns?"

"Vengeance, swift and terrible," Carred joked. "And not just for you. You're not my only lover, you know."

"I know that. Neither are you mine, by the way."

"That's good."

"That depends on which lovers you're talking—"

From outside: the unmistakable scrape of a boot.

Carred rolled out of bed and crossed to the chair that held her clothes. She started to throw on her pants and shirt.

"What is it?" Marith whispered.

Carred nodded to her lover's clothes on the other chair. As Marith rose and quickly dressed, Carred said, "Go to the back door. If anything happens to me, flee." Marith was a fierce lover, but she was no warrior.

"I'm not going anywhere. It's my house, remember? My land."

Carred felt a tickling sensation beneath her scalp—the response of her much-neglected repositories to the use of sorcery. "Is that you?" she asked.

"There's four out front, twice that number round the back," Marith said.

"Then—?"

"You take the front, Carred. Hit them hard and fast and run. Just *run* and don't look back."

"But—"

"I'll be all right. I'm moontouched, remember? I'm too much for this kind to handle."

"This kind?"

"I sensed no repositories. They're not sorcerers."

"If you're so confident—" Carred was going to say that she might as well stay while Marith saw off the threat.

"No, love. Go." Marith gave a tight smile. "Just in case." She embraced Carred, her arms trembling, then moved out through the living room toward the back of the house.

Carred strapped on her sword belt and eased the blade from its scabbard. As she crept into the living room, where the hearth fire still smoldered, she heard a definite footfall on the front porch. Her grip tightened around the hilt of her sword.

She drew in a long, slow breath, straining her ears to catch the faintest sound.

This time it was the rattle of the door handle as someone tried it.

With pounding heart, Carred remembered that Marith never locked the door. All the way out here in the countryside, there was no need.

The door opened a crack, and she thrust her sword through the gap. A man screamed as the blade plunged into soft flesh. At least he wasn't armored.

The body thudded to the ground, but she heard more feet rushing toward the door.

She stepped back to let the assailants enter one at a time, so she could fight them on equal terms. A man shoved the door open, barging his way inside. Dark clothes: all browns and blacks; a black mask covering the face; the glint of blue eyes—a mainlander, then, not a Niyandrian. Slender dagger in one hand.

Carred's blade slashed toward him. The man ducked and stepped inside the sword's arc—straight into the knee Carred threw at his face. It connected with a sickening impact. Nose crushed and gushing blood, the man fell back into the doorway, blocking the dark shapes gathering behind him.

Carred heard the back door click open. A woman screamed.

With a howl of rage, Carred ran the injured man through, then charged the two standing behind. Before they knew what had hit them, she'd barreled between them and was tearing across the field, tears blurring her vision.

She heard Marith shouting a sorcerous cant. There was a corresponding twinge in Carred's repositories. Someone else screamed—a man this time.

She glanced behind. Golden light shimmered at the rear of the house. Lightning flashed. Smoke plumed.

There were two dark figures in pursuit, though Carred was increasing her lead. Years on the run had honed her speed, not to mention her instinct for survival. Another look showed her three more assassins coming round from the back of the cabin and giving chase.

Marith!

There were no more sorcerous lights.

Carred winced at the tightness in her bad hip, but still she pulled away from her pursuers, vaulting the low fence that bordered the pastureland, slipping and skidding downhill through the trees. At the bottom, where the slope met a tinkling stream, she jogged along the bank then doubled back, making a wide loop to the stables at the rear of Marith's cabin.

She found her horse there and saddled it. She'd been concerned the assassins would have gone to the stables first, to cut off her means of escape. They had been good enough to cover all the cabin's exits, but not that good. Hired journeymen from the mainland guilds, no doubt. The sort the Order of Eternal Vigilance would want no record of. Carred took some small satisfaction from the fact that the pious fools had stooped to the use of assassins against her modest rebellion. Despite the setbacks, her resistance must be having some effect. But if the Order wasn't above using cutthroats to get the job done, what would they send after her next?

She rode from the stables, glancing at the open back door of the cabin. No sign of assassins now. No sign of—

Wait!

Marith appeared in the doorway. She was limned in emerald light like a second skin. Carred turned the horse toward the house, but Marith held up a staying hand. Then, in Carred's mind, a voice like the wind: *Go, my love. Flee.*

"But…" Carred started, not sure Marith could hear her.

This time, there were tears in the sorcerous voice. *Don't come back, Carred. It's no longer safe for you here. Go to Kovin.*

"You know about Kovin?"

I know about all your lovers, the voice in Carred's head replied. So, Marith could hear her. *What's the point of being moontouched if I can't discover your secrets while you're dreaming?*

"Why, you prying—"

I love you, Carred.

Marith closed the door.

Immediately, Carred heard the sounds of her pursuers. She wheeled her horse and set off for the tree line and the track through the forest that led to the Old Marsh Road.

ELEVEN

ANSKAR LAY ATOP HIS BED for long hours, but sleep eluded him. He missed Sareya's warmth, and hated that he'd walked away from her. But what choice had he had? Vihtor was on to them, he was sure of it. And if they continued seeing each other they would both face expulsion from the Order.

He was startled by a knock at his door. It was still dark outside. Blearily, he crossed the room to open it, heart thudding with the prospect of telling Sareya to leave him alone. But it wasn't Sareya.

"Did I wake you?" the dwarf woman, Malady, said, and a smirk spread across her wrinkled face. For a moment Anskar thought she was going to push her way inside.

"Relax, boy," she said. "I've already eaten." She cackled, then coughed, wiping spittle from her mouth with her sleeve. "Go to the east quarter and make your way up to the parapet."

"Now? Why?"

"You'll see."

"Just me?"

"All of you. Hurry. Dress yourself. It's nearly dawn."

The bailey was in darkness, save for a lone lantern high up on the parapet to the east, which Anskar took to be his destination. As he made his way up the narrow stone steps to the top of the curtain wall, he felt as if he were doing something wrong. As a child he'd been warned to avoid the walls in case he fell and broke his neck. He'd disobeyed only the once, when he'd sneaked up onto the parapet in the early hours before dawn. He still remembered trembling as he peered out into the dark, startled each time shadows passed across the faces of the moons. A ghostly howl had sent him running in terror back to his room. When he confessed the sin of his disobedience later, Tion informed him the noise had been the hoot of an owl, not the mournful cry of a ghost. And then Tion had administered a "merciful" yet severe beating, and Anskar had never climbed to the top of the walls again.

He was the last to arrive. The other eight remaining novices were already peering into the darkness between the merlons. Luzius Landav held an oil lamp, its glow casting his face in long shadow. Malady was beside him, and she gave Anskar a slow handclap as he joined them.

Sareya glanced at him, but that was all: no acknowledgment, no smile; not even a scowl. It was as if she didn't know him.

Anskar found himself a space on the parapet and looked out between a couple of merlons.

There wasn't much to see in the dark, just the hulking outlines of buildings either side of a dimly lit avenue that rolled away east from the Burg: the city of Dorinah, on the fringes of which Branil's Burg stood. In the distance was a scatter of lights, which could have been dwellings, or stores like bakeries whose owners had to rise before dawn; and farther off, at an elevation, the flicker of orange flames, which Anskar took to be campfires, probably warming the shepherds in the high pastures and keeping the night hunters at bay. There was a gentle breeze blowing from behind him to the west; it carried the tang of brine from the Simorga Sea.

"Now that Anskar DeVantte has seen fit to join us," Landav said, "I will explain what you are about to do. Or, to put it more accurately, what you are about to have done to you. For the first and most important thing you will learn about the dawn-tide is that *it* is the active principle; you are the passive. If that isn't clear enough, think of it this way: the world of Wiraya and all its forces, both visible and invisible, pre-exist us, nurture us, give us our being and substance. We, on the other hand, are but dung and offal, ashes scattered on the wind. We give nothing to the triadic tides; they give everything to us. Am I making myself clear?"

His question was met with silence.

"You surprise me," Landav said. "I didn't think you would be so well educated on the matter. Frae Ganwen, it would seem, has exceeded her remit. You, boy." He nodded to Naul. "Enlighten us. What are the triadic tides?"

Naul shrugged.

"Anyone else?"

Anskar shook his head, bewildered. "I thought there were only two tides: the dawn and the dusk."

"That is indeed what you are supposed to think. The Order of Eternal Vigilance, bless it, is the progeny of the Church of Menselas, which prefers the dawn-tide to the dusk, but would sooner have dealings with neither. As to the third tide, the Church would rather not acknowledge its existence. However, bitter experience has rendered the dark-tide not only possible but actual. This is why we must study the past, especially the war against the demon lord Nysrog. The sorcerer steeped in history is the one who comes closest to the truth."

Malady coughed loudly, prompting Landav to glare at her. "Yes?"

"The knights are just dabblers, master. Not sorcerers."

"Of course they aren't," Landav snapped. "I was merely providing context." He once more addressed the novices. "As Knights of the Order of Eternal Vigilance, you will only acquire knowledge of the dawn-tide. You are to be a force for good." He paused, a sardonic smile on his pallid face. "But like any half-decent warrior, it is to your tactical advantage if you at least know the weapons your enemy may bring to bear on you. Am I right?"

"But the dusk-tide isn't bad," Sareya said.

"Spoken like a good Niyandrian. Next you'll be telling me the dark-tide is positively benevolent and has been woefully misunderstood—a point I would be willing to debate you on, if I thought Malady would let me get away with it. In essence, you are right about the dusk-tide, but let us not run before we can walk. Or have you already mastered the replenishment of your repositories? No? Then please keep your mouth shut."

The moons emerged from behind a bank of clouds, and Anskar grew alarmed at the dark shapes flitting across their faces. Pointing a finger, he asked what they were.

"Not demons coming to gobble you up," Malady said. "Bats."

"Malady's eyes are much keener than mine," Landav said with a wry grin. "Fruit or bug bats?"

"Bug," the dwarf said.

"Good. I like bug bats. They keep the mosquitoes down. Fruit bats, not so much. Vampire bats, even less." Landav stiffened, and then sniffed at the air. "Ah, do you feel it?"

"The temperature dropped," Naul said.

"No," Sareya said. "Heat. From out there." She pointed into the darkness east of the Burg.

"Yes," Anskar said, glancing at her. "I feel it too."

Sareya ignored him.

"Good," Landav said; then to Naul, "Not so good, but at least you felt something. The rest of you?"

"Warm," someone said unconvincingly, and the others muttered their agreement.

Landav chuckled with evident amusement. "Here it comes. Embrace it. Let the dawn-tide blow through you. Let it flay your flesh and scatter your insignificant bodies throughout the cosmos. Surrender yourselves!" He arched his back and turned his face to the sky.

At first nothing happened. But then Anskar felt the first brush of hot air on his face. Not hot in any natural way. How could it be when there was no source of heat?

He saw Sareya move into the space between two merlons, using them for support. Her mouth was open wide, her black hair fanning out behind her.

The same wind blew Landav's hat from his head. Malady caught it and tucked it under her arm.

Ignoring the other trainees, Anskar copied Sareya and found his own crenel to stand within. *Surrender*, he reminded himself. Not something he found easy to do. *Surrender...* His mind took up the word like a mantra.

But before he could relax into it, the dawn-tide struck with fury and he had to clutch the merlons to stop from being hurled backward. Scorching wind snatched at his clothes and hair, pulling the skin of his face taut.

Surrender! his mind screamed. And then how, he didn't know, but he did.

Heat coursed through his veins. Particles of burning sand ripped into his marrow. A sea of virulence roiled about him, and he gave himself up to its currents, fully expecting to be torn apart and scattered across the sky. Instead, the more he gloried in the force of the dawn-tide, the more he grew attuned to it, the more solid he felt in its path.

The right side of his skull began to throb, and beneath it he felt his dawn-tide repository swell to bursting. The pressure in his head continued to grow, becoming a deafening roar. Panic rose within him, and he tried to pull back from the eldritch wind. He opened his mouth to scream, but no sound came out. He could smell blood in his nostrils.

Cold hands gripped his shoulders, and instantly the scorching winds passed and the pressure in his head eased.

"My, you are a strong one," Landav said. "Too strong for your own good. We'll have to keep an eye on you, young DeVantte."

Anskar turned to face the sorcerer. His vision was blurry, and he felt an urge to sink to his knees.

Landav steadied him and said, "Did the earth move for you?"

Some of the novices laughed, but not in mockery. It was good-natured laughter. When Anskar glanced at them, they appeared refreshed, though perhaps bewildered at what they had just experienced.

Sareya was glowing. This was who she was, what she was made for. Anskar remembered what she had told him in his room—in his bed: about her sorcerer's mark, and her spirit name, Moontouched. He felt a pang of longing for her then, but she didn't return his gaze. She was beyond him now, and he only had himself to blame. Or the Order and the Church of

Menselas, and the impossible demands they made.

"You must learn to regulate the flow of the dawn-tide," Landav was saying to him. "Your repository is significant." He leaned in and whispered, "Your dusk-tide one even more so."

"And the dark?" Anskar whispered back. "You said there are three tides. Do I have a dark-tide repository?"

Landav's black lenses held his gaze for a long while, but the sorcerer made no reply. Finally, he looked away and spoke to the group.

"Success all round, I'd have to say. Congratulations on your first full replenishment. From now on, make it part of your daily routine to rise early and bask in the dawn-tide."

There were a few grumbles at that.

"No need to come up to the parapet," Landav said. "Just being out of doors is enough, though the higher you are and the more exposed, the greater the rush you will experience and the sooner your repository will be filled."

Something had been niggling at the back of Anskar's mind. It crystalized enough now for him to give it voice. "Why haven't we felt this before? We all have the mark of sorcery, and the tide is active, you say. Surely we should have experienced this a thousand times by now?"

"Have you been up at the crack of dawn recently?" Landav asked. "Who knows, maybe you have felt the dawn-tide. Maybe you thought there was a gale blowing, even though those lacking the mark of sorcery would not have noticed. Maybe you felt queasy and shut yourself off from the sensation. But I can guarantee that without access to a catalyst none of you would have recognized the dawn-tide for what it is, let alone known how to drink from it. What little energy you had stored within you came from years of absorbing the dawn-tide that trickles into your repository while you sleep, and it doesn't penetrate much through stone walls. Certainly not enough to compensate for what you used yesterday in the cant for your swords. This is why I summoned you here today: without a full replenishment, none of you would be able to perform the feat required for the third trial. Have you any idea how much dawn-tide energy is required for the projection and maintenance of a sorcerous ward? A warrior cannot fight on an empty stomach, and a sorcerer cannot cast with a repository bled dry."

Anskar nodded. Now the giddiness had worn off, he felt elated, refreshed by the dawn-tide's washing over and through him. He could only liken it to what he'd felt with Sareya that first time, only it was stronger, purer. Not at all like the surge of energy he'd felt from his repositories when he'd made the connection to the catalyst. Was that why his crystal was discolored? Had he unwittingly drawn upon the stored energy of a different repository and tainted the catalyst with the dusk-tide—or even the dark? Was that even possible?

He almost asked Landav, but what if no one else had experienced the same thing? What if their crystals were still perfectly clear?

"We are done here," the sorcerer said. "I have things to prepare for the third trial tonight. Take the rest of the day off. Relax. Eat. Revise the theory you have been so adeptly taught by your excellent tutor, Frae Ganwen. And save your dawn-tide energy. You're going to need it. Oh, and don't forget your catalysts. Just the crystals, mind. No need to bring the box."

Anskar found Brother Tion in the Healer's chapel, helping the

Widow Glaena arrange fresh roses around the carved oak altar. Tion looked around at his approach and nodded. The priest's expression told Anskar he knew this wasn't going to be an easy conversation. Glaena smiled her encouragement as Tion led Anskar outside to the garden, where they walked among the herbs that grew in tidy rows, breathing in the different scents.

Anskar was reluctant to break the comfortable silence that settled between them. It was the last thing he'd expected. Tion also seemed reluctant to speak. But after the second circuit of the herb patch, the priest motioned for Anskar to take a seat on a stone bench and joined him.

"You're disappointed in me," Tion said with a mixture of concern and affection. "And I don't I blame you. Sareya… What can I say? I've never been a strong man, and though I pray that Menselas will spare me from temptation, he uses my weakness to keep me humble."

Anskar opened his mouth to ask why Menselas would do such a thing. And why be a priest, he thought, if you couldn't keep your hands to yourself? But Tion pressed on, not giving him a chance to interject.

"The fault is all mine," the healer said. "And you must believe me when I say it stopped immediately, after the first time. Sareya will confirm this. I'm sorry, Anskar, that I'm not the priest you need me to be. I would say I will do better, but that would be tantamount to a lie."

"A lie? What—?"

"I'm leaving Branil's Burg in the morning. Glaena and I set sail at high tide for the mainland."

"So soon? I mean, Sareya mentioned it to me, but…"

"Glaena's husband died in the war with Queen Talia. She's lived alone these past sixteen years, an example of chastity to us all. Whether it was a weakness in me or a need in her…who can say? But I'm happy, Anskar. More so than I've ever been. And I think Glaena's happy too. At least, I hope so. She inherited her husband's lands in the Pristart Combine but never wanted to return home without him. Then, only last week, she told me she was ready, and asked if I would join her there. I have requested a meeting with the bishop in Kroe. I intend to ask him to release me from the priesthood so we will be free to marry."

"You no longer believe?" Anskar asked.

"On the contrary. My faith in the goodness of Menselas is now stronger than ever."

Anskar nodded, but he was confused. Faith for him was an all or nothing decision. Either you believed or you didn't. You did Menselas's will in all things, or you did your own. How could he know if Tion was doing the right thing, or simply fulfilling a selfish desire? But then a thought occurred to him: if Tion had offended Menselas with his decision, surely he wouldn't look so at peace with himself. Maybe this was what the Five wanted, for Tion and Glaena both.

"My conscience is clear, Anskar," Tion said. His lingering look seemed to ask: *How about yours?*

Anskar swallowed. "That's good," he said, seeking to deflect the healer. "I'm glad you've found happiness."

Tion didn't smile his thanks as Anskar had expected; instead he maintained his steady stare, drawing out, as if by sorcery, that which Anskar still couldn't bring himself to reveal.

"Sareya…" Tion prompted. "When you stormed from the chapel…I know what it must have looked like."

"I was a fool," Anskar said. "Sareya told me she came to you for confession."

"I'm unable to reveal what she spoke about in confession,"

Tion said.

"I know. I wasn't asking you to."

"But what about you, Anskar? You've not sought the Five's forgiveness for a very long time. I've known you all your life. There should be no secrets between us—and before you say it, I was wrong to keep my own secrets from you. This—whatever it is—between you and Sareya: bring it into the light of day. Confess what troubles you, and trust that Menselas will forge a new balance from your honesty."

"By beating me with a stick?"

"That was different," Tion said. "You were a young boy when you climbed atop the walls. That is the time for sticks and beatings—in order to avoid far worse problems with the coming of age. You're a young man now: you require a different kind of nurture."

You nurtured me with a stick? Anskar thought.

"You already know, don't you?" he said. "About me and Sareya?"

Tion said nothing, just held his gaze.

What has she told you? Anskar wanted to ask, but there would be no point. Tion might have broken his vow of chastity, but to reveal the content of another's confession was out of the question—and decidedly dangerous, if the Patriarch ever heard about it.

Slowly, falteringly, one word at a time, then bubbling up into a stream of release, Anskar began his confession. He spoke honestly, sparing no detail, until Tion stopped him with a raised hand and advised him to lump all the sexual sins into one, and to gloss over them without being overly scrupulous.

Anskar finished his account by describing how he had abruptly brought what had happened between him and Sareya to an end when the Seneschal's suspicions had been aroused.

Tion let out a long sigh and pondered what he had heard. Eventually, he looked Anskar in the eye and said, "The Healer doesn't frown upon love. The other aspects, maybe, but ultimately the Five is balanced on the issue. But let's be clear: is it love we're speaking about?"

"How do I know?" Anskar asked.

"Then I assume it isn't."

"But what can I do?"

"You're shaking," Tion said. "Be at peace, Anskar. Above all else, Menselas is merciful, save maybe in his Warrior aspect. And the Hooded One. But the Healer…" He sighed again, and this time his expression was one of sorrow. "The Healer picks us up after we've fallen, binds our wounds, and cleanses us of every stain. Tell me, do you truly seek the Healer's forgiveness?"

"I do," Anskar said. "But what about Sareya? The Healer might forgive me, but how does that help her? How can I make things right with her?"

"You can't. But you can pray for her, and you can give her space and time. There are some things, Anskar, that are beyond our control. Now, bow your head and receive the Healer's blessing."

"Am I still worthy? Should I do penance?"

"As a healer, I'm confronted with the question of the Five's favor almost daily. Why is it that Menselas permits us to cure some people, and others, who receive the same treatment, ail and die?"

"It's a mystery," Anskar said, quoting Tion's usual response back at him.

"Then how do we know it's not the Hooded One exercising her dominion, deciding who's to live and who's to die? To be honest, Anskar, the Five's ways are confounding to me. It's why I stick to growing herbs and preparing remedies. Simple things. Natural. Tangible."

"But doesn't Menselas guide you in your work of healing?"

"I suppose the Mother sprouts the seeds, while the Healer directs us to their curative use…"

"And the knitting of bone, the spiritual light that burns out disease?" Such powers of the Five were recorded in the scriptures Tion had made Anskar read as a child.

"Both beyond me," Tion said. "But there are healers who can do such things, their abilities gifted by Menselas. Given the violence of the techniques, I wouldn't be surprised if the Warrior lent a hand."

After Tion bestowed the Healer's blessing on Anskar, they rose from the bench and returned to the side door of the chapel, where Glaena was waiting, a single yellow rose clutched to her belly. She gently touched Tion's cheek and smiled with such warmth that Anskar felt a sudden emptiness within, an acute sense of loss for something he'd never had. Not Tion—the priest had been there since Anskar was first brought to Branil's Burg; and though he was sure he'd miss his lifelong mentor, this was something else. There was a bond between the priest and his soon-to-be wife: a sense of family; of belonging.

Glaena pecked Tion on the cheek, and he blushed. When the healer met Anskar's gaze, a confusion of emotions passed across his face, and his eyes glistened.

"He'll be all right, my love," Glaena said. "Won't you, Anskar? My Tion prepared you well for life, didn't he?"

Anskar dipped his head so they wouldn't see the dampness of his own eyes. "Yes, ma'am, he did. And I'll be forever grateful."

"Goodbye, Anskar," Tion said. "May Menselas smile on

you for the rest of the trials. And don't forget: all that you've confessed is gone now, wiped out so that you can begin again. The Healer's blessing is a powerful balm. Never forget that Menselas is merciful."

"Thank you," Anskar said, lifting his head and no longer caring that the tears flowed. "And may the Five travel with you."

Glaena clasped Tion's hand and they turned away, heading into the chapel together.

TWELVE

THE THIRD AND FINAL TRIAL took place deep in the bowels of Branil's Burg, below even the chapel of the Hooded One—which, judging by the continued hammering, was still in the process of becoming a banker's vault.

With Malady the dwarf leading the way, holding aloft a smoking lantern, and the adjudicator of sorcery, Luzius Landav, at the rear, the nine remaining novices descended narrow, winding steps that had been hewn into the granite foundations. Moisture glistened on the rough, natural walls, which were veined with dark mineral deposits.

Each trainee held a softly glowing catalyst in their palm, save for Anskar, who clutched his tightly in his fist, ashamed to reveal it. The other catalysts were pure and untarnished, whereas his bore the stain of something he didn't understand, a darkness—or corruption—that could only have come from within himself.

When they reached the bottom, Malady lit the torches set

in sconces around the walls, and gradually the chamber they had entered came into focus. It was perfectly round, the floor a mosaic of white and blue tiles that depicted a gigantic skeleton with the wings of a bat.

"Kaythe Nurglich," Sareya whispered in awe.

Anskar recognized the name of the old Niyandrian god—the Corpse Maker—whom she had first suggested he name his sword after. Sareya glanced at him as though she wanted to say something more, but stopped when Landav swung his head toward her. Sareya swallowed and looked away under the empty glare of the sorcerer's dark lenses.

On the wall facing the novices were two heavy wooden doors banded with iron. The doors were twenty yards apart, the one on the left painted with a red skull, the right with an eagle in flight.

"One way in, one way out," Landav said. "Perhaps our Niyandrian friend would care to explain for the rest of us?"

Again, he directed his sightless gaze at Sareya, and this time Anskar felt a corresponding twinge within his skull—not in the vicinity of his dawn-tide repository: beneath it.

"There are crypts like these dotted all over Niyas," Sareya said. There was a strain to her voice Anskar had not heard before. She sounded compelled. "The dead would be taken in through the skull door, and should they one day rise, they would leave through the eagle door."

"Good," Landav said. "Necromantic claptrap, but terrific fun."

At once, the tingling sensation in Anskar's head abated.

Sareya gasped and touched a hand lightly to her throat. Her cat's eyes were narrowed to slits—either at the sorcery Landav had clearly used to compel her, or at the slight on her culture. Probably both.

But what kind of sorcery? Anskar glanced at the other novices, but none of them showed any sign of having noticed. Instead, they all stared with dread at the skull door.

"One at a time," the sorcerer said, "you will follow the example of the dead: you will enter the crypt. Within…well, who knows what challenges may confront you? The important thing is that you are all prepared. Frae Ganwen assures me she has drummed into you the calculations for the casting of a sorcerous ward, and you have each established a link with your catalysts. The trick now is to use the catalyst to access the stored energy of your dawn-tide repository"—he tapped the side of his head—"and make the calculations to manifest the arcane ward. Failure to do so could prove painful, or worse. If you survive"—Landav chuckled—"if you emerge through the eagle door, proceed directly to the steps and wait in the refectory until the trial is complete. Do not speak to anyone who has still to enter the skull door. Do not even meet their eyes. Do so and you will be disqualified. Does everyone understand? Splendid."

Anskar wiped sweaty palms on his pants. If they survived? Was that the sorcerer's idea of a sick joke? Or was there real danger inside the crypt? Surely not. Surely the novices would have been forewarned, better prepared?

Cail Hexal was the first to enter the skull door. When he cast a worried look over his shoulder, Landav waved him impatiently inside. At the same time, Malady slipped inside the eagle door and shut it behind her.

Long minutes passed. The novices exchanged anxious glances, but no one dared make a sound. Anskar became aware of Sareya's eyes on him. This time when he looked around, she didn't turn away. He was startled by the fierceness of her expression: determination that she would see this through; encouragement that he would too. Heat bloomed in his belly, prickled his skin.

He glanced at Landav to make sure the sorcerer wasn't watching, then mouthed, "I—"

Someone bumped into his shoulder, distracting him. Orix began shuffling from foot to foot. Through gritted teeth he muttered, "I need a piss."

Sareya smiled and shook her head. Before she turned to stare at the skull door, she mouthed, "I know."

But *what* did she know? That Anskar missed her—which is what he'd been trying to say. Did she care? Did she miss him too? Already, the effects of the Healer's blessing were ebbing away, replaced by longing; by recollections of warmth and softness and urgency.

Focus, Anskar told himself. There were challenges inside the crypt he had yet to face if he was going to pass the third and final trial. *If you survive.*

Landav took a stitched leather book from his coat pocket and leafed through it, once or twice pausing to take a pinch of brown powder from his tin and sniffing it up from the back of his hand. He didn't so much read the book as run his fingertip over whatever was written on the pages. All the while, his dark lenses were fixed on the eagle door, waiting for it to open.

Several times, Anskar felt a tug on his dawn-tide repository; he assumed it came from within the crypt: a resonance; thready, weak, stuttering. Everyone looked up as a yelp came from the other side of the eagle door. There was a patter of feet, the harsh gasp of breath, and then the door opened and a pale-faced Cail stumbled out. He was drenched from head to foot and looked thoroughly miserable. Without a word or even a glance in their direction, he crossed the chamber to the steps and left.

Orix was next, then Naul, Sareya, and the others. Each came out soaked with water or sweat or something else. All looked shaken, save for Sareya, who despite her soaking carried herself with a dignity bordering on haughtiness.

Landav grinned as she made her way to the steps, then he pocketed his book and focused his dark lenses on Anskar.

"Just you to go, Mr. DeVantte. I must say, I've been looking forward to this immensely."

At Anskar's frown, Landav merely gestured toward the skull door.

Anskar gripped his catalyst tightly and strode forward. His heart pounded in his ears, yet the catalyst throbbed to a slower tempo. He matched his breathing to its pulse, and his nerves began to settle.

As his hand clutched the doorknob, Anskar heard a soft moan. He turned, suspecting it was Landav playing tricks on him, but the sorcerer betrayed no reaction. Frowning, he turned the knob and the door opened with a gasp—he wasn't sure if he had really heard it, or if the sound had come from inside his head. A final look over his shoulder showed him Landav with his fingers steepled beneath his nose. It gave Anskar the impression the sorcerer was trying to disguise a leer.

Everyone else had emerged unscathed, Anskar told himself—save for being drenched. There was nothing to be afraid of. This was a test of sorcerous aptitude, nothing more. All he had to do was cast a ward sphere, something he'd studied inside and out. Or had he misunderstood the trial?

He slipped through the crack of the door into darkness then shut the door behind him. The air within had a peppery smell—mold and damp. Light from his catalyst bled through his fingers. He opened his fist so he could see by the crystal's glow.

As he took his first tentative step, something brushed against his hair and he swiped at it. A cobweb. Above, where wooden joists supported the rough-hewn ceiling, thick webs encrusted with dust and insects draped down. Anskar raised his crystal to get a better look, and a fist-sized spider scuttled for the safety of the shadows.

He slowly lowered his crystal, its soft light revealing flaking frescoes that adorned both walls. He moved closer to examine the one on his right: a procession of Niyandrians moving toward a pool of silvery moonlight. Not just moving, he realized: lurching; dragging themselves. The men and women depicted had been painted in elaborate detail: some were missing arms or legs; others had wasted away to virtual skeletons. All of them had milky orbs in place of cat's eyes. It was a procession of the dead.

On the opposite wall, bat-winged Niyandrians sporting crowns swarmed about the night-black sky, giving battle to horned demons with yellow eyes and forked tongues. In the foreground, a scaled giant with shadow wings and an engorged phallus loomed over a naked Niyandrian woman. Something about the image was like a punch to the stomach. Anskar reeled away from the mural and gasped for breath.

He gathered himself and looked again, avoiding the obscenity that was the demon lord and focusing instead on the eyes of its victim: they were black as pitch and speckled with silver—like a star-spangled night. And there was something else he'd not noticed before: around her head, partly obscured by her tousled hair, a golden coronet.

Something scampered over his boot, and he lowered his catalyst to see, but whatever it was had gone. A mouse? A rat? The fist-sized spider from the ceiling? Anskar didn't want to stick around and find out. And then he noticed a damp patch toward the base of the fresco—dark streaks trailing beneath it and puddling on the floor. A spill of liquid, and still wet. And the smell... He leaned down for a closer look then realized what it was.

"Orix," he muttered. "You filthy savage."

Nose wrinkled in distaste, he crept along the passageway he'd entered, holding the crystal out in front of him. There! To his right, a darker patch against the wall. An alcove—and something within it.

An exhalation passed from one side of Anskar's skull to the other. On instinct, he pounded his ear, but already the sound had gone. A slow shiver climbed up his spine, and ice clumped in his guts. He faltered. His legs grew heavy. He felt so weak. But then, like the exhalation, the sensation passed, leaving only a lingering odor of decay in his nostrils.

And then he located the source, seated on a stone bench in the alcove: a body wrapped head to toe in mildew-speckled bandages. Strands and tufts of gray hair poked between the age-yellowed wrappings on the corpse's head. The bindings that covered its face were coated with what he first took to be brownish fish-scales, but then decided were some kind of fungus. The bandages on its hands had split in several places to reveal curling, yellow nails like talons. A ripple passed beneath the wrappings on the chest and Anskar recoiled; but as he brought the light of his catalyst to bear, he saw the spiny leg of an insect withdraw inside.

Fighting for calm, Anskar reached for the connection with his catalyst and was relieved to find it instantly. As a test, he drew a trickle of energy from his dawn-tide repository and felt a corresponding twinge in the center of his skull. Eyes not leaving the mummy, he recited the calculations for a sorcerous ward in his mind, then gasped. Without his conscious control, the calculations raced about his skull in ever-decreasing circles, the numbers and symbols too fast for him to visualize or sound out. Silver flared behind his eyelids. Pain stabbed at the same place within his skull. The catalyst in his hand grew hot, and then a sphere of scintillant light sprang up around him. He felt rather than heard it thrum in time with his ragged breaths.

Anskar bit back his mounting panic. He hadn't intended to manifest the ward yet—he had no idea how long he could hold the sorcery.

The aura of light swirled around him, and as it did it changed color from silver, to gray, then to an oily combination of blues, greens, and purples. It felt wrong: bruised with corruption; discolored like his catalyst.

Maybe color wasn't important. He needed to believe that, if he was going to continue with the trial. So long as the ward was strong enough to protect him from whatever tricks and traps Landav had set for him in the catacombs.

In a hurry now, lest his repository should run out of energy to maintain his ward, Anskar continued along the corridor. He passed several more alcoves, each with its own seated mummy, then came to a low-ceilinged crypt within which were four stone sarcophagi, each with a skull-headed serpent carved in relief on its lid.

A triangle had been painted on the floor, the red pigment still glistening and wet. There were Skanuric runes around the sides of the triangle—combinations of letters that seemed nonsensical to him. At the center of the triangle was the lone letter *sythiot*, which symbolized fire. In the dust to either side, he saw footprints, presumably from the other novices.

Bracing himself, Anskar followed the passage of the footprints to the left of the triangle. He'd gone no farther than three steps when he felt pressure within his head. There was a rushing noise from above—and heat.

Anskar threw himself back—too late—as a curtain of flame

slammed into him. He ducked and covered his head, but the fire never touched him. Instead, it raged around him, following the contours of his silver sphere, and he felt nothing save a gentle warmth. Heart hammering in his chest, Anskar backed out of the flames, and as he did, they returned to a sheer curtain that extended from ceiling to floor.

He pressed on to the far side of the crypt, turning back when the flame curtain winked out of existence and plunged the chamber back into darkness.

By the glow from his catalyst, he picked out a passageway to his right, which he hurried toward. Already, he could feel the steady drip of power from his repository and knew he didn't have much time.

Something crunched beneath his boots as he made his way along the corridor. When he lowered his crystal, he could see the bones of rodents amid the rock dust that coated the floor.

At the far end of the passage was an arched opening, which he passed beneath to enter a chamber heavy with shadows. His catalyst's light glinted from something ahead of him. As Anskar approached, the crystal's glow illuminated the skeletal arm of a bronze statue. As he moved his light, he revealed ribs inscribed with unfamiliar symbols, splayed bat's wings, and a grinning death's-head.

Kaythe Nurglich.

Anskar backed away from the statue as if it might spring to life. He glimpsed the black hole of an exit to his right. The catacombs doubled back on themselves, he realized to his relief. There wasn't far to go. The question was: how many more tests remained, and how much time did his ward have left?

As he gave the statue of the Corpse Maker a wide berth, Anskar heard a scuff from the exit. A dark shape no bigger than a child appeared there, and hurled something small and shiny at him. Whatever it was hit his ward with a concussive blast, slamming Anskar into the wall. He slumped to the ground and all the air rushed from his lungs. But for the second time, his ward had saved him—though a fist-sized patch in front of him fizzed and popped and was covered only by threads of interwoven light.

Drawing upon more of his repository's energy, he began the calculations of ward-casting once more. Even before he'd finished the first sequence, the frayed patch knitted over with green, purple, and blue light.

Anskar pushed himself to his feet, and his ward flickered once then stabilized. It felt as though something pinched his brain, and almost at once he felt the dawn-tide from his repository slow to a trickle. He'd wasted precious energy repairing his ward sphere.

He ran to the exit the small figure had disappeared into, convinced it had to be the dwarf. He sprinted along a narrow passageway, only slowing when it opened into another chamber, this one lit by half a dozen ensconced torches around the walls. Other than that, it was empty, and there was one last stretch of corridor leading to a door flanked by two torches. The eagle door. The way out!

Anskar strode across the room, then half-turned at a sound from behind. A colossal impact hit his ward, sending up a shower of sparks. He twisted as he fell, and the Warrior's priest, Beof, stepped in close, a monstrous two-handed warhammer raised above his head for another blow.

This time when the hammer hit, Anskar's ward flashed and went out. He rolled aside at the last instant, and the hammer head hit the floor with a crack like thunder, splitting the stone.

Angry with himself for failing the test, Anskar pushed himself to his feet, expecting Beof to voice his disappointment. Instead, the priest pulled back the hammer for another swing.

With a cry of dismay, Anskar threw up his hands in a vain attempt to protect his face. Air rushed toward him, and he screamed in anticipation of the expected impact. Lightning ripped through his skull, and something ruptured in his brain. Blistering heat scoured his veins, and the catalyst in his hand erupted with dark fire.

He felt rather than saw the hammer's impact. Gasped at the glistening black ward that blocked it. The hammer head shattered into a thousand pieces, and Beof swore.

Anskar roared, and a fist of shadow shot forth from his ward to blast Beof in the face. The priest went down hard and didn't get up.

Anskar struggled for breath. Blood pounded in his ears. His heart threatened to smash free of his ribcage.

Beof had tried to kill him. Why? Did Vihtor know? Did Landav? Was this meant to happen?

In a panic, he ran for the eagle door, the black ward still swirling around him despite his empty dawn-tide repository. It must have sprung from another source… And it felt wrong. Forbidden sorcery. The Order would expel him, if they found out.

He stopped in front of the eagle door, but before he could lower his ward and grasp the handle, water splashed over him, passing through the ward as if it weren't there. Stunned, he spun round to see Malady holding a bucket, eight empty buckets lined up behind her against the wall.

The dwarf let out a shrill cackle then stopped abruptly as she took in his ward. "Black," she said. "Bad boy."

The eagle door opened, and Luzius Landav stepped inside.

"Well, well," the sorcerer said. "I thought I felt the tug of something other than the dawn-tide. It's all right, Anskar, you can lower the ward now. The trial is over."

"But Beof," Anskar said. "He tried to kill me."

"He did?" Landav glanced at the dwarf, though he couldn't possibly have seen her with those dark lenses and no eyes beneath.

"The Warrior's priest went too hard with this one," she confirmed.

"Did he now?" Landav tsked. "Revenge for his bejeweled mace, no doubt. Not the sort of behavior you would expect from a priest of the Warrior. Or maybe it is. Either way, the Seneschal must be informed. He will not be happy."

Malady nodded and exited through the eagle door, while Landav went to check on Beof, and Anskar felt a ripple run beneath his scalp. Sorcery—though he could not tell the type.

The sorcerer returned a few moments later saying, "Not dead, but whatever you did to him was quite unpleasant. Could take him days to recover. I've bound him with sorcery just in case. Come. We need to talk before anyone more official arrives."

Landav opened the eagle door, and Anskar stepped through into the darkened chamber at the foot of the steps.

"Hold my hand," the sorcerer said, "and I will guide you back up top."

The sorcerer's grip was damp and limp, but Anskar was beyond caring. He just wanted to get away from the catacombs and back to the safety of his room.

But it was to Landav's chamber they went, where the sorcerer seated himself in an armchair and held out his hand. "Your catalyst, if you please."

Anskar handed him the crystal. Not only was it still milky at the center, but dark threads now fractured its surface. Landav rubbed it between his palms, dipping his head in concentration. After a minute, he passed the catalyst back to Anskar.

"You have a strong connection with it, but already its attenuation has shifted in a direction the Order would not approve of, had they the ability to detect it." He smiled a crooked smile. "Show no one. I am a sorcerer, and there is little that shocks or offends me. But these knights…let's just say they don't understand. But you will, Anskar. One day. I see a bright future for you. Well, maybe bright is the wrong word…"

"So, I should keep it?" Anskar said, a sickening feeling rising from his guts as he stared at the tainted crystal in his palm.

"Of course, dear boy. You passed the third trial. Now all that remains is for the catalyst to be embedded beneath your skin." Landav leaned forward and jabbed Anskar in the sternum with his fingertips. "Here."

THIRTEEN

THE DODECAGON WAS PACKED AS Anskar entered at the head of the seven successful novices. Landav had announced in the refectory that two had failed the trial. Meli Dorana had been unable to effect the link with her catalyst at the same time as holding the calculations in her head; she would still have been standing in front of the first mummy had not Malady gone to see what the delay was and led her to safety. Cail Hexal had been the other one to fail. His ward hadn't been strong enough to withstand Beof's blow, and he'd received a mild concussion as a consequence. The other novices reported that the Warrior's priest had struck their ward spheres just the once. It was only Anskar that Beof had tried to kill.

Vihtor and the eleven senior knights were seated on their thrones, elevated above the assembled knights, the novices who had failed and would make another attempt next year, and those in the year below.

Luzius Landav stood apart with Malady. Both looked bored, as if they couldn't wait for the ceremony to be over.

The priests were there too, although only four of Menselas's five aspects were represented. The absence of any priests of the Hooded One felt to Anskar like a portent of bad things to come.

Anskar scanned the priests of the Healer, surprised at how acutely he felt Tion's absence. Perhaps it was the eruption of dark power that had erupted from within him during Beof's attack; perhaps he needed to confess. But there was no sign of his old mentor. Tion and Glaena were no doubt aboard ship for the mainland, their thoughts all on the new life ahead of them, not what they had left behind.

Haldyca was there for the Mother, along with two acolytes.

The scruffy old man who represented the Elder was alone, cataract-clouded eyes staring at nothing, beard slick with drool.

The five priests of the Warrior stood aloof, speaking only among themselves. Beof was noticeably absent, prompting Anskar to wonder what had become of him. Would Beof be punished for attempted murder? Maybe he was still in the infirmary receiving treatment for his injuries. With any luck, the Healer would withhold his blessing and Beof wouldn't recover. And if he did, Anskar prayed that the Elder's judges would quickly establish his guilt. The only pity was that with no priests of the Hooded One left in Branil's Burg, there was no one to carry out the sentence.

The room quieted as Vihtor stood.

To Anskar, it felt like being punched in the stomach, and for a moment he couldn't breathe. As the Seneschal gestured for the crowd to part around the seven novices who had passed the trials, Anskar was gripped by a sudden urge to flee. The sorcery that had risen unbidden within him, and saved him from almost certain death at the hands of Beof, made him feel a fraud, a cheat. The trials were supposed to be a test of skills learned under the instruction of the Order, the culmination of hard work and study. But this power—the only reason he had survived the last trial—was something else.

I thought I felt the tug of something other than the dawn-tide, Landav had said. That meant it was either the dusk or the dark, according to what the sorcerer had told them—unless there were other tides than the three Landav had spoken about. Use of the dusk-tide was an affront to Menselas and against the Order's rules. Use of the dark sounded demonic.

"Anskar?" It was Naul, face pressed so close that all Anskar could see was the worry in his eyes.

That was enough of a surprise to pull Anskar's attention out of his own head, and at once he saw that Naul wasn't the only one watching him with concern. Orix clapped him on the back and nodded encouragement. The Traguh-raj lad could barely contain his excitement. *We've made it!* his eyes seemed to shout. *This is it!*

Anskar glanced round till he found Sareya. Her smile was so infectious, Anskar couldn't help but return it. Her hair held a satin sheen and her red skin positively glowed. And then she turned to face the front; they all did as the Seneschal began to speak.

"Seven," he declaimed. "That is how many Menselas has given us. Seven to have passed the trials. Seven to be raised to the interim rank of knight-liminal."

"Menselas be praised!" the priest of the Elder cried out in a shaky voice.

Every priest present replied in unison, "The balance of the Five be upon these seven."

Close to two hundred knights thumped their fists to their

chests and clicked their heels together.

Knights-liminal! A lifetime at the Burg; years as a novice; and finally, Anskar had come to this. Knight-liminal: the brief transitional stage between a novice and the simple vows that would raise him to a knight-inferior. A year away from the solemn vows that would make him a consecrated knight and bind him to the Order of Eternal Vigilance for good.

Hearing Vihtor say the words "knights-liminal" was a deluge that washed away Anskar's doubts. He had done nothing wrong, only defended himself. And he'd not been in control of what had happened. Menselas wouldn't blame him for that; not the merciful god Tion had always claimed they served. If there were flaws in the Order or himself, they could be fixed. The Five himself would fix them.

Emotion flooded through him: relief, joy, pride—enough to drive out thoughts of demons and darkness. Enough to convince him that Menselas was indeed merciful; that he overlooked transgressions for those who stayed the course.

Vihtor's eyes passed from one novice to the next, and he acknowledged each with a nod and a touch of his thumb and four fingers to his forehead.

Anskar dipped his head and gripped the hilt of his sword *Amalantril*, which was sheathed in its lacquered wooden scabbard at his hip. As if in a dream, he heard Vihtor say, "Petor Vilaf," and as he looked up, he saw the older novice approach Vihtor and take a knee.

"Proof," Vihtor said, "that perseverance pays." Petor had failed the testing of his ward sphere the two years previous.

The Seneschal laid his hands on Petor's head. "In the name of the Mother, the Elder, the Healer, the Warrior, and the Hooded One, I raise you to the rank of knight-liminal."

Vihtor gripped Petor's wrist and drew him back to his feet, and the Dodecagon once more erupted into applause.

"Gar Landry," Vihtor called next, and the lad from Caronath went up.

Orix was next; then the only other young woman besides Sareya to pass, the aloof and lean Myra DeYenté. And then Naul.

Anskar's hand on his sword hilt grew slick with sweat. Inside, he was shaking, and for no reason he could tell, close to tears. He glanced at Sareya, but her eyes were on Vihtor as Naul received his blessing. As Naul stood and the knights again burst into applause, Anskar noticed Larson among them. The stablemaster beamed like a proud father and raised his thumb, and Anskar could hold back his tears no longer. He wiped his eyes with the back of his sleeve, and in that moment, Vihtor called his name.

In a daze, Anskar approached the Seneschal through the channel in the crowd, took one knee before him and bowed his head. He felt the heat of Vihtor's palms on his scalp as he received the Five's blessing. Anskar shuddered, and it seemed to him a warm glow rose from within his depths.

"Well done, Anskar," the Seneschal said, grasping his wrist and helping him to stand. "Very well done."

"Huzzah!" Larson cried out, and again the knights applauded.

Anskar bowed and turned away, narrowly avoiding bumping into Sareya, who was next in line. His heart swelled with pride for her as she took the knee, but the Seneschal glanced Anskar's way and pride swiftly turned to shame. Cheeks burning, Anskar averted his gaze and didn't even look at Sareya as she came to stand beside him in the line of new knights-liminal.

"Each of you," Vihtor said, "will be appointed a mentor to prepare you for simple vows."

The Seneschal walked up and down the line, considering,

as half a dozen knights stepped forward to receive their new charges. One by one, Vihtor paired Orix, Naul, Gar, Petor and Myra with their mentors. Anskar felt convinced that he and Sareya were being left till last for a reason: that they were to be exposed for what they had done.

But then Vihtor allocated Sareya a mentor and came to stand before Anskar. The Seneschal's blue eyes were ice-rimed ponds, hard to read, and Anskar began to flounder under their unrelenting gaze. Words bubbled up from his guts—apologies and excuses—but before they reached his lips, Vihtor turned to address the crowd.

"And I will take Anskar DeVantte under my wing." To Anskar alone, he said, "We will speak after the ceremony."

Anskar had never before been in the Seneschal's suite and was surprised at how austere it was. It held a plain wooden table and two chairs, a tatty leather couch, a covered water jug on a stand, and a mannequin on which Vihtor's mail hauberk hung. Two doors led off from the living room, presumably to the washroom and bedroom.

"Please be seated," Vihtor said.

As Anskar perched on the edge of the couch, Vihtor drew up one of the chairs, reversed it, and sat astride it. He studied Anskar for a long while, his blue eyes probing.

"You were close to Brother Tion?" the Seneschal asked. Before Anskar could answer, he raised a hand in apology. "I know you were. He virtually raised you, didn't he?"

"Since I was brought to the Burg," Anskar said.

"Yes, I…" Vihtor pressed his lips together and the merest lines of a frown etched his face. "Yes, I was told that. His departure must have affected you deeply."

Anskar shrugged. "I wish him well."

"But you have friends now who can support you? The other six who made it through the trials?" The Seneschal's eyes narrowed—only slightly; just enough for Anskar to wonder where this line of questioning was leading.

"I don't make friends easily," Anskar said. "Probably because I've been here so long."

"The mainlanders think they're better than you because you worked with the servants in the kitchens?"

"In part," Anskar said. "Some of them just resent me because I'm always at the forges. And if not the forges, the stables. And I think they don't like it that I spar with anyone who will let me— younger novices, older, some of the knights when they have the time. I've heard them say it's unfair, but no one's stopping them from doing the same."

"And sorcery?" Vihtor asked. "Frae Ganwen says you have quite the gift."

"That too," Anskar said, "though I'm far from the best in that department."

"Sareya?" Vihtor said.

Anskar held the Seneschal's gaze as his heart began to thud in his chest. His cheek started to twitch, but mercifully Vihtor looked away.

"You and the Traguh-raj boy seem to have made up."

"We have, sir. I suppose Orix has become a friend."

"Good." Vihtor still stared off into some imaginary distance. "That is good. A knight needs friends he can trust. He needs allies. Anyone besides Orix?" And now the Seneschal returned his gaze to Anskar.

And Anskar lied. "Not really. Not among the new knights-liminal. Though I will try to befriend them, sir, if you think I should."

Vihtor said nothing, merely continued to watch Anskar's face. The Seneschal's eyes glistened—they looked damp.

"That would be a good idea. You still help out at the stables?"

"I do, sir, whenever I'm able."

"And Larson is good to you?"

"Like a father, sir. At least, like I imagine one should be."

Vihtor drew in a deep breath through his nose and nodded as he let it out. "A good man, Larson. A fierce knight in his day, but hopeless with a ward sphere."

"He told me that, sir. Said he only passed the trials on the third attempt."

"Menselas is merciful," Vihtor said. "Though luck may have played a part, and connections go a long way."

"Larson has connections?"

Vihtor smiled at some private joke. "We are all connected in one way or another. Menselas builds a web of relationships around us. For those blessed enough to achieve a balance within their own natures, good things often come by way of those connections."

"Friends, then," Anskar said, concluding that the Seneschal was instructing him to make an effort with his colleagues.

"Not just friends. All our relationships combined define the person we are."

"I don't understand."

"Nor should you at your age," Vihtor said. "Pray to the Elder to grant you wisdom and beseech the Mother to help you continue to grow."

"Yes, sir. I will."

Vihtor cocked his head to study Anskar. His eyes no longer gleamed with moisture. They had once more become hard with ice.

"Tell me what happened during the combat trial," he said. "In the final bout, Clenna had you beaten, and then something happened."

Anskar swallowed. Vihtor was right, as Tion had been too: he'd been about to capitulate, but then something had erupted within him—the same thing that had effected the connection with his catalyst; the same thing that had come to his rescue when Beof almost killed him in the final trial. But to describe what he'd felt would only lead to more questions, and then Vihtor would want to see the corrupted crystal in his pocket—and all that implied.

"I'm not sure," Anskar said. "Clenna hurt me. One minute I felt weak, close to giving up, and the next…" He deliberately left the explanation unfinished.

To Anskar's relief, Vihtor nodded with recognition. "You gained a second wind. At the point of defeat, you found something within yourself—a hidden well of courage. It is the mark of a true warrior. A born fighter. That said"—he grew suddenly stern—"as a knight you must learn to curb your emotions, your…rage. A warrior is most effective when impassive. There is a place for anger, certainly. Use it to fire yourself up to come back from the brink of defeat; but then you must temper it with cold, clear thought. And most of all, you must know when to stop. When to show mercy."

Anskar remembered Vihtor's hand on his shoulder, preventing him from ramming his wooden practice sword into Clenna's throat. He lowered his eyes and muttered an apology.

"Don't be sorry, Anskar. Learn and grow. That is what I

expect from you. You have the potential to be a great knight. It's in your blood."

"It is?"

"One would have to assume," the Seneschal said with a shrug. "Now, I have spoken with Luzius Landav and with Beof—"

Anskar's heart clenched. "He attacked me with a warhammer. Tried to kill—"

Vihtor cut him off with a raised hand. "I know. Landav told me, and that dwarf of his confirmed it. I'm not accusing you, Anskar. I simply want to know what happened and how you survived."

Anskar stared into Vihtor's eyes, willing himself to find an explanation that wouldn't be another lie. *Something other than the dawn-tide.* But what could he say? What *should* he say? Somehow, either the dusk- or the dark-tide must have been unleashed from within him—it was the only thing that made sense. And he was permitted to use neither.

His lips started to form the words "it wasn't my fault," but no sound came out. It was a lame thing to say. Vihtor would expect more from him.

"Perhaps you are still in shock," the Seneschal said, standing and returning his chair to its place beside the table. He didn't sound convinced. "Let's not press the issue. Take some time; but if anything…out of the ordinary should happen to you— anything you don't understand—you must come to me. I can help you, Anskar. I *want* to help you."

Anskar stood as Vihtor opened the door for him. He wanted to ask what the Seneschal meant by "out of the ordinary." What did Vihtor know? But at the same time, Anskar felt relieved that he'd been let off the hook, at least for now, and so he held his tongue.

"Don't worry about Beof," Vihtor added. "I'm sending him to

the mainland to be disciplined by his bishop. From what I hear, the Warrior's chastisement can be extremely painful."

Anskar nodded his thanks.

"Replacements for Beof and Tion could take weeks," Vihtor continued with a sigh. "No one wants to be stationed in Niyas. It's no secret we're considered something of a backwater." He shook his head. "To think, only sixteen years ago Niyas was the heart of a burgeoning and dangerous empire.

"And I doubt we'll get a new priest of the Hooded One after this business with the vault—which wasn't my idea. Orders from on high: the Grand Master. You'll get to meet him soon enough. He's coming in person all the way from Sansor in Kaile to consecrate the vault.

"Now, get some sleep. You've earned it. Meet me after breakfast tomorrow in the horse yard. It's time you saw something of the world outside these walls."

Fellswain grew skittish as Anskar rode her alongside Vihtor's black destrier, Uhtran. The chestnut palfrey was picking up on Anskar's nervous energy, he knew that, but there was nothing he could do about it. He was excited, proud, elated; but he was trembling inside. His hands on the reins were slick with sweat, and he kept glancing over his shoulder at the keep.

Vihtor seemed to realize and offered Anskar a reassuring smile as they came in sight of Branil's Burg's east gate, and then, not giving Anskar a chance to turn back, the Seneschal touched his heels to Uhtran's flanks and cantered ahead. Fellswain, as if he knew what was expected of him, picked up his pace and, before he knew it, and with a sickening twist of his guts, Anskar found himself the other side of the east gate and in the streets of Dorinah.

Buildings he'd only glimpsed from atop the parapet now sprawled away from him as he rode with Vihtor into the sun-drenched street away from the shade of the citadel's walls. But the next thing he noticed was the stench: filth and dung, grease and cooked meat, sweat and the pungent herbs that everyone seemed to be smoking in long-stemmed pipes.

There were people everywhere, swarming like ants among the refuse piled up in the street. Most were Niyandrians, rough-looking, downtrodden. They stopped and stared at the two riders passing along the road. The few dusky-skinned mainlanders he saw were white-cloaked knights of the Order on patrol.

Most of the buildings were not dwellings as Anskar had expected: they were glass-fronted stores whose wares were hidden behind layers of grime. Many had painted wooden signs above their entrances, the paint faded and flaking, the names of the stores meaningless to Anskar, for they were in Niyandrian, which he couldn't read. In the distance, above the rooftops, he could make out a vast tower capped with a patinated dome, and farther off still, a massive wood-frame construction underway.

Vihtor slowed his horse to a plod, studying Anskar as he took in the surrounds.

"What do you think?" the Seneschal said. "It's a far bigger world outside the Burg, eh?"

"And dirtier," Anskar said as his eyes followed the rats gamboling in and out of the refuse.

"Not all Dorinah's districts are as bad," Vihtor said. "Some are even passably civilized these days."

"You mean they weren't before?"

"Before we came? To a Niyandrian they might have been, but

there are different standards on the mainland."

Before Anskar could ask anything else, Vihtor said, "Don't worry, the Order is in control of Dorinah and its surrounds. You're quite safe with me."

"I know," Anskar said. "And I'm not worried." The lie this time was to convince himself. His lips were dry, and though he tried to moisten them with his tongue, he had no spit.

"Good lad," Vihtor said, once more picking up his pace.

Anskar cast a longing look over his shoulder at the walls of Branil's Burg, literally his life's stronghold, the center of his world. But then he switched his gaze to Vihtor's white cloak pulling ahead of him down the street.

Perhaps sensing his uncertainty, Niyandrian scavengers began to crowd toward him, their cat's eyes feverish. An old woman—a crone—held out her palms to him and said something he didn't understand. She switched to broken Nan-Rhouric as she reached for Fellswain's bridle. "Coin," she said, then nodded as if he were a simpleton. "Coin."

Bile rose in Anskar's throat, and fear of contagion crawled over his skin. His hand dropped to the hilt of *Amalantril* scabbarded at his side. "Don't touch me!" he snarled as he kicked Fellswain into a canter.

"You didn't give her anything, I hope," the Seneschal said, reining in his destrier as he waited for Anskar to catch up. "It only encourages them."

"They are vile," Anskar said, heart thudding in his chest. "Not like the Niyandrians at the Burg."

"So, you don't disagree that what we offer the Niyandrians is good for them?"

"And they were always like this?"

"Left to their own devices," Vihtor said. "Niyas was an island full of filth and savagery." He narrowed his eyes at Anskar. "Try to remember that. Under Queen Talia, they would have swarmed across the Simorga Sea and infected the mainland. Not just with their barbarism, either: with their debased religion and their necromancy." Vihtor stiffened in the saddle and sucked in a sharp breath. "It's why we fought them, Anskar. Why so many gave their lives in the war."

"My parents…"

But Vihtor was already riding ahead again, and Anskar didn't want to get left behind.

As they entered a broad avenue, Anskar started to relax a little. They were flanked by enormous buildings with pillared porticos, all built from the same blue-gray stone as the citadel. The road was paved, though weeds showed through the joins, and the gutters were thick with sludge. Tributary streets were alive with better-dressed Niyandrians on their way to work, he assumed, and there was a constant clatter of cartwheels.

Vihtor called a halt at a walled compound. The only entrance was barred by a heavy iron gate, and inside there were knights of the Order at guard posts. Smoke plumed from a large chimney atop a brick building inside the compound. As much as Anskar craned his neck, he couldn't figure out what the place was.

"It's our mint," Vihtor said in response to his unspoken question. "The Order works hard, day and night, to replace the foul currency the Niyandrians use. We melt down their queens, and stamp our own copper pennies, silver talents, and gold crowns with the star of Menselas."

Vihtor urged his horse on, and Anskar followed. The stench of urine was overpowering, and Vihtor explained that there was a tannery nearby—a new business introduced by mainlanders from Kroe.

Scrawny dogs, their tongues lolling, eyed them from dismal alleys. It wasn't a place Anskar wanted to linger, and he was glad when Vihtor led them at a brisk trot toward one of the huge city gates, where more of the Order's white-cloaked knights saluted the Seneschal with a thump to their chests.

Outside the city, the sky was clear, the sun fully risen, dappling the grassland with its warm light and chasing away the shadows. It was one more step removed from the safety of Branil's Burg, but if anything, Anskar was relieved to be away from the squalor of Dorinah.

He rode Fellswain at an easy amble, not realizing how close he kept to Vihtor's horse until the Seneschal told him to relax, drink in the views, and give their horses space.

Not waiting for a reply, Vihtor kicked Uhtran into a gallop, and, after an initial twinge of panic, Anskar set off after him. Ignoring Vihtor's well-intentioned advice, he kept his eyes on the back of his horse's neck. He'd glimpsed the wide expanses rolling away into the hazy distance as they left the city gates, and had never felt so small, so insignificant. So vulnerable.

Fellswain closed the distance effortlessly, and Anskar muttered a quick thank you to Larson for allowing him to ride such a thoroughbred. Wind tugged at his face, splayed his hair out behind him. The air hitting his lungs felt cool and clean. Beneath him, the powerful motion of the palfrey's muscles, the heat of her skin. Little by little, Anskar drew courage from the horse, who seemed to yearn for the great open spaces and was only held back by good training and the tight hold Anskar had on her reins.

A shadow passed overhead and on instinct Anskar ducked. As the shadow passed, he risked a look up and smiled. It hadn't been a bat-winged demon or a marauding drakkon—if such things really existed: it was a flock of swallows undulating beneath the slow drift of cottony clouds. The sky above was so vast, a sprawling canopy now that there were no curtain walls to obscure his view.

He glanced back over his shoulder at the citadel looming above Dorinah. Beyond the expanse of the city he could see the glimmer of water rendered hazy by the heat. Fellswain missed a step, stumbled. Anskar yelped and clung to her neck as the palfrey slowed then staggered to a halt.

"You need to look where you're going," Vihtor said, riding back to check on him. "You were almost thrown."

Anskar nodded, barely registering what the Seneschal was telling him. He was too in awe of what he'd seen. Patting Fellswain's flank, he twisted in the saddle to look behind once again.

"Is that—?"

"The Simorga Sea," Vihtor said. "Yes, it is. Perhaps one day you'll get to cross it."

"In a ship?"

"Unless you plan to swim."

After that, Vihtor led Anskar across the escarpment Dorinah stood upon, which looked down upon the great forest of Rynmuntithe—the Gloaming in Nan-Rhouric.

The horses slipped and slid down a gradual scree slope until they reached the broad valley that ran through the heart of the forest.

As they passed a smallholding in the shade of the valley wall, a Niyandrian peasant woman paused in her scattering of seed for her chickens and watched them. Vihtor raised a hand in acknowledgment, and she waved back before returning to her task.

"She seems friendly enough," Anskar said.

"Why wouldn't she be?"

"I just thought…" Anskar trailed off.

Vihtor studied him intently as their horses walked side by side along the well-trodden track. "You were thinking of the Niyandrians in Dorinah?"

In part he was; but he was also thinking of the things Sareya had told him, and the defeated air of the servants in Branil's Burg's kitchens.

Vihtor looked away, scanning the trees atop the ridge of the valley. "The truth is, many of the locals see us as liberators. They weren't happy under Queen Talia's rule. It must have been horrific for them."

Anskar knew Sareya would claim that wasn't how her parents remembered it. But they were probably just bitter. It can't have been easy being on the losing side. And the servants: maybe they should consider themselves lucky to have somewhere to live and work. Even as he had the thought, he recalled the welts on Jonita's wrists, her swollen jaw and black eye.

"You ride well," Vihtor said, changing the subject. "When you're facing the right way. Is there anything you don't do well?"

Anskar shrugged, then realized that might be construed as arrogance. He thought about it. "I'm really bad at languages— especially Skanuric. And controlling my emotions."

Vihtor nodded. "Still thinking about your fight with Clenna?"

"I should have retained control."

"Yes, you should. We all should. The knight who loses his head figuratively inevitably loses it literally, too. Victory favors the calm."

"But there are exceptions?"

Vihtor smiled at him. "Very astute of you. I've seen many a knight out-thought and outclassed in a fight resort to brute rage to overwhelm their opponent—your friend Larson among them. But it's a risky strategy that leaves you open to counters from a level-headed adversary.

"It's all about balance. This is why we shouldn't devote ourselves to any one of the Five aspects of Menselas to the exclusion of the others. There will always be specialists, of course. The Five demands it. But they are the exception rather than the rule. As Knights of the Order of Eternal Vigilance, we must be many things: the strong arm of the Church, just rulers, merciful victors. We must nurture new blood in our Order through the ministrations of the Mother. And even death, the Hooded One, plays a vital role in our lives, for do we not lay to rest fallen comrades? Do we not fear the mortal wound, the invisible plague, the failure of a weak heart? And, as we age, we hope to grow wise in the lore of the Elder, so we can guide the affairs of the Order and weave a course through the politics of our world."

"Politics?"

"If—when—you visit the mainland, you'll see for yourself. Relationships—we spoke of this before—are what Wiraya turns upon. Political relationships. Alliances. That doesn't mean they are always easy."

Anskar took his time to digest what Vihtor had said. He knew nothing about politics and wasn't sure he wanted to learn. But Vihtor had twice spoken about relationships, and there were things about that Anskar still wanted to know.

"What of the other traits of the Healer and the Mother? What about family and love?"

"Why do we not take partners among our own, you mean? Why must a knight serve away from their spouse and children, often for months on end? Because Menselas demands our full attention. Because we are consecrated to his life. But it isn't as bad for us as it is for the priests—most priests," the Seneschal added in clear reference to Tion. "At least we have families to return home to."

Vihtor had misunderstood Anskar, who was again asking about his mother and father, though in a roundabout sort of way. But the Seneschal's words raised a different question. "Forgive me, sir," Anskar said. "Are you married?"

He'd never known Vihtor to be away from the Burg for more than a few weeks at a time, and then only if he was on a tour of the isle to oversee the construction of new strongholds, or visiting regional commanders to apprise himself of their progress in the fight against the Niyandrian rebels.

"No, I am not."

They rode on in silence for a while, but Anskar could feel Vihtor's eyes on him from time to time. Eventually, the Seneschal tugged on his reins and brought his destrier to a halt. Anskar pulled up Fellswain beside him.

"The girl," Vihtor said, holding Anskar's gaze. "The Niyandrian, Sareya."

Anskar's mouth felt dry. What should he say? How much did Vihtor know? He swallowed and decided it was safest to be honest. "Menselas has forgiven me."

Vihtor continued to watch him, face inscrutable. Eventually, he gave a curt nod and they set off again.

The valley floor started to rise until they emerged atop a rolling line of hills looking across lowlands teeming with sheep and cattle and dotted with farmsteads. Drystone walls formed the boundaries of pasture and, in the distance, sunlight glimmered on the surface of an immense lake. On the far shore stood a sizable settlement that Vihtor said was their destination: the fishing town of Caeltrin, which not only supplied the kitchens of Branil's Burg, but also boasted the finest tavern in Niyas—the Griffin's Rest, which had been founded by mainland entrepreneurs at the end of the war.

As they rode toward the town, Vihtor spoke at length about the virtues and vices associated with each of the god's Five aspects. He made it clear that Beof's vengefulness after Anskar had broken his mace showed too extreme a devotion to the martial nature of the Warrior without the temperance of self-regulation and mercy.

"This is why it is such a shame about the Hooded One's treatment of late," Vihtor said. "One of the chief functions of the Hooded One is to limit and moderate the other four aspects; to teach us humility, self-knowledge, recognition of our limitations and our mortality. I told the priestess Hathenor as much, but the matter is out of my hands. I tell you, Anskar—and not a word about it to anyone else, please—this desecration of the Hooded One's chapel, this turning it into a vault for the safekeeping of mainland wealth, is an offense to the Five. It can only end badly. In this—and in this alone—I disagree with the Grand Master."

"Then why—?"

"Why go along with it, when I am Governor of Niyas and Seneschal of Branil's Burg? I'm sure I could find others who share my concerns, but let this be a lesson to you: that is not how we do things in the Order of Eternal Vigilance. There is a chain of command, and it must always be respected. Always. Without fail. My allegiance is not to the individual but to the office itself. A Grand Master is sacred, beloved of Menselas, whatever his mortal failings."

Vihtor's last statement felt like a warning to Anskar: a line not to be crossed.

He trailed behind the Seneschal's horse the rest of the way

to Caeltrin, thinking about what Vihtor had said; thinking about Sareya. But as they came to the sandy shore of the lake, he pushed Fellswain to a trot to come alongside Uhtran.

"Welcome to Lake Xaranin," Vihtor said. "Don't ask me what the name means. Probably named after some Niyandrian so-called god or other."

They followed the shoreline north until they came to a well-maintained jetty where a number of small boats were moored. A larger boat—more of a broad raft, which Vihtor described as a ferry—was just coming in from the far shore.

"We timed that well," Vihtor said as he dismounted and waved at the ferryman—a gray-haired Niyandrian who hollered a greeting.

The crossing was smooth, and Anskar spent the half-hour it took lying on his belly, looking into the water at darting minnows and the occasional turtle gliding beneath the surface.

"Snappers," Vihtor said. "Make a tasty soup. Just mind your fingers; those beaks are razor-sharp."

At the far side, they led the horses along a road of hard-packed earth into town, where it became a paved high street. Vihtor pointed out the vast wooden warehouses where fish were prepared for being transported all over the island, and even as far as the cities of Kroe and Riem on the mainland.

There were awning-covered stalls selling shellfish and jellied eels, necklaces made from shells, and buckets of water containing crabs and crawfish—which Anskar had seen in Branil's Burg's kitchens when he'd served there, but had never before tasted. Farther in, there were shopfronts with painted signs—in both Niyandrian and Nan-Rhouric—promoting dried foodstuffs, lamp oil, unguents and ointments, charcoal, dried dung, twine. They passed a cobbler's displaying boots in the latest fashions from Sansor, and leather sandals in the style worn by the Jargalan Desert nomads. A dusky-skinned woman with a regional mainland accent—probably from the Pristart Combine, Vihtor commented—stood at a grindstone offering to sharpen knives.

It surprised Anskar to see how many mainlanders mingled with the Niyandrian locals, buying each other's wares, nodding to one another in the street, even sitting on the benches outside a bakery eating pastries and sipping tea as they exchanged gossip. When he wondered aloud to Vihtor how the former enemies could co-exist so peacefully, the Seneschal nodded toward a couple of white-cloaked knights patrolling the street.

"One of the Order's many roles, which you will experience once your training is complete, is to maintain law and order."

Anskar nodded, impressed, though the thought occurred to him: whose law, and whose order? Presumably the same that held sway on the mainland: the laws of Kaile, whose nobles had been the driving force behind the invasion of Niyas. His mind flashed back to Sareya's anger at the Niyandrian oppressors determined to wipe out her culture.

They tethered their horses to a rail in front of the Griffin's Rest and went inside. It was nearing midmorning and the tavern was packed. Pungent yet sweet pipe smoke filled the air, clinging to the underside of the ceiling in swirling banks of cloud. Underlying it was the stench of stale sweat and spilled beer. Sheaves of dried hops decorated the rough-carved wooden bar, atop which stood tapped kegs and rows of upturned mugs.

A passage to the bar opened up through the drinkers, who seemed to have a healthy respect for Vihtor's white cloak, whether they were Niyandrian or not.

The Seneschal ordered two mugs of beer and slapped a couple of copper pennies on the bar to pay for them, before leading

Anskar to a cozy alcove by the hearth. They sat opposite each other at a rickety round table, Vihtor sipping his beer and encouraging Anskar to do the same.

"Are you sure it's all right?" Anskar asked. Tion had repeatedly informed him he was too young to drink, but Vihtor nodded for him to go ahead.

Anskar wrinkled his nose at the first sip. It was warm and bitter, with a vaguely fruity aftertaste.

"You'll quickly acquire the taste," Vihtor assured him, taking a long pull of his own drink.

"I'm not sure I want to." Nevertheless, Anskar took another sip, then a gulp. Despite the taste, the beer brought a warm glow to his face, and he liked the look of approval he got from Vihtor.

A stocky man with very little hair and a thick bushy mustache came over to greet Vihtor by name. They shook hands, and Vihtor introduced him as Nigen Bosh, the landlord.

"And this, my friend, is Anskar DeVantte," Vihtor said.

"DeVantte, eh?" Nigen chewed on one end of his mustache. "A good Kailean name, if ever I heard one. You from Sansor, son?"

Vihtor answered for him. "Anskar was born here in Niyas. His father and mother…" He trailed off, shaking his head, and Anskar clenched his jaw in disappointment.

"I understand," Nigen said. "Hear the same sad story all the time. Good thing for you the Order was there, eh, son? To take you in, give you a bright future."

The Seneschal sighed, gazing deep into his beer before looking up abruptly. "Nigen built the Griffin, Anskar."

Nigen held up his hands. "Pish! Get away with you, Vihtor." To Anskar, he explained, "I was one of many partners—the one daft enough to leave the mainland and move here. But it's a tidy business, and I can't say I regret the choice. Now, Seneschal, will you be wanting lunch?"

"Indeed," Vihtor said, rising from his chair and brandishing his mug. "And a refill from the bar."

"Sit yourself down. I'll send one of the servers over to take your order, and he can bring you more beer while he's at it."

"Obliged to you," Vihtor said, relaxing back into his seat as Nigen left them.

By the time their food was set before them, Anskar was feeling giddy and slightly nauseous from the beer. The server had brought fresh mugs too, even though Anskar hadn't yet finished his first.

"You'll be fine once you start eating," Vihtor said, breaking off a hunk of black bread and helping himself to a piece of fried fish from the basket the server had placed between them.

Anskar bit into the meaty white fish, savoring its lightly spiced saltiness. The bread was equally good: moist and grainy, with a hint of something sweet. And Vihtor was right: the more he ate, the better he felt. Soon he was taking sips of his beer as if it were the most natural thing in the world. The interesting thing was, the more he drank, the more it relaxed him. He was beginning to see why the tavern was so popular.

As they ate and drank, Vihtor spoke about how important it was for the locals and the mainlanders to integrate, and how he believed it was part of the Order's duty to ensure that integration happened. The Seneschal's mood darkened, though, when he touched upon the matter of Carred Selenas and the disruption sown by her resistance. Almost every month there were reports of fresh attacks by the Last Cohort—usually wherever the Order was trying to establish a new stronghold to further the protection they offered the locals.

"As soon as our people mount a response, the rebels take off like startled crows," Vihtor said. "Bloody cowards."

Anskar was shocked by the Seneschal's language, and Vihtor noticed.

"Forgive me. The downside of drinking beer: it loosens the tongue and increases the frequency of confession."

"So, Carred Selenas is still a danger, even after all these years?" Anskar asked.

"Careful," Vihtor said. "That sounds like a criticism of my leadership."

"That's not what I—"

"You wouldn't be the first," the Seneschal said, staring into his beer. "But no, she's not a danger exactly. More of an annoyance. She resorts to hit-and-run tactics for the most part these days. I suspect her rebellion is thinning; that the Niyandrians have largely given up hope. For years Carred Selenas got the better of us, delayed the building of our strongholds, but we've had a recent spate of success. And her resources grow more limited year after year. Ours, however, do not."

"Because of our allies on the mainland?" Anskar asked.

Vihtor nodded and sipped his beer. "Donations from Kaile and the City States; a never-ending stream of recruits. Other things. No, the problem with Carred Selenas isn't that there's a chance she might win, it's that she won't accept defeat. Hers is a long, lingering death, but it won't be long now, not once our mainland overlords commit to the squeeze."

"The Church of Menselas?" Anskar said. "The banks and the nobles?"

Vihtor drained his mug. "And the rest of them."

"What about Queen Talia's daughter?" Anskar asked. "Surely, if the Order found her, it would deprive these rebels of any hope."

Vihtor set down his mug with a dull thud and stared into it. "Cut off the head of the serpent, you mean?"

"Well, yes." Wasn't that what the Order had been trying to do these past sixteen years? Wasn't that why they'd brought Sareya and others like her to the Burg?

When Vihtor looked up, he caught Anskar off-guard with a question. "How did you find Luzius Landav?"

Anskar wasn't sure how to answer that. *Creepy, frightening, strange* would be the truth, but was that what Vihtor wanted to hear?

"He seemed all right."

"Did he now?" Vihtor said with a wry smile. "Good. I'm glad to hear it. He'll be staying at the Burg just one more day, and then he has other business on the isle."

"With Carred Selenas?" Anskar asked. He'd overheard as much when the sorcerer had first arrived at Branil's Burg.

Vihtor ignored the question. Instead, he placed his hand over his sternum and said, "Before he leaves, he'll be fitting the catalysts."

Anskar swallowed more beer, at the same time touching the crystal in his pocket under the table.

"You have yours with you?" Vihtor asked.

Anskar's heart skipped a beat. What would the Seneschal make of the crystal's discoloration? "No, sir. I didn't want to risk losing it."

"A shame. I had hoped to bless it for you…as your mentor. It's of no matter. I'm sure the effect would be negligible at best. Come on, drink up. We should be heading back."

Anskar put his mug down. "We can go now. I think I've had enough."

As they stood to leave, a huge man entered the tavern. Last

time Anskar had seen him was in Branil's Burg, when the fallen knights had been returned to the Order. Then the man had been wearing blood-speckled plate armor. Even dressed as he was now, in plain clothes of brown cotton beneath the white cloak of the Order, he was an imposing figure.

"Seneschal," the big man said in a rumbling bass.

Rather than a formal salute, Vihtor greeted him with a firm handshake. "Anskar," he said, slurring his words, "allow me to introduce one of our finest, and the man largely responsible for our recent successes against the rebels: Eldrid DeVantte, your namesake."

"DeVantte?" Anskar asked, almost lost for words. "Does that mean…?"

Eldrid glanced at Vihtor, as if seeking permission, but it was the Seneschal who answered.

"No, you're not related. Your own family name was…it could not be…"

"Out of love for your father," Eldrid said, "I gave you mine."

Vihtor clenched his jaw and swallowed. "You should consider it an honor," he told Anskar. "Eldrid is an exemplary knight. A good friend."

"You knew my father?" Anskar asked Eldrid.

The big man sighed, and again awaited permission from Vihtor.

"We should get going," the Seneschal said, clapping Eldrid on the arm. "Have a good night."

As they stepped outside and the door closed behind them, Anskar asked, "Why won't you tell me who my parents are, sir? I have a right to know."

Vihtor drew in a deep breath, then let it out in a sigh. "I have thought long and hard about this, but I can say no more. You must trust my judgment. What's past is past. We will not blight the present by speaking of it. Not at this time."

"Then when?"

A hard look came over Vihtor's face. There was no trace of a slur in his voice when he said, "You will not ask again."

FOURTEEN

"STRIP," THE DWARF TOLD ANSKAR as soon as he entered the infirmary. "Just your shirt. No need to uncover what we don't wish to see."

It was odd being there without any priests; just Malady and her master, Luzius Landav, who stood beside a cot bed covered with a blood-spattered sheet, wiping a thin knife with a strip of cloth. The sorcerer polished the blade as if he could see it.

Malady took Anskar's shirt and folded it neatly on a chair, afterwards sniffing her fingertips and wrinkling her nose.

"You brought the catalyst?" Landav asked without looking up.

Anskar took the crystal from his pocket. If anything, it looked even more discolored: dark threads weaved through its strata like the legs of a spider trapped inside.

"Ah, yes, the tainted one," Landav said.

"You can see?"

"In a way. And I can *feel* it. Tell me, does the corruption of your crystal concern you?" When Anskar didn't reply, Landav asked, "Do you have a theory as to what causes it?"

"A few," Anskar said. He hesitated. How much did he want to share with this sorcerer, who had already told him to keep what had happened to his catalyst secret from the Order? Unless it was a flawed crystal, like Larson claimed his was, the taint had to come from Anskar himself; or the connection he had made with it.

"Yes?" Landav prompted.

Malady came to stand beside the sorcerer, rolling her eyes with impatience.

"I thought I might have accessed one of the other repositories you mentioned," Anskar said.

"You mean unwittingly? Of course you do. And perhaps you are right. My guess is that the anxiety of effecting a connection with the catalyst triggered an innate ability in you. We all know the story of the woman who lifted a wagon from her crushed child; it's much the same thing."

"But it happened twice: first during the combat trial when I faced Clenna, and again with Beof in the sorcery trial."

"Yes," Landav said. "Which is quite revealing. Baffling too. This has the flavor of the dark-tide, wouldn't you agree, Malady?"

"If I have to."

"It is a rare thing for anyone outside of the abyssal realms to have a dark-tide ability, let alone a repository—and, I can tell you, you do have one squirreled away beneath your dawn- and dusk-tide repositories. The question is, what will you do about it?"

"Speak with the Seneschal?"

But Vihtor had already broached the subject with him, and Anskar had been deliberately evasive.

A laugh exploded from Landav's thin lips. "Yes, reveal your

affliction and count on Menselas's mercy to take it from you. Do you know how many priests I've had this conversation with? Priests who possess the mark of sorcery as well as the supposed mark of the god. Do you know what I tell them? Accept who you are. Most don't, and they go on to make miserable priests, spending more time making their own confessions than listening to those of others."

"You think I'm a sorcerer?"

"We are, all of us, many things," Landav said. "Take Malady here, for example. What do you suppose she is? And don't say short, because she can get quite touchy on the subject of her height."

Anskar hadn't really considered what Malady might be. He'd assumed she was Landav's driver, his assistant, but he didn't want to risk angering her by suggesting either.

She was watching him, an amused glint in her eyes. Suddenly, she made a fist, then opened it to reveal a dancing tongue of red flame on her palm.

"You're a sorcerer too?"

Malady snorted, and Landav said, "Oh, she is much more than that. One day, perhaps, if you hone your abilities, you may be able to discern what."

"You have a catalyst?" Anskar asked the dwarf.

She scowled, and Landav said, "That is not a polite question to ask a lady."

Heat rushed to Anskar's cheeks. He dipped his head and apologized to Malady, which only made her double up with laughter.

Turning back to Landav, he asked, "So, you think I should accept what I am?"

The sorcerer watched him patiently, running a slender finger along the blade of his scalpel.

Anskar felt compelled to go on. "But what if I don't know what I am?"

No response.

"Are you offering to show me? To train me?"

"Oh, good grief, no," Landav said. "I am not in the business of charting the course of another's life. Each to his own orbit, I say, and let not worlds collide. I barely even know what direction to steer my own life in. As a sorcerer, a seeker after the secrets of the cosmos, I am somewhat envious of the certainties evinced by these knights you esteem so much. Men like Vihtor Ulnar, for example."

"You wish to be like Vihtor?"

"That is not what I said." Landav seemed to become bored by the conversation. He gestured to the cot bed. "Lie down."

"Catalyst," Malady said, holding out her hand.

Anskar gave her the crystal, then seated himself on the edge of the bed.

"Your path is your own," Landav said, "as much as anyone's is. In reality there are always invisible forces pulling us this way and that. It is how we respond to them that is important. I'm sure you never suspected you held such puissance within you that could discolor a catalyst and overwhelm a battle-hardened priest of the Warrior. Invisible forces," he repeated, "made manifest by their actions."

Malady wiped the area above Anskar's sternum with a damp cloth, leaving a yellow stain on his skin. "Numbs the pain," she explained.

"My reason for speaking of this," Landav continued, "is not to sway you one way or the other—for why would I, a master sorcerer, want to encourage someone onto the same path, knowing that one day they might surpass me? Sorcerers are like scholars in that respect: riddled with petty jealousies and seeing rivals everywhere. I merely wish to help you clarify your thinking. Show Vihtor, or any of the knights, your catalyst and I'm sure they will be horrified. At best, they'll have every priest of the Healer from here to Sansor invoking the blessing of the god on you in the hope of exorcizing some inner demon. At worst, they will expel you from the Order for your lack of purity. I offer a different perspective. Were my own catalyst not buried beneath the skin of my chest, I would gladly show it to you. I can guarantee it is not as clear as the day it was grown. I'd even go so far as to say it resembles coal more than quartz. But does that make me evil? Demonic?"

Malady shrugged, and Landav clipped her round the ear.

"I would say," Landav added, "it makes me a sorcerer. Nothing more, nothing less."

Anskar looked away, trying to process what he'd heard. But then something Landav had said brought a question to his lips. "Your crystal was grown?"

"They all are," Landav said. "And it's no simple matter, let me tell you. There are minerals that need to be mined, calculations to be made, powerful cants intoned at very specific times, if the catalyst is to be attenuated to the dawn- and the dusk-tides."

"And the dark?" Anskar said.

"Requires a different skill set. Even if they possessed the knowledge, no sorcerer the right side of sanity would prepare a dark-tide catalyst—the Church of Menselas would burn them alive if it became known."

"But you… I mean, my catalyst—"

"Is not intended to channel the dark-tide."

"Hence the corruption?" Anskar asked.

"As good a hypothesis as any."

"But who grows the crystals? They must cost a fortune to buy."

Which was presumably why the Order insisted on novices passing all three trials before the catalyst was made a permanent part of them.

"Mine was grown by a Soreshi sorcerer in the Ymaltian Mountains," Landav said. "But she's long dead."

Malady smirked, and Anskar had the uneasy feeling that Landav had been the one to kill her.

"These days I grow the great majority of crystals in Kaile," the sorcerer continued.

"You live in Kaile? But I thought—"

"I am accommodated in Kaile. Sansor, to be precise. And most comfortably, too."

"I think my parents were from Kaile," Anskar said.

Malady sniggered, and Landav allowed himself a tight smile.

"What?" Anskar asked. "What is it you think you know?"

"Not as much as you seem to believe," Landav said. "But, according to Malady, your skin tone tells a different story."

"And your scent," the dwarf added.

"My scent?"

"But I must say," Landav said, "the growing of catalysts is a most rewarding trade. I have rivals in other parts of the mainland, but the important contracts, the most lucrative, are all mine."

"Such as the Order?" Anskar said.

"A new client, and one of my most valued. Let's just say their previous supplier lost her enthusiasm for the growing and selling of catalysts. Now, please lie down. I've dallied longer than I intended to, and Malady and I are rather pressed for time."

"Are you going to find Carred Selenas?" Anskar asked. "If you kill her, the rebellion will be at an end."

"Did I say that? I may be many things, but I am not a common assassin."

"Certainly not a common one," the dwarf said.

"Malady…"

"Speak when spoken to?"

"You know the rules. No, we are not going to kill Carred Selenas; merely meet with her, have a little chat. Now, if you don't mind…"

Anskar lay back, apprehensive of the scalpel in the sorcerer's hand, and the prospect of his catalyst being inserted permanently beneath his skin.

"You think I could be a knight *and* a sorcerer?" he asked.

"You think the Seneschal, or the Order, would accept that?"

"No."

"Then," Landav said, pressing the tip of the scalpel to the skin above Anskar's sternum, "it would appear you have a choice to make. When will you be up for solemn vows?"

"Little more than a year's time," Anskar said, wincing as the scalpel broke his skin, even though he felt nothing—Malady's yellow ointment was doing its job. He tried to look, but Landav pressed his head down.

"Then there is no need to make a decision now," the sorcerer said. "You have ample time to work out who you are and what you desire."

Anskar turned his head to the side and saw Malady drop his crystal into a silver bowl. There was a sharp hiss, and a greenish mist plumed from whatever liquid was within the bowl.

"That's right, keep looking away," Landav said. "I can't stand it when people faint at the sight of their own blood."

Anskar felt a pressure on his chest. He swallowed thickly and tried to relax, but the stench of the sorcerer's black coat so close to his face made him want to gag. It smelled of loam and damp.

He heard Landav click his fingers and say, "The catalyst, Malady. Quickly now."

"Aren't you going to wash your hands first?" the dwarf asked.

"If I must." Landav moved away. Anskar heard the sound of water pouring from a jug, and then the sorcerer returned, wiping his hands on a towel, which he then carelessly slung aside.

Malady handed Landav the crystal. As the sorcerer held it above the incision, Anskar noted once again its spiderweb of dark fissures. And then Landav leaned over him, and Anskar closed his eyes.

At first he felt very little besides a weight on his chest; then he became aware of the thrum of the crystal—wild and erratic. Little by little, its pulsing synchronized with the beat of his heart: a rapid, thudding tattoo. Warmth permeated his flesh, intensifying as it hit his bones, burning, scorching. He cried out, but Malady was there, stuffing a soaked rag in his mouth. It tasted of bitter herbs. Within moments, the fire within settled into a bearable smoldering. Beat by beat, his heart slowed until it was a monotonous dull thud, distant and echoing.

"Needle," Landav said. "Thread."

Dimly, Anskar was aware of the needle pricking his skin repeatedly; the tug of the thread being drawn through.

"Is he breathing?" Landav asked.

Anskar felt the rag taken from his mouth. Drool leaked down his chin. He opened his eyes a crack, but all he saw was a gray blur.

"He'll live," Malady said.

Anskar's back arched. Fire coursed through his veins. His limbs went rigid. His heart pounded so fast he thought it was going to burst.

The spasm ended abruptly, and he sank back into the bed. But then he began to shake, and his jaw clamped shut. He tasted blood in his mouth; it trickled down his throat, and he started to choke.

"He's rejecting the crystal!" Landav cried, his voice seemingly coming from the end of a long corridor. "Don't just stand there, you useless bloody dwarf! Fetch the healers!"

The flutter of a thousand wings. Screeches. The skirl and swirl of wind. Shadows flitted behind Anskar's eyelids. He was burning up inside. Sweat-soaked sheets clung to his skin. He opened his eyes to a vortex of black shapes swarming around him. Crows beyond counting, stifling his ability to breathe; smothering him with their closeness and their stench.

He blinked and the birds were gone, replaced by a valley filled with skeletons in black—the uniforms of a once-mighty army. Skulls grinned up at him in triumph. Scattered bones shuddered on the ground, creating a fearsome clatter. New ligaments grew, joining arm bones, leg bones; forming ribs into cages, vertebrae into spines. All across the valley, the dead began to rise, tendons, sinew, muscle growing anew; black hair, cat's eyes, and red skin. Nicked and rusted swords clashed against dented shields in a distant, systolic pounding.

Anskar wanted to run, but he couldn't tell where he lay in relation to the resurrected Niyandrians. He was both present and not. He tried to sit up but couldn't feel his limbs. He cried out—a grating scream that shredded his throat and ended in a drawn-out rasp.

The sound of a chair scraping on tiles. Quick footsteps. A

damp cloth touched his forehead. A voice uttered soothing words. He peered through a crack in his eyes and saw a blurry figure leaning over him. Vihtor?

A hand behind his head raised him a little. A cup pressed against his lips. Cool water entered his mouth; trickled from the edges down his chin.

And then the back of his head was resting against a soft pillow and he was sinking into it, drifting down. Drifting, drifting.

And flames roared up to meet him.

Anskar awoke to a sharp pain in his neck. He lashed out and hit something soft and furry; felt the trickle of warm blood running down his neck. He sat bolt upright, eyes quickly adjusting to the flickering light of a candle on the nightstand.

He'd knocked something off with his blow—a dark shape that twitched and flipped atop the sheets. It righted itself, then fluttered up to the window behind his head.

Anskar stood on unsteady legs and faced the open window. In the silvery moonlight, he saw a crow perched on the sill, its eyes shining golden. Blood stained its beak. *His* blood.

He lunged at it, but the crow was too quick for him and flew away into the night.

Anskar pressed his hand to the still-oozing wound in his neck. A crow that drank blood? Could he catch anything from it— some incurable disease?

He remembered the dreams, his fever, the sealing of the catalyst beneath his skin. He'd been sick, he realized. Perilously close to death. But now... Now, he was bone-weary, but otherwise felt fine.

He became aware of a gentle, regular snore. On the chair at the foot of the bed, Vihtor Ulnar slept. Anskar recalled hearing the Seneschal's reassuring voice while semi-conscious. How long had Vihtor been here, watching over him?

Should he wake him, ask him what had happened? No, he decided; the Seneschal was clearly as exhausted as he was. Any questions would have to wait until morning.

Anskar shut the window and climbed back into bed. He'd barely pulled the covers up when he felt the misty clutch of sleep dragging him under.

He awoke to the sun glaring through the window, and the clatter of a tray being set down on his nightstand.

"Breakfast," Vihtor announced, yawning. "Don't expect this treatment in the future." The Seneschal smiled. "Your fever broke during the night. It was a close-run thing, but the healers say you're going to be all right."

Anskar's hand flew to his neck, which had been dressed with a wad of cloth. He could smell the astringent odor of a poultice to ward against infection. A quick glance at the sheets on his bed showed that they had been changed while he slept.

"What happened to your neck?" Vihtor asked. "The healers said it looked like a deep scratch."

"A crow," Anskar said. Without the wound, he would have felt certain he'd dreamed it.

"A crow?" Vihtor grimaced, then added, more to himself than Anskar, "The important thing is that you're going to be all right. Well, eat up. I have to wash and get ready for a council meeting. At this rate, I'll need sticks to keep my eyelids from drooping and a gallon of tea to keep me awake."

"I'm not really hungry," Anskar said.

"Eat anyway. The healers tell me you need to get your strength up, if you're to make a full recovery. Your body rejected the catalyst, Anskar. You could have died."

Anskar's hand went to his bare chest, where he encountered a bandage wound about his ribs. Beneath it he traced the tender ridge of sutured skin. "Is it…?"

"It's still inside you, yes. Landav said the removal of a catalyst is extremely hazardous, even for those in good health. We had no choice but to wait and hope you recovered."

"Did you pray?"

Vihtor looked surprised, then discomfited. "Of course. And thanks to the help of Menselas's healers, you're on the road to recovery."

The Seneschal left the room quickly, slamming the door behind him. Something had unsettled him, and Anskar was certain it couldn't have been the question about prayer.

Still, it had been the ministrations of the healers—and Vihtor—that had enabled Anskar to survive the night.

Or had it been something else?

He returned his fingertips to the wadding covering his neck wound and remembered his dream of black wings swarming around him, of the dead returning to life.

And all the while, he couldn't stop thinking about the crow.

FIFTEEN

TWO DAYS ON THE OLD Marsh Road, alone and grieving, sapped Carred of strength, and worse, of hope. She knew her mounting despair was in large part a symptom of fatigue, as well as the abrupt way she'd been forced to leave Marith. And she was angry. Bitter that she'd not be able to go back—at least until it was safe, and that might mean never.

It didn't help that she had the road to herself and saw no one, not even a single patrol of the Order of Eternal Vigilance. The fens the ancient road crossed were remote, and the few people who lived out here did so because they wanted to be left alone.

Carred, however, had never been good by herself. She retained vivid memories of her mother leaving her screaming in the woods that bordered their village of Bantiun until nightfall. She'd been four years old at the time. To teach her a lesson, her mother had told her, for not coming when she was called. Callous bitch. All Carred had learned was that she couldn't wait to get away from her mother and her drunken father, and that's just what she did when she turned fifteen and lied her way into the army at Naphor.

But she'd never forgotten the terror of being left alone amid the trees. Through her tears she'd seen things, blurry and indistinct. Beneath her screams she'd heard whispers. It was one of the reasons she'd never embraced the sorcery that came so naturally to her people: she was frightened of what she might see and hear if she developed her repositories. The other reason was Talia, whose compulsive pursuit of new sorceries had eaten away at her physical substance and left her skin as cold as ice.

Had it been the same for Talia's daughter? Had she felt abandoned by her mother? Did she even know who her mother was?

That was the thing that frustrated Carred the most about the path the wraithe had laid out for her atop Hallow Hill: she knew next to nothing about the girl she was meant to wait for while doing her best to keep Niyas's hopes alive. From time to time there were sightings of likely candidates for the Queen's daughter all over the isle; surges of excitement, inevitably followed by disappointment. But the girl, if she still lived, had to be a grown woman by now, living somewhere, with someone. Did they love her and look after her? Did she have any idea who she was? Not if the wraithe was to be believed; but after all this time, Carred was far from certain that it should be.

In her darkest moments, she believed that the girl—if she had ever lived at all—had fallen victim to the Order's sporadic roundups of Niyandrian girls of the requisite age. The practice had begun immediately after the conquest, and there had been occasional swoops on towns and villages ever since. If the heir had ever been identified, the whole of Niyas would have heard about it—the Order of Eternal Vigilance would make certain of that. The fact that they hadn't told Carred one of two things: either the daughter didn't exist, or she still hadn't been revealed.

She knew even less about the guardian who was supposed to protect the heir. For centuries, every firstborn child of a king or queen had been shadowed by a guardian, a sorcerer or warrior of great renown. Often it was both. But sixteen years ago, the wraithe had told her that the heir was safe—*for now*; that the guardian would be revealed when the heir became known.

And so it went on.

Carred stifled a yawn then abandoned the attempt and let it out. There was no one to hear it. No one to care.

These last two nights in the fens, with nothing but biting insects, croaking frogs, and the claw-like roots of mangroves for company, had left her rigid with fear and unable to sleep. Even now, during the day, the mire felt stuffy and oppressive. The muffled clop of her horse's hooves was almost lost amid the grating song of the cicadas, the plop and splash of creatures in the brackish waters, the rhythmic chorus of frogs. Mosquitoes followed her in clouds, and after hours of fruitless swatting at them, she'd given up and accepted their bites. Probably she'd contract swamp fever and die out here. Still, it could be worse. The mire could have been a haunt for dead-eyes.

At last she crested a grass-tufted hill and looked down upon the island amid the bog that was Halcoin. It was early morning, and the smoke of hundreds of cook fires made thready plumes in the sky, meeting in a thick cloud above the town. She could smell bacon and imagined the taste of hot coffee. She'd eaten nothing but berries since Marith's, and then only when she was lucky enough to find them among the briars and brambles threatening to choke the road.

Last time she'd been to Halcoin there had been no knights

garrisoned there, and she saw no patrols now as she rode along the cobbled high street. Halcoin, protected by the marshes and the mosquitoes, was still very much a Niyandrian town. The farther a settlement was from the Order's strongholds, the longer it was able to retain its customs and the illusion, at least, of self-governance.

One thing Carred could say for certain was that Halcoin was a damned sight cleaner than the occupied towns she'd visited. The streets had recently been washed and scrubbed, as was the Niyandrian way, and there were none of the rats that seemed to follow the Order wherever they took over. There were cats, though—lots of cats, plump and well-fed and obviously cared for. Cats were sacred to her people. Rats were not.

She stabled her horse and flipped a copper queen to the young girl on duty, then crossed the street to Kovin's stone-and-slate terraced house—a tall, thin building with three stories, narrow windows, and a flight of steps leading to a solid oak door. She didn't bother knocking: it was never locked.

Inside, she crept up the stairs, hoping to surprise Kovin, then heard the telltale grunts and cries, the rhythmic banging of the headboard against the wall that the neighbors were always complaining about. And this early in the day! Kovin was insatiable.

Carred eased through the bedroom door and crossed her arms over her chest as she watched Kovin give his latest woman a solid humping. She shook her head and smiled at his tight red buttocks rising and falling, and then noticed that the woman beneath him was dusky-skinned. Now there was a rare sight: a mainlander in Halcoin.

Carred waited until they were finished, then gave them a slow handclap.

Kovin rolled off the woman and grinned sheepishly. The woman, however, looked shocked and pulled the bedsheets up to cover herself.

Seeing the woman's discarded clothes on the floor, Carred picked them up and slung them at her. "You can go now," she said in Niyandrian.

When the woman looked at Kovin for an explanation, he merely gestured toward the door. She hurriedly dressed, cursing under her breath, then flounced past Carred as if she had been wronged. As if Kovin were *her* man and Carred had dared to come between them. Clearly she didn't know Kovin.

"How was it for you?" Carred asked, plonking herself on the edge of the bed.

"Still got more left in me," Kovin said, showing her.

She laughed. "When haven't you? But a mainlander? What were you thinking?"

"I was thinking tits. And she has…you know…"

"So I saw. But what's a mainlander doing in Halcoin?"

"There's a few now. Merchant families mainly. They bring things you can only get on the mainland."

"And our people just have to have them?" Carred shook her head.

The mainlanders had worked out it was far better to conquer by commerce, creating a need that wasn't there before—for pottery, and jewelry, trinkets of no possible use. There was nothing superior about the craftsmanship, but the items were novel to Niyandrian eyes. She glanced at Kovin. As were mainland women.

She removed her boots and lay back on the bed. "Mind if I get some sleep?"

Kovin frowned. "You know how I feel about dirty clothes on

my bed."

"I've been traveling," she said wearily.

"I can see. Looks like a bad case of the pox." He indicated her face where the mosquitoes had savaged her. "They get you anywhere else?"

Lazily, she unbuttoned her shirt then smiled as she felt Kovin's calloused hand on her breast. He was no Marith—no one was— but after all she'd been through, she deserved to find pleasure where she could. Didn't she?

"Can't feel no bumps," Kovin said, kneading her breast with appreciation. "But like I said…"

Carred shut her eyes and enjoyed his touch. "You like tits."

When Carred woke, it was evening. Kovin had picked up fresh clothes for her in town—thick-weave black pants, a black cotton shirt, and a fur-lined gray cloak with a hood. She offered to pay him for them, but he declined. He'd simply called in a favor, he told her.

"Really? And what was her name?"

Kovin chuckled. "It's been a long time," he said, embracing her once she was dressed. "Too long."

"You seem to be doing all right for tits."

"Ah, my love, but there are tits and then there are tits."

She laughed, and they embraced once more, but this time when she pulled away tears stung her eyes.

"What is it?" Kovin asked, suddenly serious. "What's happened?"

Carred wiped her tears with the back of her hand. "You know what I've missed? The Nag's Head. Take me there, and I'll tell you over a beer."

"Milady," Kovin said with a mock bow, and ushered her out the front door.

The tavern was heaving when they arrived, but Kovin persuaded a couple of young men to give up their table by the hearth and left Carred there to warm herself while he fetched them drinks from the bar.

A trio of Niyandrian minstrels played the old songs on fiddle, harp and flute, singing of gods and heroes and demons with close harmonies that left Carred feeling nostalgic while at the same time threatening to lull her back to sleep.

The thud of Kovin setting down a mug in front of her jolted her back to alertness, and she drank like a woman who'd just crossed a desert, rather than a swamp.

"More?" Kovin said, downing his own.

When he returned from the bar this time, they drank with more restraint, and slowly Carred let the words come. She told Kovin of the failed attack on the new citadel under construction at Naphor, and his face flushed with anger as he listened. Kovin, like every other true-blooded Niyandrian, bridled at the thought of foreigners desecrating their once-mighty capital.

She told him of the assassins that had come for her; how she'd narrowly escaped and ridden across the fens to reach him.

"Only because Marith held the bulk of them off," she said. The moment she mentioned her lover's name, the tears began again.

What she liked about Kovin above all other men—what she loved about him—was that he knew how to listen. He let her empty out her grief, and when she'd stopped crying, he returned to the bar. This time he came back not only with more beer, but a bowl of marinated and fried marsh eels, which tasted far better than they looked.

As he chewed thoughtfully, Kovin asked her, "What is it you want to do?"

Carred clasped her mug with both hands and stared into the white froth, considering. Finally she said, "Pay them back."

Kovin nodded. Whatever she needed, he would arrange it, she knew that.

"But not blindly," she added. "We all need to come together, share what we know, then plot the best way to hurt the bastards."

"I'll put the word out," Kovin said.

"Tell them to assemble at the Rynmuntithe Forest hideout on the feast of Theltek of the Hundred Eyes." That would give them a few weeks to organize themselves.

"Consider it done," Kovin said, rising from his chair.

"But not now." Carred took hold of his arm and pulled him back down. "Not tonight." She giggled—it had been a long time since she'd drunk so much beer. "Tonight we drink, we eat, and we fuck. Everything else can wait till the morning."

Kovin grinned. "I was hoping you'd say that."

SIXTEEN

ANSKAR SPENT MOST OF THE morning in bed, dozing on and off. Fragments of questions buzzed around his mind like insects, but before he could define one, another coiled about it and smothered the life from it.

At some point he became aware of warm wetness on his face. Like his questions, the impression was not fully present until a whine caused him to open his eyes a slit. A dog licking him.

"Rosie?" His voice came out cracked and squeaking. With an effort, he propped himself up on an elbow.

The ridgeback hound yapped and tried to jump onto the bed, but a man's hand restrained her.

"How you feeling, son?"

Larson.

When Anskar couldn't formulate a response, the stablemaster said, "I let myself in. Knew you wouldn't mind. Rosie insisted on coming. The Five knows why, but I think she missed you."

Lazily, Anskar reached out and stroked the dog's head until, seemingly content, Rosie lay down at her master's feet.

"They say your catalyst didn't take," Larson said. He pulled up a chair and sat beside the bed. "You think it was flawed, like mine?"

Anskar's mouth was dry as dust. He ran his tongue around it; tried to swallow.

"Here," Larson said, half-rising from his chair and handing Anskar a glass of water from the nightstand.

Anskar took a few sips then a gulp, then he finished the entire glass.

"You want more?" Larson asked, offering the jug.

Anskar waved it away and returned the glass to the nightstand. "I don't know," he said. "Don't know if the catalyst *was* flawed. But it is now."

"It was damaged when they put it inside you?"

"No." Anskar lay his head back on the pillow, no longer able to support his weight on his elbow. "I think it was me. I think I tainted the crystal."

"You? Is that even possible? No, I reckon they must've chipped it or something during the procedure. Or maybe you got infected, I don't know."

"So quickly? It was the crystal, I tell you. It turned milky after I first used it. Later, black veins spread within it."

"And they know what that is, do they—this mainland sorcerer and the healers? They know what caused it?"

Anskar closed his eyes. "I caused it. Me. There's something about *me*." Suddenly, he sat up in bed, causing Rosie to bark. "I know I've asked you before, but I need to know…"

"About your parents?" Larson drew in a big breath and let it out through his nostrils. "You think I've been protecting you, don't you? Though from what, I've no idea. I've told you the truth, Anskar. I've always told you the truth: I didn't know them. When you were brought to the Burg, I was still a knight; still out there fighting bloody rebels. Vihtor's who you want to ask, not me."

"I've asked him!" Anskar said. "And he never answers."

"Then maybe he knows nothing."

"And no one else knows, either? Do you really believe that?"

Larson shook his head and stood—a signal for Rosie to jump up and wag her tail expectantly. "I don't know what I believe. No one's said anything to me about where you came from over the years, and I never asked. I take people as they are and did the same with you. It's you that's important, not your parents; not what happened to them, why you ended up alone. You've got me, son, and Rosie. And Hazel and that dumb ol' donkey at the yard."

Anskar kept his eyes pressed shut in case Larson saw their dampness. "And Fellswain?" he asked.

"Well, she wasn't lame when you brought her back, so I don't think she'll object."

"Will you let me ride her again?"

"Whenever you like, so long as you muck out her stall, trim her hooves and groom her."

"I can come back to work?"

"You've finished the trials, haven't you? What other excuse do you have to be a good-for-nothing layabout?"

There was a knock at the door and Larson moved toward it. "Just rest up first, and when you're feeling better, you come and see me. Those bloody new recruits are worse than useless. I could use some decent help in the mornings."

The stablemaster opened the door, and as Rosie darted out,

Orix came in bearing a tray of food. The smell of beef broth and fresh yeasty bread turned Anskar's stomach.

"Just what you need," Larson said. "Enjoy your meal." And with that he left.

"The Seneschal asked me to come," Orix explained, setting the tray on Anskar's lap. "Sent for me personally. Said he knew we was friends."

Anskar managed a weak smile as Orix seated himself in the chair beside the bed Larson had just vacated. "I'm sorry, Orix, but I'm not hungry. I should be starving, but even the thought of food makes me sick."

Orix was up in a flash and grabbed the tray. "Waste not, want not," he said, resuming his seat and wolfing down Anskar's meal. "Don't worry," he added through a mouthful of bread, "Vihtor won't know it wasn't you that ate it."

Anskar shook his head. "Are you ever not hungry?"

"Nope," Orix said, slurping down another spoonful of broth.

After Orix had finished eating, they sat in awkward silence, broken only by Orix's occasional belch and corresponding apology. Anskar tried to think of something to say, but his mind was still foggy with fatigue, and several times he was awoken by his chin hitting his chest.

He hadn't even realized he'd been sleeping when there was another knock at the door and Orix entered bearing the evening meal. Anskar hadn't heard him leave after lunch.

"I had a word with Hubin in the kitchens," Orix said. "She said you like catfish fried in garlic and them new potatoes, so she cooked you some up with some spinach and kale—medicinal, she says." At Anskar's frown, Orix added, "The catfish was fresh caught in Lake Xaranin. Came from Caeltrin by wagon this morning."

That caught Anskar's interest. "I went to Caeltrin with Vihtor the other day."

"I heard," Orix said. "My mentor, Barris, does nothing but avoid me. Calls me a filthy Traguh-raj."

"Did you tell Vihtor?"

"Not my place. Besides, it's only words."

"Well, you are from the Plains of Khisig-Ugtall," Anskar said with mock seriousness. "And you could use a wash."

"Had one," Orix said. "Couple of days ago." He eyed the dinner tray hungrily. "Well, if you're not gonna eat it…"

"No, I am," Anskar said, propping himself against the pillows and lifting the lid from his plate. The catfish was prepared just as he liked it—crispy on the outside, with caramelized garlic coating it. The new potatoes were still in their skins and swimming in herb butter, and the greens were drizzled with olive oil and lightly dusted with salt.

He took up his knife and fork and sliced off a piece of catfish. Closing his eyes, he popped it in his mouth, expecting to be violently sick. He chewed it once, savoring the subtle spices that permeated the flesh; the tang of the garlic. He chewed again, and still wasn't sick. Gaining confidence, he swallowed his first mouthful, and in an instant found he was ravenous. Before Orix's increasingly disappointed gaze, he shoveled more food into his mouth and sighed with satisfaction. Halfway through, he stopped for a drink of water to counter the saltiness, then raced through to the end of the meal.

"You can lick the plate if you like," Anskar said once he was finished.

"Nah. Not hungry," Orix said, looking dejected.

Another awkward silence settled between them, and after a while Anskar grew concerned it wasn't just due to Orix not getting his meal.

"Is there something you want to say to me?" he asked.

"What do you mean?"

"Have I done something to offend you? Besides depriving you of seconds."

Orix managed a weak laugh, but his eyes held an uncharacteristic seriousness. "It's not you, Anskar. It's Sareya. I thought we were friends, but since…" He looked down, fumbling with his words. "She's grown cold; barely even acknowledges me."

"Ah," Anskar said. "I think that might be my fault."

"You don't say." Orix looked him in the eye. "What happened between you two? I mean, did you…you know…?"

Anskar nodded, worried about his friend's reaction.

"You sly dog!" Orix said, launching himself from his chair to shake Anskar's hand. "What was it like? I mean, no, don't answer that. But it's against the rules of the Order, and you being such a stickler, I thought… Menselas's tits and balls, Anskar! I never took you for such a dark horse."

"Orix!" Anskar said, objecting to the curse.

Orix placed a hand over his mouth. "Sorry." He looked suddenly panicked. "Do I need to confess that?"

Anskar nodded solemnly, but then laughed, and Orix laughed with him.

"Does Vihtor know?" Orix asked, serious again.

"I told him it was finished; that the Five had forgiven me."

"So, you were the one to stop it?"

"Why, what's she saying?"

"Nothing. Nothing at all. Least not to me. She spends all her time hanging around with Naul now."

Anskar felt a stab of jealousy but tried not to let it show. "Oh?"

"Like the three of us used to hang around together," Orix

continued, "until…"

"Until you all attacked me."

Orix shook his head. "I already told you I was sorry about that. I was an idiot. But this ain't about me, Anskar. How did Sareya take it when you told her it was off?"

"I didn't tell her."

Orix studied him for a long while before saying, "Well, it's done now. Probably for the best. Last thing you want is to be thrown out of the Order, having come this far. But I've got to say, I'm envious."

"You like Sareya?"

"No! I mean, yes, I like her, as a friend, but what I mean is…" His already ruddy complexion grew a shade redder. "I ain't never been with no woman. I'm seventeen, pushing eighteen—and most people are married by sixteen where I come from."

"Only another year or so and we'll be fully consecrated knights," Anskar said. "Then you'll be free to marry a woman from outside the Order."

"But what's the point of that? Only time we'd be together is twice a year when I get leave. That's not how to make a family, how to keep a home."

"You regret coming to Branil's Burg?"

Orix slumped down in his chair. "It wasn't like I had a choice. My folks weren't exactly rich, and there's not much honest work in the Plains. Anyhow, it's a moot point. I mean, who's gonna have me anyway?"

"Talking like that, you might just as well become a priest."

"Piss off!"

"Although," Anskar added, "even priests are leaving to get married."

Orix frowned. "That's unfair. If you're referring to Tion, he's one of the good ones. Not perfect, but he's doing right by the Widow Glaena."

"I know," Anskar said. "You're right."

"Course I am," Orix said. "So, you planning on talking to Sareya?"

Anskar shook his head. "Too risky."

"You mean you might not be able to keep your hands off her?"

Anskar threw a pillow at him. "No, you goose. I mean people might talk. Vihtor might suspect something."

"Crazy," Orix said, shaking his head. "Some of the Order's rules make no sense."

Something was scratching at the window.

It was dark when Anskar opened his eyes—when had he fallen asleep? When had Orix left?

There it was again—*scratch, scratch.*

Heart pounding, he rolled out of bed and drew back the curtains.

The glare of white Chandra momentarily blinded him, but as his eyes adjusted he saw a crow hovering a foot above the window ledge, raking the glass with its talons, tapping with its beak. Anskar recoiled, banging into his nightstand. He looked around for something to drive the bird off with. It was the same creature from the night before, he was sure of it: the one that had punctured his neck and drunk his blood.

There was a pinch at the base of his skull; the welling of something dark and corrosive in his guts. Heat permeated his bare chest, and through the skin and the scar line covering his sternum he could see a steady, pulsing glow of deep violet. His catalyst—but he'd not actively established a connection. It had to be his fear that had roused his power. That was disturbing. Where was the control, the volition? And whichever of his repositories the crystal was drawing on, he was certain it wasn't the dawn-tide.

The crow ceased scraping and pecking at the glass and hovered there instead, waiting for him, following his every move with its golden eyes.

Gradually, the pulse of his catalyst slowed and its inner light died down. The crow's eyes swirled and seemed to change to the color of spilled blood, before returning to their golden sheen.

As he held the bird's stare, Anskar felt the tickle of a breeze on his bare flesh, a soothing warmth within his head. He glanced toward the door—still closed—and then the window, which remained shut. Wherever the breeze came from, it wasn't natural.

His breathing slowed, and the blood rushing in his ears became a torpid slosh that left him feeling both deeply relaxed and fully alert.

He unlatched the window, and the crow flapped inside. It fluttered around his head, then sped toward the door, where it resumed its hover.

"You want me to open it?" Anskar whispered.

He threw on his shirt, pants, and boots, crossed the room and opened the door. The crow flew into the darkened corridor beyond. Pausing to strap on his sword, Anskar followed.

The crow took him along corridors and down stairs he'd seldom, if ever, trod. Anskar began to mentally backtrack in case he became lost. The only light came from the shards of moonlight shining through the clerestory windows close to the ceiling.

After a few more twists and turns, the air grew musty and the floor was carpeted with dust. At the foot of a narrow flight of stairs down, they came to a storeroom containing barrels and empty grain sacks, lanterns, oil flasks, coiled lengths of rope, shovels, rakes, and other gardening tools.

The crow waited at the door opposite, which was bolted from the inside. Feeling he had no choice, Anskar drew the bolt back, opened the door, and followed the crow outside.

They emerged into one of the Burg's courtyards—a narrow strip of lawn in the shadow of a curtain wall. There was no light from the parapet, no sign of any patrolling knights.

Set into the wall opposite the door Anskar had exited was a wrought-iron gate that looked relatively new. Probably, the entrance had been made to admit trade goods to the citadel, but in times of war it could be sealed over with mortared stone.

The crow flew between the bars of the gate, but when Anskar turned the handle he found it was locked.

The crow let out a squawk, and Anskar's catalyst once more pulsed and grew hot within his chest. He shuddered, and ropey fingers of dawn-tide mist discharged from his splayed hand. There was a sharp crack, and the gate swung open.

As he followed the crow into the streets of Dorinah, Anskar became convinced he was still asleep, dreaming. Or was he? His footfalls on the paved road were muted thuds that echoed in his ears. His breath came out in whorls of white mist. And the crystal at his sternum burned—really *burned*—and he had to check that his skin wasn't sizzling.

He was dimly aware of the rundown tenements either side of the road. In the distance, a man yelled, and a woman screamed in response. Once or twice he glimpsed shadows lurking in the alleyways he passed. An old man opened a second-floor window and tipped foul-smelling water into the street below.

As Anskar walked on, he became aware of the ache in his

knees, the sting of blisters forming on his feet. A chill wind blew, accompanied by a steady drizzle, and, despite the heat of his catalyst, he realized he was freezing.

The crow led him at last to a cobblestone wall and broad gates of blackened iron. This time there was no lock, and Anskar slipped through.

Inside the enclosure were looming statues of skull-headed devils, and others of robed men and women with beatific expressions on their carved faces. A graveyard. He walked among the tombs of Niyandrian dead and the more recent graves of mainland settlers who had fallen asleep in the embrace of Menselas.

There were squat crypts with stone steps leading down into them, and weathered sarcophagi, some missing lids or cracked open, one with a sapling growing through a breach in its center.

Anskar knew he should have been terrified; knew he should have turned and run. At the very least, he should have been wary, not languid and listless. Graveyards were the haunt of ghouls and dead-eyes—at least in Tion's stories; places where people were preyed upon and defiled. But it was a detached fear he felt—someone else's, observed from a distance. And he could feel the crow calling to his blood—the blood that it had tasted. It *knew* him inside out. It wanted him to keep up, and Anskar found that he had to obey.

The crow disappeared into a crypt overgrown with weeds and briars. Anskar followed it down the steps and through a ruined door that looked as if it had been burst apart from the inside.

The interior of the crypt was dank and utterly dark. Anskar could see nothing but the golden eyes of the crow as it hovered before him. Its gaze bored into him, and though he wanted to look away, he couldn't.

The crow's eyes expanded, flooding his vision with their glare. Invisible barbs sank into his mind, and there was a corresponding pinch at the base of his skull. This time, the sensation was unmistakable: he felt the steady flow of energy from his dawntide repository; not enough to appreciably diminish its reserves, but enough to do whatever the crow willed of him.

Anskar's hand began to glow. Startled, he held it away from him; observed a burgeoning swirl of light upon his palm. It fashioned itself into a sphere the size of an apple, then rose into the air above his head. Its radiance was soft and pearly, and extended around him for several feet in each direction.

He could hear the steady drip-plop of water—rain leaking through the cracked and sagging ceiling. Spiderwebs hung down, beaded with glistening droplets. The wall nearest him bore flakes of old paint; presumably there had once been a fresco there. Where wall met floor, cockroaches scuttled, alarmed by the intrusion of sorcerous light.

As Anskar crept farther into the tomb, the glowing sphere went with him. By its light, he saw a stone sarcophagus against the opposite wall. The lid lay in pieces on the floor, and there were broad fractures in the side of the sarcophagus facing him. The outside of it showed a bas-relief of living skeletons chained together at the ankles, and behind them the rising sun.

Anskar drew closer, a tingling chill seeping into his bones, then jumped at the flutter of wings. He turned to see the crow sitting in a niche in the wall, staring at the sarcophagus. He heard a rustling sound, like the wind blowing through fallen leaves, and was certain it came from within the sarcophagus. Steeling himself, he stooped and peered inside.

The soft light of the sphere fell on a mummified corpse wrapped head to toe in mildewed bindings. As he stared at its unmoving form, the rustling noise resolved into a harsh whisper—the same few words uttered over and over. Words he couldn't understand.

Niyandrian.

He backed away, convinced the mummy was about to grab him by the throat, drag him into the sarcophagus and devour his soul. He turned to flee, but the crow fluttered down from the wall and snagged the back of his shirt with its talons.

Against his will, Anskar's booted foot lashed out at the sarcophagus. A section crumbled to dust. He kicked again, and more of the stone disintegrated, showering rubble on top of the corpse. Still obeying the crow, Anskar grabbed the head end of the sarcophagus and pulled with all his might. Stone came away in his hands, and he dropped it and took a hold on the side nearest the wall. Leaning back and pushing with his boot against the wall, he was rewarded by the remains of the sarcophagus shifting a few inches. He gave a second, more vigorous pull, and the entire sarcophagus collapsed.

Behind it was a low opening in the wall.

A tunnel.

The weight of the crow left his back, and it flitted ahead of him down the tunnel and into darkness. Compelled, Anskar crawled after the bird, the glowing sphere so close to the top of his head he felt its heat.

The tunnel floor was strewn with rubble that abraded his hands and knees. Among the stones he saw the stripped bones of rodents and birds, and in one or two places the walls were spattered with crimson. On and on he crawled, his sword dragging, his shredded hands becoming sticky with blood. Each time he stopped to rest or to consider going back, the crow turned toward him, compelling him with its golden eyes.

At last Anskar emerged into a small cave open to the early

morning light. His glowing globe immediately winked out. Beyond the cave mouth, trees stretched away into the distance.

Anskar cursed the state of his pants—ripped open at both knees; stained with his own blood and the filth of the tunnel. His hands were a lacerated mess and stung so much it brought tears to his eyes. The sword hanging at his hip would be useless to him now; there was no way he could grip it.

The crow flew off into the trees, and Anskar was drawn in the same direction. He was high up on a ridge that sloped down to the forest floor. Behind him to the south, Dorinah's city walls dominated the landscape; within them the curtain walls and keep of Branil's Burg.

Anskar wondered who had built the tunnel, and for what reason. He estimated he had traveled at least a mile underground. To build something like that must have taken years. Given the location of the entrance via the ancient tomb, he figured it had to have been the Niyandrians—either as an escape route from the city, or for some more sinister reason. He thought back to the blood-spattered walls and the whispered voice he'd heard inside the sarcophagus.

The crow kept disappearing for long minutes at a time, then returning to shepherd him along. There was no track to follow, only the bird's promptings. Anskar descended to the forest floor and passed between the trees. From time to time he thought he heard horses, the bark of a dog, distant voices, but he pressed on without a choice. Hunger pangs clenched his stomach, and he grew faint and unsteady, stumbling over buried roots and fallen branches.

Again, he heard voices. Was that his name they were calling? Was that Vihtor?

He opened his mouth to call back but could make no sound.

He tried to halt his progress and turn toward the riders, but the crow swooped down and sank the tip of its beak into his neck. He lacked the strength to swipe it away, and merely stood there waiting for it to drink its fill.

The crow detached itself, blood dripping from its beak, and flew to alight on a nearby branch. This time, Anskar experienced the crow's urgency as if it were his own; he could feel the rapid patter of its tiny heart. Something needling wormed its way into his mind, and a woman's voice spoke inside his head, but once more the words were Niyandrian.

Onward the crow led him, through mile after mile of forest. Birds scattered from the treetops before them. Squirrels rustled through the leaves, sometimes leaping from branch to branch. At one point, Anskar heard the growl of something larger. He knew he should be wary but he was too exhausted to care. Whatever happened, happened. At times he wondered if he was even truly here, or still tucked up in bed and dreaming.

He came at last to the bank of a river, where a rotting boat lay half smothered by reeds. With the crow compelling him from its perch on one of the willows drooping over the water, Anskar forced a path through the reeds. The water came halfway up his boots, and mud sucked greedily at their soles. Freeing the boat, he pushed it out a little way, and climbed into it. There were no oars, and no rudder to steer by; the current bore it away downstream.

In the distance, a dog barked. Exhausted, Anskar lay down in the boat, and, as clouds swept across the face of the sun and a fresh rain started to fall, he drifted into sleep.

SEVENTEEN

ANSKAR WAS AWOKEN BY THE boat thumping against a mooring post, though there was no rope with which to secure it. He saw a small pile of berries on one of the boat's benches, and a handful of dead grubs. Of the crow there was no sign.

Judging by the position of the sun, it had to be past noon. The rain had stopped, but a stiff wind was blowing, and his soaked-through clothes were icy cold, causing him to shiver. One after another, he popped the berries into his mouth, breaking the skin with his teeth and wincing at the bitter taste. But the juice alleviated some of the dryness of his throat, and he finished them craving more. The grubs he left where he'd found them.

Anskar climbed out of the boat onto a dilapidated jetty and made his way to the end, where a clearly discernible trail cut through the bracken, skirting the roots of trees. Keeping to the trail when he could, sometimes losing it and picking it up again a little farther on, he repeatedly scanned the skies for the crow, but it seemed to have abandoned him. Instead of feeling relieved, he was filled with trepidation. In his mind, he was one of the children lost in the woods in the stories Tion used to tell him. Those stories never ended well, but maybe that was the point: to dissuade children from doing something foolish, like he was doing now.

What had he been thinking, to follow the crow into the wilderness?

But he hadn't been thinking. He'd been dazed, in a dream-like state. As far as he knew, he might be dreaming even now—although the stinging pain in his hands and knees, and the persistent hunger pangs, told him otherwise.

Every now and again, he would stop and strain to listen for any sound of people pursuing him or the barking of a dog. Each disappointment left him frantic, desperate to get home—but he had no idea how far he had come, and whenever he turned back, intending to return to the boat, he was overcome by guilt that he was doing the wrong thing, or dread that he'd be punished if he didn't go on.

And so, on he went, determined to reach the end of the trail before nightfall. The thought of being out here alone in the dark terrified him. Still, he had to stop sporadically to take his boots off and tend to the shredded skin of his feet. As his pants were already ruined, he tore off strips of cloth from below the knee and used them to bind his feet. It was a struggle squeezing back into his boots, but at least when he recommenced walking, the cloth soaked up the blood and weeping fluids of burst blisters, and the pain lessened considerably.

As the light faded into early evening, Anskar decided to try to experience the dusk-tide. He knew he shouldn't, but so far away from Branil's Burg, who would know? Luzius Landav had implied that there was nothing intrinsically wrong about any of the tides. The sorcerer had made them seem quite natural. What was starting to strike Anskar as unnatural was the way the Order—and the Church of Menselas—contrived to prevent people with the gift of sorcery from using it, save in the most restricted sense. Even so, he couldn't suppress the feeling of unease that came over him as he waited upon a grass-covered knoll for the sun to go down.

As the last ribbons of red sank beneath the horizon, he clenched his fists in anticipation.

At first nothing happened. Then, just as he was about to give up and find somewhere to shelter for the night, pressure mounted inside his skull, and he was blasted from his feet by a howling gust of wind—a wind that should have bent the boughs of trees and torn at their leaves, but instead left everything but Anskar unscathed. A gale screamed about him as he struggled to regain his footing; it pulled his skin taut and shrieked into his ears, threatening to burst the drums.

Something clicked within his skull, and the wind passed him by, its roar growing swiftly distant, then petering out altogether.

He could feel both his dusk-and dawn-tide repositories brimming with essence; and somewhere *beneath* them— though he couldn't pinpoint any of the three with accuracy—his dark-tide repository boiled and seethed and overflowed. It was drawing attention to the fact that night was approaching.

He knew it now: the unwholesome feel of his dark-tide repository was the same as the power that had spilled from him uncontrolled when he was under extreme stress. It was all well and good knowing that the trigger was emotion—especially fear—but there had to be more to it than that; some means to unleash it at will.

The crow had somehow guided him to open the locked gate and generate the sphere of light. Now he needed to learn how to manifest sorcerous power for himself—beyond the creation of a ward sphere and the enhancement of armor and weapons, which was all that the Order permitted. And even with the dawn-tide, Anskar's control was tenuous at best.

From somewhere behind him came a sharp exhalation. He turned just in time to see a pale shape dart between the trees. Heart hammering in his chest, Anskar set off down the knoll away from the creature, slipping and sliding his way to the bottom. He cast about quickly for any sign of the crow, but there was nothing save the limbs of the surrounding trees, almost skeletal in the failing light.

A twig snapped to his right. A blur of movement. And then Anskar was off, jogging through the woods, running, then sprinting.

An owl hooted. In the east, thunder rumbled. He could smell more rain coming and saw a bank of dark clouds closing in on the mounting wind.

He stopped to catch his breath; turned a rapid circle to scan for movement. There! A pale shape loping between two trees fifty or so yards behind him. Stalking him.

He ran on, slower now, conserving his strength. Whatever was following him could move quickly and, judging by the brief glimpse he'd caught of its gait, with half as much effort as he was using. It could have caught up with him any time it liked, which meant it was pursuing him with a purpose, waiting for him to tire. Well, that wouldn't take long. He was already more exhausted than he'd ever been, and it was fear alone that kept him moving.

Finally, he could go on no longer. Coming to a clearing, he

backed into its center and fumbled his sword from its scabbard, biting down on his bottom lip so he didn't cry out from the sting of the lacerations on his palm as he gripped the hilt. The pain was intense at first, but he found the tighter he clutched the sword, the less he felt it. Pretty soon, though, his forearm grew numb and leaden, and he had to will himself to relax his fingers.

No movement from beyond the clearing. Either the creature had given up, or it was still waiting until he was too fatigued to fight back. Realizing he must have looked a risky kind of prey standing there with sword in hand, Anskar sank to one knee, dipping his head as if he were about to pass out from exhaustion.

Long seconds passed, and then he heard the scrunch of undergrowth directly in front of him. Raising his eyes without lifting his head, he saw a pallid figure creeping warily toward him. It had long spindly limbs, curled claws, and a blunt face—almost featureless, save for boiled-egg eyes with no iris or pupil. Anskar knew at once what it was from Tion's stories: a dead-eye. A hunter of the weak. A defiler of corpses.

Fighting back the urge to scream and run, he let it prowl a step closer, then another. He could hear the gurgling rasp of its breath; smell its fetid stench. Another step, and it would be able to reach out and touch him.

Wait for it, Anskar told himself, sword arm trembling. *Wait for—*

The dead-eye sprang, and Anskar brought up his sword, intending to impale it. But the creature was quick—far quicker than he'd imagined. It swerved around the blade and slashed at him with a claw. Anskar slipped to one side, racing through calculations, muttering a cant; but as his sorcerous ward sprang up around him, he realized his folly.

The dead-eye was already inside.

It leaped on him, legs clamping around his back, claws slashing at his face.

Dropping his sword, Anskar grabbed the dead-eye's wrists, holding its claws a hair's breadth from his eyes. It shifted its weight and bore him to the ground, and his ward winked out.

The dead-eye was a crushing weight astride him, despite its spindly appearance. Anskar could hold its claws back no longer. Scooting his hips to one side, he bridged and rolled on top of the creature, hammering an elbow into its face. It howled and hissed, then raked its claws across the front of his shirt, piercing the skin beneath and drawing blood.

Anskar shoved the dead-eye down and drew his hand back to punch it, but the creature shunted him up toward its head and slid out between his legs. Before Anskar could recover, the dead-eye was on his back, legs clamped around his belly, making it hard to breathe. He fought desperately to stop it getting its arm beneath his chin, but when it slashed at his side, he dropped his elbow to protect his ribs, and in that instant the dead-eye slid its arm around his throat and proceeded to choke him. He could feel it shuddering with excitement as it clung to his back.

It added the pressure of its other arm to the stranglehold, and Anskar grew faint. A second more, he knew, and he would pass out, and the creature would be free to defile him and eat his desecrated corpse.

A flutter of wings. A piercing screech. The thud of something hitting the dead-eye. It threw up its arms to protect its head, releasing the pressure on Anskar's throat.

Twisting his hips, Anskar shoved the creature from him and lunged for his sword. The dead-eye flipped to its feet and bounded toward him—straight into the arc of Anskar's swing. Steel met flesh; crunched through bone. A viscous, milky fluid sprayed—its blood—and the creature went down.

Anskar watched, shaking, until the dead-eye stopped twitching. Then he collapsed to his knees and pitched to the ground, tired beyond words.

The last thing he saw was the golden eyes of the crow, its beak and talons dripping with the dead-eye's white blood.

Anskar came to with the stench of rot in his nostrils and the warmth of the early morning sun on his face. He was stiff from lying on the ground and winced at the prickling agony in his arm as the blood resumed its flow. His shirt and what was left of his pants were still damp from last night's rain, and a chill had entered his bones. But at least the sun was shining and the sky was blue and clear.

As he stood, he saw the dead-eye, stiff with rigor and already putrefying—which didn't seem possible. But then, the thing hadn't looked fully alive while it stalked him, and no one seemed to have any idea what manner of creature dead-eyes really were. Clotted milky blood clogged the wound he'd cleaved in its chest. No wonder it had died: his sword had almost sliced right through to the other side.

Amalantril lay where he must have dropped her, blade glistening with dew and spattered with gore. As he stooped to pick the sword up, he heard the crack of ligaments, and the dead-eye turned its face toward him. Ice flooded Anskar's limbs and he backed away. The creature began to gurgle and hiss, clack and jabber; he was convinced it was speaking to him.

He closed his eyes and shook his head, and when he looked again, the dead-eye was frozen in death, in the same position he'd found it upon waking. He edged forward so he could touch it—cold and stiff. It had definitely been dead for hours; probably the instant it had hit the ground.

Anskar turned away from the corpse, trying to figure out what had just happened. The mummy in the crypt had whispered to him in Niyandrian… Were there invisible spirits at work here? Maybe he was going mad from exhaustion and lack of food. Or had the catalyst embedded beneath his skin changed him in some way? Infected him? After all, his body had rejected it, and he'd been sick to the point of death.

He frowned, fighting down the nausea rising to swamp him. There were so many questions, and he never seemed to get a straight answer to any of them. He'd hoped to learn more from Luzius Landav, but the sorcerer's replies had been too cryptic, as if he had been playing with Anskar.

Perhaps Vihtor… But no, the last thing Anskar wanted was to admit such strange happenings to the Seneschal. There seemed no surer way to be expelled from the Order than an admission that he saw the dead move and heard them speak. Either it was from the abyssal realms, they would say, or he was crazy. Perhaps it was a little of both.

As Anskar sat cleaning his sword on the dew-laden grass, wiping it dry on what was left of his pants, the crow returned with a few berries attached to a twig. No grubs this time, which was a relief. It watched him as he ate, then guided him to a stream, where he cupped cool water in his hands and gulped it thirstily.

Anskar continued through the wilderness day after day, nourished only by the scant berries the crow found for him, and stopping to rest wherever there was water. His mind was hazy, and he moved in a delirium. He slept under the stars, and for the most part the rain kept away. The sun rose early and lingered in the evening sky. While there was light, he kept walking.

The pain in his torn feet lessened, and his hands were halfway to healing. Hunger was an ever-present companion, but he grew used to it. Oddly, the less he ate, the more energy he seemed to have, and he pressed on eastward, losing track of how long he had been away from Branil's Burg.

Some nights he was kept awake by the sounds of prowling beasts, and he was constantly on the lookout for more dead-eyes. It was well known the creatures were scarce in the vicinity of cities and towns due to the knights' frequent sallies out into the wilds to cull them. Mostly, the creatures hunted alone; but at the time of full-dark, he'd heard, when neither moon was in the sky, something drew them together to hunt in packs.

Late one morning, when the sky was overcast with swollen clouds, Anskar reached a point where the ground slowly rose toward a stepped embankment. He made the arduous climb to the top, which was a plateau of grass-tufted earth with its chalk bones showing through in patches where the soil had eroded.

At the center of the summit stood what looked like the base of a tower—a broad, squat structure made from the same blue-gray stone as Branil's Burg, save for the flat roof, which was a lighter shade of gray. The whole building was coated with moss, and there were no doors or windows.

The crow flew around the building once, then disappeared over the eastern edge of the hill. Cursing as fat drops of rain began to fall, Anskar crossed to see where the crow had gone, expecting to find it waiting for him. Instead, he saw a huge citadel under construction in the near distance: a half-finished tower of closely mortared stone surrounded by wooden scaffolding. Beneath the tower, the main body of the citadel was a vast building of many stories, with narrow windows of stained-glass and, at the bottom, huge double doors of blackwood. The whole structure sat atop a wasteland of charred ground, the site of some past devastation.

There were smaller buildings dotted about the scorched earth, all of recent construction; a corral and stables at the rear; a featureless warehouse; and a fenced-off enclosure within which stood dozens of wagons and carts. There were mountainous piles of stone—presumably from the buildings that had once existed here—at points around the site, most of them as black as the ground beneath them.

Upon the scaffolding around the tower, Anskar could make out the dark specks of people, quickly descending now as thunder rumbled and lighting illuminated the underbellies of the clouds. There was more frantic activity in and around the wagon yard and stables. Of the crow, there was no sign.

"Niyandrian slaves," a rasping voice said from behind him, "restoring Niyandrian ruins for their mainland masters. The city of Naphor rises from the dead."

Anskar spun, drawing his sword.

A cloaked and hooded figure stood by the side of the squat building, as if it had emerged from within without need of a door. A huge sword hung at its hip in a worn leather scabbard. The sword's hilt was wound with silver wire, the cross-guard studded with gemstones that seemed to swallow what scant light remained under the storm clouds.

"Who are you?" Anskar despised the quaver in his voice. He did his best to look intimidating, taking a step forward, sword extended. He tried to glimpse the face beneath the cowl, but saw only darkness there, black and absolute.

"I am one who honors an agreement," the figure said.

"What agreement? With whom?"

"The one who brought you here."

The crow? But how could that…?

The hooded figure stepped toward him. It wore heavy, armored boots, visible beneath the hem of its black surcoat, and yet it made no sound as it walked. Anskar shook with the urge to run, at the same time knowing his limbs wouldn't obey him.

"You deny what you are," the rasping voice said—a statement, not a question. "It is to be expected. I am to give you an aid to self-knowledge, but from then, your destiny is your own. So far as that can be said to be true for any of us."

With a wave of the figure's pallid hand, a section of the squat building's wall sank soundlessly into the ground, revealing a narrow corridor illuminated by a soft violet glow.

"There is something for you inside," the figure told Anskar. "Part of a larger whole that has yet to be."

"What does that mean?" Anskar said. "And why me? You don't even know me."

"You know yourself even less. Enter, and claim what has been left for you. Or leave now and forever remain in ignorance."

Anskar backed away, still brandishing his sword. "Then I'll go."

An angry screech sounded, and the crow was there, flying circles around him. A woman's voice spoke inside his skull, at first speaking Niyandrian, but then, with a thick accent, it managed a single word in Nan-Rhouric.

[Enter!]

The hooded figure chuckled. "I should not have given you the impression you have a choice. We are all of us bound, though some never know it. Fate is inexorable." It held out its arm and the crow flew to it, clinging to its sleeve. "For your own good, enter this tomb and claim that which is yours by right."

"Tomb?" Anskar said. He'd already had enough of tombs.

"An ancient one, very much diminished by the hand of decay;

its secrets jealously guarded by those with the hidden knowledge. It is a vambrace you seek within. The metal will be unfamiliar to you. Touch nothing else you might find, no matter how much it glitters."

"And it will reveal to me who I am?" Anskar asked. "Where I am from?"

"It will reveal."

Anskar gave the golden-eyed crow a long, hard look, then clenched his jaw and walked toward the entrance.

"Be mindful," the figure said. "All ancient ruins have at least one warder."

"What kind of warder?"

"You will sense it. And when you do, you must fight or run. Your choice."

"Run? With this vambrace?"

"That would be prudent."

Gripping the hilt of *Amalantril*, Anskar ran through the ward-casting calculations and cants in his mind. Previously, they had come to him the instant danger presented itself, but he was leaving nothing to chance.

He felt feverish with energy—more than should have been possible considering the scant food and the lack of sleep. Did it come from the crow's compulsion or something else: some mania fueled by his flawed catalyst, or a burning need for answers? How could he know? How could he ever know, unless he saw this through and did what he'd been brought here to do?

With a solemn nod to the hooded man, and to the crow that had drawn him here, he entered the tomb.

The flagstones beneath his feet were free from dust, and there were no cobwebs or dripping damp as he'd expected. The walls were scabbed with clusters of scaleskin fungi that gave off a soft violet luminescence—enough to see by.

There was an unnatural chill to the air, far colder than a tomb warranted, which immediately unraveled Anskar's tenuous confidence. He glanced back at the hooded man and the crow, who both seemed to be willing him on. Lightning flashed behind them, and the following clap of thunder shook the walls of the tomb.

Almost at once, the corridor began to slope downward. After twenty yards, it turned abruptly right, bringing Anskar to the top of a seemingly bottomless flight of steps. The temperature plummeted the farther he descended, and hoarfrost coated the walls, glimmering violet from the scaleskins beneath it. Deeper still, and spears of ice hung from the ceiling.

Anskar finally reached the bottom and followed a frozen passageway until he came to a circular chamber with a lone sarcophagus at its center. The sarcophagus was made from carved ebony, save for its lid, which had the distinctive orange sheen of orichalcum. The carvings were what he was coming to know as typical Niyandrian designs—skull-headed people with bat wings, a dawning sun in the background. There were letters too, similar in appearance to Skanuric runes but with subtle differences.

He was about to examine the sarcophagus further when he recalled the hooded man's warning to touch nothing save the vambrace he had been sent to retrieve. Of course, the vambrace could have lain within the sarcophagus, but it seemed safer to press on and survey the rest of the tomb first. He could always return for a fuller inspection later.

There were corridors to the left and right of the chamber. Anskar took the one on the right. He felt a rush of frigid air coming from its far end and heard the scuff of something massive scraping across stone, followed by a rasping screech. Not waiting to see what it was, he backed out and took the left-hand corridor instead.

Here, the temperature was less severe, and there was no layer of frost covering the violet scaleskins. The passage had clearly not been used for some time, for the floor was thick with dust and the husks of dead insects. Alcoves set into the walls at intervals each held a sarcophagus with an intricately carved bone statue atop it in the likeness of a man or a woman—presumably whoever was interred within. From the back of each statue sprouted the folded wings of a bat.

The corridor terminated in another round chamber. A passageway led off to the right, its opening rimed with frost. An open sarcophagus stood in the center of the chamber, its lid leaning against one side. The statue at its head was carved from a single piece of bone that must have come from some gigantic creature, for it was easily six feet tall. It showed a slender woman with long hair, wearing a tall, three-pronged crown. Her bat wings were extended as if for flight, and her arms were raised high in exultation. Upon her right forearm was a vambrace crafted from a metal with the luster of silver, yet its surface shimmered with emerald, crimson, and azure. Anskar had never seen such metal before; it held his gaze captive.

This had to be what he was here for, but he was hesitant to reach out and take it. For the first time in days, he felt fully lucid, and aware of just how crazy this all was. He looked down at the ragged remains of his pants, the dried blood on his shins and torn and scraped knees. He held up his hands and stared at the scabs forming over his shredded palms. He was so terribly empty inside, hungrier than he had ever been in his life. What had happened to him? How could he have come so far and not known what he was doing?

He glanced again at the statue. Clearly it was meant to be a queen. A Niyandrian queen. It made no sense. Why send him into the tomb to claim a vambrace from some dead queen's statue? Why had he been singled out?

He thought about the reddish tinge to his skin, about Sareya's insistence that he must be part Niyandrian. But even if he was, even if he'd been wrong about his ancestry all along, that didn't explain why he'd been chosen instead of some full-blood Niyandrian.

Or maybe he hadn't been chosen. Maybe his sickness after his body rejected the catalyst had made him vulnerable to malevolent forces. Maybe the crow had been drawn by his weakness and used it to compel him here. But why?

He looked again at the vambrace on the statue's wrist. The metal it was crafted from had the look and feel of sorcery. The crow or the hooded man, or perhaps both of them, wanted him to take it for some reason. Anskar doubted it was for his own benefit. But if they wanted it for themselves, why hadn't the hooded man come down here and taken it?

With sudden intuition, Anskar opened his dawn-tide repository and felt its connection with the catalyst embedded over his heart. He imagined tendrils of mist seeping from his hands to caress the strange metal of the vambrace, to feel something of its nature. But in his mind's eye, the tendrils were rebuffed and recoiled back into him.

He tried again, this time with the energy of the dusk-tide, and again he was thwarted.

Finally, he reached beneath those two repositories and drew upon the nebulous forces of the dark-tide. This time, the vambrace permitted his ethereal touch, and Anskar had the uncanny feeling that it belonged to him; that it was meant to be his.

Tentatively, he reached out and touched the metal with his fingers. It was colder than ice. He snatched back his hand and saw that his fingertips were raw with frost-burn.

He needed something to cover the vambrace with… He thought about ripping away more of his clothing, but he was already in rags. He didn't cherish the idea of trying to find his way back to Dorinah half-naked.

Then he had an idea. Ignoring the pain in his hands, he raised his sword and hacked at the statue's arm. It cracked off and fell to the floor, clattering where the vambrace hit stone. Anskar sheathed his sword and stooped to pick up the carved bone arm with the vambrace still attached.

Almost at once, a keening wail came from the frost-rimed corridor to his right. A violent gust of frigid air hit him full in the face, and in its wake Anskar glimpsed a shadow fall over the far end of the corridor.

His mouth was dry as he turned and ran back the way he'd come. A gale blasted at him from behind. Thunderous footfalls rocked the passageway, causing him to stumble. Still he ran, not daring to look back as sulfurous breath blasted over him. Something roared, shaking the walls and ceiling. There was an ear-shattering crack, the crash and rumble of falling stone. A cloud of dust blew over him, blinding him, but he stumbled on, clutching the bone-carved arm and its vambrace as if his life depended upon it.

Then he was out of the tomb and pelted by sheeting rain. The hooded figure glided past him and waved its hand, and a section of wall rose up from the ground to seal the tomb. Lightning forked across the cloud-blackened sky. Thunder boomed. Shaking, Anskar fell to his knees, rain soaking his skin and hair, puddling around him. He dropped the bone arm, and the crow fluttered down to land upon the vambrace, seemingly oblivious to its burning cold.

He felt the hooded presence close behind him. "You must put it on," the rasping voice said.

A flash lit up the slate skies, followed by others that flickered away into the distance.

Anskar's breath was still ragged from his flight. "It's too cold."

"Nevertheless…" The figure spoke as if he had no choice.

The crow hopped off the vambrace to stand on the ground, shaking rainwater from its wings. It glared at Anskar with its burning golden eyes. He couldn't avert his gaze. Deep within his mind he heard the woman's voice speaking in broken Nan-Rhouric:

[Put…it…on.]

Eyes still locked to the crow's, Anskar pulled the vambrace from the bone-carved arm, wincing at the searing coldness of the metal. He settled the armor over his right forearm, and cried out as it froze his flesh and sent a crushing agony through his bones. As he tore his fingers away from the metal surface, his skin ripped and bled. A groan welled within him, then erupted into a full-throated scream. He pitched forward onto the ground, whimpering and trembling.

But gradually the burning gave way to a tingling warmth that was at first painful and then pleasant. Anskar sat up and watched in awe as the vambrace grew first translucent and then began to fade. A moment or two later, there was no sign it had ever existed. He rubbed his forearm and was shocked to encounter the hard metal surface still encasing his skin. How could that be? The vambrace was both there and not.

Dimly, he was aware of the hooded man speaking above the driving rain. "You have witnessed the fulfillment of my side of the pact. I am no longer bound to support your aims."

The crow cawed in response, and Anskar heard the flutter of its wings as it departed.

The hooded man made a sound like the rustling of leaves; it might have been laughter. "The folly of mortals who would be gods. How many times have I witnessed the same futile efforts over countless centuries?"

Anskar pushed himself to his feet. "You're a wraithe?"

"That is your word, not mine; but it is sufficient."

"And the vambrace?" Anskar asked. "What am I supposed to do with it?"

"You will know."

In the distance, amid the downpour, Anskar heard the muffled thud of hooves, the barking of a dog. He stepped toward the sounds, then slipped on the slick ground and dropped back to his knees. He was too weak. He needed food. He needed to sleep.

A chill struck his back, and he turned his head to see… nothing. The wraithe had gone.

He heard riders dismounting and coming up the hillside. He tried to call out, but the effort sent him sprawling onto his face.

Someone yelled above the storm, "He's not here. Not in this lightning. We should find shelter."

Anskar clawed at the grass, willing himself to get up, but he had no strength left. They were going to miss him; pass him by. Already the voices were retreating.

And he was sinking… Sinking into sleep.

Something warm and wet touched his face. A dog whined, then barked.

"Over here!" a man yelled—Anskar knew that voice. Larson. "Rosie's found him!"

EIGHTEEN

ANSKAR REMEMBERED NOTHING OF THE long ride back to Dorinah, only that he'd been barely conscious when Larson reached his side, and right behind the stablemaster, Vihtor. He expected to be chastised, but instead the Seneschal showed only relief. He insisted on carrying Anskar down the hillside and laying him across Uhtran's saddle. The musky scent of the great destrier was instantly comforting, and Anskar drifted in and out of consciousness as Vihtor walked ahead leading Uhtran by the reins.

Next thing he recalled was waking in his room at Branil's Burg, warm beneath fresh sheets, a bowl of steaming broth beside him on the nightstand, and Vihtor once more in the chair at the foot of the bed.

"Welcome back," the Seneschal said. "I was beginning to wonder if you'd started the long slide into the realm of the dead."

Impressions swarmed through Anskar's bleary mind: the hooded wraithe; the golden-eyed crow; the statue of a queen; an unearthly shriek; fetid breath slamming into him from behind. He grasped his right forearm, expecting—hoping—to feel bare flesh; but his fingers encountered the hard, cold surface of the vambrace.

Vihtor narrowed his eyes. "Are you injured? Did you hurt your wrist?"

"No," Anskar said. "Yes, a little." He winced at the lie but Vihtor would have assumed it was from the pain. "I sprained it when I slipped over."

"Should I summon a healer?"

"There's no need," Anskar said. "It's not too bad now."

"You remember much of anything?"

"I remember lightning and rain."

"Soon passed," Vihtor said. "The journey home was almost pleasant. You have no recollection of us camping beneath the stars and Larson's caterwauling?"

"None," Anskar said. "Larson sang?"

"In a manner of speaking," Vihtor said with a chuckle. "Until Rosie barked at him to shut up."

During the long, dreary days of his recovery, Anskar was ravenous, and Orix, who alternated shifts with Vihtor, made frequent trips to the kitchens on his behalf. At first Orix asked Anskar what had happened, where he had been, but those were difficult questions Anskar wasn't sure he could answer adequately, even for himself. Moreover, he could think of no way to describe the things he had seen and felt without being thought of as mad. It was far easier to pretend he had been fevered and remembered nothing.

After a while, Vihtor came less often, limiting his visits to an hour in the evenings. He had fallen behind with the governance of the Burg in coming to find Anskar, he said; even more so with the administration of Niyas. There were councilors to keep things running in his absence, but he liked to have a hand firmly on the rudder at all times.

"Take your eye off the game even for a second," he told Anskar, "and order can swiftly devolve into chaos."

"I know that feeling," Anskar said. Everything had been going so well: he'd progressed through the trials and become a knight-liminal, and then his catalyst had been fitted and his life had been turned upside down.

"Do you remember anything now?" the Seneschal asked.

"A little. Not much."

"What possessed you to leave the Burg, Anskar? How did you survive out there for so long? How did you find your way to Hallow Hill? You know it's one of the most sacred sites in Niyas, don't you? You know it overlooks the old capital of Naphor?"

The ruined city Anskar had seen from the summit. The scorched earth. That had been Naphor, where the Necromancer Queen had made her last stand?

"I…didn't know. I mean, I saw…but I didn't know it was Naphor."

Vihtor nodded as if he believed that were the truth, and Anskar found that he cared: that he wanted to be believed. "If I knew more… If I could explain…"

"But you can't. I understand. It would worry me less if you *did* know what had happened to you and were merely lying."

"Sir, I would not—"

Vihtor raised his hand. "I know that. And I'm not accusing you. But aren't you concerned? I know I am. I will take counsel from the priests of the Elder before you and I speak of this again.

I ask only that you keep whatever happened to yourself until then. Do not discuss it, even with your friends."

Vihtor opened the door and lingered a moment on the threshold.

"Protect yourself at all times," he said. "I've spread word that I sent you on a training mission and have forbidden you to discuss it. That should stop any questions."

Standard advice for a knight, but combined with Vihtor covering for him, Anskar felt certain it meant so much more. He suddenly felt the oppressive weight of unseen forces and the dread of being left alone. As Vihtor stepped outside the room and started to shut the door behind him, Anskar scrabbled desperately for something to make him stay.

"Eldrid DeVantte said he loved my father."

The Seneschal stood rigid within the crack of the doorway, his back to Anskar. "I thought I told you not to speak of this again."

"Please, sir, it's my right. Did you know my father? My mother?"

Vihtor remained motionless in the doorway, save for the twitch of his fingers at his side.

"I need to know, sir. Please. Were they knights of the Order?" He meant, was one of them Niyandrian?

"Another time," Vihtor said. "When you're older."

"But I'm old enough now! I've passed the trials."

The Seneschal slowly faced him, jaw clenched, eyes glittering and hard. "When you have taken solemn vows in a year. We will speak of it then, but not before." And this time when he turned away, he closed the door behind him.

"But that's stupid!" Anskar protested. "I need to know now!"

He half expected, half dreaded that Vihtor would come back in and reprimand him for his insolence, but he heard the Seneschal's footsteps fading away down the corridor. Anskar's fists bunched in frustration, and he looked around for something to smash.

In a rage, he jumped out of bed and picked up *Amalantril*, drew the blade from its scabbard and raised it to hit the nightstand. But seeing the majestic sword, recollecting the research, sweat and blood that had gone into its crafting—and the arcane energy he had imbued it with—he felt ashamed. How could he speak in such a way to the Seneschal? How could he act like a petulant child throwing a tantrum because he didn't get his own way?

He lowered the sword, re-sheathed it, then gripped the scabbard tight with both hands—as a reminder of what he was supposed to aspire to; the knight he was meant to be.

It seemed so simple a request: to learn something of his parents. If Vihtor would just tell him; let him make up his own mind...

But what if Anskar didn't like what he heard? He trusted the Seneschal, respected him. If Vihtor didn't want him to know about his parents, there had to be a good reason. And whatever it was, it was surely centered upon Hallow Hill and the vambrace he'd found there...on the statue of a Niyandrian Queen.

Suddenly, his room felt cramped and stifling. Despite the late hour, he put on his cloak, and made his way through the darkened corridors to the northern courtyard. The air was crisp, but for once it wasn't raining. He'd never seen so many stars strewn across the blackness of the sky. Both moons were gibbous and shimmering, one white, the other red. He lost himself in their dazzling brilliance; felt the anger ebb away from him.

As he contemplated the moons, he felt the tug of his repositories. He sent questing tendrils to each of the three and found none was even half empty. Not only that, but his dark-tide repository seemed to have expanded. For an instant he directed his consciousness into its inky depths—and recoiled. It was an abyss of nothingness, with him teetering on its edge. Gaze too long into it and he could plummet into oblivion, never to return.

With a gasp, he drove his awareness outward, blinked to regain his sight. He saw that the vambrace on his forearm had become visible: silver with a ghosting sheen of blue. He held up his arm to direct moonlight onto it, and the metal blazed like a sapphire sun. Afraid the knights patrolling the walls might see, he covered it with his cloak, and immediately its glow died down.

When he went back inside, he was relieved to see that the vambrace had once more vanished, though he could still feel its metallic hardness over his flesh. Whatever the vambrace really was, he had no idea, but he was fairly certain it would get him thrown out of the Order if it were seen. It must remain his secret.

He recoiled from the thought: it was disloyal, treasonous. But another part of him, one he had only just started to acknowledge, instantly rejected such ideas as foolish. They were the result of conditioning imparted by those who wished to control him, to shape him in their own image.

It was a disturbing rift, and Anskar was shocked at having discovered it within himself.

"A man at war with himself cannot stand long in battle with others" was one of the maxims the Warrior's priests had drummed into him from the earliest days of his training. It bespoke the need for single-minded focus, obedience, and undeviating loyalty to the ideals and law of the Order. Vihtor had said something similar with regards to the office of the Grand Master. But how could he know such things were true? Surely the Order's statutes were written by its men and women? And the will of the Five—was that not mediated by priests like Tion and Beof, or the bishops on the mainland? People the same as he was, with their own hidden conflicts and flaws?

He knew he was changing, maturing into manhood, leaving the

ways of youth behind; but this was more than that. Whether it was an inner awakening, or something from outside that had entered him—from the catalyst beneath his skin, or the bloodletting of the crow—he couldn't say. But he couldn't ignore it.

Nor did he want to.

In the morning, Anskar resumed his training alongside the other knights-liminal. The first session after breakfast was on the efficient utilization of dawn-tide energy in the maintenance of a sorcerous ward.

"As you can see," said Frae Ganwen, "Anskar is back with us. As I announced previously, the Seneschal needed him for a mission, on which he is sworn to secrecy. Do not ask him about it. Anskar, you've missed a few lessons, but I'm sure you'll have no trouble catching up."

Curious glances followed Anskar as he joined the others for their lesson, but mercifully the trainees heeded Frae Ganwen's words.

When Frae Ganwen announced that she wished to observe each of her students casting a ward, Anskar grew immediately anxious. No one save Beof and Malady the dwarf had seen the discoloration of his ward—though Landav had undoubtedly known about it. If the Order's sorcery tutor saw it and realized her pupil had inadvertently tapped into the dusk- or dark-tide, there would be consequences.

Thankfully, he wasn't first to go up, which gave him time to observe what those preceding him did—or rather, to send out feelers of awareness to sense the flow of energy from their repositories.

At least, that was the plan. But it occurred to him that he didn't even have a theory as to what these "feelers of awareness" were. He imagined them, sensed them, and they obeyed; and as with anything he did that was vaguely sorcerous, he felt a corresponding squeeze on his repositories. In this case, from all three at once, as if this new sense perception were something the triadic tides, as Landav had called them, could agree on.

Frae Ganwen flashed Anskar a look as his feelers sprang forth, and he pulled them quickly back. Had she detected them? If so, how? But she didn't hold his gaze, instead turning her attention to Naul, who was the first to demonstrate his ward.

Anskar held back, using only his eyes to observe Naul's casting. It struck him as overly mechanical as Naul recited the calculations under his breath, face taut with concentration. Sparkles and glowing motes appeared in the air around him, gradually increasing in density until Naul was enclosed in a sphere of silver light.

Anskar tightened his hands into fists, hoping Naul's ward would change color as his own had done, but the sphere remained silver.

Orix was next. His ward manifested much faster than Naul's had, but it wavered and was pocked with what looked like craters. Frae Ganwen explained these were patches where the sorcerous light was less dense due to some occlusion in either Orix's dawn-tide repository or the intangible conduits that led from it. She urged Orix to focus his mind by verbalizing the calculations while closing his eyes and imagining a steady, pulsing flow from his dawn-tide repository.

Orix did as she asked, and soon beads of sweat stood out on his forehead. "I can't!" he said, about to give up.

"Keep at it!" Frae Ganwen snapped.

Suddenly, a dark-green tinge flowed into Orix's ward. Before it could fully establish itself, Frae Ganwen ordered him to stop.

"What happened?" Orix asked, red-faced and trembling. "What did I do wrong?"

"With the casting, nothing. But in your room at night, I shudder to think. Go see the healers, Orix. Cleanse your soul of whatever stains it, then return and try again."

If Frae Ganwen was perturbed by the mild taint of Orix's ward, Anskar thought frantically, what would she make of his? He needed a way to compartmentalize his repositories, to ensure that he only drew upon the essence of the dawn-tide.

Sareya was next up, but before she began, Anskar felt the atmosphere grow heavy like the air before a storm. He glanced at the other knights-liminal and noticed that each was tight with concentration. They were quietly testing their own dawn-tide abilities, and the room was charged with their efforts. Hoping the abundance of sorcerous currents would mask what he was doing, Anskar once more sent out his feelers of awareness, inch by inch this time, across the room toward Sareya.

Frae Ganwen was too intent on Sareya's casting to notice. Everyone knew that Niyandrians were the most naturally gifted in sorcery among all the Order's trainees, and that Sareya was head and shoulders above even her own kind. Anskar could tell Frae Ganwen was intrigued by Sareya's potential, and perhaps even a little envious. For himself, he thought, who better to learn from than the best among them?

As his feelers entered Sareya's mind, she stiffened and half-turned toward him. He felt a moment's resistance, then she relaxed and granted him access. It surprised him not only that she could resist his probe of her repositories, but that she permitted it. He'd assumed she was angry with him for discontinuing their relationship, but he felt no anger from her, only a gentle sadness.

Sareya's dawn-tide repository shuddered then rippled as power flowed from it to form her ward in one graceful motion. He couldn't see what she did, but he felt it as if he were the one doing it. She had done something to her dawn-tide repository… softened its boundaries. But how? He probed its edges, finding them malleable, fluid like water. He searched deeper, coming to the hardened shell surrounding her dusk-tide repository. No matter how hard he pushed and poked at it, he could find no access. It was fenced in with invisible barbs and briars that had an almost palpable sense of dripping with venom. The size of her dusk-tide repository stunned him: it was an ocean compared to his lake; the Five only knew how deep it was. And the dark-tide…he searched for it but found nothing within her. Did she even have one? Did any of the others, or was he the only one? If so, why…

Dividing his feelers between her two repositories, he focused his eyes on the manifestation of her ward: unwavering silver, uniformly solid. The trickle of dawn-tide energy she drew upon to create it was negligible, and he had the sense she could maintain it for hours without appreciably depleting her repository. But even more impressive was the complete lack of spillage from her dusk-tide repository. And that gave him an idea.

He'd barely withdrawn his feelers when Frae Ganwen turned her attention to him. "All right, Anskar, let's see what you can do."

Sareya's eyes were fixed on him, and she gave an encouraging smile.

Anskar took a deep breath and shut his eyes. He knew he could cast his ward lightning-quick without needing to concentrate on the calculations, but for what he had in mind he needed to focus.

He began by mentally tracing the outlines of his dusk- and dark-tide repositories, then, sending a thread of awareness toward the dusk-tide, he drew it around its circumference, feeling the corrosive energy within pushing against his cordon. The repository now felt flat, two-dimensional, and yet paradoxically it still had a depth that he could perceive obliquely with his sorcerous senses. He added another thread to the cordon, twining it with the first, then a third and a fourth. With each addition the barrier hardened, until a sturdy wall hemmed in the power contained within the repository.

Satisfied there wouldn't be any seepage, he moved deeper, to his dark-tide repository, aware of Frae Ganwen's impatient promptings. She wondered why he was stalling, encouraged him to get on with it. But he couldn't stop now. He couldn't afford to fail. He probed at his dark-tide repository, and almost cried out as the feeler recoiled and a burning agony seared his mind.

"Anskar?" Frae Ganwen said. "What's going on?"

"Nothing," he mumbled through clenched teeth. "Having trouble concentrating on the calculations."

"Perhaps you are not fully recovered. You can always try another day."

"No!" he said, harsher than he'd intended. "Almost there."

He probed again at the permeable wall of the dark-tide repository, and again he was rebuffed. He steeled himself for another attempt, then stopped. He didn't know what he was dealing with. Until recently, he'd not even known there was such a thing as the dark-tide, let alone that he held its virulence within him. All he needed to do here was contain its stored essence, stop it from contaminating the flow of the dawn-tide that he needed for his ward. But how could he contain something without knowing what it was?

The smells, scents, even the light of the room behind his eyelids retreated into oblivion as he bundled all of his senses inward, trying with all his might to open his inner eyes onto the dark-tide—to feel it, embrace it, know it.

He stiffened, smothered suddenly by an all-enveloping tar. His heartbeat was a rapid pounding; the only thing that remained of him. He latched on to it, frantic to pull himself out of the mire he'd plunged into, but even that beat began to fail. He was sinking deeper and deeper into the abyss. He tried to scream but had no voice. He wanted to thrash and kick and fight his way free, but how could he with no limbs and no body? Realizing the futility, he resigned himself to oblivion, to being nothing, to never having been…

And then he was at the heart of the darkness, and it *knew* him. Knew him and embraced him; flowed through him and begged for his mastery. With scarcely a thought, he rose upon a wave of utter blackness high above the bottomless abyss, and threw up around it a restraining thicket of thorns dripping with poison. Not to thwart intruders from without, but to contain what was within; for he had intuited from that first touch of the dark that it needed a firm hand before it would dutifully follow his instructions.

Opening his eyes, Anskar drew upon his dawn-tide repository and funneled a misty stream out through the pores in his skin. A scintillant ward of silver sprang into being around him.

"Excellent," Frae Ganwen said.

Anskar glanced at Sareya, who was watching him, the merest of frowns upon her face. Then he felt the withdrawal of her own feelers of awareness and knew that she had seen everything.

NINETEEN

"ARE YOU LISTENING, ASSLING?" SNED Jethryn said.

Anskar looked up, suddenly aware of everyone's eyes on him. He'd been lost inside his head, tinkering with the barriers he'd erected around his repositories. He shared a workbench with Petor Vilaf, who had only narrowly passed the sorcery trial this year, having failed the previous two. In the afternoon, the knights-liminal had returned to the smithing hall for the first of many classes on the crafting of armor.

"Of course, if you think you know it all now that you're a knight-liminal…" the Forge Master continued.

"No," Anskar blurted out. "I don't. I'm sorry."

Sned smiled. "Still tired from all that gallivanting around the island?"

In truth, Anskar had never felt better physically, but he couldn't concentrate. The powers awakening inside him demanded his attention; compelled it. "Yes, sir. Still tired but getting better every day."

Naul rolled his eyes, but Sareya looked at Anskar with her inscrutable gaze. Her lips quivered as if she were about to say something, then she returned her attention to the mail hauberks Sned had brought out on mannequins to demonstrate the different styles of weave.

"All right," Sned said, addressing the group, "prove to me I've not been pissing into the wind. Someone tell me why I only use sixteen-gauge and lower." He picked up one of the spindles of steel wire from the workbench behind him.

"Anything higher isn't strong enough," Gar Landry said.

That was about as much as Anskar had ever heard Gar say. He was the outcast among the trainees—mainly because he preferred his own company, but also because some of the others thought he was an inbred peasant. Like Clenna and her brother Rhett, Gar came from Caronath, which about said it all.

"Wrong," Sned said. "Anyone else?" He looked expectantly at Anskar, but it was Petor that answered. Rather than considering himself lucky to have made it through the trials at his last attempt, Petor had turned into a complete know-it-all.

"A finer gauge means you need smaller rings, and more of them. Many more."

"Which can quadruple the time it takes to make a hauberk," Sned said. "Well done. And why don't we use gold or silver? They'd make a nice, shiny suit of mail—someone else this time."

"Too soft," Orix said.

"Like that mush between your ears," Naul said, and Orix slapped him on the arm.

"Good," Sned said. "Glad I'm not talking to a bunch of complete bloody morons. Now, to make mail, you're going to need links—and I'm not talking about sausages." He held up a small ring of steel, broken in one spot with a snipped opening. "Lots of links."

"How many?" Anskar asked, determined to show that he was now fully engaged in the class.

"At least ten thousand, probably more, depending on the size of the hauberk, and whether or not you want sleeves."

"Great," Petor Vilaf said, his tone suggesting this was going to be an easy task for him. "Where do we get them?"

Sned opened his eyes wide in mock surprise. "You make them."

"All of them?"

"How else are you going to get them? And before you ask: no, you can't buy them. Not in my smithy. Where are you from, Petor? Sansor? Kyuth?"

"Nagorn City."

"Now there's a surprise. You have the accent of someone born with a silver butt plug so your priggish parents wouldn't have any mess to clean up, but Nagorn City's full of normal folk. Least it was when I was last there."

Petor's cheeks reddened, and Anskar saw him make a fist.

Sned saw too and raised an eyebrow. "Do I need to fetch my mallet?"

"No, sir," Petor said, all the haughtiness gone from his tone.

For the first time, Anskar caught the twang of a western accent, which Petor had obviously done his best to hide all the years he'd been at the Burg.

"Shame," Sned said, narrowing his eyes. He waited long enough for Petor to squirm, then let out a deep belly laugh.

"All right, everyone, grab yourselves some sixteen-gauge wire and one of these." He indicated a long metal rod held tight in a vise on the workbench, and began to wind the wire around it. "Wind it all the way to the end, keeping it tight. When you've done that, you'll need a sharp pair of pliers to snip the links and separate them. Any questions? Good," he said, not giving anyone the chance to speak. "Work through till dinner, and no stealing links from each other. Tomorrow…tomorrow you'll be doing the same. And the next day. And the one after that."

At the evening meal, the seven knights-liminal sat together at a long table in the refectory, exhausted from making mail links all afternoon. Anskar's fingers were raw, and his hands and wrists ached from winding steel wire. The others did nothing but complain about the work, and the prospect of doing the same for the rest of the week. Anskar didn't disagree that it was a long and tedious task with almost no end in sight, but he saw no sense in moaning about it like some of the others and had settled into the rhythm of the work. And once he had the technique down, he'd used the time to increase his familiarity with his repositories.

Throughout the afternoon, he'd made frequent mental inspections of the barriers he had erected around his dusk- and dark-tide repositories, and was relieved to find them both intact. He saw no reason to remove the barriers, even when he wasn't actively drawing on the dawn-tide. There was too much about the powers latent within him he still didn't understand, and with Luzius Landav gone, there was no one he could ask.

The dawn-tide was now amenable to even the slightest pull upon its power, and he could effect the connection between it and his catalyst in an instant. He didn't draw attention to what he was doing by casting a ward, but he ran through the calculations repeatedly until they formed an ever-present background to his thoughts. He needed the casting to be instinctual, in case of a sudden attack, and while he had achieved that during the third trial, he wanted to remain in control of his power and use only the dawn-tide wherever possible. Some small part of him still clung to the idea that he could become an exemplary knight.

He went up for another helping of beef pie with sweet peas and mashed turnip smothered with gravy. The food had greatly improved with their new rank.

When he returned to the table, the others were mocking one another about their catalyst scars, which they had apparently compared during the days he was absent. According to Naul, Orix's was a jagged mess, leading Petor to suggest that Landav had been drunk or half asleep when fitting Orix's crystal.

Petor's was apparently a perfect line, so fine it would be invisible in a couple of years, or so he hoped. "Of course, we still haven't seen Sareya's," he said, giving her a mock-lascivious look.

"Nor will you," she replied, not even glancing up from her meal.

"What's it like?" Petor asked Anskar.

"Sorry?"

"Her scar. You've seen it, right? In the valley between her tits."

Anskar's hand shook as he tightened his grip on his fork.

Orix tried to defuse the tension. "How about yours, Anskar? Surely it can't be as bad as mine."

Anskar's scar was nothing unusual: just a slight ridge over his sternum where the skin had knitted together. But he didn't want to show anyone. He knew it was an irrational fear, but what if they could somehow perceive the taint of his crystal?

"Don't ask him," Petor said. "Ask Sareya."

Sareya's chair scraped against the floor as she stood, her meal only half finished.

"Oh, don't play the prude," Petor said. "You're fooling no

one."

"Leave her alone," Anskar said as Sareya strode from the refectory without speaking.

"Or what?" Petor said, his accent growing thicker. "What are you going to do?"

Anskar touched a hand to his scalp. He felt something like a worm wriggling inside his skull, and knew it was his dark-tide repository. The barrier he'd erected around it was unraveling. Already, inky vitriol was starting to burn through his veins.

He pushed himself up from his chair and narrowed his eyes. Petor went pale, and a tic started up under his eye. But then Anskar took control, reinforcing the barrier around his dark-tide repository and forcing himself to resume his seat.

"As I thought," Petor said. "Nothing!"

"Shut your mouth, idiot," Orix said.

"You forgot to hide your provincial accent," Naul said, then did a good job of mimicking Petor: "As I thought. Nothing."

Petor's pale face turned red with fury, but before he could say anything, Orix leveled a stern look at him that said, *Try it, and see what you get.*

Pushing his plate aside, Petor said he wasn't hungry and left.

Anskar's appetite had also fled, but he stayed and used his fork to play with his meal, ignoring the efforts the others made to lighten the mood.

He returned to his room straight after dinner, knelt on his pillow, and looked out the open window, waiting with anticipation for the dusk-tide. The cool breeze on his face was relaxing, and slowly his mind emptied of all distractions as he watched the sky turn pink, then red, then gray.

He heard the rush of the dusk-tide inside his head, braced himself against its impact, then spread his arms wide as the eldritch forces slammed into him. Searing currents tore through his skin, muscle and bone, leaving him completely unscathed and exhilarated. He felt the throbbing of his dusk-tide repository as it stretched beyond its bounds, expanding in some ineffable manner while taking up no more space within his skull.

When the tide passed, skirling over the Burg toward the east, he slumped forward, rested his chin on his arms, and continued to stare at the darkening sky.

At some point he must have drifted off, because he came to with a start. Only the white moon, Chandra, was visible from his vantage point, and in its pale glow he once more saw the vambrace upon his forearm, silver, emerald, azure and crimson swirling together. It was clearly more than just a piece of armor.

Part of a larger whole that has yet to be, the wraithe had said. Surely, that could only mean it was one piece of a complete set of armor; but *yet to be*? Did that mean *yet to be gathered together*, or *yet to be made*?

Unconsciously, he fiddled with the vambrace's catches, but the more he did, the colder the metal grew against his skin. He could find no purchase on the clips and started to panic that he might never be able to remove the vambrace.

Anskar glimpsed movement atop the citadel's curtain walls. At first he thought it was a sentry, but then realized he'd seen no torchlight, and no one would risk walking upon the heights in darkness.

He lowered the vambrace and let his eyes adjust, blinking and squinting until a patch of blackness came into sharper focus. At this distance, and in such poor light, he could see no features, only an outline of a figure standing on the battlements, hooded and cloaked. Nevertheless, he had the keen sense that it was looking straight at him.

Swiftly, Anskar called upon his sorcerous senses and sent feelers of awareness lashing across the intervening space, but before they reached their target, the shadowy figure melted away into the night.

Anskar shut the window and drew the curtains. Almost at once, the vambrace upon his forearm vanished. His heart hammered in his ribcage, and his breaths were rasping and shallow. Had he just seen the wraithe from Hallow Hill? Or was it something else?

As he stood from the bed, he saw more figures in the scattered shadows around his room. Hurriedly, he rummaged in the drawer of his nightstand for a fire-stick and set his bedside lamp aglow. Carrying the lamp to every corner of the room, he made sure he was alone, then set it back down on the nightstand, lay on his bed and stared at the ceiling. He would run his ward calculations over and over in his mind, and perhaps that would lull him to sleep. At the very least it would improve his casting time.

After an hour he was still no calmer, so he switched to exploring his repositories, further reinforcing the barriers around the dusk- and dark-tides, snatching power from the dawn-tide and swiftly pouring it back in.

Just to make sure, he ran through his calculations again, drew the bare minimum from his dawn-tide repository to throw up a scintillant ward of pure silver around him on the bed, immediately lowered it, and cast it again in an instant. He continued to practice in this manner hour upon hour, entering into a rhythmic trance, his ward pulsing on and off as effortlessly as breathing.

Eventually, Anskar slept for a few hours, then threw open his window once more to welcome the dawn-tide. How quickly he had grown used to the arcane forces washing over and through him. But whereas the dusk- and dark-tides were still somewhat troubling to him, the dawn-tide refreshed him like a cold rain.

With his dawn-tide repository overflowing with stored essence, Anskar grabbed some spare clothes, his sword and a towel, and made his way to the bath house on the first floor. He was relieved to find the communal bath empty, and spent a good hour soaking in the scented waters and floating on his back.

When he entered the refectory, Sareya was sitting by herself at the long table reserved for the knights-liminal. She looked up at him, and he read the shock in her eyes.

"You…you're glowing," she said, then averted her gaze as if she had done something wrong.

"Glowing?"

"You look healthy." She picked at her eggs and ham, then abandoned them for a sip of tea. "It's good that you've recovered from your…fever and hallucinations."

Anskar felt an urge to tell her what had happened to him, to get her opinion on the crow, the wraithe, the statue of the Niyandrian queen in the tomb atop Hallow Hill. He was convinced now that it had to have been Queen Talia, the vanquished last ruler of Niyas. He'd remembered something Sareya had told him all that time ago—something she had painted on her fingernails: the spirit name of Queen Talia. *Blackwing*. Like the wings of a crow.

Instead, Anskar fetched himself a hot tea and some toasted bread, eggs and ham, then returned to the table. A charged silence settled between them as they ate. Mercifully, Orix and Naul arrived shortly afterwards, and then Gar, Petor, and Myra DeYenté, who seldom spoke to any of them.

Myra was from a wealthy Sansor family and saw everyone as

her servant, which wasn't an attitude that had earned her many friends. She sat by herself at one end of the table, delicately sipping her tea. As usual, she ate nothing. She claimed that where she came from, it was ill-mannered to eat in public.

As he ate, listening to Orix and Naul riling Petor, and Gar trying to keep the peace, Anskar couldn't stop himself from glancing at Sareya. For the most part she kept her head down, but once or twice their eyes met, and she even managed a half smile. He was impressed by how well she seemed to have accepted his decision. She'd made no further moves on him, and had done her utmost not only to be discreet, but to act as if they barely knew each other. He knew he'd treated her unfairly. It was true she had a reputation, but that didn't give him the right to lie with her and then dismiss her as if nothing had happened.

"You noticed it too?" Petor was saying, and Anskar realized he was speaking to Sareya. "Anskar is radiant this morning. Why do you suppose that is?"

Again there was innuendo in Petor's tone, and Anskar's fingers curled into a fist around his knife and fork. Sareya met his gaze along the length of the table.

"I did notice," she said. "And I told him it's good to see that he's recovered."

"Yes, but recovered from what?" Petor said, nudging Gar.

Orix set his knife and fork down loudly, glaring at Petor. But it was Naul who spoke.

"If you're insinuating what I think you are," he said, "I doubt you'll ever know. The closest you'll get is a callused hand."

"How dare you!" Petor thundered, jumping to his feet.

Anskar, eyes still locked to Sareya's, said, "It's the effect of the dawn-tide. Since my... While I was away from the Burg, I was exposed to the dawn-tide every morning, and I've continued to greet it upon my return."

"Is that allowed?" Gar asked.

Petor sat back down, seeming relieved that the conversation had moved on.

"Don't see why not," Orix said. "I was waiting for someone to tell us when we could do it again."

"Someone did," Anskar said. "Luzius Landav said we should greet the dawn-tide every day."

"Someone else," Orix said.

Petor, Naul, and Gar nodded in agreement. None of them had liked or trusted the sorcerer.

"How about tomorrow?" Sareya said. "We could all meet in the courtyard and replenish our repositories. Maybe bring food for afterwards."

"You mean, for a picnic?" Orix said.

Anskar shrugged. It sounded like a good idea.

"Naul?" Sareya asked.

"All right. Why not?"

"I must decline," Myra said, taking another sip of her tea.

No surprise there.

"Petor?" Sareya said. "Gar?"

They looked at each other across the table and wrinkled their noses at the same time.

"I'll do it by myself," Petor said.

Naul smirked. "Why change the habit of a lifetime?"

"I'm not sure," Gar said. "I think I'll leave it for now."

Eyes flitting from Naul to Orix to Anskar, Sareya said, "Tomorrow, then?"

"Tomorrow," Anskar agreed.

Naul gave an exaggerated yawn as he said, "At the crack of dawn."

"Before," Orix corrected. "We need to arrive before dawn."

"Better and better," Naul said. "I can hardly wait."

TWENTY

CARRED WOKE TO THE SOUND of voices outside the shelter she shared with Kovin—a simple frame of branches covered with woven creepers, sod, and leafy twigs. There were dozens of similar structures dotted about the meeting place in the heart of Rynmuntithe Forest, blending in with the trees and vegetation.

She threw off the skins that had kept her warm as she slept. It was still dark, and Kovin wasn't beside her. His was one of the voices from outside.

She and Kovin had been at the hideout for two days, and still barely half the resistance leaders had turned up: a mere thirteen men and women who carried sway in their towns and villages.

She pulled on her clothes and boots, strapped on her sword belt, and ducked outside the shelter. Her breath misted in the chill air. The twin moons shone like mismatched eyes out of the darkness, dappling the forest floor in silver and red. A steely band of gray light limned the horizon through the trees.

Two men were talking in hushed voices away from the clustered shelters that comprised her camp, and she made her way toward them.

Kovin turned to greet her, leaning over to pluck a twig from her tousled hair.

With a practiced glance, Carred took in the platforms high above in the branches where lookouts kept an eye on the tracks through the forest. Among the trees, she glimpsed a few of her people standing about talking outside their shelters, but most were still sleeping.

Maggow the Message was with Kovin, and that worried her. The old man must have walked through the night to reach the camp, and that meant he had important news.

Maggow came from Vulsin, the village on the mire, where houses were erected on stilts and people lived on eels and crawfish and all manner of things that swam or slithered. He was naked save for a loincloth colored with unmentionable stains, and he walked barefoot. He was completely bald, the skin of his face furrowed with deep wrinkles, and he had only one tooth: a vile brown stub. Maggow followed the ways of the old gods, and he and the people of the mire had eschewed Queen Talia's rule; but when the mainland knights had come, he had seen a common enemy and allied himself with the rebels.

The old man held out his hand to Carred, a tiny scrap of rolled parchment clutched between thumb and forefinger. A missive that would have been brought to him in Vulsin by one of his trained pigeons.

"From our spies in Branil's Burg?" Carred asked, taking the paper from Maggow and unrolling it.

"Came before sundown last night," Maggow said, his words wet and malformed, sloshing around the sides of his tooth.

"You should have woken me," Carred told Kovin.

"Thought I'd worn you out and you'd be unrousable," he said. When she didn't even roll her eyes, Kovin added, "I was just about to."

A soft glow emanated from Maggow's palm, enough light for her to read by. Kovin looked over her shoulder at the scrap, and Carred nudged him away. "Don't pretend you can read."

The message was from one of her agents inside Branil's Burg.

"What's it say?" Kovin asked.

Others were emerging from their shelters. Carred waited until they were all assembled—the thirteen leaders, their companions, and the two dozen rebels who tended the hideout in monthly rotations from their towns and villages.

"It's from Aelanthe," she told them.

There were murmurs and nods of respect. Aelanthe was the strongest sorcerer in a generation and had studied at the feet of Queen Talia herself.

Carred hesitated before telling the others what the message said. It would elicit demands for what she should do, and already she had acceded to too many such demands. How many times had she bowed to calls for action that had led to defeat and death? *Strike and run*, the wraithe at Hallow Hill had told her. *Hide so you may strike again… Until the Queen's return.* But many in her rebellion had grown tired of the long game. They wanted results, decisive victories. They wanted their country back.

"Carred?" Kovin prompted.

The other leaders pressed in all around, the prickle of anticipation palpable in the pre-dawn air.

Carred shivered and hugged her arms about herself.

"If you're cold…" Kovin said, glancing back at their shelter and grabbing his crotch.

No one laughed, and Carred wasn't in the mood. If anything, Kovin's attempted humor reminded her of Talia's need for warmth against the unnatural chill that had entered her bones.

"Aelanthe's still gathering information on the Niyandrian girls—young women—the knights abducted and indoctrinated. She'll report her findings soon."

"That's it?" Kovin said, turning on Maggow. "And you woke us for this?"

"I'm not finished," Carred said. "She has received word that Hyle Pausus has boarded ship from Sansor."

"The Grand Master?" Vilintia Yoenth asked—a veteran of the Last Cohort whose hair had grayed over the years, but who was still a handsome woman and a devil with a sword. "What will we do?"

"We assemble those still loyal to us," Fult Wreave said, "and attack the Burg."

Several of the other leaders voiced their agreement. Despite being an unimposing little weasel with a perpetually running nose, Fult claimed to represent the bloodline, if not the name, of the disgraced Ickthal dynasty that had preceded Talia's reign. The Queen had hunted down most of the Ickthals. Pity was, Fult had escaped her notice. Fult claimed it was time to give up chasing ghosts and restore his family's rule. Support for his cause was still scant, but it was growing.

"Idiot," Kovin said, and to Fult's chagrin the majority of the leaders laughed. "Why use the hammer when we already have our people inside?"

Vilintia's wide eyes showed that she understood what Kovin was saying before anyone else did. "An assassin's blade?"

"Or sorcery," Griga said. The scrawny woman materialized out of the dark to Carred's right, wreathed in her gossamer dress that seemed woven from shadows. Moonlight glinted from the metallic threads in her dreadlocks, and the tattoos that snaked around her arms shimmered as if they writhed.

"Too risky," Carred said. "Hyle Pausus won't be defenseless. We already know that he travels with a sorcerer—hypocritical though that might seem. And he's watched over constantly by his Elect." All of them dark-clad women who were reputed to have divinely bestowed powers. "We've committed too many agents and too much time to chance an attack on either the Burg or the Grand Master's person." Forestalling a protest from Fult Wreave, she raised her finger. "Later, perhaps. We'll keep all options open, but I want to give Aelanthe more time."

"To discover the Queen's daughter?" Fult said. "Oh, for pity's sake, Carred! How long are we going to—?"

Fult was cut off by a snatch of song that seemed to come from everywhere and nowhere.

Along with everyone else, Carred's eyes were drawn to a rippling of shadow beneath a yew tree. One moment the strange singing was a distant echo, the next it was a spellbinding chant, the words meaningless, barbarous, enthralling.

Out of the shadows stepped a lanky man in a long black coat with silver buttons, a tall hat atop his head. His eyes were covered by dark lenses. In his wake appeared a motley-clad woman no taller than a child, and it was from her lips that the mellifluous cant spilled. The dwarf's eyes blazed with scintillant, alluring colors then swiftly darkened to black and hungry pits. Carred couldn't look away from them.

She tried to call a warning, but her tongue was numb. In her peripheral vision, she saw Kovin, motionless and staring; and about him the other Niyandrians, all paralyzed, shock and wonder carved into their mask-like faces.

Sweat beaded on Carred's forehead as she strained to turn her head. It felt as though chains restrained her; but as the man in the black coat and hat ambled toward her, she managed to move her hand an inch. Encouraged, she reached for her sword, but her fingers were locked rigid.

"Carred Selenas?" the man said. He turned to the dwarfish woman for confirmation. Still chanting, the dwarf nodded. "Splendid. A successful trip, then. And, let us hope, a fruitful one. My name is Luzius Landav, and I have a proposition for you."

He spoke perfect Niyandrian, with only the slight trace of an accent that Carred couldn't place. He leaned in to inspect her, and she smelled his sour breath. Her skin tingled at his proximity, and she sensed the bristling of multiple repositories within him. A sorcerer, then.

The dwarf was something far worse, Carred sensed. What kind of power could hold an entire band of Niyandrians enthralled, scarce able to move a muscle?

"You understand this is nothing personal," Luzius Landav said.

He stood back and splayed the fingers of one hand. Tongues of flame danced upon his palm, whirling toward the center where a burgeoning radiance formed. He held it out to Carred, and she was powerless to look away. Colors swirled before her eyes, luminous, blinding, blending one into another as they raced in ever-decreasing circles. As the light shrank, so did Carred's field of vision—to a circle, a line, an infinitesimal point.

"No!" she screamed. "Nooooo!"

There was a sharp, popping noise inside her head. Carred stumbled. Cold fingers caught her by the elbow.

They were alone now, in a vague place of dismal gray. Carred felt light as a feather, as if the slightest breeze might carry her away. But there was no breeze, just as there were no objects and no other sounds than her own breathing and the sorcerer's voice.

"Traditional means have thus far failed to curtail your niggling acts of terror," Luzius Landav said, "and so my employers have requested a meeting."

Ghostly figures appeared in the gloaming around them. At first Carred thought they were wraithes, but only one of them was hooded, and he was a giant that towered above the others. Of his features, she could see nothing, but prickles of wrongness caused her skin to itch. Her *skin*. She pinched herself to make sure.

"I'm really here?" she asked aloud.

"Where else would you be?" Landav replied. "Inside your head? Please give me some credit for my abilities."

His abilities. She'd sensed more than one repository, brimming with force. The dusk and the dawn were familiar to her, even though she never used them herself. But this…this was neither. Which meant Landav was using the dark-tide.

Carred's heart thundered in her ears as she turned a slow circle, taking in the ghostly figures that stood around her and the sorcerer—twelve of them. All appeared less solid than she was, painted with a dirty yellow light just bright enough for them to stand out from the surrounding gray. Some wore robes trimmed with ermine, others, heavy chains of office. Two were dressed in long-tailed jackets and creased pants—the uniform of Kailean bankers. The three women wore elegant gowns, and one sported a mask that left only her delicate mouth exposed. A tall, emaciated man was swamped by a voluminous cassock, the fingers and thumb of one of his hands bedizened with five massive jeweled rings.

"Who are you?" Carred asked him.

"He is nobody," Landav said. "Just as these others are nobodies, and this place is nowhere."

"How can this be nowhere?" Carred let anger mask her fear. "What have you done with the others?"

"Let me show you."

A sphere materialized in the air before Carred. Within, she could see Rynmuntithe Forest bathed in pre-dawn light. Kovin, Fult, Griga and the others were locked in a frozen vignette, eyes wide, hands on swords. Griga's face was contorted into a snarl from where she had started a cant. Only one figure moved: the dwarf woman who had been with Landav. Like a predatory wolf she walked between the motionless Niyandrians, lips moving in what to Carred was a silent chant.

One of the bankers spoke, his voice echoing and distant. "You are wondering, no doubt, why we have brought you here."

"I'm wondering why I'm still alive," Carred said.

The other banker chuckled. His luminous form exuded the same feeling of wrongness as the hooded giant; it had the flavor of madness. "Rebellion is not good for business," he said.

"Oh, I'm sorry," Carred retorted.

The banker simply smiled.

The thin man in the cassock spoke next. "This rebellion is not good for you, either, my child. You look weary beyond your years."

"Thanks. You look like shit too," Carred said. "Wait"—she turned to the sorcerer—"do they all speak Niyandrian?" She could understand everyone perfectly.

"They do not. And neither do you…here. Here, all languages become one language. A language, if you like, beyond speech."

The hooded giant's robe shivered, as if he suppressed laughter.

"You could have a far better life," the masked woman said. "A good life. Filled with tranquility and lovers. And we know how you like your lovers, especially the ladies."

"Go anywhere near Marith and I'll—"

"You could have riches," the first banker said, opening his arms in an expansive gesture that took in his colleagues. "Our consortium is not ungenerous."

"It's not as if you're winning this hit-and-run war," the masked woman added. "Remind me when you had your last victory?"

Carred clenched her fist at the question. But the woman was right. "Dorinah," she said. "When we burned the carrack bringing cargo from Riem."

"Yes, I remember," the woman said. "A lot of good tea was lost that day, along with clothing and livestock and letters from the mainland to those poor, lonely knights at Branil's Burg. I don't know how we recovered! When was that, two years ago? Three?"

"Closer to four," Carred muttered.

"Four years without a victory—at least anything meaningful," the masked woman said. "Why is that, do you think?"

"Bad luck?" Carred offered.

"Perhaps," the woman said. "Although it may have had something to do with increased resources from the mainland. From us. But do you know what the really frustrating thing is? Because of you, investors are reluctant to commit to Niyas until things have settled down. For all your ineffectiveness, you are costing us dearly. And, so, we have a proposal for you: disband your dying rebellion and sail away. We'll arrange passage, so no need to be concerned about the Order's blockades."

"And we'll pay you well," the first banker said. "Extremely well. You'll never need to worry about money again."

"We will, of course, require the locations of all the rebel outposts," the masked woman said. "This is a one-time offer. Consider it carefully. Because if we are forced to continue our investment in this little war, we will. Our consortium has resources you cannot imagine. You will not prevail, not in the end."

"Unless Queen Talia returns," Carred said.

"You really believe that she will?" the thin man in the cassock said. "With your whole heart? Carred, we are all grown-ups here. Such wishful thinking is for children, and you are way past being a child."

"Thanks for the observation. But supposing I accept your offer, what becomes of Niyas?"

"It goes on, of course," the first banker said. "It thrives."

"Under mainland rule? We would be no more than slaves!"

"As I told you," the giant said in a shrill voice that sounded ludicrously incongruous, "a waste of time. Just kill her and be done with it!"

The void-steel ring on its chain beneath Carred's shirt felt suddenly like a millstone. She clutched at it through the fabric, then desisted as the sorcerer noticed.

"And create a martyr?" the man in the cassock said. "That will only shift the balance."

"What were you just doing?" Luzius Landav asked.

"Nothing." Instinctively, Carred's hand returned to her chest, where the ring lay hidden.

"Let me see," the sorcerer said.

Carred backed away, drifting like mist across formless ground. Landav uttered a cant and she grew suddenly too heavy to move.

"Kill her," the giant repeated in his piping voice.

"A moment, please," Landav said, offering the hooded figure a perfunctory bow.

The giant nodded, even as a blade of shadow appeared in his massive fist.

Landav pressed up close to Carred. He stank of mildew and

rot. With pallid fingers, he began to unlace her shirt. Carred shook with the effort of trying to move. She wanted so badly to draw her sword and gut the bastard.

She gritted her teeth against the searing cold as Landav touched her skin, then inched his hand down between her breasts. Her heart pounded in her ears, then she held her breath as something Marith had said hit her like a lightning strike.

Void-steel nullified dark-tide sorcery.

Landav's hand enclosed the ring and the world turned inside out.

"No!" he cried as he snatched his hand away.

Instantly, they were back in Rynmuntithe Forest.

"*Tereth endelios!*" Griga yelled as she ran at the sorcerer, flames leaping from her raised hands and streaking toward him.

The dwarf stood gaping, too shocked to continue her chanting.

Carred saw Maggow emerge from the trees behind the dwarf. The old man was livid with rage. He advanced on the dwarf, spitting and cursing, scoring the air with fingers like claws. Rips appeared in the dwarf's clothing. Her torn skin wept purple blood.

A sphere of deepest violet sprang up around Luzius Landav. Griga's fire died as it hit the ward and left it steaming. The sorcerer countered by unleashing a beam of thrumming sunlight from his palm.

Griga's own ward came up and the beam bounced off it to strike a tree. There was a crack like thunder, an eruption of flames and smoke, and the top half of the trunk fell, crashing into the neighboring trees.

The dwarf snarled and pounced on Maggow, bearing him to the ground and pounding him with her fists. But Maggow was stronger than he looked, and faster. He rolled out from beneath her and raised a fist blooming with crimson flames. The dwarf screeched and glanced toward the shadows of the forest. One instant she was there, Maggow's fist coming down at her, the next she was gone.

All around the clearing, Niyandrians ran for their weapons. Griga summoned a spear of flame and hurled it at the sorcerer. As it struck his ward and dissolved into soot, Carred drew her sword and charged.

Her blade crashed against the sorcerer's ward, sending jolts of agony up her arm. Lightning blasted from within the violet sphere, flinging Carred back. Her sword blazed white with heat, and she screamed as the skin of her palm blistered. She tried to release the hilt, but it was stuck to her melting flesh.

On the far side of the sorcerer's ward, she caught sight of Kovin, crumpled on the ground, skin a charred and smoldering mess. He'd borne the main brunt of the blast. Carred's scream turned from pain to loss and then to rage. She climbed to her feet, closing her fingers around the scalding hilt of her sword and drawing strength from the agony.

Landav unleashed a cloud of inky vapor at Griga, then scanned the trees for the dwarf. The rebels swarmed toward him with swords, spears, and axes; and from behind him came Maggow, spitting like a venomous serpent and scratching at the air.

Landav cried out, clutching his shoulder where blood spurted. He whirled to face Maggow. Somehow, the old man of the mire had penetrated the sorcerer's wards.

Griga struck again from the other side, a renewed assault of flame, and this time Landav's ward faltered along with his concentration. Maggow slashed with a fingertip, and the sorcerer bent double, clutching his stomach, crimson dripping between his fingers.

He lurched away, calling out, "Malady! You are bound!"

There was a ripple of shadow, and the dwarf appeared among the trees. Half a dozen Niyandrians immediately ran at her, yelling battle cries. The dwarf vanished once more.

Carred, screaming, slammed her sword two-handed into the sorcerer's failing ward. He staggered under the impact and nearly fell, still clutching his guts.

There came barrage of flame from Griga, along with quick grabs of Maggow's hands that made Landav reel and stumble.

Carred hammered her blade into the violet ward, no longer feeling the pain of her melted skin. Landav fell, and his ward winked out. He made it to his feet just as Carred swung her sword in a vicious arc. His ward reappeared in time to deflect her blow—it was now black and glistening, so dense it seemed almost solid.

And then Landav was running into the trees, far faster than a man of his age and injuries should have been capable of. Suddenly, he twisted and fell, sparks erupting from the base of his black ward. His chimney-stack hat flew from his head to reveal a bald and wrinkled pate.

As Carred advanced, the sorcerer's dark ward continued to spark and flicker. And then she saw the cause. One of the bear traps that protected the camp had closed upon the eldritch sphere, pinching the black surface. It would have crushed the sorcerer's ankle, if not for his arcane protection. And it soon would, once the ward failed. Landav knew it. His face was frenzied with concentration as he threw everything he had into maintaining his ward. He tried to move his foot out of danger, but the ward came with it, and with the ward, the bear trap.

Carred loomed over him, sword raised to strike, waiting, waiting.

Sweat slicked the sorcerer's bald head. "Malady," he muttered, though with little conviction, "I adjure you. I compel you!"

The dwarf appeared a few trees away, but the rebels saw her and immediately gave chase.

Griga closed in on one side of Landav, flinging arrows of flame at him, one after the other. Maggow came from the other side, slashing and clutching with his hands. There were dozens of rents in the sorcerer's coat, cuts and scratches on his hands and face, yet his focus on his ward didn't waver. He held it in spite of the pain; in spite of the terrible realization that his dwarf wasn't going to save him; in spite of Carred's sword raised to take off his head the minute his concentration failed.

"Spare me!" he blurted. Another cut appeared on his cheek, and he flinched. "I will aid you. I know their secrets."

Carred held her hand up to stop Griga and Maggow. "The Order's secrets, or this consortium's?"

"Both! I have no affiliation with them, save what they pay me," Landav said.

"And you would do anything for wealth?" Carred said with a sneer. Her blood boiled for Kovin.

"I would do anything for my life."

Carred studied him. Her arms ached from holding her sword aloft, but there was only numbness in her burned hand and fingers. "You've been to Branil's Burg?"

"I've just come from there." Landav leaned on one elbow, gasping with the effort of sustaining his ward while speaking.

"We seek a young Niyandrian woman," Carred said. "One of the stolen. She may show signs of exceptional power."

"A moontouched?" Landav said. "Yes, I have seen her. Her name is Sareya. Her powers are prodigious, but I don't think she knows the full extent of them. I didn't let on, and the Order are unaware."

Carred exchanged looks with Griga and Maggow. The old man of the mire resembled a hungry predator; but Griga gave a nod that said this Sareya was worth investigating.

"And you will help us to lure the girl from the Burg?" Carred asked the sorcerer.

"I will."

Carred glanced around at the eager faces of her fighters. Was this it? After all this time, all the dashed hopes? Her heart told her no; but her heart was doubly broken and couldn't be relied on. First she'd been forced away from Marith, and now Kovin was dead. It didn't seem possible that a man so virile could be reduced to a lifeless husk.

But if Landav wasn't lying, and if this really was the Queen's daughter, where was the guardian? *Who* was the guardian? They were supposed to be revealed at the same time.

She nodded to one of the men, who hauled on the chain connected to the bear trap, moving the iron jaws clear of the sorcerer's ankle.

"Thank you," Landav said, lying back on the ground. His ward dispersed into thin air.

"Pity you didn't volunteer your services before you killed Kovin," Carred said.

"Who?" The sorcerer sat bolt upright.

Carred's sword swept down, severing his head. It bounced away across the forest floor, dark lenses skittering to the side, and came to rest beneath a tree, mouth gaping. There were scarred, empty sockets where his eyes should have been. The stump of Landav's neck spurted blood onto the ground.

The dwarf reappeared from the shadows and stooped to pick the head up. She held it like a trophy, a broad grin cutting her wizened face in two.

"Free," she said, then cackled. "Free!"

This time, she didn't vanish into the shadows. A sudden frost rimed the ground around her, accompanied by a sulfurous stench. The dwarf dissolved into a shower of soot, which fell like black rain, soaking into the earth. It pooled for a moment, then disappeared without a trace. She had taken the sorcerer's head with her.

"Demon!" Maggow spat. He hurried to the spot where the dwarf had disappeared, unbound his loincloth and pissed on the ground.

Of all the things that might assail them, Carred hadn't expected a demon. All Niyandrians knew of the wars incited by the demon lord Nysrog, and Talia had imparted some further knowledge to Carred about the abyssal realms and their inhabitants. But these days, only fanatical and insane sorcerers dabbled in the lore of demons.

And then she recalled the hooded giant in the gray space Landav had taken her to. She had smelled the stench of madness on him. And not just on the giant, either, but on one of the bankers too. Were they demons aiding the mainland oppressors? Or were they bound, like the dwarf had been, forced to do their masters' bidding? What was going on? What had Talia hidden from her? Protected the people of Niyas from?

Once Maggow had finished cursing the demon with his piss and mercifully refastened his loincloth, Carred said, "Send a pigeon to Branil's Burg, to Aelanthe. Tell her to find out about this Sareya. Tell her to do nothing, only confirm what the sorcerer said about her powers. We need more information before we commit ourselves."

She couldn't afford to risk any more of her fighters, especially on the word of a mainland sorcerer. And if the knights got wind of what Aelanthe and the other three spies were up to, there would be swift and severe retribution. Carred had enough experience of the Knights of Eternal Vigilance to know that mercy was an abstract concept to them, lip service paid to their god.

She turned to the leaders of the resistance. "Bury the sorcerer's body," she told them. "Then return home to prepare your people. If you're able, mount skirmishes to keep the Order off balance and to slow the building of their strongholds. If Aelanthe confirms this Sareya is indeed moontouched and a candidate for the Queen's daughter, be ready to move as soon as I send word. The Order will retaliate with brutality and bloodshed, but with Talia's heir among us, all of Niyas will rally to our cause."

Someone cheered, and after a moment's awkward silence, the others joined in. Save for Griga, who shook her head as if they were foolish sheep. And Maggow, who was still glowering at the damp patch on the ground where the demon had disappeared.

To Carred's ears, the cheers sounded distant and hollow. She'd lost too much to be inspired by mere hope. Only when they had tangible results would she rejoice. Only when Niyas was back under Niyandrian control. Only when Talia was once again queen.

Until then, Marith was gone from her life, and Kovin was on his final journey—to the realm of the dead. Two lovers who had kept her sane throughout these years of blood and madness. Each time she lost someone, she lost a little piece of herself. But with Marith and Kovin it felt like the greater part.

If Queen Talia didn't come back soon, there would be nothing left of Carred Selenas to greet her.

TWENTY-ONE

ANSKAR WAS WOKEN BY A gentle knocking at the door. Groaning, he rolled onto his side and buried his head beneath a pillow.

The knocking grew more insistent, and then came a hissing voice telling him to open up.

Sareya.

Alert in an instant, Anskar rolled out of bed and padded to the door, only then realizing he was still wearing his day clothes, sweat-stained and greasy from the smithing hall. He didn't even remember falling asleep.

"Please," he hissed, "you must leave. Someone might see."

He heard a snigger, and it wasn't her. It was followed by what sounded like a slap, then a grumbling complaint from a male voice.

"It's all right," Sareya said. "Orix and Naul are with me. Hurry, we don't want to miss the dawn-tide. Orix went early to the refectory. He's brought us food for a breakfast picnic."

Of course! They had agreed to meet in the courtyard for the dawn-tide. Anskar felt heat rush to his face as he opened the door.

"I overslept. How long do we have until sunrise?"

"Minutes," Naul said, rubbing his arm, where presumably Sareya had slapped him.

Orix clutched a basket to his chest. It was brimming with bread rolls and cheese wrapped in waxed paper. There were strawberries too, and a corked bottle of grape juice.

"No tea?" Anskar said. He needed something to wake him up.

"Come on," Naul said. "I don't want to miss the tide."

Anskar buckled on his sword belt, and they headed out to the courtyard.

"You sleep in your boots?" Orix asked.

"He doesn't usually," Sareya said, then clamped her hand over her mouth and flashed Anskar a look with her feline eyes. "Sorry," she mouthed.

As they left the still darkened interior of the Burg for the crisp pre-dawn air of the courtyard, Anskar checked the barriers he had put up around his dusk- and dark-tide repositories. He relaxed when he found them secure.

They were just in time. The rush of the dawn-tide was a rising pressure in his head, and then it slammed into them just as Orix set down his basket.

Sareya grabbed Anskar's hand, and the four of them formed a circle, reveling in the eldritch currents coursing through them and restoring their spent repositories. In that moment, Anskar felt not only the exultation of the dawn-tide, but something extra: a bond between them all that went deeper than any look or smile, or even the intimacy he had shared with Sareya. It was as if the dawn-tide were fusing them together in some way impossible to fathom; forge-welding them into comrades; into family.

When the tide had passed over them, they stood in awed silence, still holding hands, until the spell was broken by Orix's rumbling stomach.

"Sorry," he said, plonking himself down on the grass next to the food basket.

They shared their meal in a contented reverie. To Anskar, each bite of cheese, of bread, of strawberry was a special moment. As they passed the bottle of grape juice between them, there was something almost sacramental about the act.

He glanced at the others, wanting to reassure himself he wasn't imagining it. Sareya caught him looking, and her eyes glistened as she smiled.

After the picnic breakfast came another lesson in sorcerous warding. The classes were becoming a redundancy for Anskar, though some of the other knights-liminal continued to make improvements to the efficiency of their dawn-tide usage and the durability of their wards. Sareya was easily the most proficient, her casting fluid and almost instantaneous. With all the practice he'd been putting in, Anskar was a close second, and he continued to study everything Sareya did so he could work out how to match her.

Toward the end of the class, Frae Ganwen took them outside to the bailey, where a squad of archers was waiting for them. Orix gasped and uttered a curse.

Frae Ganwen's ward sprang up around her, and she slipped away to one side as the archers drew back on their bowstrings.

Anskar's ward went first up, a sphere of silver, uniform in its strength. Sareya's was next, equally as strong.

One after another, the knights-liminal manifested their wards. Save for Orix, whose ward sputtered in and out of existence as he verbalized his cants with a stammer Anskar hadn't noticed before.

The archers unleashed a volley of arrows straight at the students. Instinctively, Anskar drew greedily from his dawn-tide repository and expanded his ward to encompass Orix—just as the arrows hit. Sparks of silver sprayed from the line of arcane wards, and the arrows dropped to the ground.

"Is everyone all right?" Anskar asked.

The question was met with steely defiance from the rest of the group. Their wards blazed, and their eyes were locked on the archers already nocking their second arrows.

"Loose!" an archer yelled, and another volley struck the wards and bounced off.

As the archers prepared for a third attack, Anskar became aware of a writhing pressure inside his skull, along with a searing rush. His dawn-tide repository was down to its last dregs of energy, on account of his protection of Orix. And the barrier around his dusk-tide repository was unraveling, as if it *knew* he needed it to keep himself alive. But use of the dusk-tide might give him away. He could be thrown out of the Order, or worse.

"Sareya," he hissed. "Ward Orix!"

With ease, she extended her ward around Orix, and Anskar let his own ward retract to cover just himself.

The arrows struck and bounced away. This time, though, Gar cried out. A frayed patch of loosely interwoven light had appeared at the front of his ward. Another couple of hits and he would lose his protection.

With that thought, Anskar felt his own ward stutter in and out of existence. At the same time, the barrier around his dusk-tide repository dissolved, and its essence coursed through him.

Sareya glanced anxiously at him. Her ward expanded further, but only a few inches—not enough to cover him.

The line of bows came up once more, arrows nocked, strings pulled taut.

The acid burn of the dusk-tide raced through Anskar's veins; welled up within him—

"Stop!" a voice cried from atop the battlements. Vihtor.

The archers lowered their bows; and the knights-liminals' wards dissipated amid sighs of relief.

"Fuck," Anskar heard Petor say. "Fuck, fuck, fuck."

Anskar felt Orix's strong grip on his shoulder, giving it a grateful squeeze; but he had eyes only for Vihtor, who was striding down the steps from the parapet, an entourage of knights behind him.

"What did you think you were doing?" Vihtor raged, stopping in front of Anskar.

"Sir?"

Vihtor gestured angrily at Orix. "Extending your wards like that. Wasting your energy. You could have been killed."

"But Orix would have died if I hadn't," Anskar protested.

"Deservedly so, if he can't cast a ward in a crisis." Vihtor turned to Orix. "If this had been a real battle, you would be dead. You both would. Give me one reason why you should remain here and be eligible to take simple vows. One reason!"

"I…" Orix stammered.

"Because he's brave and loyal, and the kind of friend I would want at my side in battle," Anskar said.

"I wasn't asking you," Vihtor said.

"I panicked," Orix said. "I wasn't expecting—"

"You think our enemies send us forewarning of when they are

about to attack? You think they will relinquish the element of surprise just because you need time to prepare your wards?"

Orix hung his head in shame.

Anskar felt a deeper anger pulsing within him now—a burgeoning of the dark-tide. It seethed with malicious intent, enticing him to unleash it, assailing him with thoughts of bloodshed.

Out of the corner of his eye, he saw Sareya glance at him.

Keeping his focus on the Seneschal, Anskar recited the litany of the Five's balance in his mind, at the same time begging Menselas for restraint. Slowly, bit by bit, he tightened the barrier he had established around the dark-tide, walling it in with the sheer force of his will.

Frae Ganwen stepped forward and dipped her head. "Seneschal, forgive me. Perhaps they weren't ready for the test."

"You have nothing to be forgiven for," Vihtor said, his tone softening. "They have been more than sufficiently prepared." He walked slowly along the line of trainees. "I'm watching you," he told Orix. "And I had better see some improvements."

He narrowed his eyes at Sareya, then gave a perfunctory nod.

To Gar he said, "Practice the efficient use of your dawn-tide. Your wards would not have withstood more than another strike or two."

"Sorry, Seneschal," Gar said, lowering his eyes. "I panicked; used up most of my repository at once."

"A knight must be calm and collected in battle," Vihtor said. "No exceptions. Frae Ganwen, is there anything you wish to add?"

"Nothing, Seneschal. I'll have them work on the things you say over the next few days. By your leave, the students should probably break for lunch."

"Very well," Vihtor said; then to the knights-liminal, "You are dismissed."

The knights who had been with Vihtor atop the parapet mingled with the archers, conversing in low voices.

"But not you two," Vihtor said, indicating Anskar and Sareya.

Anskar knew what was to come. Vihtor suspected something was still going on between the two of them. Maybe he hadn't forgiven the first transgression, or suspected Anskar of lying to him.

"Sir…" Anskar started, trying to frame an apology, to beg for lenience.

Vihtor silenced him with a raised hand. "I won't pretend to be happy about what I witnessed this morning, but let me commend you both on one thing. You each sacrificed vast amounts of your own dawn-tide to protect another. That, at least, was noble. Now, go. Enjoy your lunch."

Over the next few days, Frae Ganwen's class moved away from ward-casting and on to rote-learning the calculations they would need to imbue the mail they were still making with sorcerous resilience. Not only would the cants reinforce the steel of their armor, they would also help to insulate the wearer from attacks by the casters of tainted sorcery, which Anskar understood to refer to the dusk-tide. These calculations were more complex than those they had used to retain the keen edge of their swords, and the process of learning the cants and becoming proficient in their use would likely take days, if not weeks, Frae Ganwen told them.

The mail hauberks they were making would take longer still— if they ever finished winding steel and cutting links. But they did finish making the rings several days later; and then Sned introduced them to a simple 4:1 weave, wherein four steel rings were joined to one set in the middle.

"This is the basic unit of assembly," Sned explained. "And you're going to need thousands of them for a complete hauberk."

"Thousands?" Naul exclaimed. "But that's—"

He squealed and ducked as a wooden mallet sailed past his head.

"Boring?" Sned said.

Anskar intervened before the Forge Master could find anything heavier to throw at Naul. "Is this about teaching us patience, sir?"

"Ah," Sned said, as if he'd just had a great revelation. "The virtue of patience! Which could then be translated to the battlefield, where sometimes to rush in leads to catastrophe and slaughter?"

"Uhm, yes," Anskar said.

"No. You want to know why you're doing this, Assling? I'll show you."

Sned led the knights-liminal to the smithing hall's vast storeroom and opened the door. "That's why."

Anskar's jaw dropped. Inside, there were dozens of mail hauberks suspended from the low ceiling beams; shorter habergeons of both chain and scale; splinted armor; cuirasses of steel and bronze; padded gambesons; and a score of mannequins fully dressed in burnished plate. There were barrels of arrow and spear heads; crates of standard issue swords; racks of halberds; and on the walls hung shields, kite and round, all unpainted and awaiting an emblem.

"The Order never runs out of commissions from the mainland," Sned told them. "We even get requests for armor and weapons from as far away as Ruruc in the Wastes, and from the unknown lands across the Trackless Ocean."

"Unknown lands?" Petor Vilaf said.

"Apparently not quite so unknown to the traders of arms," Sned said. "My point is, there's coin to be made in the sale of weapons and armor, and the Order is largely dependent upon it."

"So, we'll be put to work making armor for sale?" Myra DeYenté said. "That is not what my family signed me up for."

"Just think on this," Sned said. "How long do you think most of us remain knights in the field? Five years? Ten? Sometimes it's more, but often it's less. People get injured. People get old. And then what do they do to contribute to the life of the Order?"

"Couldn't they just leave?" Sareya asked.

"And do what? A knight's only good for one thing. Two, if they learn how to make weapons and armor. It's an honorable trade," Sned said, puffing out his chest. "And lucrative. At least, for the Order."

Then it was a good job, Anskar thought but didn't dare to say, that the Grand Master was having the Hooded One's chapel converted into a banker's vault.

Since meeting Eldrid DeVantte at the Griffin's Rest, Anskar had longed to speak with the knight further. Eldrid said he had given Anskar his surname—*out of love for your father.* More than that, Eldrid would not reveal. Vihtor, Anskar had to assume, wouldn't allow it. Why? Had his father done something shameful? Had his mother? Had they died traitors? Or was it worse than that?

Something bad must have happened, else Vihtor would not have kept the truth from him. *When you have taken solemn vows in a year or two,* Vihtor had said. *We will speak of it then, but not before.*

But Anskar wasn't going to wait a year or two if he didn't have to. He *shouldn't* have to. Vihtor had no right. And so he asked around the knights he knew until he learned that Eldrid was training a cohort of men and women for some new mission down south.

Anskar skipped lunch between classes and found Eldrid at the barrack grounds on the east side of the citadel. The big man was giving a young knight a severe dressing-down, while around them armored men and women drilled with swords and ward spheres. Anskar watched curiously as the knights circled one another, exchanging blows and pulling back expertly at the last instant; then shoving against each other with flattened sorcerous wards, jostling for position and knocking each other off-balance.

His attention was drawn back to Eldrid as he slapped the younger knight around the face, then yelled for the others to stop their practice and form a circle. When Eldrid and the young knight stepped into the circle, swords in hand, Anskar realized the slap had been a challenge.

Eldrid stalked the knight, who circled away, using his outstretched sword to keep a distance between them. Twice Eldrid batted the blade aside, causing the young knight to stumble. Someone in the crowd jeered, which made the younger man angry. He feinted a thrust and at the last second flicked his wrist, turning it into a slash toward Eldrid's neck.

Eldrid swayed back out of range, at the same time taking a shuffling step to his right, then another. The young knight tried to mirror the footwork, but Eldrid changed direction mid-step, gracefully bending his knees and dipping at the waist as the young knight's sword whistled overhead. Then Eldrid rose inside his opponent's guard and pressed the point of his sword into the younger man's sternum.

Emotions churned across the knight's face—rage, fear, and shame. He tried to step back, but Eldrid went with him, until the young knight was backed up against the circle of spectators.

"Repent," Eldrid said.

"I didn't do it!"

"Repent."

When the young man maintained his protest, Eldrid pressed his sword tip harder. The knight roared and swung his own blade toward Eldrid's side, but Eldrid was too quick: his sword came down and struck the young knight's wrist. Anskar winced at the crack of bone. The knight screamed and fell to his knees, his sword thudding to the earth.

Eldrid glared down at him, then said for the third time, "Repent."

Tears of pain in his eyes, the young knight nodded.

"You admit what you did?"

"I admit it," the knight said miserably.

"Will it happen again?"

The young man shook his head, and Eldrid sheathed his sword, satisfied. "Take yourself to the healers."

The knight stood, clutching his shattered wrist. "I'll not be able to fight now."

"You won't need to," Eldrid said, turning his back on him. "You're not coming with us. There's no place in my cohort for fornicators and liars."

That was the final crushing blow. Eyes averted from his watching comrades, the knight stooped to pick up his sword with his left hand. The circle parted for him as he walked away in shame.

Anskar winced in sympathy for the pain of the young knight's broken wrist. He realized he was clutching the vambrace that invisibly encased his forearm.

Eldrid caught sight of Anskar watching and nodded his acknowledgment. To the circle of knights he said, "Dismissed. Get yourselves some lunch, then meet back here in two hours for hard sparring."

Someone groaned, but stopped when Eldrid turned his glare on the group. At his nod, they moved away in the direction of the knights' refectory.

Eldrid approached Anskar. "You're looking for me?"

Anskar couldn't find the words to answer—not after the display he'd just witnessed; not after the condemnation of a fornicator. He just nodded.

"Come, let's talk," Eldrid said. "Have you eaten?"

They went together to the refectory, where Eldrid's men and women were collecting their meals and talking boisterously. Anskar and Eldrid waited silently in line until they were served— carrots, potatoes, and a pie filled with chestnuts, chicken and gravy. To Anskar's surprise, Eldrid was also given a mug of beer.

They sat at a round table apart from the others. Anskar sipped at his water and waited for Eldrid to say something.

"I can't tell you what you wish to know," the older man said, before popping a piece of pie in his mouth and chewing vigorously. He grunted his appreciation and gestured with his fork for Anskar to start eating.

"But I need to—"

"Eat," Eldrid grunted as he chewed. He glanced at Anskar, eyes turned to steel.

Anskar stifled the urge to protest further; what would be the point? And he dared not risk an outburst as he had with Vihtor.

The Seneschal had merely shut the door on him; Eldrid might break something.

Anskar tried the pie: it was good, permeated with subtle flavors he could hardly guess at. The fare in the knights' refectory was far better than that served to the novices and knights-liminal.

"The Seneschal is wise," Eldrid said, pausing to take a slurp of beer. "Trust him. But if you wish, I can speak to you of myself and my family in Sansor. You share our name, and, with luck, one day you will share our honor."

"Is it true the streets in Sansor are paved with gold?" Anskar asked. Tion had told him wondrous things about the capital city of Kaile.

Eldrid laughed. "There are some who say that. There are some very wealthy families in Sansor, and some very poor."

"Is your family wealthy?"

Eldrid's brow furrowed. Perhaps it wasn't considered polite in Sansor to ask about a family's status.

"We want for nothing," he said. "My family come from old wealth, but these days there is far more new coin than old."

"New coin?"

Eldrid forked a carrot; he paused before putting it in his mouth. "Merchants, bankers—the sort who know how to turn a quick profit. Used to be that lineage was everything in Sansor, but now it's all about how much coin you have; which circles you move in."

Anskar had never needed coin of his own; his every need had been provided for by the Order. He resisted asking how much coin Eldrid had, then found himself wondering if the knight had reserved a strongbox in the vault being built in the Hooded One's crypt.

"The DeVanttes originally came from Thessalika in the City

States," Eldrid said, "but we moved to Kaile generations ago. There has been a DeVantte in our manse at Sansor since the time of my great-great-grandfather."

"You have a manse? And lands?"

Eldrid shrugged, as if everyone did. "A modest few hundred acres. Good pasture, though, and some forest. We breed horses, and there are sheep, cattle, chickens. As I said, we want for nothing. My wife oversees the estate, for the most part, though she hires locals to manage it. She has enough to do looking after our five children."

"It sounds a good life," Anskar said.

"For her, it is. I rarely get to see my home, or my wife and children. Each time I return on leave, the boys are taller and broader, the two girls more…womanly. It pains me to say I missed their growing up, but such are the sacrifices a knight must make." His mood grew melancholy, and he stared into his beer before emptying the mug.

"You regret taking vows?" Anskar asked.

"Not in the slightest!" Eldrid laughed at the absurdity of the idea and waved his mug overhead until a server brought him a fresh one topped with froth. "The first few days of leave are… sublime. But after a week, the novelty has usually worn off— for my family as well as for me—and I can't wait to get back. Absence breeds fondness, they say, and I'd testify to the truth of that. Give me a good horse, my armor and my sword, and I'll need nothing else. Till the next time."

Eldrid returned to his food with gusto. Anskar chewed on a potato, then washed it down with a sip of water. His thoughts skittered around inside his skull as he searched for something to say. The silence was unsettling; it made him feel guilty, as if Eldrid could see inside his mind and knew what he had done with Sareya. *There's no place in my cohort for fornicators and liars.*

Finally, Anskar could bear the silence no longer. "Why did you give me your name?"

"The Seneschal didn't know what we should call you. I merely helped him out."

"He was the one to name me?" Anskar said, surprised.

Eldrid pushed his empty plate aside. "Vihtor Ulnar is a great man, a good leader, and a friend. He takes his responsibilities seriously. As head of the Order here in Niyas, he views us all—even me—as his children. You will learn that for yourself as you advance in rank."

Anskar sat back in his chair to digest what he had just been told. Vihtor Ulnar, Seneschal of Branil's Burg, had named him as an infant. *He views us all—even me—as his children.* Hearing that brought Anskar a sense of belonging that had always eluded him. As some of the knights were wont to say, the Order was their family. It was *his* family—the only one he had ever known.

Then he recalled that he'd betrayed that family by his antics with Sareya, and again with his lies about what had happened on Hallow Hill.

"It's been good talking with you, Anskar," Eldrid said, rising. "I would suggest meeting again, but my cohort leaves in the morning. We'll be heading to the south of the island, where there have been more uprisings."

"Carred Selenas?" Anskar asked.

"Probably. And if not her personally, you can bet she's behind it. Cunning as a snake, she is, and as elusive as a ghost. But don't worry; we've come close recently—at Naphor. Take her down and who will these scum rally around? Mark my words, we'll snuff out this rebellion one way or another."

Anskar stood too. "I should be going anyway. I'm late for

smith-crafting." He tried not to show his frustration at still not being told what he wanted to know.

Eldrid seemed to realize that and gave an apologetic smile. "I don't know as much as you might think, Anskar, but I am sworn to protect even that small amount of information. A knight is only as good as his word."

That felt like an indictment.

"But you knew my father!" Anskar said.

Eldrid fixed him with a stern look—the same look he had given the young knight in the barrack grounds. "The balance of the Five be upon you, Anskar," he said, and walked from the refectory.

TWENTY-TWO

NEXT DAY, SHORTLY AFTER THE four companions had met in the courtyard to greet the dawn-tide, one of the Niyandrian servants approached Anskar and informed him the Seneschal wanted to see him. Elated by the ritual of replenishment and the time spent with his friends, Anskar raced to answer the summons.

Vihtor looked up from his breakfast table, a cup of steaming tea halfway to his lips. With a nod, he indicated Anskar should take the chair opposite.

"Have you eaten?" the Seneschal asked, taking a quick slurp of tea and setting the cup down.

"I was on my way to breakfast when I was told you wanted to see me. I came right away."

Vihtor raised an eyebrow, popped a piece of bacon into his mouth and chewed slowly. He ripped off a hunk of bread and dipped it in egg yolk, pausing with it before his lips. "Would you like me to send for some food for you?"

"I'll be fine, thank you," Anskar said. In truth he was starving, but his good mood had soured and he felt uncomfortable.

Vihtor shrugged and popped the bread and egg into his mouth. "I hear you spoke with Eldrid before he left for the south. How did it go?"

"Good," Anskar said warily. "I'm proud to bear his name." Another lie, but what was he supposed to say?

Vihtor gave a tight smile. "How's your memory now?"

"My memory?"

"The priests of the Elder say it is not uncommon to forget things following trauma, but often the memories come back over time." He annunciated the next words slowly: "Hallow Hill."

Anskar licked dry lips. He hadn't prepared for this. "There are fleeting images, sir," he said, mind racing as he tried to decide how much to reveal. "I don't know where to start."

Vihtor took another sip of tea, pausing to look over the rim of the cup. "Why not start with why you left the citadel that night?" Perhaps reading the panic on Anskar's face, he added, "The whole truth, no matter how incredible it might seem. I'm not as ignorant of these things as you might believe."

Did he know? Had the Seneschal worked out for himself what had happened? How was that possible? Or had someone told him? But who? Surely not the wraithe or the crow. Maybe the priests of the Elder had ways of working things out—it was said they could read people like books, and that some among them had knowledge of far away events. The point was, Anskar couldn't risk continuing with his lie, not if there was any chance Vihtor knew the truth.

He drew in a long breath and let it out slowly. "I told you about the crow that drank my blood," he began.

"That was no ordinary crow," Vihtor said, watching him

intently between bites of food.

"No, sir."

Vihtor set down his knife and fork. "If it were commonplace for crows to enter our rooms at night and drink our blood, we would never open our windows. Besides which, I am reliably informed that most crows prefer to eat seeds and grains."

Reliably informed. The phrase evoked memories of Luzius Landav. Maybe the sorcerer had revealed to Vihtor all that he knew, such as the fact that Anskar's catalyst was tainted, and he had defeated Beof with some manner of dark sorcery. Assuming Vihtor didn't already know that from questioning the disgraced priest of the Warrior.

"All I know," Anskar said, "is that I woke to find the crow piercing my neck. It returned later and led me from the citadel."

"And you went willingly? Did you not fear the bird was something demonic?"

Anskar shook his head. "Not willingly. I felt as though I were still asleep."

"I see." Vihtor went to stand before an open window that overlooked the healers' herb garden. "Did it speak to you?"

"Sir?" Anskar's palms were sweating, and he wiped them on his pants.

"The crow," Vihtor said, still gazing out the window. "Did it speak to you?"

It *had* spoken to Anskar—in his mind, though mostly in Niyandrian. But how could he tell the Seneschal such a thing? It might be all the proof Vihtor needed to believe Anskar was either crazy or infected with dark forces.

Anskar remembered Tion telling him about priests of the Five who had claimed to hear Menselas speaking to them. In each case they were sent before a tribunal of bishops and ultimately dismissed from the priesthood. "There are only three explanations for the hearing of voices," Tion had warned him. "Your own thoughts playing loudly in your head; a manifestation of a mental sickness; or the interference of demons masquerading as the god. The remedy in every case is to ignore them. And if you are a priest, make sure no one above you in the hierarchy gets to hear of your experience."

Of course, there was a fourth possibility—that the god was indeed speaking—but Tion's answer to that had been definitive: "If Menselas wants you to know something, he has plenty of other ways to communicate that don't involve voices in your head."

"I take it from your silence that the bird did speak to you?" Vihtor said, turning back to face him.

"No!" Anskar forced a laugh that sounded false even to him. "Crows don't speak!"

Vihtor studied him for an uncomfortably long moment, then narrowed his eyes. "No. Of course they don't." He returned to the table and stood grasping the back of his chair. "But then, crows don't enter our rooms and lead us on journeys through the wilderness, do they?"

"No, Seneschal."

"What happened next?"

Anskar described the days and nights he'd spent in Rynmuntithe Forest, the voices he had heard searching for him, the boat in the reeds.

"We almost caught up with you once or twice," Vihtor said. "With the help of Rosie. I guess the boat explains why we didn't. But aren't you forgetting something?"

"I don't think so…"

"The dead-eye."

"You found it?"

"Rosie did, and that's where she picked up your scent again after we'd lost it at the river. Quite a feat for a novice still in training to take down a dead-eye. You were lucky it wasn't part of a tribe."

"I nearly died," Anskar said, remembering just how close he'd come to being ripped apart and defiled. "The crow…it came to my aid. It attacked the dead-eye, and I was able to reach my sword."

"I see." Vihtor ran both hands through his hair and sighed.

At first Anskar thought he was angry, then he saw the concern etched into the Seneschal's face.

"One less dead-eye to cull, I suppose. And the crow led you eventually to Hallow Hill?"

"Yes, sir." Recalling what he'd seen from the summit, Anskar added, "Are we rebuilding Naphor? That citadel under construction—"

"The Order is building all over Niyas. And yes, we are reconstructing the capital. The time for war is long past. We are entering a new phase in the life of the island. But let's stick to Hallow Hill. There is an ancient ruin atop the hill. Did you enter it?"

Anskar wanted to tell the truth—about the vambrace, the crow, the wraithe, the tainting of his catalyst. He wanted to trust Vihtor enough to ask for his advice. But a change had come over the Seneschal's demeanor. That he was concerned about Anskar was obvious; but there was something more to his questioning too; some deeper suspicion.

"I didn't," Anskar said. "There was no way in that I could see, and I was exhausted. I must have collapsed soon after reaching the summit."

"I have your word on this?" Vihtor said.

Anskar swallowed and nodded. "Of course."

"Good. Have you spoken about this to anyone else since your memory…returned?"

"No, sir, I have not."

"To Orix? Larson?" The Seneschal narrowed his eyes. "To Sareya?"

"No! I swear."

"Good. I'd like you to keep it that way. Now, if you hurry, you may still make breakfast."

Anskar could tell that Vihtor was disappointed in him, but not nearly as disappointed as he was in himself. What had changed in him that he couldn't trust the Seneschal? Why did he feel compelled to keep these dark secrets? He hadn't asked the crow to come to him, nor the wraithe to send him into the ancient tomb. These were the secrets of others, not his own; and he couldn't help feeling he should reveal them to the rightful authorities—to Vihtor.

And yet he couldn't suppress the niggling worry that Vihtor couldn't be trusted. And not just him, but the entire Order, perhaps even the Church of Menselas itself. Or was that the voice of some corrupting demon hidden within his marrow, whispering words of discord to confuse him, to keep him from doing what was right? How could he know?

As Anskar opened the door to leave, Vihtor said, "Anskar…do not continue to put yourself in temptation's way." At Anskar's frown of incomprehension, he added, "Greet the dawn-tide alone. I have received word that you are spending too much time with Sareya."

The need to protest bubbled up within Anskar. He tried to formulate a response—Naul and Orix were always present; nothing had happened; he was resolved to keep the rules of the Order—but Vihtor had already dismissed him with a wave.

When Anskar arrived in the refectory, the other knights-liminal had finished eating but were still seated at their long table, those who had partaken of the dawn-tide together on one side, those who had not—Myra, Gar, and Petor—on the other. Dirty plates were stacked in the center of the table. Myra was thumbing through a book while she sipped tea; Petor and Gar stopped whatever they had been talking about as Anskar took a seat next to Orix. Sareya met his eyes briefly, then went back to speaking with Naul. She was chewing mint as she always did after a meal. The rest of the refectory was emptying out as novices went off to start their classes.

"Saved you some breakfast," Orix said, pushing a plate of eggs, bread, and bacon in front of Anskar, followed by a mug. "Tea's cold, though."

"I like cold tea," Anskar said, wincing as he took a sip before downing the tepid brew in one go.

"What did the Seneschal want?" Naul asked.

Sareya didn't look at Anskar, but he could tell she was listening intently for his reply.

"He was just checking up on me. Vihtor's my mentor."

"That's more than mine does," Naul said.

"Tell me about it." Orix folded his arms across his chest. "I don't think my mentor even knows what my name is."

Anskar set about his breakfast as his comrades resumed their conversations around him. He caught Sareya repeatedly glancing at him, and once, when he caught her eye, she queried him with a frown.

Gradually, the others began to leave. Naul lingered in the

doorway for Sareya as she leaned across the table to Anskar.

"What is it?" she asked. "What's wrong."

Anskar washed down the bread he was chewing with a slurp of cold tea. "I won't be able to join the rest of you for the dawn-tide any longer."

Sareya turned, her mouth forming the word "Why?" but she seemed to realize the answer to her question before she gave it voice. She nodded, clenched her jaw, and then set off ahead of him, slowing her pace only when she caught up with Naul.

The knights-liminal met up at the stables so they could join a group of newly professed knights for horsemanship drills: charging in formation; slamming one's lance into a straw-packed dummy; sustaining arcane wards around both rider and steed while at a full gallop.

The training was overseen by Sergeant Crosbyn, a bluff old man with the biggest, bushiest mustache Anskar had ever seen. He had a kind face, and twinkling eyes of washed-out blue.

Larson the stablemaster watched from a hay bale he'd placed outside the main stable block. He was stringing a battered guitar like a man who'd forgotten how to do it. Rosie was seated on her haunches beside him, panting with her tongue out, as if she couldn't wait for Larson to start strumming and singing. Anskar had to admit he was intrigued by the prospect too.

"A good knight," Crosbyn told the trainees cheerfully as he inspected their ragged line after the horsemanship exercises, "must know what it feels like to fight tired. Now, drink some water, pull yourselves together, and let's see some improvements this afternoon."

"Sir, are we breaking for lunch?" Orix asked, sounding concerned.

"Eventually, lad. First, water. Then you're heading outside the walls for ten circuits of the Burg—running, not walking."

"Running?" Naul said. "We've not done running before."

"Which is why you'll be running outside every day from now on, to make up for lost time," Crosbyn said.

The five knights-liminal groaned, and the newly professed knights laughed at them as they led their horses back to the stables.

"We're really going outside on our own?" Anskar asked.

"Is there an echo in here?" Crosbyn said. "Yes, outside. And yes, alone. So, be careful. You don't want a pack of dead-eyes snatching you and dragging you off into the woods. Not to mention the drakkons that swoop down out of the clouds at this time of year."

"Drakkons?" Myra said, for once seeming engaged.

"Just pulling your leg, my dear," Crosbyn said. "The biggest danger is having your pockets picked when you pass through sections of Dorinah—so you may as well empty them before you go. Now, you have five minutes to grab a drink. When you come back, the gates will be open. Ten circuits, mind, and I'll be up there"—he pointed to the parapet—"watching, in case you think of cutting it short."

Anskar's legs felt leaden from gripping his horse's flanks so long as he made his way to a trestle table that held three large water jugs and a selection of mugs. As he poured himself a drink, he caught a whiff of musk and turned to see Sareya at his shoulder.

"I need to speak with you," she said, her voice low.

"About what?" Anskar took a long drink of the cool, chalky water.

"There's something beneath my dusk-and dawn-tide repositories—a bud that wasn't there before; or if it was, I never detected it. And it's growing. I sense the same power in you, only greater. It feels wrong: an infection. Anskar, do you think…when we made love…?"

"You think you caught it from me?" Caught the dark-tide? How was that even possible?

Anskar felt an itch between his shoulder blades. He glanced round to see Crosbyn watching them. The last thing he needed was for the old knight to report to Vihtor that he and Sareya were still close.

"We shouldn't talk about this," he said, refilling his mug.

"I agree. Not here. Can we meet later, somewhere private?"

"I mean at all," Anskar said. "If you've been using your senses on me, you'll know I've walled in everything but the dawn-tide. I suggest you do the same. We're not here to become sorcerers, Sareya. We're here to become knights."

He turned away from her and headed toward the open gate, where he limbered up and prayed to Menselas that he could make it around the Burg once, let alone ten times.

The first lap was the worst. Despite Myra leading the group at a slow, steady jog, sweat poured from Anskar, drenching his shirt and pants.

Orix slapped him on the back as he overtook him. "You'll be fine after another lap or two."

On the second lap, as they were passing through the quarter of Dorinah that bordered the Burg, Anskar doubled up with a stitch, but at Orix's advice he continued to jog slowly until it wore off. Halfway into the third lap he wanted to vomit and began to lag behind. Orix held back to run alongside him, offering tips and encouragement. After a while, the sweating stopped—Anskar doubted there was any fluid left in his body to sweat out—and the sickness abated. Without thinking, he matched his pace to Orix's, and with an easy rhythm the two extended their strides and were soon moving toward their three peers.

On the ninth lap, Orix and Anskar surged past Sareya and Naul, who were also running side by side. Gradually they gained on Myra, who was surprisingly fleet of foot.

The final hundred yards were a sprint for the open gate. Anskar's blood pounded in his ears and his breath came in heaving gasps. Pumping his arms, he kicked out and put everything he had into one final effort.

Orix fell behind. "Go on!" he gasped. "Catch her!"

Gritting his teeth, Anskar barreled after Myra, lungs burning as he sucked in gulps of crisp air. Every inch he gained on Myra was a mammoth effort, and all the while she glided gracefully ahead. Near the gate, she looked back and grinned, and then, as if she'd been holding back, she lengthened her stride and reached the gate a good twenty yards ahead of him.

Anskar slowed and stumbled, but Orix grabbed him by the shirt and pulled him onward. Apparently, Orix had gotten a second wind. Together, they almost fell through the open gate, and then Sareya and Naul came in panting behind them.

Crosbyn descended the narrow steps from the parapet. "Pathetic," he said, "save for Myra. Even I could have outrun the rest of you, and I'm old and fat."

Crosbyn wasn't alone. Behind him came a hard-faced woman wrapped in the white cloak of the Order, a five-pointed star embroidered on the breast in red.

Anskar had seen, but never spoken with, Commander Noreina Lanwitch. He guessed her age to be mid-forties, but she was straight-backed and lean, and looked like she could best anyone half her age in a fist fight. Her close-cropped black hair was streaked with gray, and she had one eye of vivid green. The other was covered with a leather patch, a long scar above and below it. She wore a breastplate of form-fitting steel that had an unnaturally bright sheen, and over her riding boots, steel greaves.

Noreina strode toward the group, all of whom, except Myra, were panting to regain their breath.

"I have every confidence that Sergeant Crosbyn will have you in tiptop condition for your first mission at the week's end," Noreina said.

What mission? This was the first Anskar had heard of it.

Noreina scanned the group, her eyes hard. "You will be visiting the stronghold under construction at Quolith and, if you're lucky, doing a spot of hunting on the way."

"Hunting what?" Naul asked.

Noreina shot him a glare. She didn't need to say *speak when you're spoken to.* Naul clearly got the message by the way he lowered his head and blushed.

"Dead-eyes," Noreina said. "In case you didn't realize, the Order relies on stipends from the local councils to maintain our presence here on Niyas; and one of our contractual agreements is that we keep the dead-eye population in check. They're a bloody hazard to farmers and their animals, not to mention unattended children."

Stipends from the local councils around Niyas had to mean the occupied towns and cities whose governors came from the mainland, Anskar thought. But some remote towns and villages were still governed by Niyandrians; did they pay the stipend too? Were they forced to pay it? It seemed reasonable, he thought, if they were also to benefit from the protection the Order offered.

Anskar knew it wasn't just stipends the Order relied on; it

was also the manufacture of arms and armor, which they sold wherever they could create a need—he assumed to friend and foe alike. That much he'd already worked out from what Sned had shown them in the smithing hall. Still, he reasoned, if the Order didn't provide the weapons, someone else would. Far better for the profits to go to the Order and the Church of Menselas.

As Noreina strode away across the horse yard, Crosbyn dismissed them for lunch. Myra headed away from the refectory, apparently returning to her room. Sareya and Naul walked off together. Anskar watched them go.

"They're getting close," Orix said. "I shan't be going to the dawn-tide meeting any longer. Starting to feel like a gooseberry."

Anskar felt a stab of envy but quickly buried it. "Let them get on with it. We've got other things to worry about."

"Dead-eyes?" Orix said. "Let's hope we get picked for the Mornash patrols."

TWENTY-THREE

THEY BURIED KOVIN AND THE other dead in the woods, but Carred shed no tears. Her capacity for grief had shriveled and died.

The leaders of the resistance returned to their towns, cities and villages to await Carred's summons. After the sorcerer's attack, they needed to abandon the Rynmuntithe hideout.

Carred took Maggow the Message with her to the occupied city of Lowanin. If the Order of Eternal Vigilance wasn't above using demons against her, she had no qualms about protecting herself with the dark sorcery of the forgotten gods of Niyas— forgotten by all save the people of the mire like Maggow.

Carred rode, the old man jogging steadily behind as if he never tired; as if the rage he had unleashed against the sorcerer, Landav, somehow fueled him.

Every now and again, a pigeon would swoop down to alight on his forearm. It seemed as if the birds didn't simply travel between two or three locations but homed in on Maggow himself. It also seemed, from the way the old man made clicking sounds with his tongue before sending the pigeons away again, that they understood whatever he needed them to do.

"Our way is clear of patrols," Maggow told her. "There are no white-wings between us and the city."

"White-wings?"

"Cloaks. It is how my pigeons see the Order's knights."

"Any news from Branil's Burg—from Aelanthe?" None of the pigeons had arrived with slips of parchment wrapped around their legs.

"Nothing."

Perhaps Aelanthe was having difficulty gaining access to the Niyandrian women within the Burg. But no messages from Branil's Burg meant no further news about Hyle Pausus's visit, either. Carred had to assume that the citadel's security would be tightened pending the Grand Master's arrival. Perhaps later, once things had settled down, opportunities would present themselves.

The old Niyandrian fort at Lowanin was now garrisoned with Order knights, as was the case with other strongholds and towns across the isle. Punnit's Keep, as the knights had renamed it, was an iron fist within the once-proud Niyandrian city. At Punnit's Keep, the Order meted out justice mainland style, affecting less of the pious veneer that made Branil's Burg's knights so hypocritical. The knights of Punnit's Keep were seasoned warriors who had lost comrades in the war. They didn't balk at eking out their revenge on the servile population.

Maggow refused to enter the city. Instead, the old man set up camp in the hills outside, in a cave that had once been used by some kind of large predator, judging by the bones strewn about the floor. But Maggow didn't seem to mind, and Carred left him there sending out his summons to his pigeons—a rite that involved phlegm and urine and the entrails of whatever small mammals he could catch.

Carred passed through the city checkpoint without any trouble from the white-cloaked guards. She used the forged papers Kovin had long ago procured for her from one of his contacts—a woman named Thysianwen, who was apparently "the best in the business." Of course, Kovin said that about all his contacts. It was part of his charm. Or had been.

Carred forced herself not to dwell on his death. She wasn't strong enough.

Lowanin was a bold choice for a place to hide, right under the noses of the occupying mainlanders, but in the gray cloak Kovin had given her, Carred was able to pass herself off as a lowborn Niyandrian of no special interest. She'd had a lover in the city a long time back—a man called Shevrin. A good man, who probably had a wife and children by now. She didn't know and didn't plan to find out. Last thing she needed was someone else to lose.

TWENTY-FOUR

THE SUN WAS HIGH IN the sky when Anskar and the other knights-liminal gathered in the stable yard. After days of grueling early morning runs under Sergeant Crosbyn's watchful eye, then hours on end in the smithing hall assembling steel rings into Sned's 4:1 weave, it should have been a relief to have a change of pace, but instead there were nervous laughs and whispers that had the timbre of panic.

Anskar stood apart from the group, watching Larson nip in and out of the stalls with Rosie tagging along behind. He wished he were helping the stablemaster prepare the horses for the missions, rather than getting ready to leave the safety of Branil's Burg again.

The whispering stopped abruptly as Vihtor Ulnar strode into view from the direction of the knights' refectory. With him were Sergeant Crosbyn, Commander Noreina Lanwitch, and two more seasoned knights Anskar had seen around the citadel:

a plump woman in her fifties named Vaila, and a tall, barrel-chested man named Abizar, whose stature and almost black skin marked him as having Orgol blood in his veins. Anskar knew the Orgols from the Jargalan Desert were unsurpassed in strength, speed and ferocity, and Abizar looked a killer through and through. In place of a sword, he had a huge double-bladed axe slung across his back.

"Attention!" said Vihtor. "As you have been made aware, you are to start gaining the experience you will need to become fully consecrated knights a year from now. It's time you started earning your keep rather than being a drain on the Order's resources. You have achieved much to reach this moment, but those hardships were only the beginning. Now comes the real test of your mettle. You are to visit the new stronghold under construction at Quolith, and you will be under Noreina's command. Each of you will be assigned to a fully consecrated knight. Learn from them."

Vihtor studied each knights-liminal's face then nodded solemnly. "Furthermore, it's close to full-dark, when the dead-eyes gather. Local farmers have reported more sightings than normal and an unprecedented loss of livestock. Any time the Order's knights run into dead-eyes, we are obligated to cull them."

"If only it were that easy," Anskar whispered to Orix.

"What's that?" Noreina said. "Are you even listening to what the Seneschal is saying?"

Anskar felt his face prickle with heat. "Sorry, ma'am; Seneschal. But I've encountered a dead-eye before. Isn't this too much, too soon?"

Vihtor flashed him a glare and Anskar covered his mouth. He'd spoken without thinking.

"You've encountered one?" Crosbyn said. He frowned at

Vihtor. "When?"

Shocked whispers passed between the knights-liminal. Sareya shot Anskar a questioning look.

The Seneschal seemed momentarily lost for words. He narrowed his eyes at Anskar. *I've spread word that I sent you on a training mission and have forbidden you to discuss it.* Vihtor had lied to conceal the truth about the first time Anskar had left Branil's Burg; about the visitation of the crow and the dead-eye he'd slain on the way to Hallow Hill. Complex emotions scored the Seneschal's face, but Crosbyn simply shrugged and appeared willing to let the matter go. The silence that greeted the Seneschal's words was heavy.

Sergeant Crosbyn broke it. "So, lads and lassies, keep your eyes peeled and pray to the Warrior your swords retain their sharpness."

"They'd better," Vihtor said, "else we made a mistake passing you for the second trial. Now, the Forge Master has reported to me that your mail hauberks are still just piles of steel rings in buckets in the smithing hall, so none of you has armor. Sned's just sent out a massive order to the mainland, meaning we don't have any spare. Which is why I thought you could use an extra ward sphere."

"Sir?" Noreina said.

"I'll be coming with you."

"It's unlikely the deads will attack an armed group, Seneschal," Noreina said. "Are you sure that's necessary?"

Vihtor shrugged. "There's always the chance of running into a tribe."

Noreina gave him a skeptical look. "It's days yet till full-dark, so I doubt it."

"To be honest," Vihtor said, "I could use some time away from the Burg. I can't remember when I last cast my ward sphere, and I'm itching for something to kill."

"In that case," Noreina said, "we're honored to have you along."

They rode from the barbican at a fierce gallop, each of the seven knights-liminal paired with a fully consecrated knight for the excursion. The newly professed Jarl Soric took the lead, constantly chastising his charge, Naul, and correcting everything he did, from the way he sat in the saddle to his handling of the reins, and even the creases in his shirt.

Anskar rode Fellswain beside the Seneschal, who was mounted on his destrier Uhtran. Over his mail hauberk Vihtor wore a molded breastplate of steel; upon his head a winged helm of bronze—an ancient design. Anskar wondered if it had been replicated by the Order's armorers, or whether it was indeed a relic from a different age.

Sareya was with Sergeant Crosbyn, and Orix was paired with the giant Abizar. Vaila supervised Gar, while Petor and Myra rode a little way behind with their allocated knights: a woman in full-faced steel helm who carried a kite shield painted with the five-pointed star of Menselas; and a man in a bascinet with long, unkempt hair, who smelled like a mangy dog and swayed in the saddle as if drunk.

The retreating walls of the citadel tugged at Anskar, promising the safety of their embrace; warning of the dangers of the unknown. He schooled himself not to heed them; not to let familiar comforts hold him back. This was Anskar's third time away from the Burg and it was growing easier. The first time, he'd followed Vihtor like a frightened calf; and the second, he'd been barely aware of his surroundings, practically sleepwalking under the crow's compulsion. But now, sallying forth with his peers and accompanied by experienced knights, he felt pride and exhilaration.

As they reached the edge of the escarpment Branil's Burg and the city of Dorinah stood upon, Noreina called for them to slow to a canter for the descent to the lowlands.

When Jarl Soric continued to pull away with Naul in tow, Noreina's voice lashed out: "Soric, you idiot! I said slow!"

The scruffy man riding alongside Myra snorted out a laugh but desisted when he saw Vihtor's eyes narrow.

Jarl wheeled his horse around and trotted back up the slope. "If we are to reach Mortswain—"

"Are you questioning me?" Noreina said, leaning over the pommel of her saddle.

"Certainly not, Commander." Jarl drew his horse to a halt in front of her and sat up straight in the saddle.

Naul, a good ten yards down the slope, glanced at Anskar and made a lewd gesture behind Jarl's back.

"I was merely pointing out—"

"You have been a knight how long?" Noreina cut in.

"Thirteen months, Commander."

"Thirteen months," she repeated scathingly. "Do you know how long I've been consecrated? Or Crosbyn here?"

"By your leave, Commander," Crosbyn said, an affable smile barely visible beneath his mustache.

"Be my guest."

"You're young, lad," Crosbyn said to Jarl. "Keen to prove yourself. That is natural and good. But it is in obedience that we thrive, and in silence that we learn." Jarl's cheeks reddened and he looked about to say something, but Crosbyn continued in the same affable tone. "Rein it in, lad."

Jarl clamped his lips together, nodded, and turned his horse back down the slope to where Naul was waiting. "If I wanted you to hang back," he snapped, "I would have told you so."

"Sorry, sir," Naul said. As he and Jarl rode on ahead, he cast a smirk back over his shoulder to Anskar.

Unfortunately, Noreina saw it. "Continue with that, boy, and you'll feel the flat of my blade."

The scruffy knight was shaking with suppressed mirth. When Myra sighed at him, he blew her a kiss. After that, Vihtor gestured for the man to hang back and ride at the rear with him, where they exchanged hushed words. When the knight caught up with Myra again, he sat more upright in the saddle and kept his eyes focused ahead.

The group followed the line of hills west to the shore of Lake Xaranin. Anskar found it hard not to be disappointed when Noreina ordered them north along the shoreline, past the jetty where he and Vihtor had taken the ferry across to Caeltrin. The thought of beer and fried fish at the Griffin's Rest had him salivating.

"There'll be plenty of time for drink after the mission," Vihtor said, as if he knew what Anskar was thinking. He leaned in conspiratorially and added, "And the last thing we need is for Roj Darrow to get a whiff of beer." He nodded to indicate the scruffy knight riding with Myra.

Some miles farther on, Noreina ordered a stop for food and water. They dismounted by the lake and let their horses drink while they shared out strips of salted jerky, dried fruit, and hard cheese.

As they ate, Anskar kept looking into the trees, expecting to glimpse something watching them. Once or twice, he could have sworn he heard voices in the distance, or the cracking of twigs underfoot. But no one else seemed to notice, so he told himself to relax. It was just his previous encounter with the dead-eye preying on his nerves. He was out here with experienced knights. And the dead-eye had been hesitant to attack him even though he'd been alone.

Nevertheless, he told Vihtor of his concerns.

Rather than dismissing them, the Seneschal said, "Trust your instincts, Anskar. Sometimes they're all we have."

Vihtor moved off to speak with Noreina and Crosbyn. Anskar couldn't hear what they discussed, but the old sergeant nodded grimly, then moved among the other consecrated knights, presumably relaying whatever Vihtor and Noreina had said to him. They all grew more alert, their eyes returning often to the trees.

After everyone had stretched their legs and tended to their needs—and Roj Darrow had shamelessly relieved himself in the lake—they set off again. Crosbyn led them north along the old Niyandrian road—a perfectly straight route that did not bend aside even from hills. Vihtor explained to Anskar that in the days before the coming of the demon lord Nysrog, the Niyandrians had used some kind of long-forgotten sorcery to blast straight through the hills to create their roads.

Each time they came to a settlement, they stopped so Crosbyn and Vihtor could question the locals. A pack of dead-eyes had been seen farther north, one smallholder told them. She was so worried by the reports that she'd spent coin she could scarcely afford on hirelings to watch over her livestock. Anskar didn't think it was coin well spent. Both men were surly-looking mercenaries from the mainland who must have decided to remain in Niyas following the end of the war. They would probably run at the first sign of trouble; or worse, cause different kinds of problems for the poor woman once her coin dried up.

It was a similar story the farther they traveled from Branil's Burg. They met frightened farmers—Niyandrians and settlers from the mainland—who were doing their best to reinforce fences and shelter their animals, yet all had the despairing look of those who knew their efforts were futile. The odd thing was, not a single one of them thanked the knights or their charges for riding out to take care of the dead-eyes. Anskar was left with the feeling that the locals in some way blamed the knights for the incursions.

When he mentioned this to Vihtor, the Seneschal shook his head. "They think the Order can solve all their problems for them, and so do little for themselves. The first woman we spoke with—at least she has taken some action, but these others…" He shook his head in disgust. "I don't know what they expect. Dead-eyes are like the fire ants whose mounds spring up all over the place: no sooner do you eliminate one nest than three more appear close by. The Five only knows how these aberrations breed. Spawned in the abyssal realms, I'd wager."

By mid-afternoon they emerged into a valley and followed its winding path between the lazy hills on either side, before ascending to a densely forested ridge. They rode to its edge, and Anskar saw that the ground dropped away in a sheer cliff to a vast plain, upon which settlements were scattered about the near distance. A mile or so off, forming a sort of hub between the settlements, a massive tower was under construction atop an earthwork fortification. A wooden palisade surrounded the site, and there were dozens of pavilions inside it. Teams of Niyandrians worked high up on the scaffolding around the unfinished tower—just like Anskar had seen at Naphor.

Something fluttered across Fellswain's path and Anskar threw up an arm to protect his neck. Almost immediately, he let out a sigh of relief. It had been a wood pigeon, not a crow; he tracked its flight as it came to rest in the high branches of a tree.

Noreina reined in her horse and waited for everyone else to do the same, until they formed a line overlooking the settlements and the tower below.

"The reason for our trip," she said. "To give you a glimpse of the Order's work. Little by little we expand the balance of Menselas to encompass the whole of Niyas, replacing wooden forts and ancient earthwork defenses with strongholds built of stone."

"The construction below," Vihtor said, "will be the heart of a new city. Quolith, it is to be called, after the Quolith family of great repute in Sansor, who have provided substantial funds for—"

Knights cried out in pain. Instinctively, Anskar spoke a cant and his ward blazed into existence around him and Fellswain. He turned his mount to see arrows shooting from the forest behind. Roj Darrow fell sideways, his foot snagging in the stirrup. He hung limply, greasy hair trailing to the ground.

The woman with the kite shield arched backward, blood misting from the back of her full-faced helm as an arrow punched straight though. Jarl Soric fell forward to slump over his horse's neck. Gar took a shaft in the thigh and grunted.

Petor was quick to react, drawing his sword and turning his horse to face the threat, but an arrow thudded into his throat. He shuddered, and blood sprayed from his mouth. As he flopped to the ground, his horse bolted.

"Wards up!" Noreina cried, and scintillant spheres of light sprang up around the remaining knights.

Anskar drew *Amalantril* and glanced at his friends to make

sure they were protected. Sareya and Naul had cast strong wards of silver light. Orix's stuttered for a moment and then grew firm.

Dozens of red-skinned Niyandrians charged out of the trees. They were dressed in greens and browns that blended with the undergrowth, and screamed ululating battle cries as they ran at the group, brandishing swords wreathed in black flames.

Another volley of arrows flew at Anskar and the knights, some sailing over their heads, others sparking harmlessly off their wards. Their horses reared and whinnied as Noreina, Vihtor, Crosbyn and Vaila drew their swords; the giant Abizar tugged his double-bladed axe from his back.

The rebels were already halfway across the space between them. With the sheer drop behind them and the Niyandrians fanning out in front, the knights had nowhere to go. The voices Anskar had heard earlier, the snapping of twigs—it was a trap, and they had ridden straight into it.

"Hold the line!" Noreina cried above the din.

Still the knights and their charges struggled to control their panicked steeds, corralled like beasts in the slaughterhouse.

Not Fellswain, though. She might not have been bred for battle, but she was a thoroughbred destined for greatness and trained beyond the norm. She faced the coming tide of attackers with steely resolve, waiting for Anskar to lead.

He glanced left and right at his friends and saw they were as shocked and disoriented as the consecrated knights. If he did nothing, they would all be cut to pieces.

Anskar clenched his jaw and kicked his heels into Fellswain's flanks. Immediately, the palfrey sprang forward. Before the Niyandrians had time to check their charge, Fellswain plowed into them, pitching three from their feet. Anskar leaned out of the saddle, swinging *Amalantril* through the confines of his spherical ward. Steel clashed against steel, and a jolt ran up his arm as the Niyandrian he'd tried to decapitate parried then rolled aside from Fellswain's charge.

The palfrey burst through to the other side of the attackers, and Anskar wheeled her round. He saw with surprise that Orix had followed his lead and had knocked over two more of the rebels. Orix's face was grim, his eyes wide, as if he couldn't believe he was still alive.

There were maybe a score of rebels still standing, but their charge had been broken, and they were swiftly forming into two groups facing front and rear.

"With me, Orix!" shouted Anskar. Kicking Fellswain into action, he charged again.

This time, he saw Vihtor and the surviving consecrated knights attacking from the ridge side. Their wards sent up coruscating sparks as the Niyandrians' flaming blades hit them…and passed straight through. Desperately, the knights parried, their superior blades standing up to whatever sorcery enhanced the Niyandrians' swords. Abizar fell from the saddle, but surged to his feet unharmed, his great axe scything through flesh and bone and sending a Niyandrian's arm to the ground in a shower of gore.

And then Anskar was in the thick of battle and couldn't see what was happening beyond the snarling faces and arcing steel that trailed streamers of black fire.

Realizing his ward was useless against the sorcerous blades, he abandoned it and focused on the parry and cut of sword-work. Fellswain slowed to a standstill as Anskar blocked a hack aimed at his leg and drove his blade through an exposed neck. He swung back to the other side, meeting a strong hack then sliding his sword along his attacker's blade to nick the wrist. As the woman snatched her arm back, Anskar rammed *Amalantril* into her chest. She slid back off the blade, blood blooming at the front of her shirt.

To Anskar's side, Orix thrashed his sword left and right in bloody loops. There was a gash on his arm, but he ignored it as he wielded his blade like a madman.

Hands grabbed Anskar from behind and pulled him from the saddle. Fellswain reared and kicked out, and someone screamed.

Anskar rolled just as a sword smacked into the earth where his head had been. He got to one knee, but a boot smashed into his jaw, sending him sprawling. Before he could rise, the same boot stomped on his sword arm, forcing him to relinquish his grip on *Amalantril*. A huge red-skinned man loomed over him, black-wreathed axe raised overhead for the killing blow. Anskar cried out and shut his eyes.

Air whistled, and a stench of sulfur pervaded his nostrils. Then a great weight fell on top of him. In blind panic, he pushed the Niyandrian's corpse off him and staggered to his feet. The man's back was a bubbling mass of blisters; what was left of his clothing charred and smoking.

Stumbling away from the horror, Anskar looked about for his sword and instead saw Sareya riding toward him, hand extended, whorls of black mist pluming from her fingertips. Her eyes blazed with a white fire too bright to bear, and he had to look away. Niyandrians fled before her, scattering back into the trees.

Behind Sareya, Noreina, Crosbyn, and Vihtor dismounted amid a pile of Niyandrian dead. Abizar, yelling curses in a foreign tongue, blood dripping from his axe, gave chase until Noreina called him back.

Anskar cast about for Naul and Orix. Naul was on his back on the ground, Orix standing over him, blood-drenched sword held in both hands. Three dead Niyandrians lay before him, with another two fleeing into the woods.

Something nudged the back of Anskar's head and he turned. Fellswain. The palfrey's eyes were wide, and she pawed the earth with her front hoof. "You did well, girl," Anskar said, pressing his face to her muzzle. "You did very well."

Sareya climbed down from her horse and approached. The fire was already dying from her eyes, the sorcerous mist at her fingertips dissipating into the air.

"Are you all right?" she asked.

She was trembling, but whether it was out of concern for him, the shock of the fight, or the power she had drawn upon, Anskar had no idea.

"Thanks to you," he said, stooping to pick up his sword. He looked up at the sound of boots coming toward them.

"What in the name of Menselas did you think you were doing?" Vihtor said, striding toward Anskar, leading Uhtran by the reins. "You could have been killed."

Anskar was too stunned to reply, but Sareya spoke up for him.

"If Anskar hadn't charged, we would all have been killed. Seneschal," she added when Noreina shot a glare at her.

"You, Niyandrian, have some explaining to do when we get back to the Burg," Vihtor said. "I know the feel and look of the dusk-tide, and it has no place in our Order."

"You would rather I'd let Anskar die?" Sareya said.

"What *I* would rather," Noreina said, advancing on her, "is that you curb your tongue when the Seneschal is speaking, and that the two of you showed some discipline and awaited my orders in future. Is that understood?"

Sareya dropped her eyes.

Anskar bristled with anger. He moved to Sareya's side and opened his mouth to say something that would surely get him expelled, or worse, but clamped his lips shut when he saw the glimmer of a smile soften Noreina's face.

"I'd be lying if I said I wasn't pleased by your actions. Both of you." She glanced at Vihtor, who grimly nodded.

"You're right," the Seneschal said. "Another moment's hesitation and we would've had no chance. Whatever that black flame was on their swords, it came from the dusk-tide. One of them was no mean sorcerer—maybe even moontouched."

Anskar glanced at Sareya but she betrayed no reaction.

"But," Vihtor said, "that doesn't take away from what the Commander said about discipline. Anskar…"

He steeled himself for the rebuke.

"Control your impetuousness and your rage, and you will be a fine knight."

"I'm sorry, Seneschal," Anskar said. "I didn't know what else to do."

"Abizar?" Vihtor said.

The giant rolled his eyes and gave a self-effacing smile. "Pray." The word was malformed, his tongue not quite up to the task. "Warrior learn you, as he learn me. Well, almost, hah!"

"Now," Noreina said, "assuming you still want me to command, Seneschal?"

"This was not your fault, Noreina," Vihtor said. "You could not have been expected to know. If anyone's to blame, it's me. I should have sent scouts ahead of us."

"You shouldn't have to," Vaila said. The plump woman was breathing heavily, but it seemed more from anger than exhaustion. Judging by the blood stains on her sword, she had acquitted herself well during the fight. "The blasted rebels should have been ended years ago."

"Something else for which I am being perpetually blamed,"

Vihtor said.

"I didn't mean—" Vaila started but Vihtor cut her off.

"I know you didn't. Pressure from the mainland. You know how it is."

"So, what now?" Crosbyn asked. He stroked his mustache as he peered around at the dead. "We've lost almost half our group."

"First thing is to make sure we lose no more," Noreina said. "You, boy," she told Orix, who was helping Naul to his feet, "organize a perimeter guard. Shout if anything moves."

"Commander," Orix said.

Naul nodded that he was all right, and Orix assigned positions to him, Myra, Sareya, and Anskar. Not Gar, though, who could barely walk when they helped him down from his horse. The arrow in his thigh was lodged deep and would need a surgeon's skill to remove safely.

And not Petor either.

Petor was dead.

Anskar stared anxiously into the trees, eyes tracking every branch that swayed in the breeze, ears registering the rustle of leaves from squirrels darting through the canopy overhead. He tried to grasp the threads of his sorcerous senses to wrest them into some sort of conscious control, but they had grown slippery and eluded his grasp. He could only think that was on account of his rising panic. Out here, so far from the Burg, and with enemies close by, the fears that had been instilled in him by the stories Tion had told were suddenly immediate and real.

What he did find was an alien presence amid his thoughts:

a questing, probing feeler. He craned his neck to see Sareya at her post twenty yards to his right. She mouthed something at him—a single word. He thought it might be "Relax." Judging by her attentiveness to the woodland in front of her, he guessed she didn't mean stand down from the threat of more rebels advancing on their position through the forest. No, she had to mean relax in his attempts to make conscious use of his sorcerous senses.

He wasn't really sure how to do that. He drew in several long deep breaths and tried to empty his mind, but that just made him think about his senses all the more. Frustrated, he gave up and threw all his attention outward—taking in the spaces between the trees, the dappling of sunlight on the forest floor, the carpet of dried brown leaves. He became aware of the movements of a rabbit before he saw or even heard it. As the creature scampered away into the bracken, he wondered how he'd become aware of the animal, then realized his sorcerous senses were working in the background without any need for him to direct them.

Sareya flashed him a smile. So, she'd felt his success. He nodded his thanks then scanned the others of their group keeping watch over the forest.

Naul stood to his left; and Orix—who Noreina had placed in charge for some unfathomable reason—sat high up on the broad branch of an oak, hand visoring his eyes.

Anskar glanced behind, to where Noreina, Vihtor, Abizar, and the old knight, Crosbyn, were wrapping the dead in their cloaks and laying them over their saddles. He had the impression this wasn't the first time any of them had performed such a task. Something about the reverence with which they treated the fallen comforted him. It suggested the Order cared for its knights; that a life lost in battle wasn't forgotten.

Petor was the last to be wrapped up and placed on another's

horse. Crosbyn shook his head sadly. Noreina betrayed nothing but a clenched jaw, her sole eye glinting with steely determination.

Gar sat against a tree trunk, the bandage Crosbyn had applied to his thigh already stained red. The old knight had snapped off the arrow's shaft so only a finger's length of splintered wood projected from Gar's flesh.

"Reckon they're long gone," Orix said, clambering down from his tree.

"Nothing my end," Naul said. "But it's asking for trouble hanging around like this."

"The dead need to be cared for," Sareya said. "In case one day they rise."

"The dead don't rise," Naul scoffed. "They dissolve into stinking piles of pus and go back to the earth, nothing more."

"That's not what the *Book of Five Aspects* teaches," Anskar said. Those who suffered physical death were taken up into the balance of Menselas, where the Five existed as one undivided godhead.

Noreina shot them a disapproving look, then stepped away from the horse upon which she and Crosbyn had placed Petor's body.

Anskar was impatient to leave too. All the dead were ready to be moved out, and Gar could easily be helped onto a horse. Waiting here seemed an invitation for more trouble, but Gar cried out and clutched his stomach. He was shivering.

Crosbyn crouched beside him to inspect the wound around the arrow shaft embedded in Gar's thigh. "Doesn't look good," the sergeant said.

"You think the arrow was poisoned, Croz?" Vihtor asked.

Gar let out a whimper, his eyes feverish and bright.

"Doubt it," Crosbyn said, thought it was clear from the look he gave Vihtor that he thought it highly likely.

"This is my responsibility, Seneschal," Noreina said. "Whatever you say. I was the one in command."

"What do you want to do?" Vihtor asked.

"Make a dash for Quolith with the boy. One horse alone has a better chance of evading the rebels."

"They're bound to have the road covered," Vihtor said.

"I know that. I used to scout these lands during the war. I'll find another way."

After a long moment, Vihtor nodded. "Very well. We'll follow a little behind until you're in the clear, then we'll go our separate ways. Take Gar to Quolith, and if you make it, get them to send out a patrol to find us. We'll find a better place to make camp and sit out the night."

"And Petor!" Gar cried. He was hysterical, eyes wide with fright. Sweat dripped from his forehead. "He was my friend. We can't leave him out here for the dead-eyes to defile."

"You," Vihtor said to Naul. "You want to chance the ride to Quolith with them?"

When Naul didn't object, Noreina sighed. "Well, that halves our chances." She indicated he horse with Petor laid across its back. "Reckon you can ride with him behind?"

Naul looked as though he were going to be sick, but he nodded all the same and took hold of the bridle so he could mount.

"But no one else," Vihtor said. "The rest of us stick together and we'll get out of this alive."

"Course we will," Crosbyn said with what sounded like forced cheer.

"And the others?" Vaila said. "What about the rest of our fallen?"

"We take them with us," Vihtor said. "I'll leave no one behind for the dead-eyes."

"Good luck, Seneschal," Noreina said as she wheeled her mount to head back the way they had come.

"You, too, Commander. The Five lend you haste."

Naul leaned from the saddle of Petor's horse to touch Sareya lightly on the cheek in a gesture of farewell. Anskar looked away, a violent wave of emotion sweeping through him. He barely noticed as Noreina and Gar on one horse, Naul and dead Petor on the other, cantered away.

"He's just a friend," Sareya whispered as she brushed past him.

"Of course he is," Anskar replied.

When she turned back, her cat's eyes flashed with frustration. "I told you, I've changed."

A hand clapped Anskar on the shoulder. For a second, he feared it was Vihtor.

"Saddle up, lad," Crosbyn said. "I'll feel better without the cliff cutting off our options for escape."

TWENTY-FIVE

ANSKAR'S EYES WERE GLUED TO Vihtor's back as the Seneschal rode up front talking with Crosbyn. He didn't want to miss the slightest sign that Vihtor was unnerved; anything that might indicate how dire their situation had become.

Vaila, Myra, and Abizar rode at the rear, holding the reins of the horses that carried the dead.

Sareya brought her horse alongside Anskar's, but he barely spared her a glance.

"I meant what I said about Naul," she told him. "I'm not like that anymore."

When he didn't answer, she reached across from her saddle and gripped his hand holding the reins. "It's going to be all right," she said. "*We're* going to be all right."

Despite himself, he found himself smiling, and he gave Sareya a nod as she withdrew her hand. He wished it were true; that things between them would be all right, but how could they be when they were both under the rules of the Order? One day, perhaps, she would leave, or maybe he would! Then they would be free to be together. But was that what he wanted, he immediately wondered? And even if he did, would Sareya? She was born for things far greater than the consecrated knighthood, or marriage to the likes of him, he knew that now. During the fight with the rebels, her eyes blazing and dark vapors pluming from her fingertips, she had been the embodiment of sorcery. The way the Niyandrians had fled before her, they must have thought she was one of their ancient goddesses come down to Wiraya. The frightening thing was, Anskar felt certain she had only tapped a fraction of her true potential.

"You were taking a big risk using the dusk-tide back there," he said.

"When I saved you, you mean?"

He nodded. There was no getting away from the fact that he would have been as dead as Petor and the others had Sareya not come to his aid. "Have you drawn on the dusk-tide before?"

"Not in combat," she said, "and hardly at all before. It's too erratic, hard to control."

"It didn't look like you had much trouble controlling it to me," Anskar said. "Those vapors… How did you learn to do that?"

"I didn't think about whatever I did. The calculations and cants, they were instinctive. Maybe part of my heritage."

It had been the same for Anskar when he'd blasted Beof, the Warrior's priest, in the face with a fist of shadow: an eruption of power beyond his conscious control. He wondered if the catalyst beneath Sareya's skin hard darkened and grown cloudy as his had.

"It came naturally to me," Sareya continued. "As if I were born for it."

Which, of course, she was, according to her own people.

She was one of the moontouched. How much more could she have achieved, Anskar wondered, with the proper training and permissions?

"The power I used has changed something within me," she whispered to him. "There's a seething pool of…vitriol…just waiting for me to plunge into it."

Anskar nodded slowly, letting her see that he understood what she was referring to; that he'd experienced something similar himself.

Sareya's face paled and she swallowed thickly. "I did it for you, Anskar. I killed my own people to save you."

Anskar's heart skipped a beat, and he felt heat flood his cheeks. "You had no choice."

She shook her head. "The Niyandrians I killed… They will be within their rights to exact revenge when they rise."

"*If* they rise," Anskar said. "No one has actually risen." That's what he'd been told by Tion, and he'd seen no evidence to the contrary.

"The necromancer Tain rose," Sareya breathed.

"And you've seen him?"

"No, but… And Queen Talia will rise. You'll see."

"You don't know that," Anskar said. But neither did he know that the Necromancer Queen wouldn't rise. Perhaps she already had, in a way: in the golden-eyed crow—*Blackwing*. He remembered the woman's voice he'd heard in his head, at first speaking in Niyandrian, then in broken Nan-Rhouric.

A shiver ran along Anskar's spine. Should he tell Sareya what had happened to him at Hallow Hill? Vihtor had ordered him to speak of it to no one; but what if Sareya could help him make sense of all that had occurred since the fitting of his catalyst? Sareya was moontouched. Maybe her gift for sorcery granted her insights and intuitions he wasn't privy to. Maybe she knew something about the Necromancer Queen; about Naphor and the ruin atop Hallow Hill.

"Let's pick up the pace," Vihtor shouted from the front, and as the knights ahead sped up Anskar and Sareya urged their mounts to follow.

Within the hour, they had forded a stream and dismounted to freshen up and wolf down some rations. Orix disappeared into the brush to relieve himself but came running back blabbering like a simpleton. Crosbyn went with him to see the cause of his fright, then returned and beckoned the others to follow. At Vihtor's command, they tethered their horses and those carrying the dead to nearby trees and filed after the sergeant through the undergrowth.

On the other side of the natural boundary formed by the brush was an expanse of pasture land with the carcasses of dozens of cattle lying on the ground. Their flesh had been flayed from their bones, and pools of foul-smelling fluids spread beneath them. Flies swarmed over the dead animals.

On the far side of the field was a rough enclosure formed by drystone walls on three sides, with an open wooden gate on the fourth side. To the right of the enclosure stood a ramshackle barn, and a little way beyond was a thatched cottage with a covered verandah, upon which sat a rocking chair. Out front, a sturdy, white wooden fence defined a small garden.

The sound of Orix retching brought Anskar's attention back to the slaughtered cattle. His own guts rebelled against the stench, but he fought down the urge to be sick. The ground was still soft from an overnight rainfall, and the spoor of whatever had attacked the farmstead was clearly visible—a confusion of footprints beyond counting. Elongated footprints with the deep gashes of talons.

"Was it dead-eyes?" Myra asked. Her narrow face remained impassive, but her hands were shaking.

"Can you think of anything else that would do this?" Vihtor replied acerbically.

Orix straightened up, wiping drool from his chin. When he saw Vihtor's disapproving look, his face reddened. The giant, Abizar, placed a reassuring hand on Orix's shoulder, using his other hand to loosen the straps fastening his axe to his back.

Vaila frowned at the footprints surrounding the dead cattle. "Should've brought more knights," she grumbled. "Real knights, not callow youths who don't know their asses from their heads."

Crosbyn silenced her with a wag of his finger, then moved to stand with the Seneschal, who was gazing toward the cottage.

"She may have a point," Crosbyn said in a low voice, but not low enough that Anskar didn't overhear. The old knight was clearly going deaf and had yet to realize that didn't mean everyone else was too. "One or two slaughtered cows would be nothing out of the ordinary for dead-eyes, but so many… This must be one hell of a pack. Maybe an entire tribe. I should have listened to you."

"I was half joking," Vihtor said. "It's not even full-dark."

Anskar had heard the legends about how all night-stalkers— ghouls, changelings, the drinkers of blood—grew bold during the full-dark, the one day every month when both moons were absent from the night sky.

"Could it be all the construction?" Vaila asked. "I mean, what if we've displaced them from their nests?"

"Should we head back to the Burg?" Anskar asked, and felt heat rise to his face when Vihtor shot him a look that said he shouldn't have been listening in.

"It's not long till nightfall," Crosbyn said. "If we head back now, they may see us as prey and come after us. Not to mention, the rebels might still be out there, waiting for us to double back."

"I just hope Gar and the others made it," Myra said. "He seemed so scared."

Sareya cocked an eyebrow at Anskar that seemed to ask whether Myra was sweet on Gar. Anskar had certainly seen no sign of it, and besides, Myra wasn't the sort to risk transgressing the Order's rules. She was too much a stickler.

"Out in the open, we'd be helpless against a large group of dead-eyes," Vihtor said. "Alone, they are cautious creatures, but with the advantage of numbers, they will swarm us mercilessly."

"You know what dead-eyes do with those they kill?" Vaila asked the knights-liminal.

"I have a good idea," Anskar said.

"No, you don't."

Vihtor held up a staying hand. "Anskar faced a solitary dead-eye by himself."

Vaila snorted. "Don't mean nothing. I tell you, the things I seen them do…to friends who fell…" She looked away and spat into the dirt.

"Even if we manage to get away," Orix said, "what will they do to the other smallholders in the area?"

Abizar gave him a nod of respect, clearly understanding more Nan-Rhouric than he could speak.

"Spoken like a Knight of the Order of Eternal Vigilance," Vihtor said, and Orix couldn't hide his flush of pride. "We have a duty to protect."

"We could hole up in the cottage for the night," Myra suggested.

"Yes," Vihtor said, "we could."

Crosbyn winked at her, letting her know she had spoken well.

"I concur," Abizar said. "Defend easy. Draw deads to us."

"To which end, we will need bait," Vihtor said. "Something the deads will see as easy prey." He scanned each of them in turn, eyes coming to rest on Sareya.

"Let it be me," Anskar said.

"What?" Vihtor said.

"If anyone's to be bait—"

"I think you misunderstand the Seneschal," Crosbyn said.

"I was merely reflecting on each of our strengths and weaknesses," Vihtor said. "It is a fault of mine, being able to think of more than one thing at a time."

Anskar felt foolish. He needed to learn to keep his mouth shut, and to suspend his judgment of others. Tion had told him as much countless times, but he was only now starting to realize what the healer had meant.

"The horses?" Myra suggested.

With an air of reluctance, Vihtor nodded. "We'll have to bury the dead first. I'll not leave them for the dead-eyes. I don't like it, but what choice do we have? I doubt we could get the horses inside the cottage anyway."

"They'll be slaughtered," Anskar said, already forgetting his intention. He couldn't bear the thought of Fellswain ending up like the cows. She deserved an honorable death, not defilement.

"Vaila, check out the barn," Vihtor said. "We need planks to reinforce the garden fence and make it higher. If necessary, strip them from the barn walls. The stones from the enclosure too; as many as we have time to move. I want the horses in front of the house, and just the one way in." He pointed at the narrow gateway.

"A killing ground?" Crosbyn said, sticking out his bottom lip.

"Some are bound to get through. We may still lose the horses."

Vihtor shook his head. "Anskar and Sareya will ward them." When Anskar started to protest that it was impossible, Vihtor said, "I have full confidence in you. In both of you."

The Seneschal turned back to Vaila. "Take Abizar with you and start moving wood and stones to the front of the cottage. Orix, Sareya, Myra, fetch the horses and tether them to the verandah. After that, help Vaila and Abizar. Anskar, with me. Let's take a look inside."

Anskar immediately felt his chest tighten. As he breathed in shallow gasps, he tried to imagine the sword of the Warrior, to anchor himself in its steadfastness.

Out of the corner of his eye he saw Vaila and Abizar making their way to the enclosure; Myra, Sareya, and Orix going back for the horses. As he approached the cottage side by side with Vihtor, his vision narrowed as if a corridor had closed in on him. *Something is wrong*, his senses screamed. *Something terrible happened here.*

They entered the garden through its narrow wooden gate. Within were rectangular wooden boxes filled with soil from which sprouted cabbage, spinach and the tops of carrots. There were tomatoes growing up stakes against one side of the fence, and roses all the way around the rest of the fence. Now they were closer, Anskar could see that the windows of the cottage had been shattered. Most of the glass had fallen inside, though a scatter of shards lay on the verandah amid muddy, taloned footprints.

Vihtor reached for the doorknob and turned it. It was locked. A woman's scream sounded from inside. Anskar started, but Vihtor showed no reaction. The scream came again, this time a long, agonized wail.

"Quickly!" Anskar cried. "Someone's inside. In trouble."

Vihtor gave him a bewildered look, then put his shoulder to the door. On the third attempt, the door flew open and Anskar followed Vihtor into a narrow entrance hall.

A frayed woolen coat hung from a peg inside the door, next to an oil painting of the cottage and its surrounds—poorly executed, the paint lumpy in places, the colors thin and running into each other.

"Blood," Vihtor said, nostrils flaring.

Anskar could smell it too: sickly-sweet. And there was something else—the stench of human waste.

The screaming gave way to an anguished moan of despair. Still Vihtor showed no sign of having heard it. The vambrace on Anskar's arm felt icy cold when he touched it through his shirt.

The hallway opened into a kitchen, where a dining table and chair had been overturned. Scraps of food littered the floor, along with what looked like excrement.

There were doors either side of the hallway. Vihtor took the one on the right, which had been smashed apart. The left-hand door was intact, closed but not locked. Anskar opened it.

Inside was a cozy reading room. Unlike the kitchen, nothing seemed to have been disturbed. Maybe because there was nothing edible here. There was an armchair, a circular side table, and an open hearth, the coals long since dead and coated with ash. A bookcase covered one wall; the spines of the books were embossed with Niyandrian writing. In front of the bookcase was a stringed musical instrument on a stand—it resembled a violin, only was far larger and had twelve strings rather than the customary four.

As Anskar backed out of the room, he again heard the groans of a woman in torment. This time he was certain they came from the room Vihtor had entered. He crossed the hallway and stepped through the splintered remains of the door. There was blood in the room. A lot of blood. It spattered the walls and floor, and there were even spots on the ceiling. The stench made him gag.

Vihtor was kneeling beside the body of a woman, praying. Or rather, what was left of her. Surely she couldn't still be alive, and yet Anskar had heard someone screaming and groaning. He had to look away from her slack-jawed, sightless stare.

The room was a bedroom: its quilted bedcover crumpled and bloodstained; the pillows ripped to shreds, their downy filling all over the place. An overturned lamp had spilled oil onto the floor. Around the walls were paintings, mostly portraits of the same Niyandrian woman; some just of her face, focusing on her feline eyes, but one or two showed her full body, naked.

Anskar looked back to the corpse on the floor, noting her red skin. She must be the artist. This must have been a house of tranquility, judging by the books, the music, the paintings. A life far removed from the hustle and bustle of the towns; caring for livestock, growing her own food. An ideal way to live. Until the dead-eyes came.

Vihtor stood. "I'd say she's been dead some time…at least a day."

"And you found no one else?" Anskar asked. "No one alive?"

"No one."

"But…" Anskar was going to say that he had heard a woman scream, but with the cold crawl of dread on his skin, he remembered the desiccated corpse in the crypt that had spoken to him, and was afraid to say more. He winced as he looked again at the corpse. There were gashes and gouges all over the body, and the flaking crust of dried fluids—blood, and other things he didn't want to think about.

"But what?" Vihtor prompted.

Anskar's voice was little more than a whisper. "What did they do to her?"

Vihtor placed a hand on his shoulder. "Some questions are best left unanswered. Come, help me get her outside. If there's time, we'll bury her along with our own dead once the fence has been reinforced."

"And if there's not?"

"We have to be pragmatic, Anskar. Do what we can, not what we would wish to."

Vihtor wrapped the corpse in the quilted bedcover, and together they carried her outside, where Sareya, Myra, and Orix were leading the horses into the garden.

"Tether them to the verandah," Vihtor said. "Put the bodies on the ground. Myra, take a look in the barn; see if you can find a shovel or something else to dig with. Make a start on the graves; they'll need to be deep if the dead-eyes aren't to get to the bodies."

Myra opened her mouth to protest. "Don't tell me this isn't what your family signed you up for," Vihtor said. "You're part of a team now. My job is to give orders; yours is to obey. Now!"

Chin quivering, eyes glistening with tears, Myra hurried off toward the barn.

"After that, help Vaila and Abizar fetch wood and stones," Vihtor called after her. The Seneschal pinched the bridge of his nose. He sounded like a man in pain as he added, "Orix, go with her."

Vihtor and Anskar went back into the house to check points of entry and egress. There was only one other door, at the rear of the cottage, and they barricaded it with a large chest of drawers.

"Dead-eyes might be fast, but they're not particularly strong,"

Vihtor explained. "And we can easily move the chest of drawers aside if we need to get out in a hurry."

"What about the roof?" Anskar asked. "The thatch outside is patchy, and the ceiling's sagging in places."

Vihtor looked up. "Deads are agile; they'll get up there easy enough. We have to assume they'll come in from above. If we fall back inside the cottage, direct your ward at the ceiling and flatten it out. You know how to do that?"

"Frae Ganwen didn't—"

"Of course you don't," Vihtor said, face taut with frustration. "You've only just passed the trials. You won't learn that until next year. Do you have anything to write with?"

Anskar shook his head, then remembered the reading room. "Back in a moment," he said, and returned with a charcoal stick and a piece of parchment from the bookcase.

Vihtor squinted at the Niyandrian writing. "What was she, a librarian?" He rested the parchment on the chest of drawers and scratched out a sequence of numbers and Skanuric symbols on its back. "Here," he said, handing it to Anskar. "Memorize this, and have the others do the same. On second thoughts, just Sareya. Orix will be more use fighting with us knights. And Myra… Well, maybe she could make the tea."

"Seneschal!" Anskar said, then realized the tone he had taken. "Forgive me, but there's more to Myra than it seems. She's a great runner, and during the trials…"

"Yes, a very calculated and clever fighter. You have nothing for me to forgive, Anskar. I am duly chastised. And please, correct me if I speak ill of any of you again. This is my fault, and I've no right to take it out on Myra."

Anskar didn't know how to handle the Seneschal's apology; couldn't tell if it were a mark of strength or weakness.

He glanced at the calculations and cants. They were virtually the same as for a standard ward-casting, with one or two slight variations. He was certain he could commit them to memory without much trouble.

"I can fight," he said. "And so can Sareya."

"Only if you have to. We each have a part to play; and it's critical you follow orders, if we're to survive the night."

In the kitchen, they found a tool chest containing chisels, a mallet, a hammer, and a rusty saw. In the bottom were an assortment of nails, many of them bent from being used before.

"Not enough for the fence," Vihtor said. "Hopefully they found more tools in the barn. If need be they can reuse the nails from the planks they strip from the barn walls. What we need to do is smash up the furniture and use the wood to cover the windows. It won't keep the deads out, but it will buy us time."

"So, first we defend the garden and the horses," Anskar said, getting the plan straight in his head. "But if we're pushed back, we retreat to the cottage?"

"And if we're overwhelmed in here," Vihtor said, "there's the back door. Not that I fancy our chances in the open."

"So, we hold them off for as long as we can, and pray for morning?" Anskar said.

"That's about it."

"What about the Niyandrian rebels? Do you think they'll come after us?"

"If they were going to finish us off, they've had plenty of opportunities," Vihtor said. "I suspect they didn't like what Sareya did to them. Neither did I," he added, "but I can't deny that I'm glad she did it. Besides, if the rebels have been following us, they'll know about the dead-eyes by now. If they have any sense, they'll be far away before night falls and the fun begins.

Dead-eyes make no distinction between mainlanders and Niyandrians. We're all just meat to them."

The sound of hammering came from out front. When they went to investigate, they found Abizar adding planks to the already sturdy garden fence. Beside him sat a steel pail filled with nails he must have found in the barn. So far he had added two planks stripped from the barn, which increased the height of the fence to approximately six feet. Abizar indicated with gestures that he intended to increase the height all around, then reinforce the fence with horizontals.

"If there are enough planks," Anskar said.

Vihtor shrugged. "There should be. It's a sizable barn. The only issue is time."

Sareya was tethering the last of their seven horses to the verandah railing. The animals seemed unperturbed by the hammering and were already busy cropping the grass. She went to help Vaila, who was loading stones from the walls of the enclosure into a handcart.

Anskar took over the grave-digging from Orix, who looked worn out from his efforts. Myra was slumped on the ground beside the pit as if she'd done all the work.

"She started it off for me," Orix said.

Myra scowled. "I did more than that." She held up her palms to show where the skin was torn and red.

They had made good progress, digging a shallow hole just large enough to hold the Niyandrian and the three knights they'd lost; but it needed to be deeper, to prevent all manner of carrion eaters digging the bodies up at the first opportunity. Anskar put his back into the work, wanting it over and done with as soon as possible. Flies buzzed about the quilt-covered body, and the smell was overpowering, even outside.

Despite being fatigued, Orix made his way to the barn and stripped more planks from the walls for Abizar to use on the fence. Myra remained where she was, but she had a grim look on her face as she took out her sword and tested its edge.

"Still keen," she said. "I suppose that's something."

Vihtor coughed into his fist, causing Myra to look up. "For what I said earlier," the Seneschal said. "How I behaved. I'm sorry, Myra. You have my respect for how you've handled yourself on this mission. I would like to offer you my blessing."

Myra swallowed thickly; glanced at Anskar, then dutifully bowed her head. The Seneschal held splayed his hand above her and uttered a prayer so fast Anskar couldn't distinguish the words.

As soon as he was done, Vihtor hurried back inside the house, and Anskar heard hammering and crashing as the Seneschal broke up the furniture to barricade the windows.

TWENTY-SIX

IT WAS DUSK BEFORE VIHTOR called a break. In the steely
light, they sat on the cottage's verandah eating salted jerky and
finishing off the last water in their canteens. When she'd found
the shovel earlier, Myra had located a well beyond the barn, but
Vihtor wouldn't hear of her going alone to refill the canteens.
Crosbyn went with her, and Vaila kept watch over them from
a distance. The odd thing was, Anskar thought, that Myra had
offered to bring water for everyone. Something had changed since
her run-in with Vihtor; since the Seneschal's apology and blessing.

No one expected the dead-eyes to come until it was dark. When
Orix suggested they might not come at all, Vihtor chastised him,
saying that when it came to deads, always expect the worst. Besides
which, it was far better for the dead-eyes to attack here rather than
a defenseless farmstead somewhere else. For his penance, Orix
was ordered to clear up the mess the horses had made in the front
garden and cast their manure outside the gate.

After Crosbyn and Abizar had returned with the filled canteens, Anskar and Orix lowered the Niyandrian woman's wrapped corpse into the grave along with the bodies of their comrades.

Sareya knelt by the graveside and placed a single copper coin on the bundled-up body. Anskar saw that it was an old Niyandrian queen, stamped with the necromancer Talia's image. Vihtor's jaw clenched, but he said nothing.

Anskar assumed it must be a Niyandrian custom. Maybe there was a fee to be paid before the dead could return to life—although that sounded more like something the Church of Menselas would insist upon; and no doubt the Patriarch would put the coin toward the basilica he was supposed to be building, if he didn't spend it on himself.

Anskar stopped himself from thinking any further; whatever the truth of the matter, his mounting cynicism wasn't going to help him become the knight he had resolved to be.

He wondered briefly if the risen dead would remain sentient, or instead become slavish automatons bound to the will of one of their necromancer gods. Had that been the plan of Queen Talia, to rule over an empire of the mindless dead? If it had, he was glad the Order and its allies had put an end to her reign.

"You think it's deep enough?" Myra asked.

"You'd like to lift the bodies out and continue digging," Vihtor said, "as the sky grows darker and the dead-eyes creep nearer?" There was an uncharacteristic twinkle in his eye; the barest hint of a smile.

Myra laughed. "It's deep enough," she said, then threw on the first handful of dirt.

Taking that as his cue, Orix grabbed the shovel and began to cover the bodies with soil. Then they each took turns, as if sharing the labor also divided up the grief. As if working as a team now would pay dividends later, if and when it came to fighting for their lives.

As the first stars peeked through the canopy of night and the merest slivers of the twin moons rose, silver and red, Vihtor led them in prayers for the dead.

After the ceremony, the Seneschal spoke quietly to Vaila, who disappeared inside the house. Moments later, a soft light bled through the hairline cracks in the boarded-up window of the reading room.

"You two, go inside," Vihtor told Anskar and Sareya. "Vaila's used an illumination cant so you can study the calculations I wrote down for you. You don't have much time, so do the best you can."

Sareya frowned her incomprehension at Anskar.

"We need to be able to flatten our wards out so we can reinforce the ceiling, should it come to it," he explained.

Sareya shrugged as if it were a simple matter—which it probably was for her.

Together they went inside and found Vaila taking a rest in the reading room's armchair. Clearly, Vihtor had instructed her to stay so that Anskar and Sareya wouldn't be left alone; although what the Seneschal thought they might get up to under such circumstances was beyond Anskar.

The illumination cant took the form of an iridescent globe on the headstock of the oversized violin-like instrument; it gave off a gentle, pearly glow. Anskar drew the crumpled piece of parchment from his pocket and held it so Sareya could see it. Together, they mouthed the symbols and numbers along with the Skanuric cants.

After only one read-through, Sareya said she had it and went back outside. Anskar wondered if she had already known the calculations. Either that, or she had the ability to scan the sequence and instantly memorize it. An ability like that would make her the envy of any sorcerer.

He continued to study the parchment until he was distracted by a loud snore. Vaila had dozed off in the armchair. Trusting that he had learned the alterations to his ward's calculations, Anskar folded the parchment and tucked it away in his pocket. He shook Vaila awake, and she cursed at him, then mumbled a cant that doused her arcane light.

They joined the others on the verandah, where Crosbyn was whispering to the horses and feeding them handfuls of oats. Anskar patted Fellswain's flank and nuzzled her face.

"You'll be fine, girl," he whispered. "And when this is all over, I'll ride you back home to Larson, just you see."

Abizar handed Anskar and Vaila each a bundle of dried herbs. It smelled of sage and rosemary.

"To disguise your natural scent," Vihtor explained. "Otherwise we might frighten off the deads before we can spring our trap."

"That I sincerely doubt," Vaila said. "Not if this pack's as big as I think it is. If it's a tribe, we're done for."

Vihtor rolled his eyes. "Nevertheless, I have faith we'll see this through."

Abizar chuckled and settled himself in the rocking chair, staring out at the gathering dark, his huge war axe resting in his lap. There was a fierce glint in his eyes, as if he relished the idea of a battle with a horde of dead-eyes.

"Remember, your job is to protect the horses," Vihtor told Sareya and Anskar. "Orix and Myra, stay back behind us four knights. If any of us fall, fill the gap. If the dead-eyes get past us, protect Anskar and Sareya. And if we are overrun, everyone fall back inside the cottage. In that event, the horses will have to fend for themselves, and we'll likely be walking back to Dorinah. If we leave here at all.

"Now, don't forget: we let them into the garden, as many as possible. As soon as they're within a few feet of the horses, draw on your dawn-tide: wards up and attack. If there are more outside, Abizar and I will hold the gateway while Croz— Sergeant Crosbyn," he amended, "and Vaila will take the others in the back."

Crosbyn moved away from the horses, and he and Vihtor conferred in low voices. Vaila finished rubbing on the herb scent, then sat on the edge of the verandah, checking her sword slid free of its scabbard without effort as she muttered to herself. Orix already had his sword in hand and was casting nervous looks into the shadows. Myra, at his side, was a study in calm, hand resting on the hilt of her sheathed sword, eyes narrowed in concentration as if she were playing out in her mind all that might happen and rehearsing what she might do in response.

Sareya stood in the open doorway of the cottage. Anskar sensed her casting out feelers of dawn-tide sorcery.

"Soon it'll be too dark to see," Orix grumbled.

Vaila snorted, and Abizar let out a low, rumbling laugh.

"Once they come," Vihtor explained, "we'll be able to see by the light of our wards. But until then, we wait in the dark. Anskar, if you have any control over your senses, now is the time to cast them wide."

Anskar tried to let his senses roam out beyond the garden fence. He shook his head in frustration. He was too tense.

Anskar caught Sareya's gaze. Then he felt the merest stroke of her senses in his mind, and a wave of warmth passed through him. His muscles unclenched, and suddenly he could feel the sway of the grass outside the fence, and the attentive gaze of some night bird high up in a distant tree.

He shut his eyes the better to concentrate. He sensed the putrefying carcasses of the cattle they had found in the pasture, and withdrew. When he opened his eyes, the darkness seemed to have thickened and crept farther across the garden.

"Nothing," he muttered, then repeated it louder.

Vihtor was no more than a denser patch of darkness over by the gate, but Anskar felt certain the Seneschal had nodded.

As his eyes adjusted, he began to distinguish shapes according to their gradations of darkness: his companions, the fence, the treetops in the distance. He felt drawn to where the darkness pooled the most opaquely, shadows upon the shadow of night. He focused on a particularly black patch on the ground in front of the verandah, where they had buried the Niyandrian woman and their fallen comrades. The heavy dark tugged at him, and he felt himself drawn into it, little by little losing himself in its inky density. If only he could let go and pour himself into the thicker blackness, he would find himself in the grave with them.

The thought broke the spell and he physically recoiled.

"What is it?" Sareya asked.

"I don't know. Nothing…maybe."

Somewhere at the back of his mind, Anskar became aware of a woman whimpering. It was coming from the grave, he realized. The sound increased to a groan, a cry, a scream…

"They're coming!" he hissed.

He heard the collective intake of breath from his companions.

"I see something moving beyond the gate," Myra said.

Vihtor silenced her with a gesture.

Abizar rose from the rocking chair and walked to one side of the gate, cradling his axe.

Crosbyn and Vaila advanced halfway up the garden, keeping close to the fence left and right. Sareya remained in the doorway, the horses between her and the garden, and Anskar moved beside her.

Orix stood dithering, not certain where his position should be. Quietly, Myra directed Orix to the far side of the verandah, in front of the rocking chair Abizar had just abandoned. At least from there he had an overview of the entire garden and was well placed to go to the aid of whoever needed him most. Myra positioned herself next to Sareya, as if she had decided to protect the Niyandrian while she used sorcery to ward the horses.

"Look!" Sareya whispered.

Anskar squinted where she pointed, out past the gate, but at first he couldn't see anything. His sorcerous senses, though, writhed in agitation; and in her grave, the Niyandrian woman cried out once more then stilled, as if she held her breath despite being a whole day dead.

The rattle of the gate sent Anskar's hand to the hilt of his sword.

"Wards, remember?" Sareya whispered in his ear.

He nodded and tried to get a hold of himself. He glanced at Orix, expecting to see his friend looking anxious and unsure too. Instead, Orix had taken a step off the verandah and placed his sword tip on the ground, resting his hands on the pommel. Gone was the usual slump of his shoulders; he stood tall and proud and ready. In that moment, Anskar felt certain that no matter what happened, Orix would do his duty and do it well.

With a rasping hiss, Myra's sword came free of its scabbard. She licked her lips and swallowed, her blade wavering in her grip.

The gate rattled again, and this time Anskar saw pallid fingers curl over the top, followed by a head, and then a leg as the creature rolled over the gate and came to a crouch in the garden. Shrouded by the dark, it was little more than a pale, stick-thin ghost. As it crept forward on all fours, another dead-eye clambered over the gate, then another.

None of the knights moved; all deathly silent. Waiting…

More and more of the sickly-looking figures climbed into the garden and cautiously edged toward the verandah—at least a dozen of them. The horses began to stomp and whinny, and the dead-eyes, drawn by anxious prey, surged forward.

"Now!" Vihtor yelled, a spherical ward of silver springing to life around him.

All over the garden more wards ignited, though Orix's was stuttering and patchy. At the same time, Anskar and Sareya cast their wards wide to encompass the horses. At first, Anskar found it a strain and Sareya did most of the work; but little by little he matched her as he relaxed and coaxed the dawn-tide flow from his repository.

The dead-eyes recoiled from the silver barrier that flared in front of them. They turned and scattered—straight into the swords of Crosbyn, Vaila and Vihtor. In the glare of sorcerous wards, scintillant blades hacked, thrust, and cleaved. The garden devolved into a chaos of pallid limbs, raking claws and gurgling howls. Silvery motes flew up from the knights' wards as the deads tried to gouge through them, then fell. It was a brutal, efficient slaying; but the battle wasn't over yet.

Anskar saw the blaze of Abizar's ward as the giant swung his axe in great scything blows, cutting down the deads swarming through the gate. But in the end, their weight of numbers prevailed and the gate shattered. The creatures spilled into the garden, and Abizar was forced onto the back foot. Still he fought furiously, cleaving flesh and bone, spraying their milky blood with his massive axe.

Vihtor rushed to the giant's aid, thrusting and slashing; then Vaila and Crosbyn came to his support—a wall of three blades, their sorcerous wards overlapping, throwing off cascades of sparks where the dead-eyes struck. But they dared not draw too close to Abizar, who needed a wide arc in which to swing his axe. Although the giant reaped left and right, fore and aft, he was isolated and surrounded.

Myra saw the danger just as Anskar did, and called out instructions to Orix. With a cry in whatever passed for language in the Plains of Khisig-Ugtall, Orix slammed into the dead-eyes flanking Abizar and cut them down in a fury.

The deads were fast, though, and while many fell to sword and axe, others bounded past to crash in wave after wave against the wards Anskar and Sareya had erected around the horses. Each blow weakened the arcane barrier, and Anskar had to pour more and more dawn-tide energy into its construction. He knew he couldn't hold it much longer. It was only a matter of time.

Sareya stumbled as another wave of deads slammed into their wards. At first Anskar thought she was going to fall, that her part of the ward would collapse; but then her eyes blazed white, and he sensed the build-up of dusk-tide sorcery within her.

She threw out her palms and the ground beneath the dead-eyes erupted in a blinding conflagration. The creatures screeched in agony. The horses reared and bumped against the wards protecting them, desperate to bolt. When the fire died down, a score of charred corpses lay on the ground: dead-eyes burned alive.

The elation Anskar felt was short-lived. As he blinked flash-blindness from his eyes, he saw the four knights and Orix fighting a frantic rearguard action. Orix's ward was steadier now, as if the rage of battle had calmed him and let his sorcerous defenses flow. Abizar was tiring, his axe swings lacking power, his spherical ward frayed and flickering.

Vaila and Crosbyn fought calmly side by side, taking grudging steps back as they thrust their blades into the dead-eyes. The problem was, they were running out of room. Their retreat was taking them straight toward the sorcerous barrier protecting the horses. They seemed to be aware of the danger, trying to move laterally past the edge of the ward and toward the verandah; but then the deads attacked their flank with a fury. With a sigh of resignation, Myra ran from the verandah to help them.

Anskar's portion of the horse ward fizzed and went out. Instantly, Sareya's expanded to cover it, and at the same time she slung a blast of dusk-tide at the deads flanking Vaila and Crosbyn. But her sorcery was weaker this time, and only a couple of deads went down, thrashing in flames.

One of the creatures turned, causing Myra's advance to falter. As Myra backed away, the dead-eye stalked toward her. Anskar started forward, but then he saw that Myra's retreat had been a ruse. As the dead-eye sprang, Myra stepped to the side and slammed her blade two-handed into the creature's neck. Milky blood sprayed and the dead-eye slumped to the ground, its head half-severed.

Anskar drew *Amalantril* and moved around the edge of Sareya's ward, intending to throw himself into the group of deads blocking Crosbyn and Vaila's path to the verandah. He glimpsed Orix cutting about him with merciless blows, driving deads back from the ailing Abizar, and his heart swelled for his friend.

And then, as dead-eyes pressed in from every side, Vihtor's ward gave off a coruscating shower of sparks…and died. Vihtor had lagged behind, no doubt giving the others a better chance to withdraw. He whirled about furiously, hacking and slashing, and deads fell all around him; but no sooner had he killed one than two more took its place. Anskar cried out, despairing of reaching the Seneschal.

His eyes were drawn to the deep pools of darkness at the foot of the fence, toward which Vihtor's melee was inexorably pulling him. As had happened with the grave earlier, Anskar felt the shadows tugging at him, drawing him in. He uttered a long wailing cry as he felt himself become the very shadows. Somehow, he appeared next to Vihtor, grabbed him, and without knowing what he was doing, pulled the Seneschal with him back into the shadows. In the blink of an eye they both stood in the darkened doorway of the cottage.

A few feet in front of them, Sareya's ward still encompassed the horses, though sparks and motes flew off it from the dead-eyes' unrelenting attack.

Vihtor stumbled, then grabbed Anskar by the throat. "What have you done?"

Anskar was too stunned to respond. He didn't know what he had done—what had happened. One moment he had been staring at the shadows around Vihtor, and the next he'd been beside him, pulling him into the darkness.

Releasing Anskar, Vihtor stormed onto the verandah, crying out above the snarls and howls, "To me! Fall back!"

The Seneschal started forward into the fray, but Myra restrained him with a hand on his shoulder. "You're not protected! I'll go."

"No, I will," Anskar said. "I'll help the others."

A scintillant, multicolored ward sprang into existence around Anskar, born from the dusk-tide. Myra's eyes widened in shock at the spectacle of the tainted ward. Vihtor looked as though he had seen a ghost. Without waiting for permission, Anskar charged into the dead-eyes that were assailing Sareya's ward, hacking left and right with *Amalantril*. Milky blood arced in the sword's wake.

"No!" Vihtor cried. "Anskar!"

But the battle lust was upon Anskar, and he surged deeper into the horde, heading toward the silvery radiance of a ward.

Orix had surpassed himself, extending his ward to encompass Abizar. The big man was exhausted, bleeding from a score of cuts and gashes; barely able to support his weight on his injured leg. His war axe was drenched in milky blood, though now he leaned on its haft as if it were a crutch.

Fighting his way to their side, Anskar yelled for Orix to get back to the cottage; but in that instant, Orix's ward failed in a cascade of sparks, and a dead-eye pounced, knocking him to the ground.

Before Anskar could react, Abizar swung his axe, slicing the creature in two. The big man stumbled and almost fell, but steadied himself and pulled Orix to his feet. Beating back dead-eye after dead-eye with fluid swings of his axe, despite his wounded leg, Abizar got the two of them to the verandah.

Anskar came under renewed assault. So furious was the attack that he couldn't see beyond the prismatic sparks coming off his wards. He lashed out blindly with his sword, connecting with soft flesh and eliciting a keening howl. But the assault continued, and he staggered under the impacts rocking his ward, thump after thump after thump... And then his dusk-tide repository failed and the arcane ward vanished. With howls of triumph, dead-eyes swarmed over him.

Dark-tide erupted from within him, throwing up a ward of perfect blackness; slinging dozens of deads into the air and creating a channel through which he could see Crosbyn and Vaila. They were still fighting a tight retreat side by side, their silver wards firm. Clearly they knew the secret of managing their dawn-tide energy. Seeing the opening Anskar's eruption of dark-tide had made, they backed into it, and together the three of them reached the verandah.

Dead-eyes beyond counting continued to pour through the gate into the garden.

"Everyone inside!" Vihtor yelled. "You first," he told Sareya.

"But the horses—"

"Now!"

Darkness fell as Sareya's massive ward winked out and she ran inside the house. Orix followed, supporting Abizar; then Myra; then Vihtor.

"You next," Crosbyn said to Anskar. "We'll hold them."

With shrieks of fury, the dead-eyes tore into the horses.

Fellswain!

As Anskar dropped his dark-tide ward and ran through the doorway, he fought back tears at the whinnies and screams.

Vaila came through after him; then Crosbyn. The instant they were all inside, Vihtor slammed the door shut.

Already, Orix and Myra were bringing the bed out of the bedchamber. Despite her wiry appearance, the rich girl from Sansor seemed every bit as strong as she had been fast when they raced around the Burg. Once the others had moved into the kitchen, they used it to barricade the door.

"It'll never hold," Anskar said.

"It's not supposed to, lad," Crosbyn said. "Just need to buy some time to catch our breath."

The screaming of the horses seemed to go on forever, but eventually the dead-eyes must have finished with them, for they began a terrible hammering on the door. Clawed hands burst through the wood, then ripped away shards and splinters. The bed slowed them down a little, but bit by bit the door disintegrated and the bed quickly followed.

Down the corridor the dead-eyes came, a screeching mass of fangs and claws and boiled-egg eyes.

Vaila stepped into the open doorway of the kitchen, sword held limply in one hand, shoulders stooped with fatigue.

"Vaila!" Vihtor said. "We face them together."

"Shut it," Vaila snarled, not taking her eyes from the surge of dead-eyes. "Seneschal," she added as an afterthought.

The creatures were ten feet from her, and still she didn't raise her sword.

Five feet.

Two…

Vaila's dawn-tide ward burst forth in front of her, a wall of silvery force. With a flick of her wrist she drove it outward, slamming it into the dead-eyes and pulverizing them. Shrieks turned into howls of pain, and milky blood spattered the walls and ceiling.

Vaila drove her flattened ward down, pulping the fallen deads against the floor; then her knees buckled and she slumped.

Vihtor caught her, dragged her back into the kitchen, and Crosbyn replaced her in the doorway as a fresh wave of dead-eyes rushed in through the shattered front door.

Anskar heard Abizar groan and then growl behind him. He turned to see the big man push himself to his feet, against Orix's protests. Abizar was shivering and drenched with sweat, and his dozens of wounds wept blood.

The scratch of taloned feet on the floor made Anskar spin back toward the kitchen doorway and the renewed press of snarling dead-eyes. Many slipped in the remains of their predecessors, but they kept coming—until Crosbyn's ward hammered them from their feet and crushed them against the floor.

Like Vaila before him, Crosbyn reeled with exhaustion. Before Vihtor could support him, Abizar was there, shoving Crosbyn to one side and stepping into the breach.

Abizar glanced back at Vihtor. Their eyes met, and the big man gave a solemn nod, then turned to face the horde.

"Fall back," Vihtor ordered. "To the rear exit."

"But Abizar—" Orix protested.

Myra tried to drag Orix back, but he refused to budge.

The foremost dead-eyes sprang at the big man. Abizar's axe came down, cleaving through a skull. He slammed an elbow into another's face, shattering bone; tried to swing his axe again, but there wasn't the space. He let the axe go and pounded the dead-eyes with his massive fists.

Anskar expected Abizar to go down under a mountain of deads, but his strength was prodigious. The big man battered and slammed, kicked and roared, and earned himself a brief respite due to the wall of corpses at his feet. As the dead-eyes ripped into their own fallen, snarling and rending, Abizar took the opportunity to glare at his comrades for not having left yet.

Sareya was first to cross the kitchen and pass into the room at the rear of the house, where Anskar and Vihtor had barricaded the back door with the chest of drawers. Vaila went with her, pale and haggard, yet still clutching her sword. When Orix refused to leave Abizar, Vihtor nodded at Crosbyn, who helped Myra to drag Orix away.

Deads were now climbing over the wall of corpses and leaping for Abizar's throat. The big man clobbered them in mid-flight, but always more came. He looked every inch a giant to Anskar, an immovable object.

But then Abizar glanced back at Vihtor, gave a fierce grin, and said in his broken Nan-Rhouric, "Goodbye." He caught a leaping dead-eye by the throat with one hand, and with the other slammed the kitchen door shut behind him and was lost from sight.

"The table," Vihtor said, "quickly!"

Anskar was numb as he helped the Seneschal upend the kitchen table and wedge it against the door. With a lump in his throat and tears threatening to spill from his burning eyes, he followed Vihtor toward the back door.

For a moment, Abizar's voice rose in song above the snarls of the dead-eyes—booming, strident, full of triumph. And then he screamed, and the dead-eyes' shrieks swelled to a crescendo.

"They're at the rear of the cottage too," Crosbyn reported, stepping away from the chest of drawers that still barricaded the door. His face was gray with exhaustion.

Vihtor swore, then seemed to catch himself and touched four fingers and thumb to his forehead.

"To the death, then," Vaila growled.

Sareya flashed a look at Anskar. Still he couldn't read her eyes, but he felt certain it was a look of defiance; a refusal to accept their fate.

Myra's thin face was mask-like, her jaw set with resolve. The hand gripping her sword no longer shook as she tested her ward sphere, causing it to flicker in and out of existence.

Orix gripped his sword so tightly his knuckles were all bone. But it wasn't fear, Anskar realized. Orix's face was red with rage, his eyes hard with the promise of vengeance.

"For Abizar," Orix muttered, almost to himself. He met Anskar's eyes and said it again: "For Abizar."

Anskar nodded and drew in a long breath, which interrupted by thuds from the ceiling.

"They're on the roof," Vihtor said. "Anskar—"

"My dawn-tide repository is empty," Anskar said.

When Vihtor switched his gaze to Sareya, she said, "Mine too."

"I could—" Myra started, her ward sphere blazing around her.

Vihtor clamped a hand on her shoulder. "Save your dawn-tide essence," he told her. "This"—he indicated the ceiling with a nod—"is beyond you, just as it's beyond me."

She nodded, and her chin began to quiver.

"Stay strong," Vihtor told her. "We still need you."

"Seneschal," Anskar said, "with your permission…"

The implication hung heavy in the air. Dawn-tide wasn't the only power he possessed. And neither was the dusk. Vihtor, he knew, must have sensed that as they passed through the shadows in the garden.

The Seneschal grimaced, then gave a curt nod. "All right. Whatever it takes."

Everyone started as a claw punctured the ceiling, then another, and another.

Anskar recited the revised calculations Vihtor had given him. Within his mind, his empty dawn- and dusk-tide repositories pinched and squeezed, and he winced at the pain. But the dark-tide had already burst free of the constraints he had placed around it. Blackness vomited from the depths; flooded him with its virulence, sweeping him away. As he uttered the final part of the calculation, the dark-tide coalesced into a wave, then a stream, and finally a minuscule black speck on the palm of his hand. With a roar of exultation, Anskar flung it at the ceiling, where it burst into a flattened ward of utter blackness.

He became aware of hammering and scratching at the kitchen windows, then the shattering of glass behind the boards Vihtor had fixed there. In his peripheral vision he saw Crosbyn head to one window, sword in hand; Vaila to the other.

The ceiling was rapidly disintegrating under the onslaught of claws. Pallid figures crouched atop Anskar's dark-tide ward, pressing their snarling faces against it. Distorted by the blackness, they looked demonic. More and more dead-eyes leaped through the ruined roof, and the ward started to buckle under their weight.

To Anskar's right, the kitchen door burst apart and dead-eyes poured through. Vihtor strode to meet them, Myra on his tail, but Sareya called them back. Sheathing her sword, she walked calmly to the mouth of the corridor, while Vihtor and Myra rushed to aid Crosbyn, Vaila and Orix, who were hacking into limbs reaching through the broken boards that covered the windows.

Violet tongues of flame lapped about Sareya's fingertips. The dead-eyes' charge faltered, but they still crept toward her inch by inch. They sensed something about her; but more than that, Anskar realized, their numbers were thinning. There were no more coming through the kitchen. Or maybe they had moved the bulk of their assault to the roof. More and more dead-eyes landed on top of Anskar's dark ward, causing it to sag ever lower.

Anskar's legs shook and sweat poured from him. Another dead-eye landed atop the ward and he collapsed to his knees. His ward was a crushing weight slowly pressing him into the ground. Vihtor and the others were forced to crouch. To either side, he heard the howls, shrieks, and grunts of fierce fighting. His ward grew heavier still, and he bowed beneath its weight, using every last ounce of his will to maintain the dark projection.

As the slavering jaws of the dead-eyes pressed against the black barrier, only inches from him, Anskar yelled in defiance, and punched the ward outward, away from him. What was left of the roof exploded, and dead-eyes shot screaming into the air.

Streamers of darkness gusted from Anskar, and the last dregs of his energy went with them. His guts twisted and he tasted bile. Then his ward dissolved into sooty motes that dispersed in the air. He pitched to the floor on his back, staring up at the night sky, praying he had got all the deads on the roof.

And he had.

All but one.

As the creature flung itself down at him, Anskar threw up his arm to protect his throat. The impact of the dead-eye knocked the wind out of him. It fastened its fangs onto his forearm, and Anskar screamed…but felt nothing. In the same instant, the invisible vambrace flared golden, and the dead-eye dropped lifeless to the floor, its head smoldering.

Anskar swiftly rolled to his knees, afraid Vihtor and the others would see the vambrace—but there was no sign of its blaze of brilliance; no sign it even existed. All he saw was a rip in the sleeve of his shirt.

Vihtor and Crosbyn, Orix, Myra and Vaila turned away from their windows, the deads no longer climbing through. They all started toward Sareya, who stood at the connecting corridor facing the kitchen. The deads still crept toward her, but their confidence was growing; then, as one, they charged.

Pressure built within the atmosphere. There was a smell like burning metal, then a thunderous crack as Sareya extended her hands. Violet flames roared from her fingertips, incinerating everything in the corridor and the kitchen beyond. She swayed for a moment, then keeled over, hitting the floor with a thud.

Anskar tried to rise to go to her, but he lacked the strength. Myra reached her first, then Vaila, and together they carried her into the back room. Everything beyond where Sareya had stood was still aflame, and acrid smoke poured through the house.

Crosbyn and Vihtor pulled the chest of drawers aside so they could open the back door. There were snarls and shrieks, then the thrust of their swords and answering screams from the dead-eyes.

Smoke filled Anskar's lungs and he coughed violently. The last thing he remembered was Orix grabbing him, lifting him with a surge of effort, then the cold night breeze on his skin.

Anskar came to beneath the fang-like crescents of the uncaring moons. Orix was seated beside him, his attentive face flickering with violet light.

"Thank Menselas," Orix said. "We thought you was done for."

Anskar pushed himself up on one elbow, shivering with cold. When he saw that Orix was unperturbed by the night air, he wondered if the chill came from within him.

The farm cottage still blazed with the violet flames of Sareya's sorcery, sending sparkling motes spiraling into the sky amid plumes of iridescent smoke. The others of their group were asleep on the ground, wrapped in their cloaks. He could hear light snoring, and several times someone muttered in their sleep. He thought it might be Myra.

"How do you feel?" Orix asked.

Anskar wasn't sure. He sent questing feelers inward, probing at the edges of his repositories. The dawn- and the dusk-tide were empty wineskins in dire need of filling. The dark-tide, though, bubbled and seethed like boiling oil. He knew he had merely skimmed from its surface; that its depths remained hidden from him. At the same time, he knew he lacked the energy to access it—and for a shocking instant realized the dark-tide within him was actually bigger than he was. It was a burgeoning emptiness that could at any moment overspill its boundaries and consume him totally.

He lay back down and frowned at Orix's question. How did he feel?

"Flat," he said. "Spent."

The cottage burned till morning, its violet flames giving way to the pastel colors of dawn. The knights and their charges greeted the dawn-tide as a family, and as the invisible winds blew through him, Anskar felt fuller, more substantial. He was still like a man with one lung, but he knew that wouldn't change until he could replenish his dusk-tide repository.

As the blaze became a smolder and the house turned to a pile of ashes—even the stone walls had not withstood the heat of Sareya's flames—Vihtor led the group in prayer for the repose of Abizar. The cottage had become the giant's funeral pyre. The soot and dirt on Vaila's cheeks was streaked with the tears she shed for her fellow knight.

No sooner had they finished the prayers of mourning than Anskar heard a rumbling sound, like a distant wave ever building and never breaking. Vihtor and Crosbyn walked a little apart to talk in low voices. They gazed in the direction of the sound, clearly unconcerned.

"What is it?" Orix asked, moving to Anskar's right.

"Horses," Sareya replied.

Vihtor and Crosbyn greeted the first riders to appear, and more pulled up in a long line behind them—some twenty knights in all.

"They must be from Quolith," Myra said. There were tears streaking her hollow cheeks. "Noreina must have made it. She sent them to find us."

Orix threw an arm around her shoulders and pulled her close. "That can't have been too hard," he said, nodding toward the blazing cottage. "We have Sareya to thank for that."

Politely, but with a grimace on her face, Myra extricated herself from Orix's unwanted embrace. The sight made Anskar chuckle. Sareya noticed, then she laughed too.

She looked otherworldly, Anskar thought—as if bathed in the afterglow of the forces she had unleashed to incinerate the dead-eyes and the cottage. He sent a feeler of awareness toward her, but it recoiled before it entered her mind. Anskar winced as if he had been burned.

Sareya flashed him a warning look. Violet flames backlit her cat-like eyes. "No," she whispered, "not yet. It may not be safe for you." With a frown, she closed her eyes; and when she opened them again, they were once more brown and flecked with green.

"Are you all right?" Anskar asked.

She smiled like someone who had achieved a secret goal. "I have surpassed…" She left the sentence floating in the air.

Anskar swallowed, unable to take his eyes off her. During the fight with the dead-eyes, he had exceeded his own expectations too. But what Sareya had done—the destruction she had wrought—was on a whole different level.

"Don't worry," Sareya said. She offered him a smile that was intended to be reassuring but was anything but. "We are growing, you and I."

"Growing?"

"Into ourselves."

Anskar looked away. It didn't matter that he had been given permission by the Seneschal to use his darker powers; he still burned with shame.

TWENTY-SEVEN

CARRED'S NEW HEADQUARTERS IN LOWANIN was a so-called "suite" of rooms in a rundown building. It was a lonely base as there were few Niyandrians in the city willing to risk being part of her resistance, and Maggow was tucked away in his cave in the hills. But she had loyal men and women in the nearby village of Zolita, and between them and Maggow's pigeons, she would be kept apprised of the broad picture. When the time was right—if confirmation ever came from Aelanthe at Branil's Burg— she could send word to the leaders of the resistance.

Carred set about establishing a team of street urchins to run errands for her: grubby, forlorn orphans who begged on street corners and hated the occupiers for what they had done to their parents and grandparents. She lured the youngsters with food and coin—copper Niyandrian queens, not the Order's offensive replacement pennies—and plied them with tales of the old days under Queen Talia's rule. She spoke of the knights as demons and the urchins' parents as heroes, and within a few short days they were as committed to the liberation of Niyas as she was. One of the older children knew Zolita well from visiting his grandparents, and she planned to send the lad there once a week to bring back word from the spies who were keeping track of the knights' movements in other parts of the island.

On Carred's fourth day in Lowanin, one of the urchins arrived at her rooms with news that confirmed her worst suspicions. The poorest and most vulnerable Niyandrians in the city were being rounded up, a few at a time so as not to arouse suspicion. They were being held in a warehouse on the banks of the central canal, awaiting transport to the coast, and from there to the mainland. In contradiction of their avowed morals, the Knights of Eternal Vigilance were supplementing their income by selling Niyandrians as slaves to the wealthy families of Kaile, the City States, and the Pristart Combine.

Carred was unwilling to risk sending for help from the rebels outside Lowanin, but at the same time she couldn't sit tight and do nothing. She resolved to take a look for herself, even though she knew it was a foolish risk. But she had to do something.

A bitter wind was blowing as Carred walked among stalls that sold food, drink, jewelry and craft items. Most of the merchants were red-skinned locals: good, hardworking folk endeavoring to keep the culture alive by selling traditional Niyandrian brooches in the shape of skeletal beasts, skull rings, and multicolored canting beads. A few others sold useless trinkets from the mainland. These latter were craven opportunists making coin from the novelty value of cheap imports, uncaring of the corrosive effect such practices had on the traditions and crafts of the isle. Buy a pendant of a five-petaled rose, and next thing you knew, you were worshiping the god of the mainland—and complicit in the eradication of your own gods, your own civilization.

A fat man offered Carred a decorative piece of pottery as she passed—a blue and white vase painted with rustic scenes that was allegedly from the Pristart Combine. Carred glared and the man stepped back. She would have gutted him if she could; if there weren't white-cloaked knights perusing the stalls along with the locals.

A foul-smelling stench wafted from the brackish waters of the canal, and here and there rats scurried along the embankment, scavenging for scraps.

Carred stopped to buy a steaming mug of tea and a *khova* pastry filled with nuts, sweet cheese and honey—a Niyandrian delicacy she'd enjoyed as a child, on the few occasions her parents had treated her. While she waited for her tea to cool, she devoured the *khova*, savoring its sweetness and subtle tang, the crisp pastry and slivered almonds.

A knight approached and asked to see her papers. Heart skittering in her chest, she handed them over. The man checked them, appraised her for a long moment, then handed the papers back, apparently satisfied. With relief, Carred noted that he did the same to others gathered around the stalls—a routine security check. She hadn't been singled out. Nevertheless, she was glad for the fur-lined gray cloak Kovin had given her, which helped her to blend in. Pulling up its hood against the cold, she wove her way through the crowds until she was beyond the stalls and making her way discreetly toward the warehouse that was her goal.

The barn doors fronting the building were wide open when she arrived, and inside were stacked barrels and crates, spools of rope, nets, and bales of hay. More goods were being unloaded from a moored barge by a team of Niyandrians wearing leather gloves and aprons. They flicked looks her way as she passed, and one man whistled, but Carred ignored them and continued past the warehouse, then cut down an alleyway between two ramshackle huts so she could double back and come at the building from the rear.

The street the warehouse backed onto was cobbled, heaped with refuse, and stank of urine. A cat scampered out of her way as she approached the building, a baby rat clenched in its jaws.

The back door was locked and chained, and the ground-floor windows barred. An iron staircase led up to the next floor. Carred took it, casting looks down at the street to make sure she hadn't been seen.

At the top, she came to a narrow door with flaking black paint. It too was locked, though the frame moved when she tried the door. It was rotten and flimsy, and when she put her shoulder to the door, it splintered.

The door swung inwards, opening onto a wooden-walled room with row upon row of rails, from which hung all manner of clothes: long coats, short coats, fur coats, pants, cotton shirts, and even the kinds of elaborate gowns that had once been worn in the major cities for feast days of the old gods. There were boots, sandals, and shoes of every style lining the floor beneath the rails. The clothes looked new, and she wondered if they were headed for the mainland cities. Perhaps Niyandrian finery might end up the latest fashion in Sansor. Ironic, given the Order were intent on stamping out Niyandrian culture and identity here at home.

A man's voice came from the other side of a door across from her, then the scuff and thud of approaching footsteps.

Carred slipped behind a rail of furs and stilled her breathing.

She heard the door open, someone cautiously moving around, then swearing as he caught sight of the open outer door. More footsteps entered the room.

"Some bastard broke in," a man said in Niyandrian.

"See anything?" a woman said, also Niyandrian.

"No. Reckon they heard me coming and bolted."

"You searched?"

"Course I bloody searched," the man said.

If he had, it was half-heartedly. Carred could tell from the bluster in his voice that he was scared.

"Come on," the woman said, striding for the open door. "Let's take a look outside."

As they went one way, Carred went the other, keeping close to the hanging clothes until she reached the doorway they had come through. She entered a much larger room, lit by the flickering glow of an oil lamp on a stand. Dirty smoke plumed from the lamp housing; the thing had probably never been cleaned. She pressed her back to the wall on one side of the door and gasped.

In the middle of the room was a large iron cage, and inside it, lying atop filthy straw that stank even worse than the canal, were five Niyandrians—two men and three women. All naked and half-starved, ribs showing through their bruised and beaten skin.

One of the women grunted and craned her neck to look at Carred. Her once-brown eyes were pearly and tinged with yellow. The others shifted on the straw, watching Carred warily. If they were surprised, they weren't showing it. Probably, they thought she was a change of guard. That sent a shiver of acid through Carred's veins. What kind of person could conspire in the capture and enslavement of their own kind? But she already knew: the same Niyandrians who refused to join her resistance; who hunkered down and did as the invaders told them; who sold mainland trinkets on the banks of the canal. Traitors. Worthless pieces of—

She tensed as she heard the footfalls returning. Her hand went to the hilt of the sword beneath her cloak, and she half drew the blade. Meeting the gaze of each of the captives, she pressed a finger to her lips. At first she didn't think they understood, but then the woman who had seen her first nodded.

The man entered the room ahead of his colleague. "I tell you, they heard me coming and cleared off. And lucky for them they did." He patted the pommel of the short sword sheathed at his hip.

The woman snorted as she pushed past him and cast an appraising eye over the captives in the cage. "I'm sure it is. Well, now you can go fetch someone to fix the door."

"You go."

"I wasn't asking." The woman turned as she spoke and found herself staring straight at Carred. Her eyes went wide with shock.

Carred's sword sang as she slid it from its scabbard. She hacked into the man's neck while he was mid-turn. He dropped like the sack of worthless shit he was, blood spurting from his severed artery, spraying crimson across the walls and floor.

The woman backed toward the cage as Carred advanced on her. The bloodlust was on her now. After all she'd done for her people, after all she'd lost, these Niyandrians had chosen to stand guard over other Niyandrians who were to be sold as slaves.

The woman was too frightened even to go for her sword. Hands grabbed her ankles between the bars of the cage behind her, and she screamed. One of the slaves—a man—stood and grasped her hair, yanking her head against the bars.

"Please," the woman said. "Please."

Carred cocked her head, watching her with unblinking eyes.

"Please what?"

"It wasn't my idea," the woman said. "They made me do it." Looking past Carred at the twitching body of her colleague, she said, "He made me."

Carred smiled. She knew it was a cold smile, for the woman's naturally red face faded to pink.

"Do you know what I think?" Carred said.

The woman shook her head and swallowed a lump in her throat.

"I think you're a bright woman who knows her own mind."

Carred nodded to the man holding the woman's hair and he released her. The fingers came away from her ankles. The woman took a long shuddering sigh and muttered her thanks.

"And that makes you accountable," Carred said.

"What? No—!"

Carred thrust her blade deep into the woman's throat and watched the blood trickle from her mouth. The woman thrashed in place for a moment, then slumped to the ground, her neck opening as the sword ripped free.

One of the women in the cage spat on her body. "Bitch!"

"Traitor," said the man who had been holding the guard by the hair.

"Quickly," another woman said. "Someone will come." She indicated the body of the male turncoat. "He has the key."

Carred wiped her sword clean on the dead woman's shirt, sheathed it, and went to the man's body. She rifled through his pockets until she found the key, unlocked the cage, then directed the five within to find themselves clothes and shoes from the other room.

"Get yourselves home and lie low," she said. "Meanwhile, I'll do what I can to stop anything like this from happening again."

"We have no homes," one of the women said. "The knights took them. They're increasing their presence in the city."

"Slung us out and left us to starve," someone else said.

Taken from their homes, deprived of food, and no doubt picked up for being vagrants—and all in the name of a god of justice and balance. Carred's fists clenched, and blood roared in her ears. She had to do more. And do it now. It was too much to expect her to continue fighting losing battles until some undisclosed time when Queen Talia would come again.

She collected the lamp from its stand and carried it into the room with the clothes. All five of the former captives dressed themselves then stood waiting for her.

"What are you going to do?" asked one of the women.

"Outside," Carred said. "Wait for me across the street."

When they had gone, Carred splashed oil from the lamp onto some of the racked clothes, then threw the lamp on the floor, where it shattered. Flames erupted, black smoke billowed, and within seconds the clothes were ablaze and the high flames were reaching for the ceiling. It was a wooden warehouse. It wouldn't last long.

Carred rushed down the external stairs. Orange light flickered through the windows she passed. In a few minutes the fire would draw attention. Whistles would sound. The Watch would come, and with them the knights. But by then, Carred and the five she had freed would be long gone.

TWENTY-EIGHT

IT WAS A LONG, SLOW ride to Quolith, as the knights who had found them hadn't brought spare horses. Anskar half-slept against the cloak of the woman he rode behind, and several times she had to reach behind to stop him from falling off. As they passed through the temporary palisade marking the perimeter of the new stronghold, it began to rain, and lightning flashed in the north. Noreina was there to greet them along with Quolith's commander, an elderly man whom Vihtor clasped warmly by the hand.

"Padrin," the Seneschal said. "It's good to see you."

"Still landing yourself in trouble, I see, Vihtor," Padrin said, clapping the Seneschal on the back. "Nothing ever changes. Come on now, storm's coming. Let's get you folk inside."

Anskar, Orix, Myra, and Sareya were stationed in a temporary wooden cabin in the shadow of the partially built citadel, where they were reunited with Naul. The floor was damp from the leaking ceiling, and the place was infested with termites, as evidenced by the sawdust accumulating in the corners.

"Is Gar…?" Myra asked when they arrived.

"Alive," Naul confirmed. "Though he's still in the infirmary. He screamed half the night when they took the arrow shaft out, and he's still delirious from the poison."

Despite it being early afternoon, Orix slept like a baby, snoring lightly almost as soon as he lay down on the wooden floor with his cloak bundled up as a pillow. Anskar smiled at his friend. Surely the ability to sleep so soundly was the sign of a good conscience.

The next thing he knew, Anskar woke in the dark. He must have drifted off soon after Orix and had no idea how long he'd slept.

Naul tossed and turned in his sleep, at times crying out. Myra snored more loudly than seemed possible for someone so slight of build.

Sareya sat cross-legged and perfectly still, staring into space, her breathing barely audible. Anskar had the impression she'd not slept at all. He could only see her outline in the darkened cabin. It evoked memories of the nights they had spent together, and despite the promise he had made to Vihtor—and to himself—he wanted so much to go to her. But with the others of their group bedded down in the cabin, that was impossible. Maybe that was the Five's way of keeping him from temptation.

Without moving from his spot on the floor, Anskar sent out a probing feeler of awareness. After a moment's hesitation, Sareya permitted it to enter her mind, and he felt rather than saw what she was doing. She was playing with the dusk-tide; getting to know it better.

He withdrew his contact. Why did Menselas grant such powers

only to forbid their use? It made no sense. If not for Sareya's dusk-tide use, if not for his use of the dark, none of them would have survived the dead-eyes. Again, he wished Luzius Landav had not left so soon. There were so many questions he wanted to ask the sorcerer.

Anskar spent much of the night emulating Sareya's calm contemplation and reinforcing the barriers around his dusk- and dark-tide repositories. Through the walls of the cabin he could feel the dark-tide seeping into him, bolstering his already overflowing repository, stretching it deeper. In his mind's eye, he peered into the void and almost lost himself within its depths. He pulled back with a start and opened his eyes.

There were only a few hours until dawn, so he lay down and wrapped his cloak about him. He dreamed of falling, and of being snatched from his plummet by a gigantic crow with blazing golden eyes. It soared upward, clutching him in its claws, and the face of the white moon, Chandra, grew larger and larger, filling Anskar's vision…

He awoke to bright sunlight streaming through the cabin's windows. Orix and Naul were already awake and talking in low voices as they ate bread and bacon and drank hot tea. Someone must have brought them breakfast while Anskar slept. Sareya was curled up on the floor, asleep. And Myra… Anskar couldn't believe what he was seeing: she had finished off one plate of bread and bacon and was starting on another.

"I asked her," she said, nodding at the sleeping Sareya. "And she said she wasn't hungry."

"Isn't that your line?" Anskar asked.

Myra grinned as she chewed. "Usually, but for once I'm bloody starving."

"We saved you some," Orix said, handing Anskar a plate.

He had barely started eating when there came the jangle of horses' tack and the hubbub of voices outside, among them Vihtor's, Noreina's, and Crosbyn's.

"They're getting ready to leave," Orix said. "You'd better eat on the way."

Naul crossed to Sareya and gently shook her. "Come on, lazybones. Time to rise from the dead."

It was an odd feeling, being on the opposite side as they returned to Branil's Burg with Petor's body. Before, Anskar had been among those waiting for the dead to come home. It didn't feel right that the others they'd lost wouldn't be laid to rest in the knights' graveyard, but at least the dead-eyes hadn't gotten hold of them. And Abizar—he'd had the burning cottage for his pyre.

The eyes of the novices and the knights waiting in the courtyard beyond the barbican seemed to condemn those who had survived. Anskar knew he was likely misinterpreting due to how he felt, but that didn't make it any easier.

That evening, Anskar and the other knights-liminal were summoned to the knights' refectory, where a banquet was held in their honor.

Anskar was surprised when he was directed to sit beside Vihtor. Why he had been singled out for this special honor was beyond him—unless it was because the Seneschal was his mentor. It was Sareya who had turned the tide of the fight with the rebels, and who had ultimately won the day against the dead-eyes. And Orix and Myra had acquitted themselves with distinction, yet all three of them were seated with Naul at a lower table. Gar had been transferred to the Burg's infirmary, where the healers were attempting to speed his recovery.

"You did well throughout the mission," Vihtor said as he poured a glass of wine for Anskar and one for himself. "The way you charged the rebels—in such moments a battle is lost or won. You showed the instinct of a born warrior. And against the dead-eyes…what can I say? I'm proud of you. More than proud."

Anskar looked into his wine glass, not knowing how to respond. He felt the swell of pride in his heart; a gentle heat flooding his cheeks.

"If not for Sareya—" he started, but Vihtor spoke over him.

"This is progress, Anskar. We're winning the struggle. And I must commend you on your obedience in desisting with the dawn-tide gatherings. I have no issue with your friends continuing, but you must keep yourself out of temptation's way."

Vihtor took a sip of wine and let his eyes rove about the refectory as their food was brought to the table by Niyandrian servants. Jonita attended their table and briefly met Anskar's gaze with a half-smile. Her bruises had receded and there was no sign of the welts on her wrists.

"You're well on your way to becoming a consecrated knight, Anskar," Vihtor said, dismissing Jonita with a wave. "You must form new relationships now; focus on new concerns."

Anskar opened his mouth to protest at the way Jonita had been abused, but Vihtor's eyes were implacable. "Yes, sir," he said. "I understand."

Before they started eating, the Seneschal glanced at Anskar and asked, "While we were away, did you have any more visits… from the crow?"

"No, sir. None at all."

"That's good," Vihtor said, picking up his knife and fork and sawing into a shank of beef. "Sleep with your window shut, just in case."

"I will, sir."

"If we work together, we can get you through this…whatever it is. Teething pains, that's what we should call it. You're coming into your new abilities and learning to sort the wheat from the chaff. I need you to trust me, Anskar, so I can guide you through this difficult period. And in return, you must help me to trust you."

Anskar nodded that he would, yet the pride that had so recently suffused him ebbed away into doubt and uncertainty.

The next morning, Anskar nursed a throbbing head from all the wine he had drunk at the banquet. Vihtor had encouraged him by constantly refilling his glass. Moderation, apparently, wasn't a virtue required at feasts.

Maybe Menselas gives his devotees the odd day off. The thought popped into Anskar's head unbidden; and though he swiftly banished it, he had to admit that such inconsistencies were troubling. Not only the excesses at the banquet last night, but also Tion's behavior with women in direct contradiction of his vows. Flawed individuals failing to live up to the ideals of the Church, and yet these were the people set to guide him.

Deciding never to drink so much again, Anskar determined to do better. Menselas had already helped him with Sareya, and if he remained steadfast in his devotions and his adherence to the Order's rules, the Five would aid him again, maybe help him to snuff out the powers awakening within. It was no good looking to others for his example: there were too many half-measures; too much tepidity. Just as on a battlefield anything less than your best was likely to get you killed, the Five's way of balance was a precipitous tightrope walk that Anskar suspected only a few rare saints successfully negotiated. Well, he was going to be one of those saints. He was going to be the perfect knight.

But as he threw the covers off and grabbed a towel to take with him to the bathhouse, he became aware of the weight of the vambrace on his forearm, and his resolve began to gutter.

After dinner, Anskar and the rest of the knights-liminal made their way to the knights' graveyard in the north of the bailey for Petor's funeral. The trials had whittled their number down to seven, and then the Niyandrian rebels had reduced them to only six. Gar was back among them with his leg heavily strapped. He looked pale to Anskar, his cheeks slightly sunken, but he'd insisted on attending the funeral. Petor had been his friend, he claimed; a friend who had sacrificed his own life to save Gar's. Anskar didn't quite see it that way. In the chaos of battle, Gar had been injured and Petor slain. It was as simple as that: just luck.

The knights' graveyard was scattered with stones carved into five-pointed stars or five-petaled roses. There were fresh graves where the knights who had fallen to the rebels outside of Quolith had been buried, in a ceremony restricted to fully consecrated knights; and one open hole in the ground where poor Petor was to be laid to rest.

Vihtor was already there when they arrived. A stony-faced Noreina stood beside him; and Crosbyn and Vaila were there too. The sergeant chewed on the end of his mustache, red-faced and sniffing back tears; while Vaila looked as though she needed someone to kill.

The knights stood around the grave and stared at the coffin six feet below. One foot for each of Menselas's aspects, and another for good measure.

With no priest of the Hooded One to perform the last rites, the decrepit priest of the Elder presided, mournfully uttering imprecations to the Five, sometimes reciting entire passages in Skanuric, which mostly went right over Anskar's head.

Vihtor frowned at Petor's coffin as if he were personally responsible for the lad's death. Noreina's face was impassive, but her posture was stiff and straight, her hands clasped behind her back. No commander liked to lose knights, not to mention a trainee under their protection.

The priest of the Elder concluded the rite and motioned for each of the knights-liminal to come forward and cast dirt on top of the coffin.

Anskar was behind Orix in the line. As Orix held his arm over the open grave, Anskar heard a distant hiss and rush of wind, and felt the pressure that betokened the approach of the dusk-tide.

He glanced at the others, but none seemed to have noticed— save maybe for Sareya, who had shut her eyes and had a look of serene tranquility on her face. Maybe she had found a way to imbibe the dusk-tide discreetly, but Anskar knew he could do no such thing. The moment the full force of the dusk-tide hit him, he would be rapt with ecstasy—and Vihtor wouldn't fail to notice.

As the priest invited him to scoop up some dirt from the pile at the side of the grave, Anskar uttered a swift apology and hurried away to the nearest door.

Inside the entrance hall, he pressed his back against the wall, praying that no one would come after him. Even through the wall he felt the dusk-tide's virulence as a thousand pinpricks on his skin, though it was nowhere near as forceful as when he'd met it outside. Within, his dusk-tide repository kicked and bucked against its barrier, and only by sheer force of will did Anskar stop it from erupting in a furious discharge of power.

Holy Menselas, it was growing stronger by the day, and he had no idea how much longer he could contain it. And that was saying nothing of the deep and bubbling presence of the dark-tide.

He took a few minutes to calm himself, then went back outside. The knights-liminal were already moving away, and Vaila had already left. Vihtor, Crosbyn, and Noreina lingered at the graveside, talking in hushed voices.

A fourth voice whispered among them—louder, as if it originated between Anskar's ears. *It should have been you,* the voice said. *Not me. It should have been you.*

"Petor?" Anskar muttered.

Vihtor turned toward him and narrowed his eyes, then Orix blocked the Seneschal from view as he put a hand on Anskar's shoulder.

"What's the matter?" he asked.

"Nothing," Anskar said. "Must be something I ate."

"Well, next time leave it for me to eat," Orix said, patting his belly. "I've yet to find a food that doesn't agree with me. I've a cast-iron stomach."

In his room that night, Anskar heard Petor's voice again: *It should have been you.* This time it was a memory. But earlier, at the graveside, had he really heard the dead speak?

He shuddered. It didn't matter. Ignore it—Tion's advice again. It was enough trying to deal with the dusk- and dark-tides, but communicating with the dead… That was necromancy.

Anskar fell onto his bed. He should never have accessed the dark-tide. He should never have gone to Hallow Hill and entered the tomb. But he hadn't really had a choice, had he? He'd been drawn there against his will. Used. And it seemed unlikely that his usefulness had expired atop Hallow Hill. Why retrieve the vambrace unless it had a purpose? And was that purpose also *his* purpose, the reason he'd spent his whole life in the dark, not even knowing who his parents were? And what was his role? He was a knight who could use the dusk-tide, the dark-tide. But for what reason?

Anskar held his arm up to the moonlight streaming through his window so he could study the vambrace. As its silver form materialized, shimmering with emerald, crimson, and azure, he discerned patterns ghosting beneath the surface. Not abstract patterns, he realized, but letters. The script resembled Skanuric, but with the letters overlaid on top of each other, two or even three combined to make a new symbol—a compound letter.

Frae Ganwen had spoken about compound letters in one of their early lessons on sorcery. She'd explained they constituted a technique employed by advanced crafters of weapons and armor: a space-saving measure that ensured even the smallest items could be imbued with the requisite scripts for sorcerous wards. But the vambrace wasn't a small item. It had the surface area to hold the standard inscriptions. So why were there hundreds of compound letters inscribed *below* its surface? Anskar couldn't even begin to guess at their meaning or purpose.

He again tried to connect with the vambrace using a thread of dawn-tide essence, and again was rebuffed. Sighing, he fought the urge to dip into the dark-tide. Surely there could be no sin in using it to explore the vambrace? To find out exactly what it was he had been told to retrieve from the tomb on Hallow Hill?

Told by a wraithe, he reminded himself. *Led there by a golden-eyed crow.* But could it really hurt to find out more? No one within the Burg would need to know.

Drawing in a deep breath through his nostrils, he picked away at the barrier warding his dark-tide repository. A slender wisp of smoky essence instantly snaked out, as if it had been waiting for him. He guided its head to the surface of the vambrace and directed it to burrow inside. This time, there was no resistance.

Anskar split the strand into dozens of slender threads to encompass the vambrace. He shuddered as he felt an answering throb in all three of his repositories, then a reciprocal pull between them and the essence of the vambrace. They were tasting each other, he realized, identifying, appraising. He discerned clearly now that the vambrace contained the potency of the dusk- and dawn-tide as well as the dark; yet the dark was the principal force they were organized about.

A surge of essence from the vambrace coursed through his dark-tide feeler, traveling along its length to his repository. White light flashed behind his eyes, and he glimpsed a vision of a full suit of plate armor, intricately forged. From history tomes he'd read, Anskar recognized the fluted style favored by the ancients during the war with the demon lord Nysrog. The metal's brilliant silver surface rippled with the same reds, greens, and blues as the vambrace; and indeed, he could see that the vambrace formed part of the overall suit. The great helm that capped it off was without visor or eye-slit; and the joins between each section of the armor were virtually seamless, as if they were fused together into one whole piece.

Anskar's head started to pound, and his heart thundered in his chest. Sweat dripped from his brow into his eyes. All his nerves were aflame with the need to possess the armor. He wanted it so badly, like nothing he'd ever wanted before. He *needed* it. He began to shake, his fingers clawing at his scalp as if he could somehow dig the vision out of his head and lay hold of what he saw.

The sheer force of his need terrified him. He snatched his dark-tide thread from the vambrace, and the vision immediately faded into insubstantial wisps. He fell back, sweating and gasping, and lay there for a long time, shocked by the powerful desire that had consumed him; only slightly reassured that he'd been able to break its hold and withdraw his dark-tide thread.

All precious things require a protector, the wraithe had said. Did the creature mean the vambrace, or the entire armor? Or was Anskar being used for some other purpose? Perhaps he was meant to corrupt the Order from within. If so, did that make him an unwitting ally—a tool even—of Carred Selenas and her rebels?

Anskar shook his head. He wanted nothing to do with those heathens—especially after what they'd done to Petor. And he'd already made his choice. He was sworn to Menselas—or, at least, as sworn as he could be until he was ready for simple vows. And in another year, he would make the solemn profession that would commit him to the Order for life.

He determined never to use the dark-tide again. This time he was resolute. He had to be in control of his own destiny. Better still, he had to let the Five take control of his life. Only then could he be certain that no evil influence manipulated him.

Rising to his knees on the bed, he reached for the curtains to draw them closed. Something was pressed up against the glass. The crow, its black wings splayed, its golden eyes glaring.

Anskar struck the window to drive the creature off. Rather than flying away, the crow dissolved into a dark mist, which the wind swirled and dispersed.

TWENTY-NINE

THERE WAS A FORMAL AIR to the Seneschal's chamber when Anskar entered it the following evening. Gone was the familial atmosphere between them that had prevailed after the battle with the dead-eyes and during the prayers for Abizar. Frankincense was thick in the air, and the only light came from a votive candle in a blue-glass holder. If not for the lingering hint of musk underlying the incense, Anskar would have assumed the Seneschal had been praying. But from the scent it was obvious Sareya had been given her dressing-down first.

Anskar couldn't help wondering if the prayer-like atmosphere was an attempt to remove the taint of the dusk- and dark-tide sorcery Vihtor had been complicit with during the battle. The Seneschal had permitted Anskar and Sareya to use the forbidden sorcery in the name of survival, but it was a sin he would have to confess. And Vihtor had never struck Anskar as a man who could abide even the slightest stain on his conscience.

"Sit," the Seneschal commanded from his armchair by the hearth.

Anskar took the chair opposite, perching on its edge, fingers alternately clenching and splaying above his knees. It was impossible to see Vihtor's expression in the guttering candlelight, but Anskar could feel it: solemn and stern. Something like anger radiated from the Seneschal. Or perhaps it was disappointment tinged with grief.

"Sareya has been issued a formal warning," Vihtor said with no preamble. Before Anskar could protest, he went on, "I have accepted the blame. After all, I granted you both permission."

"And you were right to, sir, else we would all have died."

Vihtor said nothing for a long moment. Anskar could almost hear his thoughts turning over. Eventually, the Seneschal said, "Death is not the worst fate that can afflict a knight. It is true none of us would have survived without the use of forbidden sorcery, but what have we lost as a result?"

Nothing that Menselas can't remedy, Anskar wanted to say. But that was the voice of Tion, he knew at once. Tion, who was no longer a priest. Tion, who had reneged on his vows to the Five so he could lead an ordinary life. Part of Anskar still condemned the healer for that decision, but a growing part admired him. These past few weeks, Anskar's eyes had been opened to the world outside Branil's Burg: a world of mystery and danger, but also joy and adventure. It was like emerging from a dingy cave into the full spectrum of daylight; and while the cave still felt like home, it was hard to forget all the things that did not fit into its confines.

"I will issue the same warning to you, Anskar DeVantte," Vihtor said formally. "That which is tainted within you must be closed off from your mind. Seal it in. Bury it. Forget about it.

We are Knights of the Order of Eternal Vigilance, and we can only serve one master. He is Menselas, the god of Five aspects. Our allegiance is to him; if not, it is to the abyssal realms. Do I make myself clear?"

Anskar clenched his fists as he nodded. "Yes, sir."

Vihtor let out a long breath. The waves of tension coming off him instantly eased. "Good. I will see to it that both you and Sareya are shielded from the Grand Master when he arrives. I have already written my report, and was very clear that if there is any blame, it is mine."

"Will he punish you?"

Vihtor shrugged. "It will not be the first time. We will know soon enough. He arrives from the mainland the day after tomorrow. There is one last thing I would discuss with you, Anskar. The stench of the dusk-tide is not unfamiliar to the Order. Indeed, many of us had to fight the temptation to use it in our early days; and many times we have defended ourselves against foes who have wielded it. With a firm hand and discipline, the dusk-tide repository will close up and atrophy, leaving nothing but a kind of scar-tissue, figuratively speaking. But what you did back there—the black ward, and when you appeared at my side during the fight with the dead-eyes and pulled me to safety—perhaps I alone among the knights here have felt the touch of such evil before. It must never happen again. *Never.* For your sake as well as mine. I could not bear—" He broke off and stared into the flickering darkness.

Anskar had the impression Vihtor was about to say something of great moment, but when the Seneschal spoke again, all he said was, "You must make me a promise never to use such power again…*even* if I command it."

Anskar wetted his lips and nodded. "I promise."

But how could he, really? How could he be expected to stand by and do nothing while his friends and comrades perished? He knew he couldn't. Not when he had the means to save them.

It came as a surprise when, next morning, the Seneschal sent word that the knights-liminal were to take the entire day off. The message, conveyed by an elderly knight during breakfast, was that they should ride out of the Burg and explore the local area at their leisure. The knight handed them each a purse containing three silver talents that Vihtor had sent for them. "The Seneschal says to think of it as wages for a job well done," he told them.

It was the first time Anskar had ever had his own coin to spend. At once he knew where he wanted to go. The Griffin's Rest at Caeltrin. After all the knights-liminal had been through, he could think of no better way to unwind than to sit in the tavern with his friends, eating fresh-caught fish and sipping beer.

He told the others. Gar said he wasn't up to the ride, and Myra had once again given up eating in public, but Orix never needed encouragement as far as food was concerned, and Sareya said she'd always wanted to go to the tavern. She'd been told they still sang the old songs of Niyas there, despite the tavern being built by mainlanders.

"I know the landlord," Anskar said, though in truth he'd met Nigen Bosh just the once. "It's a nice place he runs. Naul, are you coming?"

Naul shook his head. "Reckon I'll keep Gar company. And I'd sooner not spend the money."

"Are you sure?" Sareya asked.

Naul couldn't meet her eyes. "I'm sure."

"He's jealous," Orix whispered to Anskar on the way to the stable yard.

Anskar shook his head. "He's got nothing to be jealous of."

When they arrived at the stable yard, Larson was taking a break, lolling in a rocking chair outside the main stall block.

"Give me a moment," Anskar told Sareya and Orix, then, with a mounting sense of trepidation, went to speak with the stablemaster.

Rosie lay at Larson's feet, half asleep. The Niyandrian ridgeback opened one eye a slit then closed it. No wagging tail greeting for Anskar. No jumping up to lick his face.

"About Fellswain…" Anskar said, but Larson silenced him with a raised hand.

"Sergeant Crosbyn told me all about it, son. You're not to blame."

"I'll find a way to repay you," Anskar said.

Larson chuckled. "How? You planning on robbing one of the Ethereal Sorceress's depots? Not something I'd advise. Or maybe you're going to muck out all the Burg's horses by yourself for the next fifty years?"

"If I have to."

"Then it's a good job you don't. Fellswain cost me nothing, son, so there's nothing to be repaid."

"But you could have—"

"Yes, I could have sold her to some rich bastard from Kaile, but why would I do that when she had you to ride her? Coin isn't everything, Anskar, and that horse loved you. Loved you a lot—and I know a thing or two about horses."

"Thank you," Anskar said, not even trying to disguise the dampness in his eyes. He doubted he would ever forget the terrible screams of the horses as the dead-eyes ripped into them.

"Now, what is it you're after?" Larson said, eyeing Sareya and Orix.

"Well…"

Larson laughed as he rolled out of his chair and clapped Anskar on the shoulder. "I've got just the nags you're looking for."

Mounted on three mature horses that Larson was happy to spare, Anskar, Sareya, and Orix rode south out of Dorinah, heading toward the fishing village of Caeltrin. It was a glorious morning, the sky clear, the sun cheery and bright. Gone was the menace they had all experienced under the threat of the dead-eyes. The one reminder that all was not entirely well was the weight of the vambrace on Anskar's forearm, but given that he couldn't see it, he was able to keep it largely out of his mind. Vihtor had rewarded them the whole day off, and he intended to make the most of it.

"You think the Seneschal feels guilty about reprimanding us even though he encouraged our use of forbidden sorcery?" Sareya asked, cantering alongside Anskar. "Is that why he's let us out for the day?" She spoke like a woman who had not had fire in her eyes; who had not blasted aside dead-eyes and burned a cottage to the ground.

"Who cares?" Orix said from Anskar's other side. "As long as I get to eat something soon."

"Just think," Anskar added, "we could be in the smithing hall this afternoon, making more mail."

Orix groaned. "I don't think I can take much more of that."

They tethered their mounts outside the Griffin's Rest and went inside where the air was thick with pipe smoke and smelled of the bittersweet tang of hops. It wasn't as packed as when Anskar had come with Vihtor, and he said as much to the landlord.

"Start of gavelfish season," Nigen said, his mustache rising and falling with each word. "Early bird and all that, but they'll be in soon enough, once they've snared their fill. Place'll be heaving later on. So, tell me… Anskar, isn't it? I forget the surname… something Kailean."

"DeVantte, sir."

"That's it, DeVantte. Orphan, raised by the Order." He tapped the side of his head. "It's all in there somewhere, waiting to come out. Memory like a fishing net, but the important things stay put. So, tell me, Anskar DeVantte, how is my old friend the Seneschal?"

"He is well, sir."

"Sir, pish! It's Nigen." He clapped Anskar on the back and grinned at his companions. "And these two?"

Anskar made the introductions, then told Nigen they had come to sample his most excellent beer. The three friends settled at the table in the nook Anskar and Vihtor had shared, and Nigen himself brought over three frothing mugs.

"Will you be eating?" he asked.

Anskar opened the purse with the three silver talents, but Nigen wouldn't hear of him paying. "On me, lad. You can pay next time you come. Is fresh gavelfish all right? It's today's special. Served on a bed of greens with a side of new potatoes topped with butter."

"Sounds good," Orix said, slurping his beer and getting a froth mustache to rival Nigen's bushy one.

Sareya wrinkled her nose as she sipped her beer, but she tried again, and this time raised an appreciative eyebrow.

"The Five only knows what gavelfish is," Orix said, "but the potatoes sound good."

"Bugs," Sareya said. "Big bugs in shells."

Orix looked at Anskar as if he thought Sareya was joking.

"Food's food," Anskar told him.

"Well, maybe this once you can finish off my meal rather than the other way round," Orix said, clearly deflated. "But *only* this once, mind."

When the meal came, the gavelfish meat was pink and succulent, the smell tantalizing. Orix picked at his, but like Sareya with the beer, he appreciated it more and more with each bite.

Anskar tucked into his with gusto, fearing if he didn't, Orix would be demanding seconds. The potatoes were soft but not too soft—they popped when he bit into them, filling his mouth with creamy, salted butter.

Nigen sent a server over with more beer, and by the end of the meal, all three were slurring their speech and laughing at bad jokes.

Orix asked for the coins Vihtor had given Anskar and insisted on going to the bar to pay for a third round out of appreciation for Nigen's hospitality. He came back with the beers and a bemused look on his face. "He wouldn't take my coin," he said, returning the coins to Anskar. "It's embarrassing."

"Make the most of it," Sareya said, snatching a mug from the tray Orix was carrying and taking a long pull. "Because tomorrow it's back to making mail."

"Maybe not," Anskar said. "I'm sure Vihtor said there was something else happening tomorrow." He racked his brain for whatever it was, but the beer made him feel dumb. Eventually he dredged it up. "The consecration of the new vault! The Grand Master is coming from the mainland."

"He is?" Orix said, setting down his beer. "Shouldn't we be getting back? I need to prepare."

"Prepare what?" Anskar asked.

Orix shrugged. "You know, make sure I have clean clothes, check my sword, oil my scabbard… I don't know, just prepare."

"You might want to start with a haircut," Sareya said.

Orix's usually tight curls were getting long and unruly, and even starting to form ringlets. He also had a healthy growth of downy stubble on his chin that hadn't been there a few days ago.

"And shave," Anskar said.

"Come on," Orix said, pushing his chair back. "We're leaving."

"Orix, we're joking," Anskar said. "The Grand Master won't be conducting the ceremony until tomorrow evening. We have plenty of time."

"You're sure about that?"

"I'm sure."

"Right, then," Orix said, reseating himself and lifting his mug. "Let's see who can finish their beer the fastest. Loser goes to the bar for the next round."

It was during the fourth round that Orix let slip that Vihtor had come to see him before they'd set out from the Burg. With a big smirk, he said, "The Seneschal told me to keep an eye on you two. He said I wasn't to leave you alone together, even for a minute."

"Did he now?" Sareya said, taking a sip of beer. She grinned and looked at Anskar.

"I gave him my word," Anskar said, angered that it clearly carried no weight with Vihtor.

Their tutors were constantly telling them: *A knight is only as good as his word.* Then again, Anskar had made Vihtor a promise he couldn't possibly keep—to never use his dark-tide sorcery, even if it meant losing a comrade. Maybe Vihtor could tell Anskar hadn't meant that promise; and if so, who could blame him for applying the same distrust to the situation with Sareya?

Even so, Anskar didn't like being doubted. It irked him that to be a man of his word he had to be false to himself—to what he was; the powers he carried within. If Tion had been there, would he have told Anskar he was the way Menselas had made him, complete with his ability to draw on the dawn-, dusk- and dark-tides? He doubted it. Tion would have been horrified by the powers seething within Anskar. No doubt the healer—former healer by now—would have considered them demonic, and subjected Anskar to endless rituals of exorcism and purification. None of which would have worked, Anskar was sure. You couldn't deny what you were. And he couldn't deny that without his and Sareya's sorcerous abilities, the three of them wouldn't be sitting here now drinking beer and laughing. They would have been dead, defiled, eaten.

The effect on his mood was like a bank of cloud smothering the sun. He stared sullenly into his beer, and Sareya and Orix retreated into themselves, giving him space. The three of them sat there with their empty mugs until Anskar could bear it no longer. He stood up to leave, and Sareya and Orix followed suit.

At the same moment, the tavern door flew open and a long line of men and women wearing knee-length, water-stained boots and greasy leather aprons came in. They stank of fish, and had the garrulous voices of people who had worked hard all morning and were starving and in need of a drink. As they pressed up against the bar, a troupe of Niyandrian musicians entered behind them, all dressed in somber blacks and browns, with floppy black caps atop their red-skinned faces. They carried fiddles and pipes, hand drums and lutes, and set themselves up in a half-circle on the far side of the tavern from Anskar and his companions.

"We should stay for this," Sareya said.

"I'm not in the mood," Anskar grumbled.

"You will be."

"We ought to get back," Orix said.

"Just wait a minute," Sareya said. "I promise you won't regret it."

The musicians were already tuning their instruments, laughing and joking with one another with a good humor that belied their appearance.

"You've seen them before?" Anskar asked Sareya.

"Not these particular ones, but as a child I loved being taken to see the bardic troupes."

"My parents were musicians," Orix said. "Back in the Plains of Khisig-Ugtall."

Sareya nodded, impressed. "It's songs and stories that keep our culture alive from one generation to the next."

"And that's allowed, is it?" Anskar said. "I mean, Niyas is ours now, isn't it?"

"By 'ours,'" Sareya retorted, "I assume you mean the Order's, and the mainland nobles and bankers who benefit from its presence here?"

"I don't know anything about that," Orix said. "Only that Niyas was evil till the Order and its allies came."

Sareya drew in a deep breath, and Anskar was shocked that he could so easily feel the roiling of the dusk-tide within her.

"The Order is wise," he said tactfully, "to encourage mainlanders and Niyandrians to live side by side. I agree with Sareya. We should stay."

"Only if you fetch the next round," Orix said, slumping into his chair with a scowl.

Anskar went to the bar, and this time managed to pay for their drinks. The sour-faced woman who had taken over from Nigen didn't seem to share his need to give everything away for free.

When Anskar returned with the tray of mugs, Sareya complained about how much he'd spilled. It struck him as odd that, out of the three of them, she was the least affected by the beer. Orix was vacant-eyed and slurring his speech, and Anskar wasn't faring much better. Maybe it was a Niyandrian thing, he reasoned; or maybe Sareya was used to beer. He discounted the latter immediately. When would she have had the opportunity?

When she was servicing the knights at the Burg, a snide voice in his head answered. He immediately quashed it. That wasn't something he wanted to hear. And besides, Sareya had changed; she'd told him that. More than changed: *I have surpassed...*

"Something I've been meaning to ask you," Orix said to Anskar, missing his lips at the first attempt to drink from his mug. "What happened...you know, when you went missing from the Burg? I mean, I know you were in a bad way after, and Vihtor was worried, but why did you leave in the first place?"

"And where did you go?" Sareya asked.

Anskar remembered another of his promises to Vihtor. "I can't say."

"Can't or won't?" Sareya countered.

"I'm not permitted to."

Sareya lowered her eyes and chuckled into her mug. "Since when has that ever stopped you?"

"Everyone's asking about it," Orix said. "You should hear the rumors. Everything from a lovers' tryst to a drunken binge. Of course, I told them they were wrong; that most likely Vihtor had sent you on a secret mission." He held Anskar's gaze, hoping to hear his assertion confirmed.

"You're my friends," Anskar said, "and I will tell you. But not now. Please, let it rest."

Orix shrugged and took another pull of beer.

Sareya reached across the table and squeezed Anskar's hand. When he met her eyes, she smiled with what looked like sympathy. Perhaps it was the effect of the beer, but he felt a strong urge to kiss her. Before he could act on the impulse, the musicians struck up a song.

"Oh, I used to sing this as a child!" Sareya said.

It was a mournful ballad, the words of which Anskar and Orix didn't understand. Sareya outlined the story for them as the somber music washed over them and the atmosphere in the tavern grew dream-like and unreal. It was about a Niyandrian princess whose parents had both died of plague. The girl watched them fester and die, and when she became queen she devoted her reign to the obliteration of death. So obsessed was she with her quest, which led her into ever deeper and darker mysteries, that her kingdom started to come apart. She consorted with demons, and, following the suggestions they gave her, she assembled alchemists, artisans and sorcerers from all across the isle to construct an egg of "divine metal", as the demons described it, large enough to contain her. Inscribed with sigils and wards in the demonic language of Nazgrese, it would bring about her death and rebirth into immortality. She did everything they said, and entered the casing of divine metal. Her sorcerers incanted the barbarous words that would trigger the transformation, and there was an eruption of luminous forces. But when the sorcerers opened the casing to free their immortal queen, it was empty, save for the stench of brimstone.

"Sounds like Queen Talia," Anskar said when the ballad ended.

"It wasn't. The queen's name was Pavenuta. Pavenuta the Damned."

"And you sang this as a child?" Orix asked.

"Pavenuta's was a noble quest gone wrong. But others built upon the lore she gathered. Others, indeed, like Queen Talia."

"What is the divine metal in the ballad?" Anskar asked.

Unconsciously, he rubbed the invisible vambrace on his forearm.

Before Sareya could answer, the musicians changed to a jaunty jig, instantly sweeping away the somber mood. The tavern came alive with the banging of mugs, the stamping of feet and the clapping of hands.

Sareya leaped from her chair and invited Anskar and Orix to dance. Orix declined, complaining that he couldn't feel his legs—although that didn't stop him taking another swig of beer.

Anskar stood unsteadily, but when Sareya clasped his hand and showed him the steps of a traditional Niyandrian folk dance, he was swept up in the energy of the music, the musky scent of her perfume, the proximity of her warm flesh. After a few stuttering moments where he almost tripped over his own feet, the two of them whirled and turned, stomped and clapped along with the rest of the dancers. And in that chaotic and carefree movement, Anskar felt the connection between him and Sareya stronger than ever before. They were set apart from their peers by their mysterious gifts of sorcery. They could do things others could only dream of; and yet both had sworn not to use their talents again on pain of being expelled from the Order.

During a lull in the music, they returned to their table to find Orix asleep in his chair. Anskar sat to catch his breath. To his surprise, Sareya moved behind him and kneaded his shoulders.

"Vihtor likes you, Anskar," she said. "He likes you a lot."

"What makes you say that?"

"Nothing. I just get the feeling he does. I wonder why." She pressed her lips close to his ear and whispered, "I like you too. I always have done."

Anskar did his best to laugh it off and stood. "Come on, let's get the lummox home."

Orix grumbled when they woke him and half-carried him

outside. He was promptly sick all over the verandah, then sagged unconscious, held up only by his friends. With much effort, they managed to roll him over his horse's saddle. Anskar filled a bucket from a nearby well and washed the vomit away. Then he led Orix's horse by the reins as they rode back to Branil's Burg.

It was dark when they made it back, and the guards at the barbican rolled their eyes with amusement. Once they had stabled the horses, Anskar and Sareya dragged Orix along the corridors and up the stairs to his room, where they lay him on the bed, not even bothering to remove his boots.

Anskar pulled Orix's door shut, then walked in silence with Sareya until they reached her room. She pressed her back against the door and looked up at him to wish him a good night.

Disinhibited by the beer, he kissed her, and she responded hotly. Together, they tumbled through the door and ended up on the floor, their cloaks a makeshift blanket.

"Wait," Anskar gasped. "Let me close the—"

His scalp prickled as Sareya spoke a cant and the door slammed shut.

"How did you—" But this time she stopped him with her lips.

Anskar's hands fumbled at the front of her shirt as he tried to free her breasts.

"Slow down," she said, and with a laugh, unleashed another stream of dusk-tide, this one even more tightly controlled. Fiery manacles of ghostly blue surrounded Anskar's wrists.

"What are you doing?" he cried, but she altered her cant and a cord of fire shot from each manacle to the ceiling, yanking Anskar upright so he was dangling with only his toes touching the floor.

"You're not going to tell Vihtor, are you?" Sareya said as she circled him like a predator. She winked as she passed his face;

bared her teeth in a lascivious grin.

Desperately, Anskar tried to remember the words of her cants, to follow the weave of her sorcery; see how she had done it; work out how to counter.

"It's not funny!" he protested as she unlaced his pants and pulled them down around his ankles.

Sareya widened her eyes with exaggerated shock. "The mind protests," she said, "but the body does not. Now, my poor, sweet, innocent knight, what am I going to do with you?"

Anskar spoke an improvised cant. Dusk-tide streamed from his repository and dispersed the blue flaming manacles in a shower of sparks. He tried to grab Sareya, but she stepped back. His legs became tangled in his pants and he tumbled to the floor.

Sareya grasped his shoulder and rolled him onto his back. He felt her senses brush over his dusk-tide repository.

"Spent so quickly?" she said. "I'm disappointed. But you do look silly with your pants around your ankles."

A third cant and burst of dusk-tide essence, sublimely controlled. The eldritch blue fire danced over the fabric of his pants, then along his bare legs. Anskar winced, expecting pain, but all he felt was a tickling, gentle warmth.

"I could make it hotter," she said. "Enough to burn. Would you enjoy that?"

"I… No!"

"Impressed yet?" she said, stepping out of her pants and tugging off her shirt. She sat astride him and lowered her face to his. Her breath smelled of beer.

Suddenly she yelped and cried out as Anskar reached into the dark-tide and dragged her with him into the shadows, to reappear atop her darkened bed. The ease of the transition shocked him. In the fight against the dead-eyes, when he'd rescued Vihtor by stepping into the shadows, he'd not even known what he was doing.

Sareya pushed up from him. "What in Theltek's name did you just—"

"Theltek?" Anskar said. "Of the Hundred Eyes? That sounds like apostasy to me!"

Before she could respond, he pulled her down and smothered her mouth with his own. He felt her senses skimming over his dark-tide repository, but blocked her access with a wall of briars—just as she had done to him that time in Frae Ganwen's ward-casting class.

Sareya drew back and playfully slapped his shoulder. But then she pressed down with her hips, causing Anskar to moan, and within moments they were both lost in the rhythm of their lovemaking, all thoughts of sorcery dispelled from their minds.

In the morning, Anskar woke with a pounding head and slipped out of Sareya's room without waking her. It angered him that he had to sneak around like this. More than ever, he was convinced he had done nothing wrong; and he had Tion's example to back him up.

It wasn't as if Anskar had chosen the strictures of the Order—he'd been brought to the Burg as an infant and forced to walk the path of the Five. It was a good path, he knew that, but was it the path for him?

He admired men like Vihtor—even more so after their experiences on the way to Quolith; men who embodied the ideals of honor and self-sacrifice. But Anskar was different. He only needed to think about the dawn-, dusk- and dark-tide repositories inside him to know how different. Luzius Landav had spoken of the triadic tides, but did anyone at the Burg, Frae Ganwen included, even know what that meant? Either they were ignorant by choice or they were just ignorant. Maybe, he thought, they were supposed to be. But *he* wasn't, of that he was certain. He was meant for so much more. Yes, he had a lot to be grateful to the Order for, but he'd been born with unique gifts for a reason. It seemed unfair that he was expected to bury them. And to deny the feelings he had for Sareya.

But what could he do? He'd known nothing but the Order of Eternal Vigilance all his life. If he left—or was expelled—where would he go? What would he do? Whenever he thought about it, all he could envisage was darkness, emptiness. Without the Order, he was no one. Nothing.

But without Sareya, he risked being even less.

Perhaps they could run away together. What if she refused? Even if she didn't, how would they live? *By sorcery*, an inner voice told him. They could travel the mainland and use their talents in return for coin. For a brief moment he felt elated by the idea, then dismissed it as a childish fantasy. More than a fantasy: a temptation to turn his back on Menselas, the same way Tion had done, despite his claims to the contrary.

Orix wasn't at their table when Anskar entered the refectory for breakfast. Probably, he was still sleeping off the beer. As Anskar collected his food—bacon and eggs and a thick wedge of bread smothered with butter—he caught sight of Vihtor poking his head in and scanning the novices and knights-liminal seated in the refectory. Their eyes met briefly, but Vihtor's expression was stony, inscrutable.

He knows, Anskar thought. *About last night. But how can he know?*

THIRTY

CARRED HAD GIVEN THE FREED slaves a few days to settle in to her new headquarters in Lowanin, and by and large they had made themselves useful, cooking, cleaning, doing menial chores. But they couldn't go on like this. Choices had to be made.

All five of them sat with her now on cushions strewn around the hearth. Flames crackled and spat as they took hold of the logs. The man who had held their captor's head against the bars was called Taloc, and Carred had already decided he had the makings of a warrior. The other man, Kalij, she was not so sure about. He was scrawny, with sunken cheeks and thinning gray hair. And as for the women—Mala, Noni, and Olana—it remained to be seen.

"We're grateful for what you did," Noni said, as if she already suspected what this meeting was about.

Noni had the piercing-eyed look of a witch, but when Carred asked if she was moontouched, the young woman shrugged. "If

I am, no one bothered to tell me." She dipped her head as if she were nothing, a nobody.

Carred lifted Noni's chin and nodded. *You're somebody now.* They all could be, if only they joined her.

"By now, I imagine you've worked out who I am," she said.

The others exchanged looks, but it was Taloc who answered. "Captain Carred Selenas. I guessed from the scars."

Carred gave a wry grin. "So, you know what I'm going to ask?"

"We know," Taloc said. "Though what good we'll be to your cause, I can't say."

"*Our* cause," Carred said. "Or are we not all Niyandrians?"

"Our cause," Taloc agreed.

"I can cook," Kalij said.

Carred already knew that. The scrawny man might have eaten like a sparrow himself, but he'd kept the rest of them well fed and had shown a knack for turning the most bland rations into passable fare.

Taloc nodded. "You wouldn't tell it from the look of him, though."

"You don't like your own cooking?" Carred asked.

"It's not that," Kalij said, eyes glistening. "I ain't been hungry, see. Not since they took my wife and children."

"Grabbed them from the streets while Kalij was foraging for food," Taloc said. "They'll be somewhere on the mainland by now, if they were lucky."

"And if they weren't?" Carred asked.

Olana spoke up, a quiver of fear in her voice. "They've been selling folk to the Jargalan nomads."

"But that's—" Carred was going to say it was impossible. The mainlanders considered the Jargalan nomads to be savages, and the devotees of Menselas, most especially the Knights of Eternal

Vigilance, condemned them as heathens, little better than demons. But she'd seen enough of the Order's duplicity to realize that if they'd established a lucrative trade arrangement with the nomads, it would cover up a multitude of sins. Hypocritical bastards.

She laid her hand on Kalij's arm. "Once we've driven the mainlanders out of Niyas"—she neglected to say, *Once the Queen has returned*—"we'll find your family and bring them home."

Kalij's eyes were dull and tinged with yellow as he studied her face. He gave the semblance of a nod, as if he took her words for what they were: empty promises.

Carred tightened her grip on his arm. "And if we can't find them, we'll avenge them. On that, you have my word."

That put a spark in his eyes, and he clasped her hand warmly.

"So, what do we do now?" Mala said. "We can't hide away in your rooms forever."

"No, you can't," Carred said. And neither could she. Sooner or later, the Order would pick up her scent again, and her exploits at the warehouse would only hasten the process. "But you can come with me."

"Come with you where?" Taloc asked.

Noni shut her eyes in concentration, then opened them wide on Carred. "You still serve the Queen," she said.

"Common knowledge," Carred said. But there was still something about Noni that unsettled her. "As to where I go next, I've not figured that out yet. But we need people. We always need people."

"Not long to wait," Noni said in a whimsical voice. "Queen Talia is grateful for your service."

Ice churned in Carred's guts.

"The Queen's dead and gone," Olana said, as if talking to a child who refused to accept reality.

Noni shook her head. "She will return. Not long now. She'll soon come back."

"Says who?" Taloc asked. "The voices in your head?"

"Them and others." Noni bit her top lip and stared balefully into the flames.

"The Queen speaks to you?" Carred asked.

No answer.

"Look," Taloc said, "we're all grateful to you for freeing us, but…" He sighed and looked to the others for support, but they wouldn't meet his gaze. "We're not fighters. We're none of us rebels. We're just ordinary people trying to go about our lives."

"And look where that got you," Carred said. She knew she was being unfair, but the sooner they faced up to reality, the better. To her mind, none of them had much of a choice but to join the resistance—not if they called themselves Niyandrians. Not if they wanted Niyas back for their own. And not if they wanted to live out the rest of their lives in freedom and dignity. "The mainlanders killed our queen and took our towns and cities. Now they are taking our families and selling them into slavery, and you think this is not *your* fight?"

"They wouldn't have come," Olana said, "if Queen Talia wasn't…" She trailed off at the look Carred flashed her.

"Wasn't what?" Carred asked coldly. "If Queen Talia wasn't what?"

"Don't worry about what Olana says," Noni said. "She's been listening to the lies the knights spread. They say Queen Talia was a demon lover and a witch. They call her—"

"The Necromancer Queen," Carred said. "I know. And what if I told you she was? Would you have a problem with that?"

Noni smiled—the mad smile of a simpleton or a lunatic, though Carred guessed the young woman was neither. "I would be proud to serve such a queen."

"You will join us, then?"

Noni nodded.

"As will I," Taloc said slowly, like a man who thought he would come to regret it. "Kalij?"

"Don't see as we have much choice."

"Mala?"

"How many people do you lead?" Mala asked.

Carred knew her sort: she would lend her support if she was certain of winning. When had Niyandrians become so weak?

"Enough," she replied. She no longer knew with any accuracy. She had hoped to muster ten thousand, but when the time came for all of Niyas to rise up against the Order, she had no guarantee of how many would heed her call. Ten thousand? Five? A few hundred? Or no one at all. "And today I would like to say I have five more," she added, looking pointedly at Olana.

The older woman puffed out her cheeks and said, "Fine."

"Good." Carred turned to Kalij and slung him a coin purse. "For supplies. Prepare something for the road. I'll soon be sending you all away from Lowanin."

When Olana protested, Carred said, "The chance of recapture is too high here. Besides, you have been too long in an occupied city. You need to go where Niyandrians still live as Niyandrians. Relive our culture, hear our stories sung in the taverns, and then you'll remember what we're fighting for."

As Kalij rose unsteadily on his bird-like legs and pocketed the purse, there came a knock at the front door.

Carred gestured for silence as she stood, fingers wrapped around the hilt of her scabbarded sword. She moved to the window and peered through the shutters, then breathed a sigh of relief. It was Davon, one of her street urchins.

She opened the door and the freckle-faced young boy came inside. One hand held a rolled-up message from one of Maggow's carrier pigeons, and the other hand was outstretched ready to receive payment.

"Wait while I read it," Carred said, slapping a copper into his palm. "I may need to reply."

"That'll be two coppers," Davon said. He never missed a trick.

Carred unrolled the scrap of parchment and moved closer to the fire for light to read by. Maggow wrote that, a few days ago, the rebels had attacked a group of knights from Branil's Burg and their trainees on their way to the old Niyandrian settlement that was now named Quolith, where a new citadel was under construction. The rebels had sprung the perfect trap, but had been driven back by a young knight who bristled with sorcerous energy and had two—maybe more—powerful repositories. Carred covered her mouth with a hand before she could utter a curse. Were the Order training a new breed of knights? Knights who were also sorcerers?

She scanned the remaining few lines of the message. A young woman had helped this knight-sorcerer—a Niyandrian who had used the dusk-tide to rout the rebels. Maggow believed her to be moontouched.

Carred scrunched up the parchment and dropped it in the fire, watching as it curled and browned then slowly reduced to ashes. Another defeat.

At this rate, no one would answer her summons when the time came. No one would believe they had a fighting chance. Carred was starting to feel the same way herself.

But the Knights of Eternal Vigilance were up to something, and it didn't bode well. First the sorcerer and his demon who had come for her in Rynmuntithe Forest, and now this: a trainee knight steeped in sorcery, and a moontouched Niyandrian aiding him. It had to be Sareya.

Was this the moment she'd been waiting for? But Talia's daughter, fighting for the Order? That would never happen… unless…

Sareya didn't know who she was.

The guardian will be revealed when the moment is right, and at the same time the heir will be known.

Even after all these years, the wraithe's words were burned into Carred's mind.

And the Order wouldn't know either, else the heir and her guardian would already be dead.

Unless they had been converted…

"What is it?" Taloc asked, a deep frown etched into his forehead.

Carred ignored him, looking instead at Noni. "Did you know Queen Talia had a daughter?" she asked.

Noni's eyes opened wide in surprise, then she narrowed them and rolled her head from side to side. "Some say she did, some say she didn't."

"What does that mean?" Carred snapped.

"Niyas will rise," Noni said, then shuddered and started to sob like a baby.

Olana put her arms around Noni and shot Carred an accusing glare. Carred was sorely tempted to drag the older woman outside and leave her in the street for the knights to find. She decided against it, because Olana would probably reveal Carred's location to anyone who asked.

Instead, she told Davon to return to Maggow and tell him to send a pigeon to Aelanthe at Branil's Burg. "You can remember a message for me?" she asked the boy.

He nodded. "For another copper."

Carred slapped two more coins in his palm, then told him what she wanted Maggow to write to Aelanthe.

The moontouched at the Burg may be the one. Sareya. Get her away from the citadel, and send word when you have her. Be wary: there may be a guardian. Perhaps a young knight who is also a powerful sorcerer.

THIRTY-ONE

ANSKAR STOOD WITH HIS FELLOW knights-liminal among a large group of novices and knights-inferior in front of the shelves covering the west wall of the newly completed vault.

Naul, Myra, and Gar were there with him. Gar's leg was still heavily bandaged, but he could walk now without pain. Naul seemed sullen, as if the attack on the way to Quolith had jaded him; and Myra…well, if it was possible, she looked even thinner.

On the eastern side of the vault stood Vihtor with at least fifty consecrated knights, among them Crosbyn, Vaila, and the Forge Master, Sned. The center space was occupied by priest representatives of the Healer, the Elder, the Warrior, and the Mother. Anskar didn't recognize any of them and assumed they must have traveled to Dorinah aboard the Grand Master's ship. An acolyte in a white robe, wearing thick leather gloves and a white mask over his nose and mouth, stood with the priests. Beside him was a brazier piled with smoking gray coals. The handle of an iron tool stuck out of it; the head buried in the coals.

The massive chamber was deep in the roots of Branil's Burg, where the stonework was ancient and built to last. The vaulted ceiling, fluted pillars and granite arches were all reminders that the space used to be a chapel. It was also clear from the bas-relief on the north-facing wall depicting a raven, wings outstretched between two full moons, that its original dedication had not been to the Hooded One.

The only indication that the fifth aspect of Menselas had ever been worshiped here was a ruby skull mounted on an ebony post at the center of the chamber. The skull now seemed to watch over the shelves with their locked iron boxes, and the dozens of vast orichalcum safes arrayed in a broad circle on the glistening black floor.

Anskar couldn't believe the skull was fashioned from a real ruby: it was too large; human-sized. But from what other material it had been intricately sculpted he could not decide. Perhaps a common crystal ingeniously colored? Presumably the red signified blood, given the Hooded One's dominion over death.

Grand Master Hyle Pausus entered the chamber from the southern door, trailed by the dozen or so Niyandrian carpenters and stonemasons who had converted the chapel into an impregnable vault. Oddly, they were naked from the waist up— both men and women—their red skin on full display.

The Grand Master wore a mirror-bright breastplate of steel, greaves, vambraces, and oversized pauldrons that made his shoulders look huge. On his head was a winged helm of silver and gold, though Anskar suspected it was constructed of some far harder metal, if it wasn't ensorcelled. His white cloak, embroidered on the back with the five-pointed star of Menselas, trailed too far behind him to be practical in battle. He was dressed like a god, but the man beneath the finery was of advancing years, nothing like the imposing figure Anskar had imagined. His gray beard was wispy and stained yellow from pipe smoke. His even grayer eyes were rheumy, and his nose was bulbous and spider-webbed with purplish veins. Beneath his breastplate, his stomach was distended, and he waddled like a duck.

Still, Anskar told himself, the strength of a man was not in his appearance. Maybe the Grand Master was a skilled swordsman, or a great tactician. Or maybe he was that rarest of things: a scholar knight, whose wisdom guided the Order of Eternal Vigilance from strength to strength.

Or maybe he was what he looked like: a fat old man, ridiculous in his showy armor; a fraud; a pretender.

Anskar knew he was being critical to the point of sinfulness, but he was starting to not care. It was this man, this supposed Grand Master, who had commissioned the vault and offended the priests of the Hooded One. Just how much wealth was stored within the vault, Anskar could only guess at, but it was a great deal; and more was arriving daily on ships from the mainland cities of Sansor, Kyuth, and Riem. Anskar was inclined to side with the priests: how could the head of a holy Order place the needs and wishes of the noble elite of the mainland above those who represented Menselas's fifth aspect? It was an affront at best, and a demonstration of blatant hypocrisy at worst. No wonder priests like Tion were abandoning their roles for a life among the ordinary folk. How could anyone make the sacrifices the priesthood demanded if leaders like the Grand Master placed coin above their god?

Hyle Pausus stopped before the ruby skull mounted on its post and bowed slightly to it. At least he was showing the Hooded One that respect, Anskar thought, but he figured it would take more than a bow to appease the Hooded One's priests, not a single one of whom was present.

The white-robed and masked acolyte gestured to the Niyandrians, and they fanned out into a semicircle facing the skull. A second gesture had them kneeling on the black stone floor. *Why?* Anskar wondered. Was it a forced show of obeisance to the Grand Master? To the Order? An acceptance of Niyandrian inferiority? That didn't seem likely. The Niyandrian trainees at the Burg had always been treated with dignity and respect…at least formally.

One of the Niyandrians, a woman, glanced toward the assembled novices, then the knights-liminal, and stopped when she reached Sareya. As soon as the woman saw Anskar had noticed, she lowered her eyes to the floor. Did Sareya know the woman? Or had the Niyandrian been intrigued to see a red-skin like herself among the trainees? Sareya wasn't the only Niyandrian standing with the group of novices and knights-liminal, though: there was Niv Allund, the young woman everyone used to say shared Sareya's bed; and there were several others Anskar didn't know well.

The priests of the four aspects began an elaborate ceremony, each in turn blessing the orichalcum safes that circled the center of the chamber. Anskar let the droning Skanuric litanies drift over him and studied the safes instead of the priests' complex hand gestures as they inscribed divine wards of benediction in the air. The burnished orange of the orichalcum suggested the safes were newly built, but the design looked as if it came from a previous age. Each safe was roughly the height of a man and half as wide. The edges were gilt with grape-bearing vines—the symbol of fecundity; and the doors were beveled and reinforced with bands of steel. Each was set with a brass dial within a circle of Skanuric runes.

Once the priests had completed their blessing of the safes, they moved around the perimeter of the chamber to bestow a general benediction on the shelves with their locked boxes. The contents of these were presumably of lesser value and therefore didn't warrant the same degree of attention as the safes, Anskar thought wryly.

Finally, the priests returned to their initial places. The Grand Master walked a slow circle around the safes, invoking in turn each of the Five aspects—though he seemed to hesitate at the fifth—before facing the ruby skull and once more dipping his head in a bow.

As the Grand Master straightened, he caught Anskar watching him and slightly raised an eyebrow. Anskar immediately looked away, but he had the uncomfortable feeling that the Grand Master continued to stare at him for several seconds before addressing the entire group gathered in the vault.

"This marks a great day for both the Order of Eternal Vigilance and the island of Niyas," the Grand Master said in a nasally voice. "Not only has the Order expanded its capacity to serve the merchants, nobles, speculators and banks who form the backbone of our society—but it has done so with the cooperation and expertise of Niyas's finest artisans, men and women who were once our foes, held enthralled by the dark theurgy of a depraved queen."

Anskar noticed one of the Niyandrian men tighten his fingers into a fist at that. He glanced at the woman who had eyed Sareya, but she remained impassive, her green-flecked eyes inscrutable.

"Niyandrian craftsmanship," the Grand Master continued, "has created this secure and blessed home for the wealth of the nobles of Kaile, the City States, and the Pristart Combine.

While the Order's strongholds throughout the mainland offer similar services, none have such impregnable safes, recreated from Sandoval's original design by the most skilled metalworkers Niyas has to offer, and installed within this orichalcum-lined vault. The feat is nothing short of magnificent; but it pales in comparison with the true miracle of what we are gathered here today to witness.

"I traveled to Dorinah from Sansor to consecrate the new vault, and instead I am humbled by the prospect of fulfilling the will of Menselas by expanding his flock. These carpenters, stonemasons and metalworkers are the first fruits of a renewed Niyas. During the time they have worked here inside Branil's Burg, they have soaked in the blessed atmosphere of the Five. They have eaten our food, slept within the protection of our walls, and witnessed the way the Knights of the Order of Eternal Vigilance conduct themselves.

"That is a lesson to be remembered by us all, for it is not with words that we convert others to the beauty of a life in Menselas. Rather, it is through our actions. Under the leadership of Seneschal Vihtor Ulnar, the knights of Branil's Burg have grown to be truly exemplary servants of the Five, and a beacon of holiness to the liberated people of Niyas. It is because of your example, and because of the generous time the Burg's priests have devoted to these Niyandrian men and women, that upon my arrival the spokeswoman for these workers"—he indicated the woman who had looked at Sareya—"Aelanthe—did I pronounce that correctly?"

The woman smiled and nodded.

"Aelanthe," the Grand Master repeated, savoring every syllable, "requested an audience with and, to my great delight, begged that she and her colleagues be received into the family of Menselas."

"He's lying," Sareya whispered. "No Niyandrian would willingly forsake the old gods."

Anskar flashed her a look that said he was trying to listen to the speech. He didn't bother retorting that she had forsaken the old gods, because he knew what her answer would be. She hadn't come to the Burg willingly; she'd had no choice. Not only that, but Anskar couldn't state with any certainty that Sareya *had* abandoned her old gods—or anything else of her native culture.

"Let us thank Menselas," Hyle Pausus said, "for bringing us to this momentous occasion: the first tempering of Queen Talia's reign, which has lingered even beyond her death. Let us pray to the incomparable god of Five aspects that those who pledge themselves to his service today are but the first swallows of a new springtime."

The Grand Master gestured toward the white-robed acolyte and the brazier beside him. "In case anyone here doubts the veracity of this conversion of our Niyandrian brothers and sisters, Aelanthe and her colleagues have agreed to the primitive ritual of initiation, during which postulants are branded to show who they belong to."

Hyle Pausus went to stand beside Vihtor, while the masked acolyte plucked his slender tool from the coals of the brazier. The end that had been buried in the heat burned red: it was a brand in the shape of the five-pointed star of Menselas.

The first to undergo the branding was the woman, Aelanthe. She rose and walked steadily to the acolyte, then kneeled once more, bowing her head and closing her eyes. The acolyte adjusted his face mask, then pressed the red-hot metal to her shoulder. Aelanthe flinched but did not cry out, though her face was contorted with pain.

Anskar winced at the sizzling hiss and the stench of charred meat. Beside him, Sareya groaned.

One by one the Niyandrians received the mark of Menselas in the flesh of their left shoulders. Anskar wanted to look away, but the grisly ritual held him enthralled. Most were as stoic in the face of searing agony as Aelanthe had been, but a few cried out, then winced with shame. One man lost consciousness and had to be dragged back by his colleagues so the initiation could continue.

Fighting back rising bile, Anskar focused on counting those who received the brand: fourteen in all. Was that all the Niyandrians who had participated in the construction of the vault, or had others left without pledging themselves to Menselas?

His eyes flicked to Vihtor, who stood beside the Grand Master, chin tilted proudly. All things considered, Vihtor was a man defined by his role, Anskar decided. A complex man beneath it all, but when it came to the Order and his duty, he knew how to toe the line. The Seneschal had made it clear that his obedience was to the office of the Grand Master. It did not matter to him that the supreme head of the Order of Eternal Vigilance was a fat old man who may have offended the fifth aspect of Menselas. All that mattered was the chain of command, and blind, loyal obedience.

There was a large part of Anskar that wished he could do the same: quiet his unruly mind and the roiling forces within him; learn to serve with humility. The simplicity that implied, the serenity, was a lure to his warring nature, but how could he succeed when he had failed to keep himself from Sareya's embrace?

You fail because you rely on your own strength, Tion would have told him. *To succeed, you must give yourself up to the will and mercy of Menselas.* Easy for Tion to say, given that he now had a wife and lands, and was free from the daily sacrifices a priest had to make.

When the acolyte's work was done, he returned the branding tool to the coals and stepped back.

The Grand Master was staring at the shelves of locked boxes opposite, apparently bored by the proceedings. But when the prolonged silence touched him, he jerked alert and addressed the Niyandrians, who now stood before him.

"Your own legends speak of death and rebirth, and today they have been fulfilled. Today, the lies and superstitions that kept your people from the light of truth have died. Today, your old selves have died, and your new selves are risen to the life of the Five. You bear the mark of Menselas in your flesh. You are his now. I commend each of you for the choice you have made, and for your willingness to suffer for Menselas. But ask yourselves this: what is a moment's pain compared with an eternity of bliss?"

The Niyandrians didn't exactly break out in joy and celebration. Maybe that would come later, once the pain of their branding wore off. Instead, they stood sullenly, heads bowed. To Anskar, they looked not so much like people who had abandoned themselves to Menselas, as people who had been cowed and made slaves. But the Grand Master had said they had asked for this; that they had witnessed the holy life within Branil's Burg and chosen it for themselves.

Turning from the converts, the Grand Master spoke to the knights, priests, and novices. "Truly, this is a great day. Our new brothers and sisters will remain among us for the next few weeks so they may be fully instructed in the ways of the Five. After that, they will return to their own people bearing the message of their salvation, and we will see an end to the senseless uprisings and the continuing devotion of certain factions to the cult of the Necromancer Queen."

Anskar felt Sareya bristling beside him; but what if the Grand Master was right? Under the rule of the Order, the isle had known more than a decade and a half of peace, save for the isolated attacks by Carred Selenas's rebels. Wouldn't it be better for everyone if these Niyandrian converts carried the message of peace and solidarity back to their people, and perhaps even softened the hearts of the rebels themselves? The old ways of Niyas were coming to a long-overdue end and a new day was dawning. Already, the Order had shown a great tolerance of Niyas's culture—the musicians at the Griffin's Rest last night had been proof of that. And a peaceful Niyas would draw further enterprise and investment from the mainland. That prosperity would spread, and within a few short years the Niyandrians would be thankful to Menselas that they had been conquered.

He turned to Sareya to reassure her with a smile, but she wouldn't meet his gaze. As soon as the Grand Master departed, signaling an end to the ceremony, Sareya left the chamber too. Anskar noticed that the Niyandrians who had newly given their lives to the Five watched her leave, but Sareya ignored them.

Anskar found himself rubbing at the invisible vambrace on his forearm. Something of its icy chill had returned—unless that was his imagination. It was beginning to feel less like an intriguing mystery and more like an unwanted growth or contagion. Or a shackle for a slave.

Heart pounding in his ears, he considered what he should do. Maybe he should go to Vihtor, tell him the full truth of what had happened on Hallow Hill. Maybe the priests of the Elder would know how to remove the vambrace. Surely Anskar would not be blamed…he had not traveled to Hallow Hill by choice.

Patience, a thought told him—he wasn't sure it was his own. *You do not know enough yet. Wait a while longer.*

THIRTY-TWO

THE DAY AFTER THE CONSECRATION of the vault, training resumed as normal—except for the continued presence of the Grand Master and his entourage. This included a squad of twenty knights in immaculate plate armor; and a handful of dark-clad women known as the Elect, who lurked in the shadows wherever Hyle Pausus happened to be. The Grand Master was lingering at the Burg, Vihtor had told Anskar, to speak with Luzius Landav when the sorcerer returned from whatever business he had on the island.

As the knights-liminal made their way to their morning sorcery lesson with Frae Ganwen, they passed the Seneschal and the Grand Master in the bailey, deep in conversation. From what Anskar caught of the discussion, Luzius Landav should have returned the day before yesterday. Indeed, the sorcerer had been expected at the consecration of the vault.

Anskar noticed that the portcullis at the far end of the barbican was half raised, and a contingent of the Burg's own knights formed two lines outside, as if expecting an arrival. With any luck, it was Landav returning from his trip. Anskar hoped he might be able to speak with the sorcerer again. There were so many questions he needed to ask, and guidance he hoped to obtain.

In their lesson, Frae Ganwen taught them how to use their wards offensively—the way Crosbyn and Vaila had done during the fight with the dead-eyes. Anskar wondered if Vihtor had instructed Frae Ganwen to include it earlier than originally planned as a consequence of the near-disaster of the culling mission.

After what he'd achieved inside the cottage, flattening his ward to reinforce the ceiling, Anskar had little trouble coalescing the energy that comprised his ward into a massive fist and punching it outward. It was a draining technique, though; one that required a flood rather than a steady trickle of dawn-tide energy. That explained why Crosbyn's and Vaila's repositories had been emptied after just one such feat.

Anskar was spent after a single offensive blast; though his projection was so powerful, the target mannequin disintegrated on impact. Frae Ganwen nodded gravely, obviously impressed by his success.

Orix barely mustered enough of a sorcerous fist to topple his mannequin; and Naul and Myra couldn't manage the feat at all.

Sareya, on the other hand, destroyed her mannequin, then asked for a second, and then a third. When Anskar sent out feelers to probe her dawn-tide repository, Sareya smirked as she gave him access. It was still half full. He wondered how she had managed to control the release of power required to generate such force.

After the lesson, the trainees headed to the refectory for lunch. They passed a priest of the Mother hunched over beneath her shawl on a bench outside; she was speaking with one of the Niyandrian converts—a man who seemed to cling to every one of the old woman's words.

The other Niyandrian converts were seated together at a long table in the refectory, eating, drinking, and talking with each other in their own language. They seemed completely at ease, Anskar thought, as if they belonged. And in a sense, they did— at least for the few weeks the Grand Master had allotted them for instruction in the ways of Menselas. The woman Aelanthe glanced at Anskar as he entered, then immediately resumed her conversation.

Anskar collected his food: a thick-crusted pie filled with chestnuts, leeks and a strong-smelling cheese, sitting on a bed of greens. He pulled up a chair next to Orix, who acknowledged him with a grunt—all he could manage with his mouth full of pie. Naul was seated beside Sareya, the two of them talking in low voices and laughing at some secret joke. It turned Anskar's mood to acid, and he did his best to not look at them. Myra had her head in a book and a cup of water before her on the table. Her meal appeared untouched, save for where she might have picked over the greens.

Aelanthe rose and approached the trainees' table. She was dressed in a plain white shirt and black pants, and her dark hair was swept back in a ponytail that exposed her sharp, angular cheeks. There was something a little mannish about her, Anskar thought: she was flat-chested and broad-shouldered, and through the sleeves of her shirt he could see her arm muscles clearly defined. Her lips were thick and full, and her green-flecked eyes were almond-shaped. Like Sareya's, they betrayed no emotion.

She directed her gaze first at Anskar, saying in broken Nan-Rhouric, "I Aelanthe. Work stone. Learn Five now. Hello."

Anskar paused with his fork halfway to his mouth. "Anskar DeVantte," he said, and popped the piece of pie in his mouth.

Aelanthe's brow furrowed slightly, and she made virtually the same introduction to Orix. The Traguh-raj lad only nodded at her, his mouth too full to speak.

"Myra," Myra said, barely glancing up from her book.

Naul rose and shook the woman's hand—a gesture Aelanthe seemed unfamiliar with. And then she spoke in Niyandrian to Sareya: a long flurry of words.

Sareya replied in Nan-Rhouric: "How do you like being a Niyandrian in the Burg?"

Aelanthe frowned and looked to the others at the table for an explanation. Clearly, she didn't understand enough of the common tongue to know what Sareya had said. Anskar glared at Sareya, willing her to explain in Niyandrian, but she resumed her conversation with Naul as if Aelanthe didn't exist.

Swallowing his food, Anskar rose and gave the woman a slight bow. "Welcome," he said. "May Menselas resolve all that wars within you and bring you to his balance."

Whether or not she understood his words, she understood the tone and the body language, and smiled her gratitude. She returned to her own table, but her eyes repeatedly flicked to Sareya, and it was clear that when she spoke in low tones to the other Niyandrians, she was talking about her. And who could blame her? Sareya had been rude beyond all belief.

"What?" she asked, catching him studying her.

"Nothing. I just thought you could have been a bit more… you know, welcoming, that's all."

Sareya's face twisted into a snarl. "It's a betrayal of our race, what they've done. A rejection of our culture, our gods."

"You are too harsh," Myra said. "Especially given that you remain at the Burg when it is no longer required of you."

"Isn't it?" Sareya snapped. "Don't believe everything they tell you, rich girl. Come on, Naul, I don't need to listen to this."

Sareya and Naul found themselves another table, where they continued to laugh and joke as if they were lovers. Anskar understood the need for discretion with Vihtor watching his and Sareya's every move, but Sareya seemed to see no problem turning her attentions to Naul. It made Anskar's blood boil to think that she could so casually hop from his bed to another's. After all, he had risked much by again spending the night with her.

By the Five, he wished he had never succumbed to her advances the first time.

After lunch, Anskar trailed Orix into the bailey. They still had some time before the afternoon's session in the smithing hall, where Sned would be expecting them to begin assembling their steel rings into the 4:1 weave pattern that would constitute the basis of the hauberks. It was the easiest single-sized ring pattern and used the least wire. Once they were done with their first mail shirt, they could progress to other patterns using two different ring sizes and even 6:1 weaves.

Anskar was twitching with hurt and anger about Sareya, and Orix seemed to sense that, staying silent as they walked across the bailey. Anskar knew his jealousy meant he still cared for Sareya, but it was clearly over between them. She had moved on to Naul, and who could blame her? Anskar hadn't exactly made it easy for her. The true culprit, though, he was coming to believe with more and more certainty, was the Order itself, and the inhuman demands allegiance to the Five made on people.

He understood now what Sareya had meant when she'd said she had nowhere else to go. Either he surrendered himself fully to the demands of the Order, or he would be cast out. If he was lucky, he might land a position as a laborer or a hired hand aboard a ship. If not, he would starve to death. Or, if he reached the mainland, he might end up a servant in some wealthy noble's mansion. None of those possibilities were particularly alluring.

He had to do better. He had to forget Sareya and work harder to ascend toward perfection as a knight. But as much sense as that made, he found it difficult to muster the enthusiasm. It would come, he told himself, so long as he prayed for it.

"Something's going on," Orix said.

Anskar looked up and saw a flurry of activity around the inner gates of the barbican; and at the far end, the portcullis was being winched down. Knights of the Burg, as well as those of the Grand Master's entourage, emerged from the barbican into the bailey. Among them Anskar glimpsed a few dark-garbed women of the Elect. The knights fell into twin lines leading away from the barbican, and along the passage they formed came Vihtor and the Grand Master, and behind them…Luzius Landav's dwarf assistant, Malady. Her motley clothes were besmirched and frayed; her face fixed in a scowl. In one hand she clutched the neck of a sack, the underside of which was stained dark. Three Elect followed the dwarf, their cloaks thrown back to reveal baldrics loaded with knives that glinted in the midmorning sun.

"What's this about?" Orix asked.

Anskar shrugged. No one had registered their presence yet; all eyes were on Malady and the sack she carried.

"I take it you have something to show me?" the Grand Master said. "What's in the sack?"

With almost casual disdain, the dwarf tipped its contents onto the ground. The silence that followed was deafening.

Anskar strained to see what the sack had held, but Vihtor was standing in his line of sight. At last, the Seneschal dropped to one knee and made the sign of warding. The assembled knights did the same, save for the Grand Master and the dwarf.

Anskar heard Orix gasp before he had fully registered what he was now able to see.

There on the ground, drenched in blood, empty eye sockets staring, was the head of Luzius Landav.

Help me! the head cried.

Anskar glanced around, but no one else seemed to have heard the anguished wail. They just stared in horror at the grisly sight.

"Carred Selenas did it," Malady told the Grand Master. "But not before my master had determined what she was up to. A plot is afoot within the very walls of Branil's Burg. You have been hoodwinked."

"In what way?" Vihtor said, rising.

"I have fulfilled my final service," Malady said. "More I will not say."

"The Niyandrian builders who were branded for Menselas?" the Grand Master asked. "Will they betray us?"

Malady ignored the question. "I was compelled by the bindings of my master to bring him to hallowed ground in the event of his demise."

"Compelled?" repeated the Grand Master. "Bindings?" He flashed a look of horror at Vihtor.

As one, the three Elect drew blades and advanced a step.

Malady continued unperturbed. "It's a risky business, binding a demon who is already in the service of another, especially when that other is a demon lord. Luzius was safe so long as he still lived; but dying without releasing the bindings he placed upon me…not the most sensible thing to do. Still, it's his essence, or soul as you would call it, and I'll lose no sleep over it."

"What plot?" the Grand Master demanded, as if he hadn't heard what Malady had just said. As if he couldn't accept it.

The dwarf ignored his question. "Despite his hubris, Luzius was a fearful man who hoped to escape the torments of the abyssal realms while acknowledging that he duly deserved them. He staked his eternal soul on the mercy of Menselas, for whom, it is said, no sin is too great to forgive. And so, for my last act of servitude, I bring him to you—well, a bit of him, but he'd say it was the most important—for burial in hallowed ground. And maybe it will work; maybe the Five will free him from the clutches of his new master." She stuck out her bottom lip. "I'm not convinced, but what do I know?"

Anskar! the head of Luzius Landav said, but again no one else betrayed any reaction. *For pity's sake, Anskar!*

This time, Anskar was sure he had seen the lips move. He glanced at Orix for confirmation, but his friend's attention was all on Malady.

"I compel you to reveal what you know, demon!" Hyle Pausus said.

"You have no power to compel me," Malady sneered. "Only a sorcerer does—a real sorcerer who has not stunted their own growth by using only the dawn-tide. Like him." She kicked the severed head; then she raised her eyes to meet Anskar's. With a wink and a smile, she might just as well have said, "And him," but she released his gaze without a word.

Anskar felt a chill start at the base of his spine and work its way upward. Orix grabbed his arm and tried to pull him away.

The Elect behind the dwarf advanced another step, and her nostrils flared, as if she smelled them.

"Kill it!" the Grand Master said.

The three Elect leaped forward, but in the same instant, the temperature dropped to freezing and frost rimed the ground of the bailey. A filthy, sulfurous stench made Anskar gag.

Malady dissolved into a cloud of soot that swirled into a vortex and spiraled down into the ground until nothing of her remained.

"Round up every last Niyandrian in the Burg!" Hyle Pausus snarled, his breath steaming in the cold air. "Bring them to me."

Vihtor held out his hands in placation. "Grand Master, surely not the trainees?"

"All of them, Seneschal. Too much has been invested in this isle to risk it now. Carred Selenas will rue the day she crossed me. Kill my sorcerer, would she? I'll show the bitch!"

"I implore you, Grand Master," Vihtor said. "Temper your rage. We must act with caution, not haste."

"Sareya!" Orix blurted.

One of the Grand Master's plate-armored knights turned at his outburst; strode toward them. Vihtor glanced over his shoulder and met Anskar's gaze. The Seneschal looked ashamed.

"Inside, both of you," the Grand Master's knight snarled as he drew near to Orix and Anskar. "Say nothing of what you have seen here."

Anskar's hands shook as he assembled units of five interlinked rings for his mail hauberk. He couldn't stop thinking about

Luzius Landav's severed head. *Help me! For pity's sake, Anskar!*

Had he really been the only one to hear it? To see its lips move? It wouldn't be the first time he'd heard the dead speak. Was he going mad, or was it his tainted catalyst playing tricks on him?

He kept glancing at Sareya, who was working on her own assembly across the hall from him, next to Naul. At any moment Anskar expected the Grand Master's knights to come in and drag her away. Or worse still, the dark-garbed Elect.

But no one came; and as the afternoon wore on and he started the task of joining his five-ringed units together to form the front of his mail hauberk, he began to relax. Perhaps Vihtor had succeeded in calming the Grand Master's ire.

During a water break, Orix led him outside the smithing hall, where they spoke in hushed voices. He was still visibly shaken by Landav's severed head and the revelation that Malady was a demon, but more so by the Grand Master's reaction.

"You think he'll go through with rounding up all the Niyandrians in the Burg?" Orix asked.

"I don't know," Anskar said. "We'll find out soon enough. At least they haven't come for Sareya."

"Yet," Orix said glumly. "What will we do if they take her?"

Anskar didn't want to think about that. His heart told him one thing; his head another.

"Sareya isn't our problem," he said.

Orix shot him a disapproving glare. "She's my friend. *Our* friend."

Naul's lover.

"You're right," Anskar forced himself to say. "But what could we do? We can't fight them—we're sworn to obey, and in any case, there are too many. We should pray," he added lamely. By the Five, he was starting to sound like Tion. "Pray to Menselas that the Grand Master will see sense."

"You think that will work?" Orix asked.

Anskar could tell his friend wasn't being dismissive; he looked too worried. "What concerns me most is how Carred Selenas and her rebels were able to kill a sorcerer of Landav's caliber," he said.

"Maybe he wasn't as good as he thought."

"No, he was good. You saw what Malady was capable of, and Landav had the power to bind her."

"I saw, but I still don't believe it," Orix said.

Anskar did. The dwarf had dissolved into the earth—a feat that reminded him of when he had stepped into the shadows during the battle with the dead-eyes. No wonder Vihtor had reacted so strongly to the action.

He fought back the climbing dread that threatened to engulf him. He was no demon. If anyone besides Malady deserved that label, it was the Grand Master himself. It was Hyle Pausus who had desecrated the Hooded One's chapel by turning it into a banker's vault. It was he who had branded the Niyandrians. And it was he who now demanded they all be rounded up and punished in retaliation for something they couldn't possibly have done.

Unless they really were spies. Anskar had to admit it was a possibility, which meant that Carred Selenas's agents had been within Branil's Burg all this time, with no one any the wiser. But where was the proof? Would the Grand Master even bother looking for evidence?

"I thought demons were just myths," Orix said.

"The way I see it," Anskar said, "if there are gods—and Brother Tion said many ancient gods were once worshiped across the mainland, before the spread of the Church of Menselas—then it only stands to reason there are demons too. And there's the histories detailing the demon lord Nysrog and his armies."

Orix shuddered. "So, a demon helped fit my catalyst…"

"Mine too," Anskar said. "But she was serving Landav. She was bound to him, she said."

"But why would Landav, a sorcerer in good standing with the Order, bind a demon to his service?" Orix asked.

"Good question. And one I don't think we'll get a straight answer to, even if we could think of anyone to ask."

"Vihtor?" Orix suggested.

"I think not," a voice said.

Anskar turned, startled. It was Sned, and his face was stern and forbidding.

"Come on, lads, back to work. I heard what happened outside, and it leaves a sour taste, but best not to talk about it. Especially here, where the walls have ears."

Orix frowned at the smithing hall. "They do?"

"Them Elect have been snooping around since they got here," Sned said. "Makes me feel I've done something wrong. I'll be glad when the whole lot of them piss off back to Sansor. Good riddance, I'll say."

Anskar opened his mouth to speak, but Sned stopped him with a raised finger. "Not a word more. Knuckle down and get on with your work. We'll be imbuing the armor with sorcery and testing it within a couple of days. Leave other issues for those best qualified to deal with them."

But within the hour, one of the Grand Master's polished knights appeared in the doorway of the smithing hall. Sned went to speak with him and came back with a face like thunder— and something else besides, Anskar thought. The Forge Master wasn't just angry at the interruption; he was concerned.

"Put down your tools," he told the knights-liminal. "We've been summoned."

"All of us?" Myra asked. She sounded affronted at possibly being accused of some wrongdoing.

"The entire Burg," Sned said.

The knights-liminal followed the Forge Master to the bailey behind the barbican. Already the area was packed with knights—the Burg's and the Grand Master's own; half a dozen Elect; priests of the four aspects that were still represented in the citadel after the desecration of the Hooded One's chapel; postulants; novices; knights-liminal and inferior; and servants—most of them Niyandrian—huddled together and looking decidedly anxious.

The throng was arranged in a rough circle, at the center of which stood the Niyandrian converts, stripped naked, heads lowered, hands bound behind their backs. All were bloodied from the bite of a multi-tailed whip, which the white-masked acolyte brandished. Some sported other welts and abrasions too, presumably from putting up a fight. But all were cowed now; broken.

Vihtor stood stiffly beside the Grand Master, his expression unreadable. Crosbyn's face was flushed with anger and disapproval; and Vaila's lips worked constantly, either in prayer or curses. Their reactions told Anskar this was not what the Order did—at least not at Branil's Burg. But no one had the courage, it seemed, to step up and complain.

"Menselas has rejected the conversion of these dogs," the Grand Master said, once Sned's group had taken their place in the circle. "They are beyond redemption. Not through any fault of their own, but because of the sins of one Carred Selenas, leader of the so-called rebels. A fanatic and a cultist who would see Niyas suffer once more under the demonic rule of the Necromancer Queen. Some of you assembled here already know that a beloved son of Menselas, the sorcerer Luzius Landav, was brutally murdered by Selenas. His head was returned to Branil's Burg by his loyal servant."

No mention of Malady being a demon, which struck Anskar as odd. But not as odd as Landav, a sorcerer, being referred to as a beloved son of Menselas.

"Today," Hyle Pausus said, "I intend to send a reply to Carred Selenas; one designed to put an end to this foolish rebellion of hers—a rebellion not endorsed by the majority of Niyandrians." He fixed a smile on his pudgy face and turned to take in all the Niyandrian servants and trainees, including Sareya.

It was a cynical gesture, Anskar thought, considering the Grand Master had initially ordered his knights to round up all Niyandrians in the Burg. Probably none of them knew how close they had come to the same fate as the converts. Surely only Vihtor's intervention had saved them. Anskar watched the Seneschal closely, wondering what that action had cost him; but Vihtor stood silently beside the Grand Master, tacitly offering his support.

"The message I will send to Carred Selenas is this," Hyle Pausus continued. "For every one of Menselas's people she murders, nine of her own will suffer the same fate, and one more will be maimed and sent to bear her the news."

Mutters passed among the Niyandrian servants, swiftly curbed when a dark-garbed Elect woman turned a glare on them. They realized the threat now: once the converts had been slain, they would be next in line, unless the rebellion ceased.

"How long this goes on—a day, a week, a month—is up to

Carred Selenas. Sooner or later she will realize the futility of her cause, but before she does, perhaps the people she claims to represent will rise up and say 'Enough!'"

The Grand Master flicked a look toward his own knights. One of them—a huge man with a two-handed sword—strode into the circle.

Dropping his whip, the masked acolyte grabbed one of the bound Niyandrians and forced him to his knees.

The knight's sword went up. And came down.

Anskar looked away—straight into Sareya's eyes. For once he could read them: they were wide with fright; appalled; livid. Tears spilled down her cheeks, and she visibly shook. Naul discreetly tried to take her hand, but she snatched it away.

Again Anskar heard the rush of air as the sword swept down; the pulpy crack of steel meeting flesh and bone; the muffled thud of a head hitting the ground. Gritting his teeth, he forced himself to watch, lest he be singled out as a dissenter. Blood pumped from the necks of the two headless corpses and pooled upon the grass of the bailey. The heads were snatched away and slung into a large sack.

Again and again the sword fell, and each time Anskar felt a little piece of himself die. His nostrils filled with the cloying, metallic scent of blood. The grass was slick with gore, the images of slaughter forever burned into his mind. He knew this execution was an affront to the faith Tion and the other priests had taught him. No god would exact such retribution. At least, no god worthy of worship.

Another Niyandrian was forced to his knees. In the brief moment of life remaining to him, he shouted his defiance: "The heir will rise. Talia's daughter!"

It took two strikes of the sword to completely sever his head.

Either he was a tough man to kill, or the knight-executioner wanted to make him pay for his remarks.

Only one Niyandrian convert remained to carry the grisly message to Carred Selenas: a woman. It wasn't Aelanthe. In fact, Anskar didn't recall seeing Aelanthe among the group. And then he realized: only ten Niyandrians had been assembled here in the bailey. But there had been fourteen of them at the conversion ceremony. Where were the other four?

Anskar studied the Grand Master. Surely he must know there were four unaccounted for. Why had he said nothing about them? Had he let them go? Doubtful. Probably he had chosen not to mention it. If four Niyandrians had evaded capture, it showed weakness; it said Hyle Pausus wasn't fully in control. But if they had fled, how had they escaped the confines of the Burg? Or evaded the Grand Master's Elect?

The acolyte threw the last remaining Niyandrian to the ground, then invited the knights to kick her with their armored boots. First came the Grand Master's knights, and then it was the turn of the Burg's own. Anskar hoped they would refuse, but at a stiff nod from Vihtor, they stepped forward one after another and meted out their punishment. Even Crosbyn, though his kicks lacked conviction. Even Vaila. Even Vihtor himself.

The Niyandrian woman lay curled in a ball, arms bent at impossible angles, legs broken and useless, blood drooling from her mouth.

A horse was brought through the circle, led by Larson the stablemaster. His eyes were downcast, and as soon as he had delivered the horse, he left.

A couple of the Grand Master's knights lifted the Niyandrian woman and draped her over the horse's back. The acolyte secured her in place with rope. The bulging sack containing the nine Niyandrians' heads was placed on top of her and tied in place. One of the Grand Master's knights took the reins and led the beast toward the barbican, where the inner gates were slowly opening, and the portcullis was beginning to rise. Three more knights took up the rear.

"They will lead the horse through the streets of Dorinah," the Grand Master said, his tone weary, as if this were an act of tremendous self-sacrifice, "then drive it out into the wilderness. Either the rebels will find it or they will not; but it *will* be seen. Word will reach Carred Selenas. Let us hope she learns her lesson without us having to repeat it."

THIRTY-THREE

THE ATMOSPHERE WITHIN BRANIL'S BURG deteriorated over the next few days. Lessons became somber affairs. Frae Ganwen displayed an irascibility that had not been there before; and Sned obviously spent more time in his cups than usual, often coming to the smithing hall red-eyed and slurring his speech. The Forge Master looked like a man whose conscience had been pricked but not acted upon. Vihtor might have lacked the drunkard's appearance Sned wore so easily, but there was a new hardness about him that made him aloof and unapproachable. To Anskar's mind, none of them were to blame. The longer the Grand Master's knights and Elect remained in the Burg, unsuccessfully searching for signs of the missing Niyandrians, the worse the atmosphere became.

Sareya withdrew into herself, seldom speaking and barely eating. Even Myra started encouraging her to eat and drink. Naul trailed Sareya like a shadow, but she rarely acknowledged his presence. Anskar could see how much her concentration wandered during their lessons, but she persevered all the same.

For himself, Anskar mourned the loss of Luzius Landav like a missed opportunity. Certainly, he'd had no affection for the sorcerer, but Landav had raised the specter of a different life for Anskar; perhaps one in which he wouldn't be forced to lie. If the sorcerer had asked it, Anskar would have followed him. Not because he rejected the Order and the Five—far from it. But because Landav had seen deep into his core and recognized things about him that others would condemn. Recognized them and not even flinched.

Despite the atmosphere, the knights-liminal continued to assemble their mail hauberks, link by link, unit by unit; and each morning they memorized the sorcerous cants that would imbue the steel with unnatural toughness. There was no need to add astrium this time, Sned told them; it was already a component of the steel wire they had used to construct each individual link.

Finally, at the week's end, it was time to apply the sorcery. Anskar drew upon the dawn-tide as he uttered the words of the cant and ran through the calculations in his mind. The only discernible effect was a ghostly shimmer that coated the mail before fading away to nothing.

"That'll do," Sned said, as if Anskar hadn't spent hours and days working on it. Probably, the Forge Master was nursing a hangover. "Good work."

Sned surveyed the hauberks of the other knights-liminal. Some he praised; others he merely sniffed at. Gone was his usual rigor, replaced by an indifference that bordered on despair.

"Will you be testing the armor like you did the swords?" Naul asked.

Sned shook his head. "Either you followed my and Frae Ganwen's instructions diligently, or you didn't. You'll find out soon enough when you fight your first battle. Those who weren't listening, or skimped on the details, will regret it when they feel the bite of cold steel in their guts."

It was a sobering thought, but Anskar knew he had done all he could with the armor. His confidence in his dawn-tide sorcery was growing by the day.

"Seriously, though," Sned added, "you've all done me proud. The Seneschal will hear only good things from me, and I expect you all to be put forward for simple vows. Count yourselves lucky," he said drily, "that Grand Master Hyle Pausus is here to preside over your swearing in."

It should have been an honor, but to Anskar it felt anything but. The Five only knew what Sareya must be thinking.

As the knights-liminal left the smithing hall wearing their new mail hauberks to get used to the weight, Sareya drew Anskar to one side. Instinctively, he cast about in case Vihtor should be passing by.

Sareya rolled her eyes. "You still care if you're seen with me?"

Anskar crossed his arms over his chest. "I need to be above suspicion. We both do. And besides, I thought you were with Naul now."

Sareya scoffed. "He'd like that, I'm sure. We're friends, nothing more. You'll be pleased to know I've been taking things more seriously. Since the battle with the dead-eyes, if not before, I've really been trying."

"You've accepted Menselas?"

"I thought I had, but the other day…in the bailey…"

"I know," Anskar said, flinching at the memory of bodies without heads.

He gestured for Sareya to walk with him to the refectory. If anyone spotted them, they had the excuse of walking together after finishing their lesson in the smithing hall. Besides, what could they possibly get up to out in the open?

"I've heard of mass conversions of Niyandrians in Dorinah and beyond," Sareya said, "following the passage of the horse bearing the lone survivor. It's wrong, Anskar. There's a demonic feel to what has happened since the Grand Master's arrival here."

Anskar silenced her with a sharp look. The Grand Master's Elect might hear. But he knew what she was saying, for he had felt it too. The stench of wrongness pervaded the entire Burg, and he couldn't wait for the Grand Master and his entourage to set sail for the mainland.

"They seek not only the conquest of our land but of our entire culture," Sareya continued in a whisper. "First, our old ways, our religion; then it will be our language, our customs, everything that defines us as a race. They plan to make us as they are, only on a lower level because of the redness of our skin."

It was hard to deny. Anskar had seen the way the knights within the citadel treated the Niyandrian servants; and there was always an undercurrent of condescension toward the Niyandrian novices. And woe betide any who showed a glimpse of their innate sorcerous ability, as Sareya had done in the fight with the dead-eyes. Vihtor had been lenient that time, because everyone knew none of them would have survived without her dusk-tide sorcery; not to mention the even darker sorcery Anskar himself had unleashed. What that told him—and presumably Sareya, too—was that the knights were willing to disregard their moral standards in the interests of survival and victory. It wasn't the absolute moral code Anskar had come to crave and respect. If anything, it was Tion all over again, only far, far worse. Tion was a weak man with normal human longings. Ultimately, he'd shown strength in accepting what he was and stepping down from the priesthood; but these others—Vihtor, the Grand Master and their ilk—they continued with the facade of purity while doing whatever they felt they needed to in the name of their cause. As the entire Burg had witnessed the other day, this included the murder of innocents.

Assuming, of course, the Niyandrian converts had been innocent, Anskar reminded himself. What if Malady had been telling the truth about a plot from within the very walls of Branil's Burg? Surely, that would go some way to explaining the hard line the Grand Master had taken? Even mitigate, in some small way, the cruelty he had inflicted upon them? And if there had been a threat, perhaps it was still present. There were four Niyandrians still at large.

"What if these rebels aren't the devils the Order makes them out to be?" Sareya continued. "What if they really are fighting for the freedom of Niyas? They may be all that stands between my people and being devoured by the demons of the mainland. How can I abandon my childhood beliefs? It would be a rejection of my people; my own parents."

Anskar frowned. "Carred Selenas's rebels are cultists sworn to bring about the return of Queen Talia. That's necromancy, Sareya. Can't you see that?"

"All I see is confusion. The Niyas I was born into is slipping away."

"Is that such a bad thing?"

She shot him an inscrutable look, then sighed. "But what will replace our culture? Are we Niyandrians to be no different from the mainlanders, with their love of wealth, their iron grip on power?"

"The love of Menselas serves as a balance to the greed of people," Anskar said, quoting Tion. It sounded lame, even to his ears.

Sareya didn't seem to hear. "I have been insulated from my culture for so long, I can barely recall my parents' faces any more."

"At least you knew them," Anskar said.

Sareya reached out to touch his arm, then thought better of it. "I'm sorry. That was insensitive. You still believe they were mainland knights? Or have you considered what we spoke about before?"

About how the reddish tinge to his skin might denote Niyandrian blood? Anskar was beyond caring either way. "I don't know what to think any more."

They stopped outside the refectory and Sareya said, "What do we really know, Anskar?"

He frowned, not understanding.

"You've never seen the mainland. And neither have I. We know so little of the world outside Branil's Burg; beyond Niyas. How can we judge what is right and just, and what is evil? All I know is what I feel…and I don't want to see my culture die. I don't want to lose my memories of childhood. Not if I can't be certain of the Order, of the Church of Menselas, and all they stand for."

"Will you proceed to simple vows?" Anskar asked. The vows would bind them for the period of one year, after which they would be expected to either take solemn vows or leave the Order and never return.

Sareya's usually unreadable eyes seemed to convey a profound sadness. Or maybe it wasn't her eyes; maybe it was despair suffusing the very skin of her face. "What other choice do I have? I've no doubt my rejection of the Order would be seen as a betrayal, and we all know how that would end."

Flayed flesh and broken bones; the stroke of a two-handed sword.

The simple vows ceremony saw the return of the knights-liminal to the Dodecagon. The cavorting forms of the masked Niyandrians depicted in the stained-glass ceiling blazed with almost supernatural brilliance in the light of the rising sun. The twelve-sided chamber was filled with all the Order's trainees and a good number of its knights, along with the Grand Master's plate-armored bodyguards. Of the Elect, there was no sign. Anskar assumed the dark-clad women were still scouring the Burg for any sign of the escaped Niyandrians.

Blosius, standing at the front of a group of novices, waved to Anskar, beaming as if he were the one about to take simple vows. Anskar acknowledged him with a nod.

Beside Anskar, Orix shifted nervously. Naul seemed to be taking it all in his stride; he'd worked for this, his expression said, and now he was collecting his just deserts. Myra's mail hauberk threatened to swamp her.

Sareya was so still, so devoid of expression, she could have been carved from stone.

For himself, Anskar knew he had to turn a blind eye to the Grand Master's shameful treatment of the Niyandrian converts. Hyle Pausus was just one man—a flawed one; he was not the office of the Grand Master. In time, he would grow feeble and die, and then the ideals that defined the Knights of Eternal Vigilance would be reborn under a new head. Someone like Vihtor perhaps; certainly not someone like Anskar himself. He already knew there was an irreparable schism between the pious ideals he'd grown up with and the revelation of the roiling forces within him. Whoever he was in truth, whoever his parents had been, he was resigned to the fact that he could not ignore his nature. He would do his best to be the knight Vihtor expected him to be, but in his mind he had already failed. It was only a matter of time before that became clear to everyone else.

The Grand Master and Vihtor entered the Dodecagon through the double doors. The white-masked acolyte followed them, laden with the white cloaks to be given to those taking vows.

Vihtor called each of the knights-liminal forward. Naul was first, barely suppressing a grin of pride as he went down on one knee. The acolyte passed a white cloak to the Grand Master, who draped it over Naul's shoulders and fastened the clasp. He rested a hand on Naul's bowed head and muttered the invitation, to which Naul responded with the vow they had been instructed to learn overnight.

As Myra, Gar, Sareya and Orix went up in turn, Anskar thought the Grand Master looked bored, as if he couldn't wait for the rite to be over.

When at last his own turn came, he kneeled, and the Grand Master fastened the cloak about his shoulders. He touched Anskar's head and asked, "Do you seek admission to the knightly ranks of the Order of Eternal Vigilance?"

Anskar recited the vow: "I, Anskar DeVantte of Branil's Burg, do so wish. I swear to uphold the statutes and the honor of the Order of Eternal Vigilance and the law of Menselas for the period of one year, and I dedicate myself to the nurture of those beneath me, and obedience to those above."

The words were bile. Lies. The whole ceremony was a sham, and anyone with eyes could see that. But what else could he do? He had nowhere else to go; and while he'd fantasized about how he could make a living, all his ideas now seemed so unrealistic; someone else's dreams. He had no choice. He'd been nurtured for this. Manipulated all his life. Looking back, he'd never had a choice. And neither had Sareya.

The Grand Master's hand lingered on Anskar's head, then squeezed his shoulder. As Anskar stood, Hyle Pausus gave him a curious look—at once questioning and filled with amusement. Anskar glanced at Vihtor, but the Seneschal was looking down at his feet.

"Well done," Hyle Pausus said, clasping Anskar's hand and giving it a limp shake.

"Thank you, Grand Master," Anskar mumbled, then dipped his head and backed away. When he was sure he was not being watched, he wiped his hand discreetly on his pants.

The Grand Master left with his acolyte in tow, and immediately the Dodecagon devolved into a hubbub of voices as the tutors, novices and postulants congratulated the newly professed knights-inferior. Crosbyn winked at Anskar and raised his thumb, while Vaila gave him a curt nod.

"Just one more short year," Vihtor said as he shook Anskar's hand—far more firmly than the Grand Master had done—"and you will be taking solemn vows."

Anskar didn't know how to respond to that. He swallowed and settled on a perfunctory nod.

A troubled expression flitted across Vihtor's face, and he leaned in close to whisper, "Have there been any more visits… from the crow?"

Anskar shook his head.

"That is good. And the girl?"

"I gave you my word," Anskar said, but he was barely able to suppress a cringe at the statement. His word was worthless.

"The struggles you face…" The Seneschal trailed off, sounding uncertain. He still had not relinquished his grip on Anskar's hand. "At your age, I mean…all of you trainees…it is not easy. There is much that we must renounce: urges, an inclination to sin… I am pleased with how well you've taken to the task, Anskar. More than that, I'm proud of you."

Vihtor released Anskar's hand and passed him a coin purse. "Here: your first week's stipend. The citizens of the mainland realize our worth and pay their gratitude in taxes. Remember their generosity in your prayers." He clapped Anskar on the arm and walked away to congratulate the other new knights-inferior.

Shame, or rage, or indignation, burned like acid through Anskar's veins. For as long as he could remember, he had craved Vihtor's approval, but now he had it, he despised it. Vihtor didn't approve of who Anskar really was, what he had done, what he continued to do. He approved of the facade Anskar had presented to him. Either the Seneschal was easily misled, or he was turning a blind eye.

But the child that still clung to life in Anskar longed for Vihtor's words to be true. Longed for approval. The Seneschal believed he could make it as a knight, but was that really possible? A consecrated knight, unblemished, truly holy? Was such a path still open to him, despite his inclinations, his urges, the powers that threatened to engulf him?

He grasped the neck of the coin purse Vihtor had given him—a sign of his new worth as a knight-inferior. Perhaps the Seneschal believed Anskar could rid himself of the bubbling dark within him. Maybe one day he would.

He looked up, straight into Sareya's eyes. She had been watching him, no doubt reading the play of emotions on his face.

"I can do it," he wanted to say to her. "Vihtor approves of me!

We can do it—we can both become knights."

But he said nothing.

His words would have sounded false; hollow.

Sareya had the look of the damned about her, and it was contagious.

THIRTY-FOUR

THE FIRST BENEFIT OF BEING a knight-inferior was that Anskar no longer had to endure Frae Ganwen's monotonously detailed lessons on dawn-tide sorcery. Continuing with her classes was optional, and encouraged, but to Anskar's mind he had outgrown the sorcery lessons with their limited use of the dawn-tide, and he had little doubt that he already exceeded Frae Ganwen's modest abilities.

On the other hand, he decided he would continue to attend Sned's smithing and metallurgy classes until he had achieved full mastery—if ever anyone could. And even if he did, he would probably still spend time in the smithing hall. He enjoyed the work, and he enjoyed Sned's company, in a strange way.

But not today. Soon enough, Anskar and the other new knights-inferior would receive instructions from Vihtor, but today he had to himself.

He needed solitude, time in which to reflect. Was it possible to become what he had aspired to be as a child, despite the rot within the Order? Or was there indeed another way—a way he felt certain Luzius Landav had implied? He needed to get away from the Burg so that he could think clearly; feel the wind in his hair, the sun on his face. The citadel was no longer a protective mother for him; it was an overbearing father.

He left the refectory after breakfast, before his peers had gotten halfway through their meals. Orix stood, cramming his mouth with sausage and bread, obviously intending to go with Anskar, but Anskar told him he needed to be alone.

At the horse yard, Larson was yelling at a novice for not cleaning the stalls out properly—Hazel's stall and Monty's. Anskar's old job.

"Useless bloody idiot," the stablemaster said as he saw Anskar and ambled over. "Him, not you."

The novice was red-faced and trembling after his dressing down. He wiped his eyes and disappeared inside the stalls with a rake.

"Newly arrived from Sansor and can't take a shit without a servant to wipe his ass with silk." Larson must have seen the loss on Anskar's face, for he said, "You can visit Hazel and that dumb ol' donkey anytime you like. I just figured you'd be too busy now that you're a knight-inferior."

Anskar nodded, surprised at how sad he felt. "I was wondering…" he started, but Larson took hold of him by the arm and led him to the main stable block.

Anskar craned his neck at the sound of barking and snarling.

"Cut it out," Larson yelled over his shoulder at Rosie. "Stupid dog. Don't know what's gotten into her of late."

"Maybe she's rabid?" Anskar suggested. They both knew that wasn't the case. Maybe it was him.

Larson led Anskar into a stall and patted the flanks of a huge gray destrier.

"Every knight must own and care for their own horse," the stablemaster said. "This here's Old Thunder. Consider him yours."

"But I've only taken simple vows," Anskar said. "I'm just a knight-inferior."

"We all have to start somewhere," Larson said, clapping a hand on Anskar's shoulder and looking him in the eye. "If you don't move on to solemn vows a year from now, you can give the horse back." The stablemaster smiled and his eyes glistened. He turned away and stroked Old Thunder behind the ear.

"He's a good horse but a willful one; known to bite. Used to belong to Hafdin Scorce"—Larson touched four fingers and thumb to his forehead—"Menselas grant him balance. Remember the fallen brought back from a skirmish with the rebels a while back?"

Anskar nodded. It was difficult to forget.

"Hafdin was one of them. Old Thunder brought him home; and word is, he killed the man who did for Hafdin. Like I said, a good horse."

Anskar rode alone from the Burg, unchallenged in his white cloak by the knights stationed at the west gate. He had expected resistance from Old Thunder, given what Larson had said, but besides a stomp and a snort when he mounted, the horse proved perfectly obedient.

As he rode at a trot through Dorinah, Anskar noticed a team of Niyandrian laborers in the process of erecting a timber frame for a large building. Directing them was a priest of the Elder, which suggested the building was to be a new church. The priest was cursing and yelling in a manner at odds with his venerable appearance. Rather than answering back, the Niyandrians bent to their tasks with quiet resignation. Anskar wondered if these were some of the converts Sareya had spoken about—the first fruits of the conversion of all Niyas. If they were, he only hoped their fate was better than that of the converts back at the Burg.

Anskar headed north through the city. In the distance, a bank of dark clouds rolled in from the Simorga Sea. Already, a light patter of rain was falling, but that didn't bother him; if anything, he found it cleansing. Thunder rumbled way out to sea, and Old Thunder whinnied in response, then bucked and tried to bolt; but when Anskar pulled tight on the reins the destrier settled back into a trot.

The north of the city was far more impoverished than the other areas Anskar had seen. Storefronts were boarded up, and the houses were little more than hovels in states of disrepair. The drainage ditches cut into the packed earth roads were overgrown with weeds and likely to flood at the first decent rainfall—which was probably going to be quite soon, judging by the gusting wind bringing the storm clouds ever closer. Urchins playing in the streets stopped to watch Anskar's passage with bright cat's eyes staring out of their grubby faces. Disheveled adults lurked in doorways, or congregated on rotting verandahs. The large groups of Niyandrians might have been threatening had they not seemed so listless and cowed.

Rarely did Anskar see a mainlander; and those he did see appeared no better off than the Niyandrians. Several were drunk, seated by the roadside drinking from brown bottles. The few knights he saw were unkempt, their white cloaks begrimed. They cast suspicious glances at him as he passed.

There was nothing to mark the northern boundary of Dorinah, only the rubble of the wall that had once stood there. No doubt the stones had been carried off to repair buildings elsewhere in the city. The remnants of a gate lay flat on the ground, smothered with grass and creepers.

Anskar rode between the leaning gate posts and across a humped bridge that spanned a foul-smelling stream. Free of the city, he kicked Old Thunder into a canter toward the northern woods, which were split wide by an ancient paved road. As they hit the road, he pushed the horse to a gallop. Frigid air scorched his face, and his white cloak flapped behind him with a sound like heavy wings.

He had hoped the gallop would clear his head, but instead he felt even more torn between despair and hope. Part of him believed he could succeed as a knight, even excel; the other part mocked him for his naïveté. How could he forget the burgeoning forces within him, the things he had seen at Hallow Hill, the vambrace on his forearm? If it was all a temptation by Menselas to see if Anskar had the strength to reject forbidden knowledge and power, it was too hard a test; too unfair. It would have helped if he knew who he was, where he came from; but more and more he had the sense that if anyone at the Burg knew the truth—even Vihtor—they would never tell him. He had been kept in the dark for a reason, he decided: either his parents' shame, or the Order's.

He pushed Old Thunder until the horse's flanks were soaked with sweat despite the rapidly falling temperature; then slowed as the road deteriorated into a muddy track carpeted with fallen leaves.

When they came to a clearing, Anskar dismounted. The space was oddly circular, surrounded by a ring of oaks, all roughly the same size and presumably the same age. Planted deliberately, then. Another mystery of the ancient Niyandrians that was doomed to pass into oblivion as the Order's dominion increased.

He tethered Old Thunder to a trunk and fed him a handful of oats. It was then he realized he'd brought no food for himself, and nothing to drink. Resolved to head back after an hour or so, Anskar seated himself among the roots of an oak, pulled up the hood of his cloak, and tried to find the still point of prayer. Somehow, prayer still comforted and calmed him despite his newfound cynicism.

Beneath the oak, miles from Branil's Burg, and with a storm closing in, he knew peace. But it was brief. No sooner had he grown aware of his tranquil state than he felt a niggling sensation like the crawl of insects' feet on the back of his neck.

He opened his eyes and looked into the branches above.

Golden eyes stared back at him.

It was the crow, perched on a thick limb. Watching him.

A frigid fist clenched Anskar's heart. He jumped to his feet, clutching the hilt of *Amalantril*, and strode to Old Thunder. He untethered the horse and remounted, then, without a backward glance at the crow, took a weaving path through the trees. Not toward Branil's Burg, but west toward Caeltrin.

He needed a drink. Something to make him numb.

The storm broke as he reached the edge of the fishing town. Heavy rain pelted him so hard it felt as though it was cutting through his clothes and skin. The sky was thick with black clouds, and the wind whistled down the main street, churning up sodden leaves in its fury.

As Anskar went to tether Old Thunder outside the Griffin's Rest, the landlord, Nigen Bosh, poked his head out the door and told him to hang on a minute. Nigen disappeared back inside, leaving Anskar to shelter under the verandah's pitched roof, which spilled rainwater in torrents. Anskar could hear Nigen yelling out back, then a Niyandrian boy in a leather apron came round the side of the tavern, cap clutched tight to his head, and led Old Thunder to the stables.

Anskar stepped inside the tavern, drenched and shivering. He thought he heard a woman's mocking laughter, but a quick scan of the interior showed him the tavern was empty—save for Nigen, who rushed toward him and ushered him over to the blazing hearth.

Anskar muttered his thanks; and then again as a dusky-skinned server brought him towels to dry off.

"A fine day," Nigen said with a rueful smile. "But you've come to the right place. Beer? Food? I'll have them sent out to you."

Nigen bustled away, but the server lingered, palm out, and Anskar realized the man wanted paying for bringing him towels. With a barely suppressed sigh, he pulled out the coin purse Vihtor had given him and placed a copper in the server's hand. When the man still didn't move, Anskar gave him another, and to his relief that did the trick.

Once he'd toweled the worst of the rain from his hair, Anskar removed his cloak and hung it over the back of a chair beside the hearth, then seated himself at a nearby table, enjoying the penetrating warmth of the flames.

He ate his meal of fish and potatoes and melted cheese in silence, sipping his beer, thoughts consumed by the crow.

He had started to believe himself free of the ungodly creature. Why was it back now? How had it known to wait for him in the branches of the oak tree? What did it want?

Blackwing.

He recalled the statue of the Necromancer Queen. A space in

the tomb atop Hallow Hill had clearly been prepared for her in advance of her death, but there had been nothing left of Queen Talia to bury. She had ended her own life with a violent blast of sorcery that had reduced Naphor to ruins and killed hundreds upon hundreds of her own people, as well as her enemies.

But there was a connection, that much was clear; some reason the crow had led him to the dead queen's empty tomb and the vambrace.

More unsettling was the involvement of the wraithe—a creature from beyond the dawn of history. What did such a being want with Anskar, a trainee under the protection of the Order of Eternal Vigilance? The whole sequence of events played out again and again in his mind, and he wondered, not for the first time, if he had been possessed by some malevolent spirit. Either that or he'd been cursed. But why? Why him, of all people?

His fist tightened around the handle of his mug, and beer sloshed over his hand. It wasn't fair. He hadn't asked for this; and all it had done was bring him into conflict with who he once was; who he aspired to be.

Perhaps he should have been more truthful with Vihtor and told him about the vambrace.

"Why so pensive, son?" Nigen asked, reversing the chair opposite and straddling it. The landlord's eyes flicked to Anskar's sodden white cloak hanging to dry in front of the hearth. "Stresses of commitment, eh? A knight-inferior now, I see. Congratulations."

"Thank you," Anskar said, making an effort to break out of the sucking mire of his ruminations. "It's been a long path."

"But worth it, eh?" Nigen said. "I haven't always been a landlord," he added. "Tested my vocation on the mainland—in Sansor." He grimaced and looked away. "Wasn't cut out for the life of a knight. But you…you have a bright future ahead of you."

His words sounded hollow to Anskar, as if they echoed from the far end of a long tunnel.

Nigen frowned with concern. "I've a good ear for listening, if you've a mind to talk."

Anskar looked at him dumbly, then smiled. "Thank you, I'll remember that. I'm all right. Just tired. The training has been long and hard."

"I'll bet," Nigen said. He flicked a look at Anskar's glistening mail. "You made that yourself?"

"I did. The final test before simple vows."

"Very nice. Listen, Anskar, you won't hear word of it back at Branil's Burg, but we get a lot of knights here at the Griffin's Rest—men and women wound tight by hard discipline. It's a huge sacrifice you folk make; and speaking for myself, I'm grateful for it. Just think what it would be like without the Order's patrols, or the strongholds going up all over the place to keep us safe." He made a show of shivering. "Doesn't bear thinking about."

"And they talk to you, these other knights?" Anskar asked.

"Some do. Others use the drink to relax. And others…" He fixed Anskar with a penetrating stare. "There are women upstairs who know how to ease tension. Men too, if you know what I'm saying."

Anskar nodded slowly. This wasn't what he wanted to hear. He'd left Branil's Burg to reflect on the things that divided him, not add to them. Setting down his mug, he stood and reached for his cloak.

"I didn't mean to offend you," Nigen said, rising too.

"I'm not offended. Just tired. I should be heading back."

"It'll be dark by the time you reach the Burg. For a silver, I can give you a room here for the night."

"Thank you," Anskar said. "Perhaps another time." He fastened his cloak and turned to leave, then turned back at a cough from Nigen.

The landlord held out his hand. "For the food," he said. "Just a couple of coppers. Beer is on the house."

Anskar smiled in appreciation, handed over two coppers, then headed for the door. As he made for the stables in the sheeting rain, he wondered whether Vihtor made use of the tavern's services, besides its food and beer.

The stable hand was surprised to see Anskar, and looked annoyed at having to re-saddle Old Thunder and lead him out into the rain. Anskar mounted and nodded his thanks; and for the third time since he'd arrived at the Griffin's Rest, a hand was held out to him for coin.

The ride back was miserable, his vision reduced to only a few feet by the heavy rain and the churning clouds that blotted out the setting sun. But as Anskar rode along the lamplit streets of Dorinah, the rain softened to a steady drizzle.

He rode through the Burg's western gate in utter blackness and dismounted, leading Old Thunder by the reins toward the denser dark of the stables.

Unsaddling and leaving his horse there, he entered the citadel, making puddles on the stone floor as he trudged along the corridors toward his room. It was unusually dark inside and he had to tread warily, hand trailing the wall for guidance. He could smell sulfur and oil, and guessed it was later than he'd thought: the lamps had burned out a short time ago.

He proceeded along the corridor, counting off the doors on the way to his room. One of them was open a crack, the wavering light of a candle coming from inside. He heard a sharp gasp and then a voice, cracking and spitting like kindling set alight.

"Anskar," it rasped. "Help her."

On the floor of the passageway outside the open door—Naul's door—something was sprawled on the floor. A body, Anskar realized as he inched closer, heart pulsing in his throat. Naul!

Naul's head cranked round to face him, the eyes rolled back. A dark line across his throat wept blood. "Anskar," he said again. "Help her. Sareya."

"Naul?" Anskar dropped to one knee and felt for a pulse. Nothing. He leaned over Naul's mouth to detect his breath. Again nothing.

And yet still Naul spoke. "They think she's Talia's daughter. Niyandrians…"

Dizziness flooded Anskar's head. He blinked and refocused, and the terrible permanence of Naul's death confronted him again. Once more, he had heard the dead speak.

Unsteadily, he pushed himself to his feet. Farther down the corridor he heard the sounds of a scuffle. A woman cried out.

Sareya!

He started toward the sound, then hesitated. Niyandrians, Naul had said. They believed Sareya was Queen Talia's daughter and heir. There were four Niyandrian converts still at large, but Sareya should have been able to overcome them with sorcery. The fact that she hadn't caused him to worry.

He backtracked to Orix's room, tried the door handle and found it unlocked. Swiftly crossing to the bed, he awoke his friend.

"Sareya's in danger," he said. "Niyandrians. Get help."

Orix leaped out of bed and grabbed his sword. At the door, Orix ran one way, yelling the alarm, while Anskar went the other. Drawing *Amalantril*, he sprinted for Sareya's room. Voices erupted in panic in response to Orix's shouting. Already doors were opening all along the corridor.

The scent of sulfur hit Anskar's nostrils again; it was coming from beneath Sareya's door. Again she cried out, weaker this time; muffled.

Anskar threw his shoulder against the door, assuming it would be locked. The frame juddered, and a woman barked words in Niyandrian. Anskar barged the door again, and this time it flew open, the jamb splintering.

The first thing he saw was Sareya, bound and gagged, kneeling at the center of a circle formed from a golden chain on the floor. There was a brilliantly glowing stone at each of the cardinal points—rose, amber, crimson, azure. Light streamed from the stones, converging overhead and showering the circle's perimeter with luminous sparks.

Within the circle stood four Niyandrians, one in front of each glowing stone. All were armed with daggers and dressed neck to toe in black bindings that left only their red-skinned faces visible. It was enough to recognize them: three men and a woman: the four escaped converts. The woman was Aelanthe.

Two of the men sprang at Anskar, daggers thrusting. He blocked one and slid out of the way of the other. Already the other two were advancing. He parried again, countered with a slash, but his blade met air. All he could think of was reaching Sareya, but the Niyandrians gave him no quarter.

He batted aside a dagger and ripped his blade up toward his opponent's throat. The Niyandrian slipped aside and punched Anskar full in the face. Anskar reeled into the wall and *Amalantril* clattered to the floor. Two daggers came at him, and behind them he glimpsed Aelanthe and the other Niyandrian rushing forward then dissolving into the shadows.

Anskar threw his hands up to ward himself from the blades. A scream erupted from his throat, and at the same time the dark-tide roared within him, bursting its bindings. Vitriol burst from his pores.

The first Niyandrian it struck shrieked and dropped his sword, nursing a withered hand. The second's face putrefied in an instant, and he fell wailing to the floor, crimson steam rising from his flesh.

A rustle of movement behind him made Anskar turn, and he shielded his eyes against a brilliant glare. At once the dark-tide within him stilled, bound by something far stronger than his own restraints.

In front of him stood Aelanthe, her dagger a streak of lightning, dazzling with silver fire. He tried to lash out with the dusk-tide, but that repository was blocked too.

The other Niyandrian touched the tip of his dagger to Anskar's throat. Aelanthe shouted something at him in Niyandrian, and the man's eyes flicked to hers.

Aelanthe looked at Anskar and uttered a stream of Skanuric words. His vision blurred for an instant, and when it returned, she gasped and said with reverent awe, "*Melesh-Eloni!*"

The man's eyes widened and he dropped his dagger, grabbed Anskar around the neck and pinned his arm behind his back. As the man dragged Anskar to the center of the circle, Aelanthe advanced on Sareya, dagger raised.

"No," Anskar cried. "What are you doing?"

He struggled to break free, but the man slammed him to the ground and put a knee in his back. Anskar screamed as Aelanthe's blade slashed toward Sareya's neck. At the last instant, she pulled back and reversed the dagger, instead hitting Sareya in the temple with the handle. Sareya toppled, and Anskar saw blood pooling from her head on the floor before Aelanthe dragged her out of the circle.

From beyond the shattered door came the tramp of booted feet; cries of challenge.

Aelanthe stepped back inside the circle. Showers from the convergent beams of the glowing stones dazzled Anskar's vision. Aelanthe raised her dagger and spoke a cant. The blade once more erupted with fire: this time a prismatic blaze of every conceivable color.

A knight appeared in the doorway, and Anskar's heart swelled with hope. It was Crosbyn, and behind him, Vihtor.

But then Aelanthe rammed her dagger high above her head, into the point of convergence of the four streams of light.

And the world exploded.

Anskar was dragged roughly to his feet. The first thing he felt was the cold rain. He blinked flash-blindness from his eyes and saw that he was outside the Burg in a lamplit street.

Aelanthe took one arm, the man the other, and they manhandled Anskar into a waiting carriage and sat him between them.

A second carriage parked alongside immediately set off down the street with a fierce clop and clatter. Aelanthe called Niyandrian words to the driver, and then they were off too, heading in the opposite direction from the other carriage, along the deserted road.

"Calm self," Aelanthe said in broken Nan-Rhouric. "Safe now, *Melesh-Eloni*."

"Sareya!" Anskar snarled through tears of rage.

"We wrong about her."

"The perfect concealment," the man said, shaking his head. His Nan-Rhouric was fluent and far less accented than Aelanthe's.

Aelanthe silenced him with a sharp hiss. She opened her mouth to say something more to Anskar, but he had seen the man's sheathed sword lying on the floor and she had noticed. Anskar slammed an elbow into Aelanthe's face, rocking her head back. He launched a kick to the man's knee, and it broke with a loud crack. Anskar grabbed the sword, then booted the carriage door open. As he leaned out, the wind whipped his hair and the cobblestones blurred beneath him. Taking a breath and uttering a swift a prayer to Menselas, he rammed the sword into the spokes of the wheel.

Multiple cracks sounded and spokes shattered, sending splinters and chunks of wood flying. The carriage veered sharply to the right, pitching him back inside. Horses shrieked and the carriage careened onto its side. There was a chaos of limbs and bodies rolling over and over. One door was ripped clean off as the carriage screeched against the road in a wide arc.

As it came to a halt, Anskar tried desperately to orient himself; battered from being thrown about. The Niyandrian man was unconscious beside him, blood trickling from his lips, leg bent at an impossible angle. Aelanthe was beneath Anskar, groaning and dazed. She had unwittingly cushioned him against the worst of the crash.

Wincing at the pain of his bruised limbs, Anskar climbed over the man and out through the open doorway. He rolled onto the road and, as he got to his knees, a cold presence fell over him.

He looked up at the hooded form of the wraithe he had first seen on Hallow Hill.

It inclined its head as if about to speak, then Aelanthe crawled out of the carriage and cried, "*Tresunios*! Betrayer!"

"Not so," the wraithe said. "I fulfilled my part of the bargain at Hallow Hill. Now, my actions are my own."

It raised its clenched fist, opened its fingers, and dropped something dark on the ground, before it melted away into the night.

Anskar heard Aelanthe's sharp intake of breath, but his eyes were riveted on what the wraithe had dropped on the road. Beady golden eyes stared back at him, slowly narrowing to slits. Black-feathered wings twitched uselessly. The crow emitted a pathetic caw. In his mind, Anskar felt it begging him for help.

Rage and regret burned through him. If this…thing had not come to him, had not led him into the wilds and onto Hallow Hill, his life would still be his own, his purpose known. He hated those golden eyes. Hated the cruel beak; the black wings.

Every muscle in his body stiffened. Aelanthe must have seen, for she cried out in Niyandrian. Anskar's boot came down, answered by a dull splat and faint crunch as he ground his tormentor underfoot.

A sound like rolling thunder approached from the other end of the street. It took Anskar a second to realize it was horses' hooves.

The knights had come for him.

As he backed away toward the din, Aelanthe staggered after him. Once more she drew her dagger, and the blade ignited with iridescent flame.

Behind Anskar, the hooves slowed and stopped. He heard the chink of mail, the rasp of swords being drawn from scabbards.

Aelanthe raised her dagger and shouted a cant. Anskar's knees buckled. He dropped to the ground. Against his will, he began to crawl toward her. She reached out a hand to him.

"Come with me," she said, the words thick and awkward on her tongue. "Safe."

Compelled, Anskar lurched to his feet and extended his hand. Their fingertips met, and instantly he felt the burgeoning tug of the shadows in an adjacent alley.

"Closer," Aelanthe said, the strain evident in her voice. "Closer…"

Anskar inched toward her; took her hand in his. Aelanthe gazed toward the alley and began the words of a cant—then slumped to her knees, releasing her grip on his hand. Blood bubbled from her mouth. Her eyes implored him, her lips feebly uttering, "*Melesh-Eloni*," as she slid back off the sword projecting from her chest.

Aelanthe hit the ground, dead, and Vihtor stepped over her, blood drenching his blade. When he saw Anskar, the Seneschal immediately backed up a step.

"Menselas!" Vihtor breathed. "What have they done to your eyes?"

THIRTY-FIVE

THE DODECAGON WAS WREATHED IN shadows when Vihtor, Crosbyn and Vaila brought Anskar there to await the Grand Master. The moons had forced their way through a bank of clouds and cast a feeble glow through the stained-glass ceiling; the silver light lent the depictions of cavorting Niyandrians a ghostly cast, as if they were lost souls in the realm of the dead.

"This is absurd," Crosbyn grumbled into his mustache. "The lad needs to be taken to the infirmary."

Vaila shook her head as if to say the sergeant was wasting his words.

No one had told Anskar what was wrong with his eyes, but it sounded bad. He could only assume Aelanthe had worked some sorcery when she uttered the Skanuric cant that had caused his vision to blur. He had begged Vihtor to tell him, begged for a mirror to see for himself, but the Seneschal had ordered him to silence. "I will deal with this," was all he would say.

Now, Vihtor made his way to one of the twelve thrones around the walls and slumped into it. "While he is here," he said, "the Grand Master is the supreme authority. It is our duty to tell him what has happened."

"Pah!" Crosbyn muttered, but he said no more on the subject.

"I'm not hurt," Anskar said. "Just a few bruises." He rolled his shoulder and winced at a shooting pain; probably from when the Niyandrian man had jammed his arm behind his back. Still, it was nothing that required the attention of the healers. He seated himself on the step beneath Vihtor's throne and looked up at the Seneschal. "Is Sareya…?"

"She lives," Vihtor said, chin on his fist, eyes far-off and brooding. "The healers arrived before we came after you."

"Can I see her?"

Vihtor glared at him, then softened it to a frown.

Realizing he would get no answer regarding Sareya, Anskar asked instead, "What of the glowing stones in her room? And the golden chain that made the circle?"

"We stored them away for safekeeping," Vaila said. "The priests of the Elder are accustomed to dealing with such artifacts of evil."

"Anskar," Vihtor said, "I hoped this day would never—"

The Seneschal stopped as the double doors parted, and in walked the Grand Master, trailed by his white-robed acolyte and a pair of plate-armored guards carrying flaming torches. Anskar caught a glimpse of dark-garbed Elect in the corridor outside.

"Spare me the details," the Grand Master said as Vihtor stood to greet him. "My people have already apprised me of the situation. A cowardly attack, no doubt born of revenge. You have prisoners, I take it?"

"All dead," Vihtor said.

"Even the drivers?" Anskar asked.

Vihtor waved him to silence and addressed the Grand Master. "The second carriage was a decoy, but we dealt with it swiftly. The driver fought like a demon. We had no choice."

"And the driver of the other carriage?" the acolyte asked.

"Died in the crash."

"I see," the Grand Master said. "A shame. There are questions I wanted answers to."

Anskar could imagine how Hyle Pausus would have extracted those answers. It was as well for the Niyandrians they had all perished. But had the driver of the decoy carriage really fought like a demon? Surely he could have been overpowered and bound?

"What caused the carriage to crash?" the Grand Master said. Vihtor looked at him blankly, so he turned to Anskar for an answer.

"I did," Anskar said.

He flinched at the memory of the crash; saw again the wraithe gliding toward him as he climbed out of the wreckage, opening its hand and dropping the dying crow to the ground. Why do that, when at Hallow Hill the bird and the wraithe had seemed in some way allied?

Even as Anskar thought about it, he felt a vague presence at the back of his mind, and knew with certainty that he had not killed the crow when he crushed it underfoot; only destroyed its body. Whatever it was remained in essence; and it now felt close to him. Too close.

"Come nearer, where I can see you," the Grand Master said, and Anskar complied.

Hyle Pausus studied him for a long moment. "You look different. Your eyes…" He glanced at Vihtor. "Does he look different to you?"

"They did something to him," Vihtor said. "Some kind of sorcery."

"To what end?"

"I don't know, Grand Master."

Hyle Pausus nodded thoughtfully. "Are you a half-blood, boy?"

"No!" Anskar said.

"His eyes were normal until tonight," Vihtor said, clamping a hand on Anskar's shoulder. The Seneschal was trembling. Why? "They did something to him, I tell you."

"What for?" the Grand Master asked his acolyte.

The man in white shrugged. "To alter him for some purpose? Or to reveal that which was hidden?"

"Show me!" Anskar said, pushing Vihtor's hand away. His heart was racing, and he found it hard to breathe.

"Soon," Vihtor said. "Once we're finished here."

"Well, thank Menselas you are otherwise unscathed," the Grand Master said to Anskar. "And the girl?" he asked Vihtor.

"With the healers. She sustained a heavy blow to the—"

"No, no, not that," the Grand Master said. "I meant what was her involvement? Why did they target her?"

Anskar opened his mouth to say that they thought Sareya was Queen Talia's daughter, but Vihtor spoke right over him.

"Vengeance pure and simple, Grand Master. A blood feud of sorts."

The Grand Master nodded. "Yes, I see. Carred Selenas killed Luzius Landav; I killed the converts in retaliation; and the fugitive four tried to kidnap one of our own. Odd, though, that they chose a fellow Niyandrian."

"They abandoned her for Anskar," Vihtor pointed out.

"But why?" the Grand Master said.

Melesh-Eloni. What did that even mean?

Vihtor knew why, Anskar was sure of it. The Seneschal knew more than Anskar did himself, and certainly more than the Grand Master. The Niyandrians had believed Sareya to be Queen Talia's heir, but they had left her behind once they witnessed Anskar's use of the dark-tide. And they had done something to his eyes. But why was Vihtor holding things back from the Grand Master? What was it he knew?

"Clearly they thought Anskar of more worth as a prisoner," Vihtor said.

The crow. The wraithe. Hallow Hill. The vambrace. Anskar clutched at its metal around his forearm.

"Do you think they will try again?" the Grand Master asked.

"If they do, we'll be ready," Crosbyn said, hand on the hilt of his sword.

"And if they use more sorcery?" the Grand Master said. "Will you be ready then?"

Crosbyn chewed on the end of his mustache.

"There is mystery afoot here," the Grand Master said. "And I abhor mystery. Get to the bottom of it, Seneschal. But until you do, I would say it is not safe for Anskar to remain at Branil's Burg, or anywhere else on Niyas for that matter."

"But—" Anskar started, but he may as well not have been present.

"I sail for Sansor on the morrow, and Anskar will accompany me."

Anskar looked pleadingly at Vihtor. *I hear the dead,* he wanted to say. *Naul spoke to me!* But no words came out. His jaw trembled; then his arms; his legs. *The Necromancer Queen. Oh, sweet Menselas! The Necromancer Queen!*

"There are associates of the Order who are wise in these

matters." The Grand Master's voice continued from a far-off place. "And by all accounts, young Anskar here is a gifted knight-inferior. He'll benefit more under my personal guidance."

Vihtor swallowed thickly. He looked as though he wanted to say something—needed to—but discipline forbade him.

Hyle Pausus strode for the door, his acolyte and his two knights trailing him.

"Sansor?" Anskar said as soon as they had left. "I can't go to the mainland. I need to speak with Sareya!"

"You'll do as you're told," Vihtor said. Then, in a softer tone, "We are all bound to do the Grand Master's will. And maybe he's right. It could be dangerous for you to remain here."

"Dangerous how? What is it you're not saying? Sir, what won't you tell me? My eyes, you said. What did they do to my eyes?"

Vihtor made a fist; swallowed; unclenched his fingers. "You will leave on the morrow, Anskar." He strode to the double doors, then turned back to speak to Crosbyn. "Take him to the infirmary. Have the healers look at his eyes. Show him."

Crosbyn nodded.

"What's going on?" Vaila asked.

The old knight shook his head. "Get some sleep, Vaila. Tomorrow, with any luck, things will return to normal."

"Huh," she snorted, but she left without another word.

In the infirmary, the healer on duty expressed bafflement at Anskar's eyes, asking him how this had happened. When Anskar mentioned sorcery, the healer looked at Crosbyn for confirmation.

"Don't ask me," Crosbyn said. "You're the healer."

"Well, there's nothing to heal," the woman said. "They look perfectly normal. For a Niyandrian."

Finally, an auxiliary brought a mirror and Anskar was

permitted to see for himself.

His eyes were a golden-flecked brown, the pupils shaped liked almonds.

Sareya looked more at peace than Anskar had ever seen her. She was asleep in an infirmary bed, gently snoring, the sheets pulled up to her neck, a bloodstained bandage around her head. He had hoped to find her awake so he could say goodbye. So he could question her.

As he turned to leave, a feeler of awareness stroked the inside of his mind. He stopped in the doorway. Looking back, he saw the trace of a smile on Sareya's lips.

Anskar returned to her bedside, and one of her eyes opened a crack, widening slightly as she focused on his face…his eyes.

"Told you," she said in a thin, rasping voice. "Half-blood."

"Sareya," he said, taking her hand and leaning in close so he could be sure she heard him. And then he got to it, the real reason he had come: "What does *Melesh-Eloni* mean?"

The smile fell from her lips and her eye closed. "Godling," she breathed.

"Godling?"

Anskar listened for more, but the light snoring resumed.

There was a footfall in the doorway. One of the healers stood there, a stern-looking woman who glared that it was time for him to leave.

There was a biting breeze, and the air was heavy with brine when early next morning the Grand Master's ship, a majestic galleon named *Exultant*, passed out of Dorinah's harbor and headed for the open sea.

Sunlight glinted from the armor of several hundred of Branil's Burg's knights standing in disciplined lines to watch the galleon leave. Behind them stood the trainees, and with them Gar and Myra, and a scatter of priests.

In the garden of a tavern that overlooked the harbor, Anskar could just about see Larson seated upon a bench, strumming his guitar and singing in a shaky voice while Rosie howled along. It was a song of farewell, which the stablemaster must have learned in his youth in the highlands of Valborg, and it brought tears to Anskar's eyes. Thank Menselas the Order had accepted Larson on his third attempt at the trials, Anskar thought. The stablemaster would have died a pauper by now if he'd pursued his dream of singing for a living.

Orix leaned over the gunwale, spewing his guts up. The one concession Vihtor had made to Anskar: a friend to accompany him on the trip to Sansor. Orix, of course, had seen it as a commission to keep Anskar safe. He was to be the loyal sword, the protector, until they returned to Branil's Burg at some undisclosed time in the future. But it looked to Anskar as though their roles were to be reversed as long as they remained at sea.

Leaving Orix to his misery, Anskar walked the swaying deck and climbed the steps to the aftcastle. It was a fighting platform, he'd been told, in case the ship was ever boarded; but it also provided the second-best view of the receding white cliffs of Dorinah and the sprawl of the city, with the citadel of Branil's Burg—the only home he had ever known—looming above it. The best view, he fancied, was from the crow's nest, but nothing would possess him to climb all the way up there, especially with the ship starting to lurch in the open waters.

He stood leaning on the rail, enjoying the feel of the breeze ruffling his hair, the tang of the brine, the splashes of sunlight on the waves and white foam. For a time, he managed to clear his mind of skittering thoughts—but they always returned to haunt him.

Melesh-Eloni.

Godling.

Sareya's translation had opened up a void within Anskar; a deep well at the bottom of which mysteries coalesced. All he had to do was let go, but he kept drawing back from the brink. Give credence to those half-formed thoughts and they would snag him. And then the nightmare would come true.

By the time the galleon cleared the turbulent waters and caught a strong headwind, the harbor walls were a black line in the retreating distance. Anskar turned to see Orix watching him. His friend was pale, and vomit streaked his face and shirt, but he looked better than he had earlier.

"Can't see me ever getting used to you with those Niyandrian eyes," Orix said. "It's putting a creep in my crotch."

"You're not the only one," Anskar said. "It's worse for me: they're my eyes."

At least he thought they were. Had they always been this way, disguised somehow by sorcery? Or was it sorcery that had changed them? There were so many questions—only a few of which he dare ask—and every league nearer to Sansor took him farther from the answers.

Anskar had no trust in these "associates" of the Order in Sansor that the Grand Master had mentioned. Sareya could have told him more, perhaps. But if anyone knew what was really going on, Anskar was convinced it had to be Vihtor.

"I tell you, it ain't natural," Orix said, still staring at Anskar's eyes. "You think they'll ever change back?"

Anskar shrugged. There was no way of knowing, at least not yet.

He turned to face the front of the ship and caught sight of the white-robed acolyte standing like a figurehead at the prow.

To alter him for some purpose? Or to reveal that which was hidden?

The acolyte turned to look at Anskar, his dark eyes penetrating, a thin smile on his face. Anskar felt a tremor within his repositories and didn't need to send out feelers of awareness to discern the truth. The man wasn't a mere acolyte. He was a sorcerer.

That shed a whole new light on the Grand Master's associates who were "wise in these matters." Clearly the recruitment of Luzius Landav by the Order of Eternal Vigilance hadn't been an isolated case.

Lies within lies, Anskar thought as he wrenched his eyes away from the acolyte.

The *Exultant* pitched, and he stumbled and threw out a hand to steady himself on Orix's shoulder. In that moment, he was glad of Vihtor's concession to let Orix come along. Anskar had a feeling he was going to need his friend. Not so much for his sword, but as an anchor in a sea more treacherous than the one they currently sailed on.

THIRTY-SIX

A CHILL MIST ROSE FROM the escarpment, unaffected by the breeze coming off the Simorga Sea. Carred stood with Taloc, Noni, Griga and Maggow atop the highest elevation overlooking the former Niyandrian city of Dorinah. She'd had all about she could take of Mala's complaining and had left her behind to help Kalij prepare the food the foragers brought in. Olana, the last of the slaves Carred had freed, had disappeared a few nights ago. Probably, she had gone to sell what she knew to the Order of Eternal Vigilance. Well, good luck to her with that, because the morning after Olana had gone missing, Carred had ordered yet another change of camp.

The citadel of Branil's Burg towered above the dwellings of the city and the outer walls, a triangular pennant showing the five-pointed star whipping and snapping on a pole atop the parapet.

Carred's eyes tracked the passage of the lone galleon as it entered the open sea, its prow rising and falling in the waves and troughs, its keel skirted by frothing white.

"Maybe things will calm down now he's gone," she muttered to herself, though she knew Taloc was listening.

She was speaking of the Grand Master, Hyle Pausus. Things had gone from bad to worse when he and his entourage had arrived from Sansor. Carred had to assume the Grand Master's visit, the new vault at Branil's Burg, and the assassins that had come for her at Marith's had been part of a push by the shady mainland consortium Luzius Landav had introduced her to.

And then there were the Grand Master's brutal reprisals within Branil's Burg: the execution of nine Niyandrian laborers, and one—Estri—beaten so badly she had later died; but not before Carred had held her broken body and pieced together what had happened from Estri's blood-choked account.

Aelanthe, and Carred's three other operatives, had evaded capture then, but something had gone wrong, because Carred had lost contact with them shortly after she'd sent her message for them to snatch the moontouched woman they suspected of being Queen Talia's daughter.

"I still don't get why you didn't strike while the Grand Master was here," Taloc said.

Carred bit her tongue. If only it were as simple as one man being the root of all Niyas's problems. She'd glimpsed the powers behind people like the Grand Master and his Order, but she felt certain the roots of this consortium went deeper than she could even begin to imagine.

Taloc shot her an anxious look. He knew he'd put his foot in it. He was out of his depth: he didn't have the military training she'd had, and certainly didn't have the experience, but given time he'd be a useful addition to the resistance. Time and instruction, and the right amount of nurture.

With a sigh, she said, "We are tasked with preparing the way for the return of the Queen, not igniting another major war. A war we have no chance of winning."

Taloc dipped his eyes in shame and nodded. But Carred wasn't in the mood to let him fully off the hook.

"What do you think the knights would do if we killed their supreme leader? There are still Niyandrians among the trainees at Branil's Burg. They'd be the first to suffer. And then, when they'd all been slaughtered, the ships would come again—from every major city in Kaile, the City States, the Pristart Combine; even from Nagorn City in the west. Gods, they would probably form an alliance with the Jargalan nomads too, just so they could descend upon Niyas in such numbers that we would be totally erased. All they need is an excuse to break their thin veneer of morality, and they'll do what they've always wanted: kill every last Niyandrian on the isle and replace them with their own kind. Is that what you want, Taloc?"

She knew she was being melodramatic, and she wasn't even sure that was how the Order would react to the assassination of their Grand Master. But that wasn't the real issue. The consortium had threatened her, and she'd turned down their ultimatum. Whatever she did or did not do from now on, things were bound to be grim for Niyas.

"I'm sorry," Taloc said. "I spoke out of turn."

"Yes, you did. Remember, you're here to observe and learn."

"I said I was sorry."

She touched him lightly on the arm. "In time, you'll become the man the gods want you to be: a hero of the resistance, a champion of Niyas. But first you must be trained, tried, and tested. It'll be worth it, Taloc. Just think of how the Queen will reward you when she comes back to us."

"How?" he asked, looking up. "How will she reward me?"

"Eternal life. For you, for me, for all Niyandrians."

He frowned slightly, then nodded, but Carred could tell he wasn't convinced. And, in truth, neither was she. The more years that went by, the more people she lost, the less she believed in the promise of her queen. But it was all she had left.

Carred glanced skyward as a speck drew near. It resolved itself into a pigeon and alighted on the arm Maggow held out. She watched as the old man of the mire unfastened the rolled-up parchment from the bird's leg and read it, before passing it to her.

"You still have eyes and ears in the citadel," he said.

The message was from a Niyandrian woman named Niv Allund—a novice of the Order. She began with *Argensi Volo*—Silver Fox—which was Aelanthe's soul name. It was proof that Aelanthe had recruited Niv to the cause. The message was short and to the point: *Failed. Aelanthe and others dead. Moontouched injured. Knight-sorcerer sails with Grand Master. I know them both. More soon.*

Carred swallowed the lump in her throat. Aelanthe had been a good friend and a trusted agent. She was also the greatest sorcerer Carred had known, other than Queen Talia herself. With Aelanthe's death, the resistance was severely hampered. And Talia's daughter—if indeed that's who this moontouched was—had been injured. How badly? And if the knight-sorcerer was her guardian, why was he sailing with the Grand Master? That made no sense.

This Niv Allund claimed to know them, which was useful. But could she be trusted? She'd disclosed Aelanthe's soul name, but she'd still need to be tested. More messages would have to be sent, trick questions asked.

Carred shared the message with the others and asked for their opinions.

Of course, now that he had permission, Taloc said nothing.

Griga was adamant they should find a way to get more of their people inside the Burg and make another attempt to get the moontouched out.

"And if she's too badly hurt?" Carred asked.

Noni chuckled. Everyone looked at her, but she covered her mouth and shut her eyes.

"I could heal her," Griga said lamely.

Carred shook her head. "With what? Leeches?" And besides, after all that had happened, it would be impossible to get their people inside the citadel. The knights had fallen for the ruse last time, but that was only because they'd needed their vault built and greed had overridden common sense.

And taking Branil's Burg by force was out of the question. Even if the entire resistance gathered, they had no siege engines, and too few sorcerers to even scratch those mighty walls.

"I do," Noni said.

Carred frowned at her. "You do what?"

But Noni still had her eyes closed, and her bottom lip was trembling. "I do," she said again. "I accept."

"Griga?" Carred said, flashing the sorcerer a look.

Griga approached Noni, one hand outstretched. Carred felt the flow of the dawn-tide from Griga's repository.

Noni's eyes snapped open, and she laughed hysterically, causing Griga to recoil.

Slowly, Noni turned until she was facing the trees where the embankment sloped away to the north. Carred followed her gaze, and a tingling chill crept through her bones. Just inside the tree line, half obscured by the eerily still mist, stood the wraithe she had first seen on Hallow Hill.

Carred heard Taloc's sharp intake of breath. Griga cursed and made the curled hand sign of warding. Maggow crouched down, averting his eyes from the wraithe and scratching on the ground with his finger.

The wraithe glided toward them out of the mist. Taloc half drew the sword Carred had given him in Lowanin, but she stayed him with a sharp look.

Noni chuckled, then gasped, then sobbed.

Fighting the fear-paralysis in her limbs, Carred advanced to meet the wraithe. She was the leader. She was responsible. And the wraithe had visited her before, so she had to assume it was here to speak with her now.

"Carred Selenas," it said in a rasping voice, coming to a standstill half a dozen yards from her.

Carred avoided looking into the void beneath its cowl. Instead, her eyes rested on the huge sword at its hip, on the gem-encrusted cross-guard—dark gems, like crystalized blood and venom and storm clouds.

"*Melesh-Eloni*," Noni said, causing Carred to turn to look at her. The young woman was staring once more out to sea, where the Grand Master's galleon was but a distant speck.

Carred faced the wraithe again. It too was watching the receding ship.

"She hears well," it said, inclining its cowl toward Noni.

"She hears you?"

"Among other things. *Melesh-Eloni*. An echo. The utterer now dead. The one it signifies very much alive. *Godling*."

"You mean the Grand Master?"

The wraithe chuckled—a gurgling sound like the draining of a ditch. "He would like that."

"Then who?"

"Sixteen years," the wraithe said. It seemed to draw closer, its presence smothering; but when Carred blinked, she saw it remained in the same place. "Have you never wondered why, in all that time, you have not found Queen Talia's heir?"

"We almost had her—the moontouched woman," Carred said, hating how shrill her voice came out.

"Yet you failed. Always you fail."

Carred scowled, and her hand drifted to the pommel of her sword. Her fear of the wraithe was strong, but her anger was growing stronger. "You were the one who told me to wait… until the time was right. You did this. You're to blame."

The wraithe lightly touched the hilt of its own sword. It let Carred's words hang between them for a long moment, as if considering a course of action. As if daring her.

Eventually, it said, "I bore a message, nothing more. The fulfillment of a pact."

"Between you and Queen Talia?"

"On behalf of my kind."

"And is that why you're here now? To fulfill your pact?"

A subtle shake of the cowl. "The pact is already fulfilled."

"Then why are you here?"

"Even shadows have a claim to the land. A vested interest."

"And that is?"

The wraithe didn't answer. It looked out to sea again, but the Grand Master's ship was no longer visible. "The moontouched woman is not the one."

"Then who?" Carred spat the words in anger. "Who is the Queen's daughter?"

"The less anyone knows, the safer the child will be," the wraithe said, repeating the words it had spoken atop Hallow Hill sixteen years ago.

Carred had had enough of riddles and games. "Griga," she snarled, "can you banish it?"

Griga's hands curled into claws. The wraithe's arm whipped out, and Griga shrieked as she was flung back across the embankment, landing with a sickening thud some twenty yards away. She twitched and grew still, and Carred felt the dawn and the dusk-tides leave her.

"She cannot," the wraithe said.

Carred backed away and saw that Taloc was doing the same. Maggow, though, still crouched in his spot, drawing on the ground with his finger and keeping his eyes averted.

"The servant of the old ones knows my kind and is wise," the wraithe said.

"Why did you come?" Carred said through gritted teeth. This time she did draw her sword. She was done with the wraithe's games. Done with false hope and endless fights…and for what? Had life really been so good back then when Talia was alive? So glorious? It wrenched her insides to think that way, but grief and endless struggle had wearied her.

"You're right," she told the wraithe. "I've failed. I always fail. Everyone I ever loved. The people I lead. This island. Gods, I was even a failure to my own parents. So, let's end this now. Put me out of my misery."

She became aware that she was crying as she shouted the words. Ashamed of her weakness, angry and flooded with vengeful thoughts—for being parted from Marith, for Kovin, and now for poor Griga—she hurled herself at the wraithe, swinging her sword in a wild and murderous arc.

The blade struck nothing but mist.

The wraithe was gone.

Carred fell to her knees, shaking and sobbing. Her sword

pierced the earth before her, her hands on the cross-guard the only thing keeping her upright.

"There is no daughter," Noni said from behind her. Her voice was deeper than normal, harsh and grating.

With a shudder, Carred pushed herself to her feet using her sword, then pulled the blade from the ground and turned.

Noni was staring at her, feverish and trembling. The young woman's eyes were wide with fright as her lips struggled to speak with another's voice.

"Talia?" Carred said. The blood froze in her veins.

"You have failed, but he will not," Noni said, her face contorting. "He will find you upon his return."

Carred shook her head to clear it. "He? What are you talking about?"

"I didn't have a daughter," Noni said, turning to gaze out to sea. "I had a son."

"A son?" Confusion once more gave way to anger. How could Talia have done this to her, kept her in the dark for so long? Carred took Noni by the shoulders and spun her round. "A son?" she repeated.

The less anyone knows, the safer the child will be.

Talia had fooled them all.

The knights had been rounding up Niyandrian girls all these years but had never found Talia's heir. No wonder.

"*Melesh-Eloni,*" Noni said. "Godling. The son of a god."

"And you're a god now?" Carred asked. The question could have sounded mocking, but she was deadly serious.

Noni—Queen Talia—chose not to answer. "The knight-sorcerer. His name is Anskar DeVantte."

"DeVantte?" Carred said. "You didn't! With Eldrid DeVantte?"

"Of course I didn't! And don't sound so hurt, Carred."

Not Eldrid? Then who? Some other knight? Some demon?

"There is still the matter of the guardian," the Necromancer Queen said through Noni. "Anskar was protected at Branil's Burg, I made sure of that, but things have changed now."

"Who?" Carred asked. "Who is the guardian?"

"Oh, Carred. Need I spell everything out for you?"

"Me?"

"I think so," Noni answered in a tremulous voice. She was once more herself, shivering and crying. "She won't say. The Queen has gone."

Carred stumbled away from the group.

Anskar DeVantte, the knight-sorcerer, was Queen Talia's son? Did he know? How could he? Who would have told him?

And the heir her people had given their lives for had turned on his own kind.

Talia said he was protected at Branil's Burg—*I made sure of that, but things have changed now.* But what had changed? Had the protection ended? Was that why Hyle Pausus had taken Anskar aboard his ship? But that implied the Grand Master knew…

It made no sense. If the Order knew Anskar was Talia's heir, he would already be dead. They had to be taking him to the mainland for some other reason.

Whatever it was, it was out of Carred's hands now. She'd fought and she'd failed. Failed as the heir's guardian as with everything else.

…*but he will not*, the Queen had said through Noni.

Anskar would not fail.

Had Carred given up too soon?

Talia must have still believed in her, to have appointed her guardian. There had to be more she could do, some way she could bring the heir back to Niyas. The Order controlled all the ports around the isle, and their galleons patrolled the sea, but she would find a way. By the hundred eyes of Theltek, she would find a way.

Then the entire country would rally to her cause. Under Anskar's lead, the rebels would take back Niyas for Niyandrians.

Perhaps then the Queen would return.

And the dead would live forever.

END OF BOOK ONE

TO MY READERS

As always, if you enjoyed the read, leaving a review supports the books and helps keep me writing! You can return to where you purchased the novel to review it or simply visit my website and follow the links: WWW.MITCHELLHOGAN.COM

There are also websites such as Goodreads where members discuss the books they've read or want to read or suggest books others might read: WWW.GOODREADS.COM/AUTHOR/SHOW/7189594.MITCHELL_HOGAN

If you never want to miss the latest book sign up here for my newsletter. I send one every few months, so I won't clutter your inbox. MITCHELLHOGAN.COM/NEW-RELEASE-ALERTS/

Having readers eager for the next installment of a series, or anticipating a new series, is the best motivation for a writer to create new stories. Thank you for your support and be sure to check out my other novels!

ABOUT THE AUTHOR

Photo copyright © 2018

When he was eleven, Mitchell Hogan received *The Hobbit* and the Lord of the Rings trilogy, and a love of fantasy novels was born. He spent the next ten years reading, rolling dice, and playing computer games, with some school and university thrown in. Along the way, he accumulated numerous bookcases' worth of fantasy and sci-fi novels and doesn't look to stop any time soon. For ten years he put off his dream of writing; then he quit his job and wrote *A Crucible of Souls*. He now writes full-time and is eternally grateful to the readers who took a chance on an unknown self-published author. He lives in Sydney, Australia, with his wife, Angela, and his daughters, Isabelle and Charlotte.

Printed in Great Britain
by Amazon